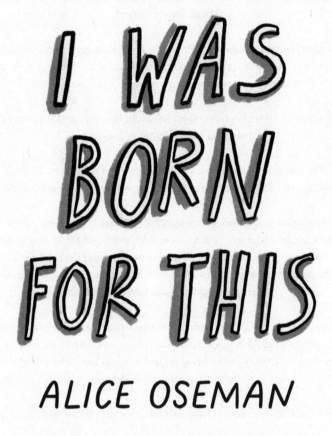

# I WAS BORN FOR THIS

## ALICE OSEMAN

Scholastic Press / New York

Library of Congress Cataloging-in-Publication Data available

ISBN 978-1-338-83093-4

10 9 8 7 6 5 4 3 2 1          22 23 24 25 26

Printed in the U.S.A.          37
First edition, October 2022
Book design by Stephanie Yang

"CHILDREN SAY THAT PEOPLE ARE HUNG
SOMETIMES FOR SPEAKING THE TRUTH."
—JOAN OF ARC

# MONDAY

"I WAS IN MY THIRTEENTH YEAR WHEN I HEARD A VOICE FROM GOD."
—JOAN OF ARC

# ANGEL RAHIMI

"I'm literally dying," I say, putting my hand on my heart. "You're real."

Juliet, having just escaped my hug, is smiling so hard it looks like she might tear her face in half.

"So are you!" she says, and gestures to my body. "This is so weird. But cool."

Theoretically, this shouldn't be awkward. I have been talking to Juliet Schwartz for two years. On the internet only, yeah, but internet friendships aren't that different to real ones nowadays, and Juliet knows more about me than my closest school friends.

"You're a physical being," I say. "Not just some pixels on a screen."

I know almost everything about Juliet. I know that she never falls asleep before 2 a.m. and her favorite fanfic trope is enemies-to-lovers and she's secretly a fan of Ariana Grande. I know she's probably going to grow up to be the sort of wine-sipping middle-aged woman who calls everyone "darling" and always looks slightly like she's giving you evils. But I still wasn't prepared for her voice (posher and deeper than it sounds on Skype) and her hair (she genuinely is ginger, as she's always said, even though it looks brown on camera) and her size (she's a full head smaller than me. I'm seventy feet tall so I should have been prepared for that one, really).

Juliet flattens her fringe and I adjust my hijab and we start walking out of St. Pancras station. We're silent for a moment, and I feel a sudden wave of nerves, which is a bit irrational, since me and Juliet are practically soulmates—two beings who found each other in the depths of the internet against all odds and, just like that, we were a duo.

She's the sharp-witted romantic. I'm the whimsical conspiracy theorist. And we both live for The Ark, the best band in the history of the world.

"You're gonna have to tell me where we're going," I say, smiling. "I have no sense of direction at all. I get lost on my walk to school sometimes."

Juliet laughs. Another new sound. It's clearer, sharper than on Skype. "Well, you are visiting *me*, so I think I'm supposed to be in charge of directions anyway."

"Okay, *true*." I let out an exaggerated sigh. "I genuinely think this is gonna be the best week of my entire life."

"Oh my gosh, I *know*, right? I've been counting down." Juliet pulls out her phone, clicks the screen on, and shows me a countdown timer. It says *3 Days Left.*

I start babbling. "I've been, like, freaking out. I don't even know what I'm gonna wear. I don't even know what I'm gonna *say*."

Juliet flattens her fringe again. It makes me feel like she knows exactly what she's doing. "Don't worry, we have today, tomorrow, and Wednesday to formulate a plan. I'm going to make a list."

"Oh man, you *will*, won't you?"

Neither of us have any friends in real life who like The Ark, but that doesn't matter, because we have each other. I used to try to get people to talk about The Ark with me—my school friends, my parents, my older brother—but no one really cared. They usually just found me annoying, because once I start talking about The Ark, or anything really, I find it kind of hard to stop.

But not Juliet. We've spent hours upon hours talking about The Ark and neither of us get tired or annoyed or bored with each other.

And this is the first time we've ever met.

We exit the station and step out into the air. It's pouring with rain. Tons of people. I've never been to London before.

"This rain is so horrible," says Juliet, wrinkling her nose. She unhooks her arm from mine so she can put up an umbrella—one of those fancy plastic ones.

"True," I say, but that's a lie, because I don't really mind the rain. Even weird August downpours like this one.

Juliet continues to walk without me. I'm just standing there, one hand on my rucksack, one hand in my pocket. There are people smoking outside the station and I breathe it in. I love the smell of cigarette smoke. Is that bad?

This week *is* going to be the best week of my life.

Because I'm going to meet The Ark.

And they will know who I am.

And then I will be worth something.

"Angel?" Juliet calls from a few meters away. "You okay?"

I turn to her, confused, but then realize that she's using my internet name, instead of my real name, which is Fereshteh. I've been going by Angel online since I was thirteen. I thought it sounded cool at the time and, no, I didn't name myself after a *Buffy the Vampire Slayer* character. Fereshteh means *angel* in Farsi.

I love my real name, but Angel feels like a part of me now. I'm just not used to hearing it in real life.

I hold out my arms and grin and say, "Mate, I am living."

⇄  ◄◄ ⏵ ►►  ♥

Despite our first-meeting nerves, it turns out that real life really isn't that different to the internet. Juliet's still the cool, calm, and collected one, and I'm still the loudest and most annoying person in the world, and we spend the whole walk to the tube station talking about how excited we are to meet The Ark.

"My mum freaked *out*," I tell her as we're sitting in a tube carriage. "She knows that I love The Ark, but she just said *no* when I told her I was coming."

"What? Why?"

"*Well* . . . I'm kind of missing my school leaver graduation thing for this."

It's more complicated than that, but I don't really want to bore Juliet with the details. I got my A-level results last week, and *just* scraped the already quite low grades I needed to get into my first university choice. Mum and Dad congratulated me, obviously, but I know they're pretty annoyed that I didn't do better, like my older brother, Rostam, who got at least an A on every exam he's ever taken.

And then Mum had the absolute cheek to demand I *not* go to the Ark concert, just so I could go to a pointless school leavers' ceremony, shake hands with my head teacher, and awkwardly say goodbye to the classmates I'm probably never going to see again.

"It's on Thursday morning," I continue. "The same day as the concert. My mum and dad were gonna come." I shrug. "It's stupid. Like, we're not American; we don't *have* school graduation. Our school just does this stupid little leavers' ceremony that's completely pointless."

Juliet frowns. "That sounds like the worst."

"Anyway, I told my mum there was no way I was going to this thing instead of seeing The Ark, but she just kept saying no and we had this huge shouty argument, which was weird, because, like, we *never* argue. She kept finding all these excuses for me not to go, like 'Oh, it's not safe in London,' 'I don't even know this friend,' 'Why can't you go another time?,' blah blah blah. In the end, I just had to leave, because obviously there was no way I was gonna take no for an answer."

"Jesus," says Juliet, but it sounds like she doesn't really get it. "Are you feeling all right about it?"

"Yeah, it's fine. My mum just doesn't understand. I mean, all we're going to do this week is sit at home, watch movies, go to one fandom meetup, and then go to the meet-and-greet and concert on Thursday. It's not exactly dangerous. And this school thing is absolutely pointless."

Juliet puts a hand dramatically on my shoulder. "The Ark will appreciate your sacrifice."

"Thank you for your support, comrade," I say in an equally dramatic tone.

⇄  ◄◄ ⊙ ►► ♥

Once we reach the top of the Notting Hill Gate station steps, my phone buzzes in my pocket, so I take it out and look at the screen.

Oh. Dad's finally replied to me.

**Dad**

Mum'll come around. Just check in with us when you can. I know this school event isn't very important ultimately. Mum just worries whether you're making good choices. But we understand you want your independence and we know you only make friends with good people. You're eighteen, and you are a strong, sensible girl. I know the world is not so bad, whatever your mother thinks. You know she was raised with different values to me; she respects tradition and academic achievement. But I had my fair share of youthful antics when I was a boy. You must be allowed to live your life, inshallah!! And you must give me some writing material, boring girl!! Love you xx

Well, at least Dad's on my side. He usually is. I think he's always hoping I'll get myself into a mildly unfortunate situation so he can write about it in one of his self-published novels.

I show the text to Juliet. She sighs. "*The world is not so bad.* How extremely optimistic."

"I know, right?"

⇄  ◄◄ ⊙ ►► ♥

We are spending the week at Juliet's nan's house. Juliet herself lives outside London, but Juliet suggested it'd be easier for us to go to the fandom meetup and the concert if we stayed in London for the week. I didn't have any complaints.

The house is in Notting Hill and Juliet's family is rich. I became aware of this not long into our friendship when she bought over £500 worth of The Ark merch in an attempt to win a giveaway competition and then didn't even bat an eyelid when she lost. Over my many years of being in the Ark fandom, I've just about been able to save up enough money to afford an Ark hoodie and a poster.

And, of course, a meet-and-greet ticket to see them this Thursday at the O2 Arena.

"Mate, this is fancy," I say as we walk through the door and into a hallway. It's tiled. Everything is white and there are actual paintings on the walls.

"Thanks?" Juliet replies, a slight lilt in her tone suggesting that she has no idea how to reply. Most of the time I try not to bring up how much richer she is than me, because that would be awkward for both of us.

I take my shoes off and Juliet lets me dump my stuff in the bedroom we're sleeping in. There are a couple of other rooms that I could sleep in—a spare bedroom and an office—but half the fun of staying at a friend's house is those late-night deep conversations while you're tucked up in bed with face masks on, eating Pringles, with a terrible rom-com on the TV in the background. Right?

After that, I'm introduced to Juliet's nan, whose name is Dorothy. She's short, like Juliet, and looks much younger than she probably is, her hair dyed a sandy blond and kept long. She is wearing designer wellies while sitting at the kitchen table typing away at a laptop, glasses perched on the end of her nose.

"Hello," she says with a warm smile. "You must be Angel?"

"Yep! Hi!"

Okay, yeah, people calling me Angel in real life feels weird.

"Excited about the concert on Thursday?" asks Dorothy.

*"So excited."*

"I bet!" She closes her laptop and stands up. "Well, I'll try not to get in your way too much. I'm sure you and J have lots to talk about!"

I assure her that she definitely wouldn't get in our way, but she leaves the room anyway, which makes me feel a bit guilty. I never know how to behave around grandparents, since mine are all dead or overseas. Another thing I don't bring up around anyone, ever.

"SO!" I say, rubbing my hands together. "What food do we have?"

Juliet swishes her hair and slams her hands down on the kitchen counter.

"You're not ready," she says, raising one eyebrow.

She takes me on a tour of all the food and drink she bought for this week—pizzas and J2Os being the main features—before asking me what I want right now, and I go for a classic orange-and-passion-fruit J2O, because I feel like I need to be holding something. I hate not having anything to hold while I'm not talking. What do you do with your hands?

And then Juliet says something else.

"So, if we head out again at around six, I think that should give us enough time to get there."

I scrape the J2O bottle label with my thumbnail.

"Er—*wheeeeere* are we going?"

Juliet freezes, standing over the opposite side of the counter island.

"To pick up—wait . . . have I not told you about this?"

I shrug exaggeratedly.

"My friend Mac is coming down as well," she says. "To stay. To see The Ark."

I immediately begin to panic.

I don't know who Mac is. I haven't heard of Mac. I don't really want to hang out with someone I haven't met before. I don't really want to have to make any new friends when this week is supposed to be dedicated to Juliet and The Ark. Making friends is effort, making friends with Mac will be effort, because he doesn't know me, he isn't used to me and my incessant talkativeness and my deep passion for a teen boy band, and this week isn't about Mac. This week is for me and Juliet and our boys—The Ark.

"Did I really not tell you?" asks Juliet, running a hand over her hair.

She sounds like she feels pretty bad about it.

"No . . ." I say. I sound rude. Okay. Calm down. It's fine. Mac is fine. "But—it's fine! More pals! I'm good at making new friends!"

Juliet puts her hands on her face. "God, I'm *so* sorry. I could have sworn I told you. I promise he's really, really nice. We message, like, every day."

"Yeah!" I say, nodding enthusiastically, but I feel guilty. I want to tell her that I'm not really okay with this, and I hadn't been expecting this, and to be honest I probably wouldn't have come if I'd known I'd have to spend the week socializing with some guy I don't know. But I don't want to make things awkward when I've only been here for ten minutes.

I'll just have to lie.

Just for this week.

Hopefully God will forgive me. He knows that I need to be here. For The Ark.

"So, we'll head out at six, back here for pizzas, put a film on, then the awards start at two, yeah?" I say, words tumbling out of my mouth.

It's 5:17 p.m. We're staying up tonight to watch the West Coast Music Awards, which start at 2 a.m. UK time. Our boys are performing there. The first time they've appeared at an American awards show.

"Yes," says Juliet, nodding decisively. Nodding is starting to lose its meaning. I turn round and start pacing the kitchen, and Juliet takes out her phone.

"Looks like the boys have arrived at their hotel!" she says, staring at the screen. Probably on @ArkUpdates on Twitter—our usual source for everything Ark-related. It's incredible I haven't checked it in the last hour.

"Any pics yet?"

"Just a blurry one of them getting out of their car."

I lean over her shoulder and look at the photo. There they are. Our boys. *The Ark.* Blurry, pixelated smudges, half blocked by huge bodyguards in dark suits. Rowan is leading them, Jimmy in the middle, Lister behind. They seem connected. Like the Beatles on Abbey Road, or a group of toddlers holding hands on a preschool trip to the park.

# JIMMY KAGA-RICCI

"Wake up, Jimjam." Rowan kicks me in the shin. Rowan and Lister and I are all in the same car, which makes a pleasant change. Usually we have to arrive at these award shows separately and I have to endure a car ride with a bodyguard who keeps glancing at me like I'm a rare Pokémon card.

"I'm awake," I say.

"No, you're not," he says, and then waggles his fingers above his head. "You're up there."

Rowan Omondi is sitting opposite me in the back of our Hummer. He looks hot. Always does. His hair's been in twists for the last couple of months and his glasses—new—are aviators. His suit is red with white and gold flowers on it—fire against his dark brown skin. His shoes are Christian Louboutin.

He links his fingers together over one knee. His rings make a jangling sound.

"It's nothing new. We've done this before. What's whirring?" He taps his temple and looks at me. What's whirring. I love Rowan. He says words like he made them up. Probably why he's our lyricist.

"Anxiety," I say. "I'm anxious."

"About what?"

I laugh and shake my head. "Not how it works. We've been through this."

"Yeah, but, like, everything has a cause and effect."

"Anxiety is the cause *and* the effect. Double whammy."

"Oh."

The anxiety thing isn't new. By this point, it's pretty much the fourth member of the band. I've been trying to get on top of it in therapy, but I haven't had the time for many sessions this year what with the European tour and the new album, and I *still* haven't really warmed up to my new therapist. I haven't even told her about the massive panic attack I had at Children in Need last year yet. Still sang anyway. It's on YouTube. If you look closely, you can see the tear tracks on my face.

We fall into silence. I can hear the screams in the distance. Sounds a bit like a tide. We must be nearly there.

My weird bad feelings are probably half anxiety and half genuine nerves about tonight, plus all the other things I'm sort of constantly dreading. I tend to constantly dread things, even when the "things" aren't actually dreadful. Currently up there on Jimmy's List of Things He's Dreading the Most are *signing our new contract* and *coming home from tour*, along with *tonight's performance at the West Coast Music Awards, aka our first-ever live performance in America*. It'll be no different to our normal concert performances except that our audience will be the greatest musicians in the world and people who haven't really heard of us rather than teenagers who know all our lyrics by heart.

Everything's sort of changing and happening and I feel excited and scared, and my brain doesn't know how to deal with it all.

"I don't know how you have room to be anxious when we're finally performing at the Dolby," says Lister, who is literally bouncing up and down in his seat with a wild grin on his face. "I mean, I feel like I'm gonna shit myself. I think I might, actually. Stay tuned."

Rowan wrinkles his nose. "Can we not talk about poo while I'm wearing Burberry, please?"

"If we can talk about anxiety, we can talk about poo. They're basically the same thing."

Allister Bird. Easy for me to tell he hasn't had a drink or a cigarette since yesterday—while he does look like he's about to explode from excitement, he's subconsciously gritting his teeth and has bags under his eyes. Cecily, our manager, enforced a no-alcohol-for-five-hours-before-events rule on Lister after the Incident at *The X Factor* that We Do Not Talk About Anymore, and he's not supposed to smoke on singing days, even though he usually does.

No one else can tell that, though. To everyone else, he's beautiful, perfect, flawless, etc. He's got the James Dean, Calvin Klein model, I-just-tumbled-out-of-bed look. Tonight, he's wearing a Louis Vuitton bomber jacket and ripped black skinny jeans.

Lister pats me a little too hard on the back.

"You're at least a bit excited about it, right?" he asks, grinning.

It's hard not to grin back. "Yeah, I'm a bit excited."

"Good. Now, back to the important topic at hand: What are the chances of me running into Beyoncé and what are the chances of her knowing who I am?"

I squint out of the car window. It's tinted, and Hollywood looks darker than it should, but the too-fast beating of my heart is an indiscernible mix of anxiety and excitement and I get a sudden wave of *I can't believe I'm here*. It happens less and less nowadays, but sometimes I remember how weird my life is.

How good it is. How lucky I am.

I glance back at Rowan. He's looking at me, a faint smile on his lips.

"You're smiling," he says.

"Shut up," I say, but he's right.

"You boys should all just try to enjoy yourselves," says Cecily. She crosses her legs and doesn't look up from her phone as she talks. "After this week, things are gonna get five hundred percent more hectic for you guys."

Cecily, who is sitting opposite Lister, is the only one of us who looks anything like a normal person—she's wearing a blue dress, tight black curls swished to one side, and she's got a lanyard round her neck. The only seemingly expensive thing about her is the massive iPhone in her hand.

Cecily Wills is only about ten years older than us, but she comes everywhere with us and tells us what to do, where we're going, where to stand, who to talk to. If we didn't have her, we'd have literally no idea what we were doing, at all, ever.

Rowan rolls his eyes. "So *dramatic.*"

"Just keeping it real, babe. The new contract is very different to your current one. And you'll be adjusting to post-tour life."

*The new contract.* We're all signing a new contract with our record label, Fort Records, once we return home from our European tour later this week.

It'll mean longer tours. More interviews. Bigger sponsors, flashier merch, and, above all, it'll mean *finally* breaking the US. We've recently had a top-ten single in America, but the plan is to get us a real audience here, a US tour, and maybe even worldwide fame.

Which is what we want, obviously. Our music spread across the world and our name in the history books. But I can't say the thought of *more* interviews, *more* guest appearances, *more* tours, *more everything*, is making me feel particularly thrilled about my future.

"Do we have to talk about that right now?" I mutter.

Cecily keeps tapping away at her phone. "No, babe. Let's get back to poo and anxiety."

"Good."

Rowan sighs. "Now look what you've done. You've made Jimmy grumpy."

"I'm not grumpy—"

Lister drops his mouth open in faux shock. "How is this my fault?"

"It's both of you," says Rowan, gesturing to Lister and Cecily.

"It's none of you," I say. "I'm just in a weird mood."

"But you're excited, yeah?" asks Lister again.

"Yes! I promise I am." And I mean it. I am excited.

I'm just nervous and scared and anxious as well.

The three of them are all looking at me.

"Like, we're performing at the Dolby!" I say, and find myself grinning again.

Rowan raises his eyebrows a little, arms folded, but nods. Lister makes a whooping noise, then starts to unwind the window before Cecily smacks his hand and winds it back up again.

The screams coming from outside are piercing now, and the car comes to a halt. I feel a bit sick. I don't really know why all this is bothering me so much more today. I'm normally fine. Wary, always wary, but fine. The screams don't sound like a tide anymore. To me, they sound like the metallic screech of heavy machinery.

I'm sure I'll enjoy myself once we get in there.

I rub my fingers over my collarbones, feeling for my tiny cross necklace. I ask God to calm me down. Hope He's listening.

I'm wearing all black, as usual. Cigarette trousers, Chelsea boots that are giving me blisters, a big denim jacket, and a shirt that I have to keep pulling on because I feel like it's choking me. And the little transgender flag pin I always wear to events.

Rowan undoes his seat belt, pats me gently on the cheek, pinches Lister's nose, and says, "Let's walk, lads."

⇄ ◄◄ ⊙ ►► ♥

The girls aren't anything new. They're always there, somewhere, waiting for us. I don't mind, really. I can't say I understand it, but I love them back in a way, I guess. The same way I love Instagram videos of puppies tripping over.

We get out of the car and some woman touches up our hair and makeup and some other woman brushes down my jacket with a lint roller. I sort of love how they always seem to appear out of thin air. Men holding massive cameras, wearing jeans. Bald bodyguards wearing black. Everyone's got a bloody lanyard on.

Rowan puts on his Serious Face. It's hilarious. Kind of a pout, kind of a smolder. He's not so smiley in front of the cameras.

Lister, on the other hand, is flashing his smile all over the place. He never looks miserable in photos. He's got the opposite of a resting bitch face.

The screams are deafening. Most of them are just screaming "Lister!" Lister turns round and holds up a hand, and I dare to take a glance too.

The girls. Our girls. Clawing at a chain-link fence, waving phones, crushing each other and screaming because they are so happy.

I hold up a hand and salute them, and they scream back at me. That's how we communicate.

We get ushered on by the adults that escort us everywhere. Bodyguards and makeup artists and women holding walkie-talkies. Rowan walks in the middle, Lister walks slightly ahead, and I linger at the back, finding myself more excited than I usually am at these awards ceremonies. This is our first step into the American music industry, worldwide success, and a musical *legacy*.

We've made it from a run-down garage in rural Kent to a red carpet in Hollywood.

I glance up at the California sunshine and find myself smiling again.

⇄  ◄◄ ⊙ ►►  ♥

Photos are very important, apparently. As if there aren't already enough high-quality photos of us in the world. Cecily tried to explain it to me once. They need up-to-date HQ photos, she said. They need HQ photos of my hair now that I got the sides buzzed. They need HQ photos of Rowan's suit, since it's something special that fashion magazines will talk about. They need HQ photos of Lister. Because they sell.

The three of us reconvene at press photos. I still feel like it's just us three here, sometimes, even though we're surrounded by other people constantly—adults swarming round us, putting their hands on our backs and pointing where to stand, before jogging out of the way so the fireworks show of camera flashes can begin. I catch eyes with Lister and he mouths the words "shitting myself" at me, before turning away and sending a blinding smile to the cameras.

I stand in the middle, always, holding my hands together in front of me.

Rowan, the tallest, is to my left with a hand on my shoulder. Lister is to my right, his hands in his pockets. We never really discussed this. It's just what we do now.

The photographers, like the girls, all scream mainly at Lister.

Lister hates this.

Rowan thinks it's hilarious.

I think it's hilarious.

But nobody except us three knows that.

"This way!" "To the right!" "Guys!" "Lister!" "Over here!" "To the left, now!"

It goes on. We can't really do anything but stare into the flashing lights and wait.

Eventually a man gestures for us to move on. The photographers continue to scream at us. They're worse than the girls because they're doing it for money, not love.

I automatically walk close to Rowan and he turns to me and says, "Lively bunch tonight, aren't they?"

"California, baby," I say.

"It's a funny old world." He stretches out his arms to adjust his sleeves. "And I'm sweating one out right now."

"I'm the one wearing all black!"

The camera flashes reflect in his glasses. "At least you're wearing socks. I think I can smell my feet already." He waves a foot at me. "Leather shoes with no socks is a fucking disaster. I've got a sweat swamp growing down there."

I laugh and we walk on.

⇄　◄◄　⊙　►►　♥

This is where most of the girls are. A long line of red carpet stretches out before us with the girls on either side, leaning over the fence, waving phones. I used to wish there was time to talk to every single one of them.

Lister dives straight in, walking along the left side of the carpet, stopping every so often to lean into a girl's selfie. They grab at his arms, his jacket, his hands. He smiles and moves on. A bodyguard hovers a few steps behind him.

Rowan hates the girls, hates the way they scream and grab him and cry in front of him and beg for a follow-back on Instagram. But he doesn't want them to hate him. So he goes to take some selfies too.

I don't anymore. I don't go anywhere near them anymore. I don't mind waving and smiling, and I'm grateful, definitely grateful that they're here and supporting us and loving us, but . . . they scare me.

They could just reach out and hurt me at any moment. Someone could have a gun. No one would know. One evil person shows up and I'm dead. And I'm a big target. Being a member of one of the most successful and well-known boy bands in Europe makes you a big target.

Typical me. Paranoia, dread, and too much overthinking all crammed into one tiny brain.

Instead, I walk slowly and wave. They wave back at me, smiling, crying, so happy. This is a good thing. They are having the best time.

Near the end of the carpet, we all walk together again, the three of us in a slightly spaced-out line. Sometimes I wish we really could hold hands. You couldn't give me a billion quid to be a solo artist and do all of this by myself.

It's stressful. It's scary. That never goes away. The girls scream and they claw at you. A lot of them only like us because we have nice faces. But as long as we are here, the three of us, and we get to make music, and we get to live this life—playing our music in a new city every week, bringing smiles to millions of faces, leaving our mark upon the world—then everything is good, and fine, and okay.

Rowan glances my way and nods. He pats Lister on the back. At least I'm not alone.

# ANGEL RAHIMI

Since Juliet announced that I am not the only internet friend who is coming to stay, things have gotten seventy times more awkward, because she feels bad about it, and I feel uncomfortable about it, and nobody is fully happy about anything anymore.

Fortunately for us, I'm excellent at faking being okay with things, even when inside my brain there is a tiny screaming gnome who is definitely not okay.

I keep the conversation flowing as we walk to the tube station, where we're meeting Mac, whose surname and entire personality I do not know. I'm good at that—talking, even when there's nothing to talk about.

Juliet seems happy to go along with it. Especially when I bring up Rowan's Instagram.

We turn a corner and I spot the red-and-blue underground sign at the end of the road.

"So," I continue, "what's Mac like?"

Juliet stuffs her hands into her pockets. "Well . . . He's in the Ark fandom, he's the same age as us, eighteen, he's . . ." She falters. "He's really into music?"

"Hmm!" I nod along. "How long have you known him?"

"Only, like, a few months, but we pretty much message every day, so I feel like I've known him for *years*, you know? I mean, hopefully he doesn't turn out to be a forty-year-old fedora-wearing stalker."

She mimes tipping a fedora, which makes me snort out a laugh. "Yeah, hopefully not!"

I wonder whether Juliet feels like she's known me for years. Even though we *have* known each other for two years.

"There he is!" Juliet points into the crowd pouring out of the tube barriers. I have no idea who she's pointing at. I spot various guys of our age, and Mac could be literally any of them. Due to Juliet's very bland description of him, my expectations are low.

And then a guy waves in our direction.

My expectations, as it turns out, are fairly accurate.

He is the definition of an average British white boy.

He sees us—well, he sees Juliet—and waves in our direction. He smiles. I think he's attractive. Sort of averagely spaced-out facial features. That haircut that all the lads are wearing nowadays. Bit like he was designed in a lab. I don't know, really. He looks like the sort of person I should think is attractive.

Juliet walks slightly forward as he approaches, leaving me standing behind her.

"Hey!" she says. She sounds nervous.

"Hey!" he says as he reaches her. He sounds nervous too.

They both grin at each other, and then he holds out his arms for a hug, and she stands on her tiptoes and hugs him.

Ah. Think I might have an idea of what's actually going on here.

"How was your journey?" asks Juliet after they separate.

"Not too bad!" says Mac. "You know. *Trains.*"

She laughs in agreement.

You know. Trains.

They small-talk for an exasperating two minutes before I'm introduced.

"Oh! Yeah!" says Juliet, spinning round in absolute *amazement* to find that I am, in fact, still there. "So this is my friend Angel."

I feel another flash of weirdness at being introduced as Angel, not Fereshteh. Then again, that's who I am with these people. The internet people. *Angel.*

Mac drags his eyes away from Juliet and properly focuses on me.

"Hey, you all right?" he asks, but his eyes say, *Why the fuck are* you *here?*

"Hi!" I say, trying to sound cheerful. I hate it when people say "You all right" instead of "hello."

He looks a bit like an older version of the boys who bullied me on the school bus.

After a long pause, I clap my hands, stop looking at them, and say, "Well! Painful introduction aside, let's get back, because I want to put pizza in my mouth."

I half expect Juliet to make some sarcastic comment, or to at least agree with me, as she would do if we were talking online, but she doesn't. She just laughs politely with Mac.

⇄  ◄◄ ⊙ ►►  ♥

"Oh, Radiohead are so good," Mac is saying on the walk back to Juliet's nan's house. I am walking slightly behind Mac and Juliet. Can't fit three people in a row on the sidewalk. "I know they're kind of old now, but they're still relevant. I think you'd really like them."

Juliet chuckles. "Well, you know me, I'll listen to anything that's mildly miserable."

"I'll have to send you a link to 'Everything in Its Right Place' so we can talk about it," he continues, and runs a hand through his hair. "It's so creepy."

His accent isn't far off Juliet's—posh, like the people on *Made in Chelsea*, but it sounds so much worse coming out of his mouth. Juliet sounds like the kids from the Narnia films, but Mac sounds like a movie villain.

"Yeah, do," says Juliet, nodding enthusiastically.

I wouldn't have thought Juliet would be at all interested in Radiohead.

Obviously her number one is always going to be The Ark, but overall she's more of a fan of pop rock and upbeat stuff. Not miserable old *Radiohead*.

"I just really like that sort of classic nineties indie stuff," Mac continues. "I mean, I guess it's unusual to be into that sort of music, but, you know, it's better than being too obvious."

"Oh yeah, definitely," says Juliet, smiling at him.

"Anyway, I'm glad I have you to talk about music with." Mac grins. "No one at my school is really into the stuff I like."

"Like The Ark?" asks Juliet.

"Yeah, exactly."

Mac launches into a monologue about the similarities between The Ark and Radiohead and how he's sure that they must have been inspired by Radiohead in some of their less upbeat songs, but I switch off from the conversation. This guy talks nearly as much as me but has ten times more opinions. I'm sure Juliet sees him as a quirky music nerd, and I'm sure I'm only being negative because I thought I was getting Juliet all to myself this week, but I can't stop myself imagining him getting some sort of emergency phone call, having to rush back to the train station, get on a train, never to see either of us again.

⇄  ◄◄ ⊙ ►►  ♥

Not even the presence of Juliet's nan prevents me from feeling like a third wheel. There's no avoiding it. Mac and Juliet are Ferris Bueller and Sloane, and I'm Cameron. Except they're dull and I don't have a fancy car.

I'm extremely relieved when I retreat upstairs to perform my evening prayers, just because I get to stop listening to Mac's voice for ten minutes. I ask God to give me strength to be kind and not judge him too hard when I've known him for, like, an hour, but a girl can only listen to so many monologues about obscure old bands before she snaps.

Eleven p.m. rolls around and Dorothy has long gone to bed. We've had food, and now we're sitting in the living room, Mac and Juliet on one sofa and me on an armchair, TV playing something on Netflix I've never seen before, waiting to watch The Ark walk the red carpet on a livestream at 2 a.m. I'm used to having to lead conversations with most people, but Mac and Juliet seem to be doing perfectly fine now that they're together.

At five past midnight, the worst happens.

Juliet goes to pee, leaving me and Mac alone in the living room together.

"So," he says once Juliet has left the living room. He smooths his hair back with one hand and looks at me. So? What am I supposed to do with "so"?

"So," I say.

Mac looks at me, smiling. He's got an awkward sort of smile. Clearly fake, but at least he's trying to be nice, I guess. And I can see why Juliet's got a thing for him. His hair's swishy and his awkward smile is kind of cute, I suppose. He's almost got some Ark vibes about him, if you put him in some ripped black jeans.

"Tell me about yourself, *Mac*."

He laughs, as if what I've said is really weird. "Wow, a big question!" He leans forward, putting his elbows on his knees. "Well, I'm eighteen, I just finished sixth form, I'm off to Exeter Uni in a few weeks' time to do History."

I nod as if I am super interested in these facts.

"And, er . . . well, I guess I'm just a big music fan!"

He laughs and scratches his head, like this is a really embarrassing thing to admit.

"That's so interesting," I say. I've learned absolutely nothing about him at all. "So you and Juliet started chatting on Tumblr?"

He grins sheepishly. "Oh, yeah, well, I messaged her a few months back, just to start up a conversation, you know? And we got talking. I think we're quite similar."

"Mmm, yeah, totally!" I try not to say this in a sarcastic way. Juliet and Mac couldn't be more dissimilar. Juliet likes memes and dissecting fandom theories. Mac looks like he posts #like4like selfies on Instagram.

"How about you?" he asks. "*Tell me about yourself.*"

"Okay, then," I say, eyebrows raised, as if I have accepted a challenge to duel. "I'm also eighteen, I've also just finished school, and I'm going to uni to study Psychology in October."

"Psychology? That's pretty cool. Do you want to be a psychologist? Or, like, a therapist or something?"

I hold up my hands and shrug. "Who the heck knows, man!"

He laughs, but he looks a little panicked, not knowing whether he should laugh or not. Easier than telling him the full truth, anyway, which is that I chose psychology because it's the only subject I'm even slightly good at or interested in at school—I'm below average at everything else—and I have no idea what I want to do with my life.

Which is a bit shit, to be honest, especially when your older brother is in his third year of a medicine degree at Imperial College London, and your mum and dad are *both* teachers, and really you should have ended up with better genes than this.

But I don't need to think about any of that right now. This week is for The Ark. This is what I've been waiting for. I can deal with the rest of my life after.

"Honestly," says Mac, "I barely know what I want to be after uni. I mean, I chose history because I find it interesting, but, like, it's not the sort of subject that leads you into a straightforward career path, unlike what Juliet's doing, which is *so* brave obviously, not going down the lawyer route like her parents and going for backstage theater stuff instead . . ."

He rambles on for a couple of minutes without leaving pauses for me to speak, and I find myself switching off again. I can actually see why he and Juliet get along. She's more of a listener.

"Hey," he says suddenly, "we should follow each other on Tumblr!"

"Oh," I say. "Yeah, cool, sure."

We both get our phones out of our pockets.

"What's your URL?" he asks.

"Jimmysangels."

He laughs. "Like *Charlie's Angels*? That's cool. What a classic."

I've actually never seen *Charlie's Angels*. "Well, my name's Angel, and, you know, I love Jimmy, so, there you go."

"Is your name actually Angel? Because that's really cool."

I pause, but I end up saying with a smile, "Yep!"

Not technically a lie.

"Mac's short for Cormac, which is so stupid, because Cormac's an Irish name and I'm not even slightly Irish—"

"What's your URL?"

"Oh, yeah, it's mac-anderson." I assume that's his full name. Cormac Anderson. His description reads *mac, 18, uk. i live for good music and cool shoes.* This makes me have a look across the room to see what shoes he was wearing earlier, and I'm disappointed to find that they're Yeezys. Why does everyone have Yeezys? Aren't they like £800?

"There," he says.

"Cool," I say.

We sit in silence for a moment, nodding at each other.

The door opens, and Juliet comes back to us. Thank actual God. Mac looks up at her with immense relief.

She freezes in the doorway and grins, moving her head from me to Mac.

"You two look like you've had . . . a conversation," she says.

"That is accurate," I say.

"Yeah, we're BFFs now," says Mac, smiling. "We don't need you anymore, Jules."

Jules? I want to die. First "You know, trains" and now "Jules"? *Jules?*

She walks into the room and sits back down on the sofa next to Mac. "That's too bad because it's only a couple of hours until we see The Ark, and you will literally have to kick me out if you think I'm gonna miss that."

He nudges her and murmurs something I can't hear from my armchair. She laughs. I get a weird thought that they're laughing at me, but obviously they wouldn't do that right in front of my face. Would they? No. They continue their flirty banter and I open up Twitter for the hundredth time in an attempt to escape from the romantic comedy I seem to have ended up in as the comic-relief ethnically diverse side character.

I miss the Juliet from earlier already.

⇄ ⏪ ⏵ ⏩ ♥

By 1:00 a.m. I'm constantly refreshing @ArkUpdates for any sign that The Ark are on their way. The red-carpet livestream doesn't start for another hour, but you never know when someone might get a quick shot of them in their car, or leaving their hotel, or whatever, wherever.

You can never really guess what's going to happen next in the Ark fandom.

The fandom is one of the biggest on the internet, and I've been here since the beginning. Fans range from ten-year-olds who just tweet the boys with "FOLLOW ME BACK!!!" to fans in their late twenties writing fanfiction longer than five novels put together and fans my age, constantly discussing and theorizing and loving and hating and always, always thinking about our boys.

I got into it when it started, five years ago, back when The Ark were just posting covers on YouTube. I was there when they got their record deal after one of their videos went viral. I was there when they first performed on Radio 1 and when their first single went to number one in the UK.

I was there through the media shitstorm that occurred when Jimmy, aged sixteen, revealed that he's transgender—he was assigned female at birth. I was there through all the think pieces. The good ones:

*Jimmy Kaga-Ricci: A New Trans Icon*

And the many bad ones:

*Has "Diversity" Finally Gone Too Far?*

*The Ark: A Black Guy, a White Guy, and a Mixed-Race Trans Guy*

*Is The Ark's Newfound Fame a Response to Millennials' Obsession with Diversity?*

*Is Political Correctness Destroying the Music Industry?*

Most of it was a load of middle-aged whining, but there were a few sensible people who could see the good in the fact that a trans guy was becoming one of the most famous and well-loved musicians in the history of the world.

I was there through the *GQ* magazine cover and their first festival gig at Glastonbury. I was there when the Jowan shipping began—people wanting Jimmy and Rowan to be in a relationship—and I was there when the *Lister is bisexual* rumors began. I was there through the Jimmy-and-Rowan-friendship-origin discussions and the second-album-bonus-track theory and, of course, the "Joan of Arc" video discourse.

Maybe not always physically. But spiritually, mentally, and emotionally, I was there.

There's a new picture of Jimmy on @ArkUpdates, posted on Twitter by one of The Ark's stylists. Jimmy's smiling, looking off to the side. He's wearing all black, as we thought, but he's in a denim jacket, which is new. It looks good against his skin. His hair, silky and brown, is buzzed at the sides now, making his face look even more elfin, but older, somehow. Sometimes it's hard to believe we're almost the same age. Other times, I feel like we've grown up together.

He's my favorite. Jimmy Kaga-Ricci.

I wouldn't say I was attracted to him, or to any of them, really. That's not what this is about. But God, if anyone's the angel around here, it's him.

# JIMMY KAGA-RICCI

"I am here tonight on the West Coast Music Awards red carpet with three of the UK's greatest musicians—it's The Ark's very own Lister, Rowan, and Jimmy!"

The suited, smiley presenter—I don't know his name—turns to us, and so does the camera. This area of the red carpet is specifically for interviews, and everyone wants to talk to us. We always just walk through and stop when Cecily points at an interviewer.

I say, as upbeat as possible, "Hi, you all right?" Lister says, "Hey," and Rowan just nods and smiles.

"How are you boys doing tonight?"

I'm standing closest to the man, so he thrusts the microphone at me. I grin and glance at my fellow "boys." "We're doing good, I think! Yeah!" Lister adds his agreement and Rowan nods again.

"So The Ark's been nominated for the ever-so-prestigious Best Newcomer award at the WCMAs after your single 'Joan of Arc' hit the top ten just three months ago, is that right?" The presenter doesn't wait for us to confirm this before continuing. "How do you guys see your chances tonight?"

He asks this with a sort of sly, cheeky grin, as if this is a dangerous question to ask. It's not. We won the BRIT Award for British Group two years ago and none of us really gives a shit whether we win any awards anymore. Being here and spotting Beyoncé from afar is reward enough.

"Well," I say, "I mean, I think it's pretty funny, first of all, that the WCMAs have been calling us a 'pop' band in all their tweets, when we're not really a pop band." I say this all with a laugh, but I do actually wish people thought we were a rock band. We're a rock band. Electropop at a stretch. I'm not a music snob. Shut up.

The interviewer laughs too. "Oh, really! That's *so* interesting." His eyes move away from me and he thrusts the microphone at Lister. "What about you, Lister? Any thoughts about how you're going to do tonight? There are some big contenders!"

Lister nods thoughtfully and starts to speak in his chirpy interview voice. "Oh yeah, well, you know, whether we win or don't, we put our hearts into our music and it's something our listeners love, and that's really what matters, isn't it? We're all just honored to have been nominated by the WCMAs and we're really excited to be performing here."

I resist the urge to laugh. Lister is so good at spouting this bullshit.

"Now, about your recent single, 'Joan of Arc.' Your fans *adore* it, don't they?" The interviewer turns to Rowan. "It's sprouted some pretty *crazy* conspiracy theories, hasn't it?"

Rowan shifts uncomfortably beside me.

Here we go.

"What do you guys say about all these, I mean, frankly *insane* rumors about . . . what is it?" The interviewer makes quotation marks with his fingers. "*Jowan?* I know a lot of these *conspiracy theories* have a lot to do with the 'Joan of Arc' video."

Lister audibly sighs. I freeze, mid-grin, trying to work out what the diplomatic thing to say is. What to say that's not going to make the fans angry but not directly lying. What to say that isn't going to land us on the front page of every single gossip magazine *again*.

The "Joan of Arc" video. Somehow, the fans think the entire thing is a metaphor for my and Rowan's supposed "romantic" relationship. Which is a load of absolute bullshit, of course, but the fans like to overthink everything we do.

It's only a minor annoyance in the grand scheme of things, but it's particularly annoying right now, when we're trying to be proud of one of our best songs and yet all anyone cares about is *Jowan*.

"Our fans," says Rowan, getting in there before I can start, "our fans are super passionate." I can hear the strain in his voice. "And we love them for that. But like all fans throughout time, from the Bible to the Beatles, they can take some things kind of overboard, you know?" He's reaching a dangerous line. "And it's all from a place of love, yeah?" Rowan pats his chest. "It's all love. It's just because they love us. And if they wanna . . . yeah . . . tell these stories? Then I'm not gonna stop them. Because we love them back, don't we, lads?"

Lister chuckles and nods his agreement. I add a "Yeah, absolutely."

When did we get so damn good at this?

"And Jimmy here," Rowan continues, clapping me on the shoulder in a manly fashion, "Jimmy's like my *brother*, you know? The fans know that. The world knows that. I think that's what's so special about being in The Ark. We might not be related, but the three of us are *brothers*, yeah?"

Interviewer puts a hand on his heart and says, "That is so sweet to hear," but Cecily and security are already gesturing at us to leave this guy and he only has a few seconds to say "Thank you very much for joining us tonight, boys, and good luck!" before we're gone, on to the next one, time to do it all over again, and Lister is patting Rowan on the back as a silent "well done" when we're away from the cameras, and Rowan's snorting and saying, "They're gonna overthink that one as well."

But it doesn't matter, really. It's all part of the job. And when the next interviewer asks me what musicians I'm enjoying at the moment and I get to ramble about how much I love Lorde, I feel a bit better.

"Not being funny," says Rowan to Cecily during the applause for one of the other artists performing tonight, "but are you going to raise your head away from your phone while we're at one of the biggest and most important award shows in the world?"

The four of us have had the absolute misfortune to be seated in the front row. Cameras always on us. I've been trying not to move my lips too much while I'm talking.

"I mean, I could," says Cecily, raising her eyebrows but not looking away from her phone, "if you didn't mind several large blogs running the Bliss story tomorrow morning."

Rowan groans. "They're *still* threatening to do that?"

"Yep. They want that Bliss story, babe. They've been pestering me with emails for days."

"Well, they're not having it."

"I know."

Bliss is Rowan's girlfriend. She's a normal person, and a secret. Bliss doesn't want to be famous. Several large blogs and magazines have a lot of information on Bliss, and have been threatening to run a story on the relationship for several weeks, but our publicity team (headed up by Cecily) is one of the best around and have managed to keep them at bay. For now.

The press don't care what *we* want. They just want more clicks.

Cecily looks up at Rowan. She pats him on the leg.

"Don't worry about it, babe," she says. "I'll sort it."

She will. She always does.

There's another thunderous round of applause, and then the lights dim. Time for another performance. The giant LED screen at the back of the stage starts showing rain falling on a window, and the auditorium explodes into the sound of rainfall but at the same time, everything feels oddly quiet too. It surprises me for a second, makes me feel like I've been taken out of the room, not really here. I half expect to feel cold drops of fresh water on the back of my neck, instead of the stuffy air of a packed theater and the hum and the

31

glare of the stage lighting. Makes me think of England. I miss England. When was the last time I saw it rain? Two months ago? Three? When was I last in England again?

I stop thinking when a tiny red light catches my attention and I realize a camera is pointing directly at me.

# ANGEL RAHIMI

Two a.m. comes and we sit and watch them walk the red carpet.

Jimmy and Rowan and Lister. Our boys.

As soon as they appear, I can't stop smiling. They look so happy to be there. So excited. So proud of themselves and their achievements.

They look like they were born to be together.

I love them. God, I love them.

Rowan is the serious one. The adult of the group. He seems a little more grown-up and composed and eloquent in interviews. He's probably the quietest of the three.

Lister is the most popular. The one on all the posters. Personality-wise? People call him the "bad boy," but that phrase honestly makes me cringe. He's extroverted and cheeky. And he wins all the "most beautiful" magazine contests.

But Jimmy's my favorite because he feels so real. You can tell he gets a little nervous at events like this. His voice shakes a bit in interviews and when they accept awards. He tries his best to smile even when he's not totally comfortable. He's more complex than Rowan or Lister, or maybe I just understand him better, and I *relate* to him, the way he tries his best even when he feels awkward and smiles even when he's not okay.

I wonder if I'll be able to tell him that when I meet him at the meet-and-greet on Thursday. I wonder what I'll be able to say when faced with Jimmy Kaga-Ricci.

"So which one is your favorite?" Mac asks Juliet with a sly grin after the livestream cuts to the adverts.

The three of us are now huddled under blankets, an array of demolished snack foods surrounding us. Juliet has hooked her laptop up to the TV so we can watch it on a big screen. I don't even feel slightly tired yet.

"Rowan," says Juliet without any hesitation whatsoever.

"How come?"

"He's . . . so protective of the other two," says Juliet, and there, in the eyes, while she's talking, I can see the Juliet who I have fangirled about The Ark with for the past two years on Facebook Messenger. "He's like the dad of the group. Which is adorable."

Mac seems to think that she's joking or something. He nudges her in the side. "Not because you think he's *attractive* . . . ?"

I resist the urge to roll my eyes. It's obvious Mac has a thing for Juliet, sure, but does he have to be so gross about it?

Juliet laughs, as if what he has said is a very cute and cheeky joke. "No! Oh my God, shut up." She playfully slaps him on the arm. Literally what the fuck? The Juliet I know would have probably made a throwing-up noise and then asked Mac which one *he* found attractive.

Juliet continues. "Jimmy and Rowan are together anyway. There's no hope for anyone wanting to get into those pants."

"Jimmy . . . and Rowan?" Mac gives her a clueless look.

Juliet and I both stare at him.

"Yeah, Jimmy and Rowan," Juliet says. "Jowan. You know. *Jowan.*"

"Oh! Oh, yeah. Of course. You meant *together* together."

It's impossible to be in the Ark fandom without knowing about Jowan—the infamous shipping of Jimmy and Rowan. It originated back in their YouTube days, as soon as Jimmy and Rowan revealed the barest of details about their childhood friendship.

Is it real? Are Jimmy and Rowan really in love with each other and concealing a secret relationship? No one knows, to be honest. There've been signs. Convincing signs. A lot of them simply being the way they look at each other, the way they hug each other and look out for each other and stay by each other's side.

I do ship Jowan. I'll admit it. I ship it a lot.

Whether it's real or not, I think they love each other very much.

I look at Mac and wonder how much he really knows about that side of the fandom. How much is he *in* the fandom, anyway? Does he check @ArkUpdates? Does he take part in discourse and theory discussion? What's his take on the "Joan of Arc" video, the suitcase conspiracy from two years ago, the bonus-track theory?

I could force his opinions out of him now, but I don't feel like it because The Ark will be performing in a minute and I don't want to be in a bad mood.

"Angel?" asks Mac, his voice a little more forced. "Who's your favorite?"

"Definitely Jimmy."

"Why Jimmy?"

I smile sweetly and rest my chin on my hand.

"It's such an interesting concept to think about," I say. "People think boy-band fangirls all just want to kiss the boy-band boys and marry them and live happily ever after. Whereas if you actually asked a lot of fangirls, they probably wouldn't even say that they had a crush on the boy-band boys. It's a different sort of love, to be honest. It's an *I'd probably take a bullet for you but I'd probably feel a bit weird if we just started kissing* sort of love. Add that to the fact that there's an extremely high percentage of LGBTQIA+ people in fandom, particularly queer girls, usually because it's a much more diverse and accepting space than real life, then the percentage of fangirls who are just in it because *Lister's soooo hot* is actually quite small. And that's just one of the many things that outsiders don't get about fandom."

Mac's sly smile drops gradually as I speak. Juliet seems to have momentarily snapped out of her weird flirty persona and is looking between the two of us, intrigued.

"So . . . wait . . . you're gay, or . . . ?" he asks.

I laugh. He couldn't even keep up with what I was saying.

"Well, no," I say, even though I probably would go out with a girl, but I don't really ever get crushes on anyone, so I just don't know what I am right now, to be honest. "I'm just saying there's more to fandom than *I want to kiss a famous boy.*"

He fidgets on the sofa. "Oh, yeah. Yeah, I guess so."

"So who's *your* favorite, Mac? Who would you want to marry and live happily ever after with?"

Juliet finally laughs, and grins at Mac, who clearly looks uncomfortable. Mac then forces out a laugh and just says, "Would you really take a bullet for them?"

The adverts end and an announcer comes onstage. When he reads the name of the next act, *The Ark*, I feel a spike of joy in my heart, a stabbing burst of love and happiness that makes me feel like everything's going to be okay, as long as our boys are in the world.

"Yeah, I think so," I say.

# JIMMY KAGA-RICCI

Someone's given me the wrong guitar, but I can't try to find the right one because one of our stage crew is fixing my angel wings onto the back of my jacket while we stand backstage during an ad break. Someone is combing Lister's hair for him. Rowan's changing into something black so we're all matching.

The Ark likes theatricality.

"Hey, where's my guitar? This is Rowan's spare," I ask the air around me. Someone swaps the one I'm holding for my actual guitar and I hang it round my neck. It's not even really "my guitar," anyway. My guitar, a lower-end Les Paul that my grandad snagged for £50 from a flea market for my birthday when I was eleven, is safely locked away in my apartment. The guitar I'm holding right now is probably worth over five grand.

Rowan, changed now into a black bomber jacket with embroidered doves on the front, comes up to me and grabs me by the arms.

"How you doing, Jimjam?"

"What?" I ask, not understanding the question.

He squeezes my arms, then rubs them soothingly. "Are you calm?"

"Am I calm?"

No. I am never calm.

"I'm calm," I say.

"Sure?"

"Yeah."

Rowan pats me on the head, just to be sure. I brush my fingers over my cross necklace again.

Lister joins us. He's swapped his burgundy jacket and white T-shirt for a black button-up. He looks the most excited out of the three of us, which is no surprise.

"Remind me, what are we doing?" he asks, bouncing up and down on the balls of his feet. "'Joan of Arc' or 'Lie Day'?"

Rowan laughs and I groan.

"Do you *ever* pay attention to *anything*?" I say. "Were you high during sound check?"

Lister shoots me an offended look. "God, sorry, Dad!" This kind of makes me chuckle, and then Lister smiles, a real old rare Lister smile, and continues, "Okay, for real . . . which is it?"

⇄  ◄◄ ⊙ ►►  ♥

We are used to this now. Maybe a little too used to it. We won Best Newcomer earlier. Of course we did—everyone on the internet said we were going to. When we step up to perform, everyone cheers, even though we're newcomers, even though we're only just starting to get known in America. None of that fazes me, though. Overexposure, I guess.

But when we step out onto the stage, shrouded in darkness, I get a rush of adrenaline and I can't stop smiling because *finally we get to play our music.*

Like I said, The Ark likes theatricality. We don't just stand there and play—which is fine, but it's not us. Lister is center on drums and Rowan and I stand behind him on a raised platform, playing various instruments depending on the song—keys, guitar, Launchpad (me), cello (Rowan). We always wear black.

I am always wearing angel wings. It's a tradition.

When we started out, we'd play with shoddy instruments in the back of pubs and post videos of our garage recordings to YouTube. But tonight, we stand on a stage wider than three houses, and when Rowan gives us a nod and starts to strum the screechy opening bars of "Joan of Arc," the LED screens behind us light up a bright, blinding orange, and we're lost in the dry ice mist.

Then begins our intro—a low, distorted robot voice that we play at the beginning of every tour show. It was my idea at the start of our last tour.

*I am not afraid, said Noah*
*I was born for this*

I mouth along. It always makes me smile, reminding me of all the Bible stories Grandad used to read to me when I was little. It's a slight variation of a Joan of Arc quote too. I love tying all the parts of ourselves together.

I find myself shouting "West Coast!" just because I'm so excited, and the audience cheers right back at me. Weird how it never seems to hit me until the music starts. Until the music starts, I'm just floating through it all. Waiting to get to the next song so I can breathe again.

*Born to survive the storm*
*Born to survive the flood*

Our platform starts to rise into the air. The light changes and I glance around to look at the LED screen. It's a giant Renaissance painting of an armored woman wielding a sword. Joan.

Then lights are on me, just as the voice speaks its final words.

*Believe in me*
*Said Noah to the animals*
*And two by two, they ascended*
*Onto the ark*

# TUESDAY

**"THE VOICE HAD PROMISED ME THAT, AS SOON AS
I CAME TO THE KING, HE WOULD RECEIVE ME."
—JOAN OF ARC**

# ANGEL RAHIMI

I am jump-scared awake at 11:14 a.m. by Juliet making a sound resembling that of a goose passing into the afterlife.

I sit up. Juliet and I slept in one of her nan's spare rooms. Mac slept in another. Weirdly, Juliet seems to have brought most of her possessions with her—the wardrobe is overflowing with potential outfits for Thursday and the floor is littered with assorted Ark merchandise.

"Did I just dream that," I say, "or did you just shriek very loudly?"

"I think *I'm* dreaming," says Juliet.

Juliet is staring at her phone like it's a solid bar of gold.

"What's happened?" I ask.

"Jowan," she says, and then turns her head and stares at me. "Jowan."

I take a moment to process.

Because saying *Jowan* like that, like it's a magic spell, like it's the name of an entire country—there is only one thing that she could mean.

"You're joking," I say.

She simply thrusts the phone at me.

On-screen is a news article.

### THE ARK'S JIMMY KAGA-RICCI AND ROWAN OMONDI CAUGHT SLEEPING TOGETHER AT LONDON APARTMENT

My heart starts to hammer. My palms start sweating.

I scroll down.

While their fandom's theories concerning a relationship between The Ark's Jimmy Kaga-Ricci and Rowan Omondi have previously been considered naught but the sexual fantasies of fourteen-year-old girls, a new piece of interesting evidence has emerged from the depths of the internet.

We've acquired a photograph appearing to show Jimmy and Rowan sleeping next to each other in a bed. They appear to be inside their SW3 apartment (in which Jimmy, Rowan, and Lister live), as a London skyline can be clearly seen through the large window next to them.

Is this fandom conspiracy real? You decide! Jimmy and Rowan look pretty cozy to us!

The photo does indeed show Jimmy and Rowan sleeping next to each other on a bed. Rowan is on his front, one arm slung over Jimmy's chest. Jimmy's head is tilted ever so slightly towards Rowan.

It's adorable.

It's like it's been Photoshopped.

It's better than any piece of fan art I have ever seen.

"I have died and gone to heaven," I say. I put the phone down on the bed and turn to Juliet. "What is happening right now?"

Juliet has both of her hands on her face. "I'm dying," she says.

"You don't think—I mean—the title of the article was kind of misleading, but—"

"Look at them. *Look at them.* They're *cuddling.*"

I look at the photo again. They are sort of almost nearly cuddling.

"They're cuddling," I say.

Juliet flops down onto the bed.

"This is the beginning," she says, "isn't it?"

Of course it's the beginning. It's the beginning of everything we ever dreamed of. Jimmy and Rowan standing up and showing everyone that love is real. That even amid all the shit, there is some pure goodness in the world.

Juliet suddenly flings herself out of bed. "I need to tell Mac."

Having forgotten that Mac exists for the past few minutes, I am suddenly sprung back to reality.

"Oh yeah. Don't bring him in here, though."

Juliet gives me a confused look until I point at my scarf-less head, and then she gives me a thumbs-up and leaves the room.

Once she's gone, I load up the image on my own phone. When did this happen? There was nothing about this when I checked Twitter after I got up to pray earlier this morning. Amazing how everything can change within the space of a few hours.

I stare at it. It's beautiful. God. It's so beautiful. Jimmy is so beautiful. Rowan is so beautiful. They love each other so much. I want to cry. Nobody will ever love me like that. Doesn't matter. Jowan exists. There's something good in the world. There's a point to being alive.

Every single day I wish I knew the full story. I wish I knew how they met. I wish I knew the things they say to each other. Who's louder. Who's the joker. I wish someone had recorded their every interaction and I could sit down and watch them all from start to finish.

I'll never know, though. But at least we have this.

Enough to make me believe.

When Juliet calls "Angel, do you want breakfast?" through the door, I realize I have been sitting in bed looking at the photo for over ten minutes.

# JIMMY KAGA-RICCI

Please don't let me die in a plane crash. Please. I mean, I'm on a plane every other day, so if it's going to be anyone, it's going to be me. Can you imagine dying in a plane crash? All those people screaming in an oversized tin can. Knowing they're gonna die. Can't even call your grandad on the phone. Sounds like something that would happen to me.

I'm curled up in my first-class seat, clutching my cross necklace, counting down the minutes until we land safely back in London and the chance of me dying a fiery metallic death is back to "relatively low." I know the chance is low anyway. I know that. But I can't stop thinking about it, and the more I do, the faster my heart beats and the harder I find it to take a full breath. At this rate, I'll flood the plane with my own sweat. Create a self-fulfilling prophecy.

Suddenly, Rowan yanks up the blind that shields my seat from the rest of the cabin. He looks furious, but then his expression drops into something softer, and he says, "Jesus. You all right?"

I release my necklace and wipe my hand on my joggers.

"Planes," I say.

"Oh, yeah." Rowan opens the compartment door and sits down on the table next to my seat. "You know you're more likely to—"

"To die in a car crash, to get struck by lightning, or to get eaten by a shark than to die in a plane crash. I know."

"Oh."

There's a pause. My breathing has calmed down.

"Anyway," I say. "What's up?"

He sighs, then glances around the cabin. There are a few people staring at us, which isn't unusual. I've already caught two people taking photos of us when they thought we weren't looking. Not that I confronted them about it.

Rowan shuffles farther inside my compartment, shuts the door, then pulls up the blind so no one can see or hear us. He drops his iPad into my lap and touches his fingertips to his lips.

I look at it, confused. "Did you get stuck on *Candy Crush* again?"

He gestures at the iPad and doesn't say anything. The expression on his face suggests that this is not a *Candy Crush*–related issue.

I pick up the iPad and look at it.

On screen is a picture of me and Rowan sleeping in my bed in our London apartment.

I laugh. It's kind of funny. We look like we're a couple or something. Lister must have taken it as a joke.

I look up at Rowan, expecting him to be laughing too. But he isn't. His eyes are wide. His hand is gripping the back of my seat.

"I don't understand," I say.

"Haven't you checked Twitter today?" he says, shaking his head almost manically.

"No?"

Rowan snatches the iPad back and swipes the screen. The image minimizes and the screen returns to Rowan's Twitter notifications, which seem to be full of people tweeting him the photo. He starts to scroll through them, holding the iPad in front of my face. Everyone is tweeting him about the photo, and the link to where it came from.

I sit upright in my chair, take the iPad from Rowan, and click on the nearest link.

It takes me to a big but gossipy news site, the usual sort of place that jumps on any Ark news for easy clicks. And there, in the center of the page, is the photo of me and Rowan, accompanied by the title:

### THE ARK'S JIMMY KAGA-RICCI AND ROWAN OMONDI CAUGHT SLEEPING TOGETHER AT LONDON APARTMENT

"Well, that's misleading," I say.

"Quality clickbait," says Rowan, nodding solemnly.

It's almost chilling, actually. Where did they get this photo from? How did Lister slip up this time?

"I can't believe he did something like this *again*," groans Rowan.

He's referring, of course, to the fact that Lister is the sole reason I came out publicly as trans when I was sixteen. He tweeted a photo of our open suitcases while we were packing for a tour with a cheerful "PACKING FOR TOUR WITH THE BOYS #TheArkEuropeTour." This included my suitcase, which had my hormone-blocker medication in it, very clearly visible in one of the suitcase compartments. And so the speculation and coming-out pressure began.

I got over it pretty quickly, but Rowan barely spoke to Lister for two entire months.

Coming out at sixteen was probably a bit too soon for me—I wasn't completely sure whether I was ready for everyone in the world to know—but it wasn't a total disaster. There was hate, obviously, but most of our fans were amazingly supportive and it actually brought in a whole new load of listeners, ones who looked up to *me* specifically. Which was kind of cool.

Suddenly we weren't just a teenage boy band playing fun, upbeat tunes. Suddenly we were something a little bit more important than that.

"Didn't think he was quite that dumb," Rowan continues.

"Are you talking about me?"

Rowan and I turn to look at Lister, who is leaning over the compartment wall and peering down at us. He has sunglasses on and has his hood up, concealing around 80 percent of his head.

The smell of alcohol immediately fills the air.

Rowan gives him a look of disdain, and then holds his iPad up in front of Lister's face. "Explain."

Lister squints at the screen. There's a pause.

"Mate, that's touching," he says. "Very sweet. Romantic." He looks up at the two of us and puts his hand on his heart. "I wish you both every happiness."

Rowan sighs. "Come on, man. Why'd you do it?"

"Do what?"

"Send them the picture."

Lister's smile drops. "I didn't."

Rowan groans again, throws his hands in the air, and turns round. "Oh my God, now you're gonna stand here and *deny* it for half an hour."

"What?" Lister chuckles nervously, but Rowan just shakes his head and ambles back to his own compartment, which is opposite mine.

Lister takes Rowan's place and sits down, looking at me. He takes his sunglasses off, revealing eyes with dark circles underneath them. I knew he was drinking too much at the after-party last night, and the cocktails he's had on the plane today probably haven't been helping.

"You guys think I took a picture of you two in bed together and then sent it to some gossip blog?" says Lister. His smile is wobbly.

I stare at him.

"Jimmy," he says. "Come on."

"Did you, though?" I ask.

"*No.* I swear. I would take a blood oath with one hand on your Bible if you had it with you."

"You're literally the only one who could have taken it." I load up the photo on my laptop. "Look, we're in my bedroom. It's nighttime."

"It could have been someone at a party—"

49

"I wouldn't be asleep if we had anyone else in our house. Obviously."

Lister slumps back against the compartment wall. He actually looks a bit annoyed. "I can't believe you think it's me. I know I'm stupid, but I'm not *that* stupid."

"You've done stuff like this before. The Twitter suitcases thing."

I instantly regret mentioning it when Lister looks up at me, hurt.

"I— That was an accident—" he stammers. "And I'm still really, really, *really* sorry about that. I swear I don't think I'll ever forgive myself—"

"You seriously swear it wasn't you?"

"Jimmy, I *swear*. I think I'd remember sending a photo to a gossip website." He shakes his head. "That's such a weird thing to do, why would I do that?"

Okay.

I think I do believe him.

"Who else could've taken it, then?" I look down at the photo. Whoever took it was literally standing right next to my bed, staring down at us. Lister leans forward and looks at it with me.

"What if," he says, sitting back up and staring at me with wild eyes, "someone *broke in*?"

"What?"

"Yeah. It happens all the time to celebrities. Fans break in and just . . . spy on them. Take photos. Steal a couple of things, maybe. I've heard so many horror stories about K-pop band members where they got home and there'd be a fangirl hiding in their wardrobe or they'd wake up in the middle of the night and there'd just be a girl watching them from the other side of the room—"

"*Lister*," says Rowan sharply without looking towards us, but it's too late. My palms have started to sweat again. A fangirl, dying to know whether Jowan is real, sneaks into our apartment and hides, waiting for the proof that she desperately wants. And we hand it right to her after falling asleep midway through a *Brooklyn Nine-Nine* marathon. Next, she installs a camera in our bathroom, films us naked, posts it online. Then there's a camera in our bedroom, which films us doing other stuff, personal stuff. Then she hides in my wardrobe, ready to step out and stab me in the neck—

"*Jimmy*," says Lister, snapping his fingers in front of my face. "You're spacing out."

"What?"

"It's not a big deal. You know what? I bet you just fell asleep when we were having a party and forgot about it and someone walked in and thought you looked cute."

I don't believe him.

All I can see is some girl waiting to kill me in a wardrobe.

⇄ ◄◄ ⊙ ►► ♥

Rowan continues to give Lister the silent treatment for the rest of the flight. He still thinks Lister took the photo.

The shipping itself isn't a major inconvenience to any of us. If anything, it keeps the fans interested. They think Judgment Day will eventually come and there'll be a big reveal that Rowan and I are secretly in love.

There won't. We're not.

I suppose sometimes it makes me feel a bit awkward. Knowing that a fair percentage of the people who come to meet us or see our concerts have probably read extremely explicit fanfiction about me and my best friend having sex. I got curious once and had a look at some of it, which was a mistake, because it just made me feel really uncomfortable.

But it doesn't matter. They keep believing and we know the truth and keep on going. Nothing really changes and everyone is happy. So that's fine.

Lister escaped most of the fanfiction stuff, somehow. He's always been a bit separate from Rowan and me. Rowan and I are generally considered attractive, by magazines and blogs and stuff, but Lister is so lusted over that he's been asked to model for Gucci *four* times. Rowan and I have been friends since we were seven, but we only met Lister when we were thirteen.

Rowan and I wanted to start a band, and we forced Lister to be part of it at the last minute because he was the only kid we knew who could play the drums.

It's always sort of been Rowan and Jimmy, plus Lister.

We still love him, of course.

But that's just the way it is.

When we land at Gatwick and start collecting our stuff together, Lister walks over to Rowan, perching on his table, and says, "Come on, Ro, you know I wouldn't do something like that."

Rowan shrugs and doesn't meet Lister's eyes. "It doesn't matter."

Lister stands up and wraps his arms round Rowan's chest. "*Ro Ro.* Don't be angry at me. I'll do the washing-up for a week."

Rowan can't stop himself smiling. "There's a higher chance of The Ark winning Best Country Artist than you doing the washing-up for a *single day.*"

Lister lets him go and smiles and, for the moment, all seems to be forgiven, but when Lister skips away to his own chair, I watch Rowan's smile fade away into nothing.

# ANGEL RAHIMI

"And they're giving you enough to eat?" asks Dad.

"No, Dad, they're refusing to give me any food and I'm having to survive on the packet of crisps you gave me yesterday."

"Well, that would make quite an adventure, at least."

I sigh heavily and lean against the hallway wall, switching my phone to my other hand.

"You don't need to worry. I'm having a good time."

"I know," says Dad. "But after that big argument with your mother yesterday . . . I just wanted to check up on you. And she's been telling me all about this TV show *Clownfish—*"

"I think it's called *Catfish*, Dad."

"Well, according to your mother, whatever kind of fish it is, it's one that could kidnap you and sell you into sexual slavery."

"Juliet and I have talked to each other on Skype loads before now. She's very nice and is looking after me perfectly fine and she isn't a middle-aged man looking to drug and kill me."

Dad laughs. "I'm very glad to hear that."

"Is Mum still angry at me?"

"I think so, yes. She was typing very loudly at her computer this morning."

We both laugh.

"I think," says Dad, "she's just frustrated because she feels like you've been keeping this from her."

"I talk about The Ark *all* the time. I don't know why this was a surprise."

"Fereshteh, it was a little bit of a surprise to me too."

"Why?"

"I suppose . . . I suppose I never thought you actually cared about this band *that* much. And to see you just . . . just start *shouting* at your mother like that—"

"She shouted at me too!"

"I know, I know. But I've never seen you so angry, my girl. You're not a naturally angry person. It was a bit of a shock for everyone."

There's a pause. I guess it had been a major argument. One of the worst I've had with my parents. I usually get along with my parents really well. I don't tell them everything about my life, obviously, but I share stuff with them and we have a laugh sometimes.

But the argument yesterday. I can sort of see why Mum and Dad were a bit taken aback.

"Well, sorry, I guess," I say. "This is just really important to me."

"I know," he says. "I know. But we're worried it might be *too* important."

"What does that mean?"

"Well . . . more important than your education."

"I told you, that school leavers' ceremony thing isn't important—"

"Not just that. You are growing up now, my girl. You'll be studying at university, then finding yourself a job, starting a new life. And we just want to make sure . . . you have that in mind too. Because all you seem to talk about or care about is this boy band."

"That's not all I talk about!" I say, but now that I think about it, it does seem to come up in conversation quite a lot with my parents. And they listen politely, but they don't care about The Ark.

"We're just concerned, Fereshteh."

I laugh, not knowing what to say. "I'm . . . I'm just going to a concert."

Juliet wanders into the hallway, a cup of tea in her hand and her hair pulled back into a loose French plait. She notices the serious expression on my face and mouths, "Everything okay?"

I give her a reassuring nod.

"Fereshteh? Have you gone?"

"No, I'm here, Baba."

"Just stay safe. We worry."

"I know you do. But I'm not stupid. I won't do anything stupid, I promise."

"You are a smart girl. Smarter than us, probably."

I smile a little. "Nah, you two are the smartest of them all."

I reassure him again that I'll be fine and hang up.

"What was all that about?" asks Juliet, perching on a radiator and looking up at me.

"That was my dad. My mum's still angry."

Juliet grimaces. "Oh."

I laugh. "Don't worry. Parents, am I right? She'll chill out when she realizes she's in the wrong."

Juliet chuckles weakly and looks away. I know she's had some bust-ups with her parents in the past—they're both very important lawyers, as are Juliet's older siblings, but Juliet wants to go to uni to do theater set design.

"Oh," she says. "Yeah." There's an odd expression on her face, as if this is an awkward thing for us to talk about. Maybe it is. I guess we don't talk about our families *that* often.

Mac chooses this moment to thunder downstairs, adjusting his belt. At the sight of Juliet, he immediately starts running his hands through his hair.

"What are you two talking about?" he asks. Nosy.

"You, behind your back," says Juliet with a sly smile that is most definitely the Juliet I know.

They start talking and wander off towards the living room. I stay and stare down at my phone, thinking about what Dad was trying to explain about Mum.

Mum doesn't understand me. She doesn't understand why I reacted so strongly about a boy band.

And I know they're both worried about my future. They don't ever say it, but I know they know I'm average, and average is disappointing for them. Especially compared to my brother. The pinnacle of ambition and success.

Don't worry. I know that. I'm fully aware I'm average. God, I'm so, so aware I'm average.

But I'm not going to think about any of that right now.

I don't need to.

This week isn't about my life.

I don't have to think about it at all.

This week is about The Ark.

I spend a greater part of the day talking about Jowan. With Juliet, and on the internet.

Tumblr is awash with theories and opinions and discourse. Whether Jowan is real is split approximately fifty-fifty. I suppose Jimmy and Rowan being asleep in the same bed, cuddling, isn't *exactly* official proof, but in my eyes it's close enough. It looks pretty damn romantic to me. I'm an optimist. I like to believe that love exists.

Twitter won't shut up either. #Jowan has been trending for hours. My whole timeline is flooded with people screaming and crying in caps lock. Neither Jimmy nor Rowan have tweeted about it, but they'll have to say something soon, won't they?

I wish I could ask them in real life.

I wish I could see them and tell them everything will be okay and everyone is happy for them.

"Do you think they're upset?" asks Juliet, while we're both sitting on the same living-room sofa, our laptops open in front of us, *Brooklyn Nine-Nine* playing on the TV across the room. Mac sits alone on the other sofa, scrolling through his phone.

"Maybe," I say.

"I feel bad . . . feeling so happy when they're probably upset," says Juliet.

"We don't really know what they think about it yet, though," I say, forcing a chuckle, but it's obvious to both of us I'm just trying to justify our joy at the situation.

Once I've read every opinion one could possibly have on the subject, I wrap myself in one of the blankets from last night and reread one of my favorite Jowan fanfics. It starts when Jimmy and Rowan met in primary school, and ends when they're both twenty-seven, having left The Ark and gone on to solo careers. They fall in and out of love multiple times, always finding their way back to each other.

I know it's not real. The details, anyway. But I like to imagine.

I like to hope.

I like to feel happy.

# JIMMY KAGA-RICCI

I have had a lot of bad days (I know, shocking, right?), but today really is making a strong case to join The Day I Had a Panic Attack at Children in Need, The Day I Passed Out at a Meet-and-Greet, and The Day I Fell off the Stage at the London Palladium as all-time worst days of my life.

These probably don't sound very bad, but they were bad. Please take my word for it.

During the drive into London, I contemplate the strong possibility that someone was able to break into our apartment and take a photo of me while I was asleep, meaning that literally anyone could break in at any time and do . . . anything. It could be anyone. A deluded fan who'd do anything to see us. A journalist wanting to uncover our deepest secrets. A transphobe who just wants me to *die*. God knows there are people like that out there.

Cecily makes five different phone calls throughout the journey, each one pestering a different person about how this photo made international news, but she just seems to get angrier each time. She ends the final phone call with a heavy groan and a shake of the head at Rowan and me.

Looks like not even Cecily has the answers this time.

The fans don't seem to think anything's wrong. The only thing they're talking about in my Twitter notifications is that they all think "Jowan is real." It makes me feel sort of sad for them. They're only going to be disappointed, one way or another.

When Rowan reveals he has a girlfriend, maybe.

Bliss Lai.

The girlfriend who's stayed a secret for the past two years.

"You've got that look on your face," says Rowan, midway through the journey. He's sitting opposite me in the car, like he had been on the way to the WCMAs, and for a moment I feel like we're back there, before I remember we're already five thousand miles away.

"What look?" I say.

"The constipated look. The sweaty-palms look."

I rub my forehead. "Someone's going to break into our apartment and kill me."

Rowan sighs and pats me on the knee. "Come on, Jimjam, don't think stuff like that."

"We could hire a full-time bodyguard?" says Lister, who is sitting next to me sipping from a Starbucks cup.

Somehow the idea of having a huge suited person loitering in our apartment 24/7 makes me feel even worse.

Cecily glances up at me from her phone. "Why don't you just focus on the important stuff this week, huh, babe? We've got the final show on Thursday and then the contract signing on Friday."

"Do you think if we hired a full-time bodyguard they'd do the hoovering for us?" asks Lister.

Rowan turns his head slowly towards Lister. "If you can name me one occasion that you have *ever* hoovered our apartment, I will give you five hundred quid right now."

Lister opens his mouth, then freezes, then closes it again, and we all laugh at him, and for a few moments I stop thinking about being murdered.

⇄ ⏮ ⏯ ⏭ ♥

Cecily only tells us that we have an interview with *Rolling Stone* today when the car pulls up at a fancy hotel and Lister asks, "Why the *fuck* are we here?"

None of us are particularly surprised. We're used to just being told where to go and what to do.

"It's the Bliss thing," she says with a sigh. "I've promised *Rolling Stone* an interview with you so they don't run the Bliss story."

I shoot a glance at Rowan. He looks a little sick.

We sprawl ourselves around one of the hotel's conference rooms and a few hair and makeup people arrive to make us look less dead. This thankfully includes Alex, who is one of my favorite hair and makeup people because he treats me like I'm a real human being and not one of those posters you pull out of a magazine.

He gives me a pat on the shoulder after he finishes doing my hair.

"You looked tired today, Jimmy."

I chuckle. "Sorry."

"You getting enough sleep?"

"What counts as enough sleep?"

"I dunno . . . six to eight hours a night?"

I just laugh at him.

Across the room, Rowan is reading the copy of our new record contract that Cecily's just given him. He's frowning deeply, which is not a good sign.

"It's different," says Cecily while standing at the sink, handing Lister another cup of water. I think the water is just making Lister, who has passed drunkenness and has entered a full-on middle-of-the-day hangover, feel worse.

"*Different*," says Rowan, raising his eyebrows. "It's, like, ten times more work than we normally do. They want us to do a two-year-long world tour? *Two full years?* Why didn't you mention that earlier?"

"We don't have to talk about this now," says Cecily, holding up her phone and tapping on it.

"We've only got three days left before we sign, though," says Rowan. He points at a page. "I just . . . this is a lot more than we normally do, publicity-wise. More interviews, more appearances, more collabs. I don't know whether we're even gonna be able to deal with all this."

"Babe, don't worry about it. We'll talk about it after today."

Lister leans over the sink and dry-heaves, then drools a bit.

"If you throw up," says Cecily, "I will actually smack you."

"Can't we just go home?" Lister mumbles.

"No," she says.

⇄ ◄◄ ⊙ ►► ♥

"Jimmy, turn your head to the left a bit? That's it."

The camera flashes. Pretty sure I blinked.

Our stylists are magic. They transformed the three of us from greasy and sleep-deprived lads into pop icons in under an hour. The bags under Rowan's eyes have disappeared entirely. Lister looks positively healthy. I barely recognize myself in the mirror.

And we're wearing outrageously beautiful designer clothes. That always makes me feel like magic.

The camera flashes again. I wonder what the time is. Not even sure whether it's the morning or afternoon.

"Jimmy, just look at the camera, now. That's it."

It's a good thing everyone likes the "dead behind the eyes" look.

"Rowan, can we get you in the middle now?"

Rowan stands next to me. He's been scarily quiet since he started flicking through the contract. Normally he'd be the one trying to cheer us up when we're all tired, making sarcastic comments or messing around, distracting us when we were trying to pull serious expressions.

But he's too lost in thought today. We all are, a bit.

"Rowan, can you just put your arms round Jimmy and Lister for me?"

He does, and the camera flashes.

"Hold on, just pause for a sec, please." The woman directing the shoot calls at the photographer to pause. "Lister, you all right? You need to break for a minute?"

Rowan and I turn to Lister.

Lister's eyes are watering and his skin is pale white.

"Er, yeah, just need to go to the loo," he mumbles, and then walks swiftly out of the room. Rowan and I follow him immediately, like there's a string attaching us, just in time to hear him run into the nearest bathroom and throw up in a toilet.

We enter the bathroom. Lister tells us to go away, but Rowan just walks up to him and starts rubbing his back as he throws up again. I don't really know what to do—there's not much I *can* do—so I just sit down on a radiator and wait.

There's a big window on one side of the bathroom. Big enough to climb out, probably. We're on the ground floor. We could just climb out and run. Get up and go.

⇄ ◄◄ ⊙ ►► ♥

"So, lads."

We're with the interviewer now, back in the hotel conference room. He's white, middle-aged, balding, and his name is Dave. Dave looks evil.

He has put a Dictaphone on the table between us, and it is recording everything we say.

He nods at us slowly.

"The Ark has always had something special," he begins, as if he's already writing the article in his head. "YouTube success. Then chart success. And you're a strong example for the diversity everyone craves in today's media"—he gestures at Rowan—"a young man, born to two immigrants, in the height of success and fame"—he gestures at Lister—"a young man who grew up in a single-parent, working-class family on benefits, only to make himself a millionaire before he turned eighteen"—he gestures at me—"and a trans-gender guy of both Indian and Italian heritage, proving to the world that being transgender is just one tiny part of you."

I resist the urge to roll my eyes. Being trans has been a pretty big part of my life so far, thanks, but that shouldn't be particularly relevant here, in an interview about our music. Younger interviewers usually like to chat about music and fans, but older interviewers, like Dave, are always obsessed with how many adjectives they can put before our names.

"And now a European tour, huh? *Started from the bottom, now we're here?* How does it feel to be at the absolute top of your game?"

Lister, having thrown up several times, looks once again like a god, and begins his We Are So Lucky to Be Here and We Love Our Fans spiel.

The interviewer nods along, like they usually do.

Then he says, "Now, guys. I know you know you're very fortunate people. You've won several prestigious British and European music awards. Gone gold on two albums. A sold-out European tour." He leans forward onto his elbows, like he's the CEO and we're three underperforming interns. "But I want to know the *real* Ark. I want to know your highs"—he gestures vaguely towards the ceiling—"and your lows." He points at the ground and narrows his eyes. "I want to dig into your hearts and your minds. I want you to tell me what it's *really* like being a famous *boy band.*"

None of us say anything.

"Why don't we start at the start, huh?" Dave continues. "I've heard it from Wikipedia but I want to hear it from you. How did you meet?"

I wait for either of the others to speak, but Rowan still seems distracted after reading the new contract, and Lister looks a little like he didn't understand the question.

I smile widely at Dave and begin the story of how Rowan and I met at primary school, and when we were thirteen we wanted to start a band. We needed a drummer, so we got Lister to join, after some persuading. He didn't want to hang around with two music nerds, but he was the only person we knew who could play drums.

"Must seem like a world away now, huh?" Dave chips in. "Three school-boys starting a band." I don't really know whether to continue the story, but then Dave holds up his palms and says, "Sorry! I interrupted. Carry on."

"When we were thirteen, we starting uploading our songs to YouTube. A year and two hundred thousand views later, Cecily Wills from Thunder Management found us and took us straight to Fort Records, and that was that."

"Ah, the power of the internet," says Dave after I've finished. There might be something sinister about the way he says it, or I might be imagining it.

We talk for a while more about the formation of The Ark. I do most of the talking, which is a little unusual, but Lister keeps fidgeting—he probably still feels a bit ill—and Rowan is still acting weird and silent.

"Now, I want to delve a little bit into your relationship with your fans," says Dave. "Particularly your *online* fans."

Here we go.

"The Ark has a well-established online fan base. Perhaps one of the biggest in the world. You've got people watching and analyzing your every move, perhaps even invading your privacy, in certain areas."

He pauses, so I nod at him.

"In particular, The Ark's online fan base is famous for its conspiracies and overanalyses." He leans back in his chair. "How does stuff like that make you *feel*?"

None of us say anything.

Cecily watches on from the corner of the room.

"A difficult question, I suppose," continues Dave, unfazed by our silence. "Let's look at it a different way. I'm a journalist. I write serious articles, and, yes, I hope that they affect people, in a similar way your music does. I hope that they change people's way of thinking. Teach them something. Make them *feel* something." He crosses his legs. "But at the same time, I am, for the lack of a better phrase, a 'normal person.' I send off my article to my editor, go home from the office, and nobody cares." He holds up his hands and laughs. "Nobody cares! And there's freedom in that. But you three—you don't have that freedom anymore. You don't have the freedom that normal people have. You barely even had the chance to experience it at *all*."

There's another pause.

"And I want to know how that makes you feel," says Dave.

Rowan sits up in his chair.

"We love our fans," he says, but it sounds wrong. It sounds like he's lying. "Everything they do, they do out of love, and we love them back for that."

Dave nods, smiling. He knows.

"Love is a strong word for people you've never met," he says. "For people that watch your every move, that talk about you behind your backs, that formulate their own opinions of your personalities and relationships and behavior, all without having spoken to you, or often even *seen* you, in real life."

Rowan doesn't drop eye contact. "Appreciate, then. We appreciate our fans. We wouldn't be here without our fans." It sounds like he's reading from a script.

Dave waits.

Rowan says nothing.

"And that's all you have to say about your fans?" says Dave.

Lister leans forward and laughs, though it's obviously fake, trying to defuse the tension. "Look, mate, what are you trying to get us to say?"

Dave laughs back at him. "I just want to hear some honesty. That's sort of what I do."

"Well, if you're looking for some easy drama, you picked the wrong band, mate." Lister laughs some more. "We've nearly finished our second European tour. Let us fucking rest. I just want to fucking rest."

"Now *that's* honesty." Dave points at Lister, and then looks back at me and Rowan. "I like him."

Rowan scoffs and looks away.

"Jimmy," says Dave. "How do you feel about your fans?"

The photograph flashes in my mind before I can stop it. A fangirl standing over Rowan and me asleep in my bedroom, eyes empty black pits, a grin with spiky shark teeth.

"I love the fans," I say in a robot voice.

"You don't feel irritated that they keep insisting on knowing everything about your personal lives?" Dave leans back. "I mean, take the photo that emerged on the internet today. You guys must have heard about that, right? How did that make you feel?"

I force the words out. "I . . . felt . . . anxious, because . . . people now think that . . . my and Rowan's rela—friendship is something more than . . . friendship. It looks like we're lying to our fans." My palms are actually sweating. "We'd never lie to our fans."

"Do you not blame your fans for overanalyzing incidents like this?"

"Why would we . . . blame our fans?"

"Because it's their fault," says Dave, raising his hands into the air in pretend innocence. "You can see it. I can see it. Your fans take any scraps of evidence they can for their wild theories—whether that's 'Jowan' or anything else—and manipulate it into something they can't *not* believe. They're believing lies, Jimmy. Not just believing—putting *hope* in these lies, caring *deeply* about these lies. Doesn't that bother you?"

My mouth has gone very dry. I glance at Cecily again. She is still looking at me.

"Look, what do you wanna hear?" says Rowan suddenly, interrupting. "Me and Jimmy are not in a relationship. We're friends. No matter what the fucking fans say. They can do whatever they want. We can't stop them. We know we're telling the truth. That's enough."

"Oh, I know that's the truth," says Dave. "Don't you think I'd rather be publishing the truth?"

Everyone in the room is silent.

"About Bliss Lai, I mean," he says. "Your girlfriend."

"Yeah, I got that," Rowan growls.

"You Ark boys are getting yourself tangled up in this huge web of lies," says Dave, leaning back into his chair and smiling sadly at us. "And I just worry, I suppose, that the fans—all these hundreds of thousands of, let's face it, impressionable teenage girls—are the ones who are going to suffer in the end. And I want to know how you all feel about that."

"We've done nothing," says Rowan. His voice is calm, but somehow, he's never sounded so scary.

"You've lied all this time. Lies by omission, lies by *not telling the truth*. About Bliss, and Jowan." Dave smiles and looks directly at me. "Even Jimmy lied for a long time to his audience about *what he was—*"

And it all seems to happen in under a second. Lister shoving his chair back, standing up, and grabbing Dave by the collar, hoisting him out of his seat, his free hand curling into a fist. Cecily jumping towards us and crying out at him to stop, and Rowan standing too, shouting garbled swear words and *"How fucking dare you?"* Me sinking farther and farther and farther into my chair, hoping it might swallow me entirely, transport me to another dimension where none of this is happening.

Dave laughs and says again, "Now *that's* honesty."

# ANGEL RAHIMI

Honestly, thank God today is a game-changing day in Jowan fandom history, because if it wasn't, I would be having an awkward time, instead of a great time, which is what I'm definitely having, because it's impossible to be unhappy knowing that Jimmy and Rowan are in love with each other.

The only plan for the day is the Ark fandom gathering at a Wetherspoons in Leicester Square tonight. Mac has been skulking around, talking to Juliet at every single opportunity. He talks all the way through us trying to rewatch last night's WCMA performance. Then he talks all the way through us trying to watch some of their old YouTube videos.

But no. I'm not going to rise to it. I am not going to let Muliet ruin any of it.

I ask God to give me a bit of extra patience. Because every time Mac speaks, I sort of want to put an entire bag of cotton wool in his mouth.

I didn't exactly tell Mum about the nature of the fandom meetup—that it's at a pub in the evening—because if I had, she'd have been even more eager to stop me going. But I'm eighteen. I can make my own choices. I'll be going to uni next month, living my own life.

And I know Mum still thinks I'm a kid. Most adults see teenagers as confused kids who don't understand much, while they're the pillars of knowledge and experience and know exactly what is right at all times.

I think the truth is that everyone in the entire world is confused and nobody understands much of anything at all.

Juliet has been deciding what to wear for twenty minutes. Relatable. Thankfully, I planned ahead and only brought a few outfits with me, otherwise I too would have been hurling clothes around the room and groaning at the wardrobe.

"But it's not like a *party*, is it?" she says.

"No, but we'll be at Spoons."

"Spoons isn't *fancy*, though."

"Definitely not."

"But it's not a *dress* event, is it?"

"Nah. Smart-casual, I reckon."

I myself am wearing black mom jeans and a loose stripy top—my go-to outfit for when I think I might come into contact with cool people. And the other Ark fans are people I definitely want to impress.

"Mac's coming tonight, right?" I ask her.

She turns to me, a black-and-white skirt in one hand and high-waisted shorts in the other. "Yeah, of course. Why?"

I shrug. "I dunno. He doesn't seem like he *actually* likes The Ark that much."

Which is true. There was barely any reaction from him while The Ark were performing last night, while Juliet and I were trying not to scream too loudly or say "I love my boys" too many times. Mac had just sat and watched.

I'm not going to go as far as to say he's been *lying* about liking The Ark just so he can get with Juliet, but . . .

That's exactly what I think.

"Also," I continue, "he's very annoying."

Juliet snorts, thinking I'm joking. Then she realizes I'm not. "What! What d'you mean?"

"He just . . . He tries to make every conversation about *him*."

Juliet frowns. "*Nah*, I think he's just nervous." She flicks her hair, strikes a pose, and raises her eyebrows at me. "I mean, who wouldn't be nervous to meet Juliet Schwartz, am I *right*?" She starts to strike several fashion poses in a row, which does kind of make me laugh.

"And," she continues, "he's just not as . . . I don't know. He's not as fangirly as we are. He's not as weird as us."

He seems pretty weird, in my opinion, but in more of a conventionally attractive way, like the protagonist of an indie movie, which I expect is why Juliet likes him. Being a male fan of obscure old bands is, for some reason, more acceptable than being a female fan of a twenty-first-century boy band.

There's a pause, and then I say, "Anyway, I cannot *believe* you brought this many clothes with you! It's like you're planning to stay at your nan's for the next four months!"

Juliet freezes on the spot and turns to me. She opens her mouth, and for a moment, I feel as though she's about to say something very serious, but then she just chuckles and says, "Yeah, I know, right?"

⇄ ◀◀ ⊙ ▶▶ ♥

The only person who seems to have no degree of nervousness about tonight's event is Mac. Must be easy to socialize when you're a cute boy with cool taste in music, I suppose.

We hop on the tube and arrive at Leicester Square at around 7:30 p.m.— a sensible half hour later than the start of the event—and The Ark fans are immediately visible. A gathering of at least fifty people of our own age are scattered around one side of the square, sitting or standing in little groups, chattering and laughing and taking selfies.

I've never been to anything like this before. I stayed well away from the kids at school who started cruising the clubs at fifteen, armed with fake IDs and bottles of Archers. I don't drink. Even if I wanted to go to a club, I don't think I could face going into a club sober. I've never actually been drunk, but from what I've seen it does make you a little bit more enthusiastic about entering a dark, sticky cave-like building and jumping up and down to DJ Snake.

Doesn't mean I didn't socialize. But most of my friends from school were like me—not interested in that scene. And none of them wanted to talk about The Ark with me.

So, I never really had much to talk about at all.

"Holy shit, are you Angel? @jimmysangels on Twitter?"

I spin round. Hearing someone say my Twitter and Tumblr username out loud is pretty much a spiritual experience.

I recognize the girl immediately. She's a little shorter than I expected, but I've seen her in pictures she's posted on both Twitter and Instagram—curly hair dyed green, thick-rimmed glasses. Goes by the name of "Pops," username @superowan. Next to her, someone else I recognize—"TJ," @tinyteej—cropped hair and a polo shirt, holding their phone in one hand like it's got a treasure map on it. Both are pretty big-name fans. If I recall correctly, they each have over ten thousand followers on Twitter. Like me.

I point dramatically at both of them and say, *"DUDE."* Then I hold out my arms. "Look at us, meeting in real life!"

⇄  ◀◀ ⊙ ▶▶  ♥

When fans get together, there's little we actually talk about apart from the thing we're all fans of. In this case, obviously, it's our boys.

When I was at secondary school, I didn't have any friends who cared about The Ark as much as I did. And dear God, I tried. I talked about The Ark to anyone who would listen, thinking maybe, maybe one day *someone* would understand why they're so important.

No one ever understood, though. So I was alone.

But here—here is different. People get it. People understand. I keep checking Twitter and seeing a load of tweets tagged #TheArkLondonMeetup. People putting internet usernames to faces. Meeting their best friends in real life for the first time. I start talking to a girl about the Q & A video Jimmy and Rowan made together three years ago, talking about our favorite moments—the little shoulder nudge, the spontaneous harmonized rendition of an old song, the synchronized laughs. The girl lights up, she talks back to me. She gets it. It's magical.

⇄　◄◄ ⊙ ►►　♥

By eight o'clock, most people have moved into Wetherspoons and I'm having a great time, but Mac and Juliet, it seems, are not.

Juliet hasn't spoken to many people. I think she wants to, but Mac won't leave her side or stop talking to her, so it's a bit difficult for her to get involved in any conversations. I keep trying to include her, but somehow Mac keeps dragging her out of the conversation again every single time. Then again, Juliet doesn't seem to mind talking to him.

After a while, they just go and sit at a table together, by themselves. Juliet's showing Mac something on her phone. I'm pissed off at Mac for not letting Juliet have fun and I'm pissed off at Juliet for not seeing how annoying Mac is.

I didn't think I could dislike him any more than I already did.

This was supposed to be my and Juliet's week. The week where we became *real* best friends, not just internet best friends.

I've always had friends—people I sit with at school, people I talk to, people I hang out with sometimes. But I've never had a best friend. I've never had a friend, or anyone, really, who I could talk to about anything and everything, someone who actually cared about the stuff I'm interested in. Someone who didn't roll their eyes when I got too excited about stuff, someone whose eyes didn't glaze over when I told a lengthy anecdote. Someone who actually liked me for who I am, not just because I'm easy to talk to and good at filling awkward silences.

Until I started talking to Juliet.

"Are they your friends, or are you intensely in love with one of them?" a voice asks in my direction, causing me to spin round on the spot and find myself facing a girl with a big smile on her face holding a glass bottle of J2O.

"Definitely friends," I splutter, suddenly imagining ever being in love with either Juliet or Mac. Absolutely laughable.

The girl chuckles to herself and takes a sip of her drink. She doesn't actually look like she's here for the fandom meetup—she's wearing an oversized All Time Low T-shirt and a casual pair of jeans. And she just looks older. No, not older—more *mature*. Someone who doesn't spend every night of their life watching The Ark videos or reading fanfiction.

"Are you here for the meetup?" I ask, genuinely curious.

She leans onto the bar. "Sort of. I'm here with a friend who's a massive Ark fan. I'm not really one myself, but . . ." She grins to herself. "Well, I wanted to see what it was like. I've never been to anything like this."

"If it makes you feel any better, neither have I!" I say. "But . . . I am an Ark fan. If you couldn't already tell." I flash my phone at her, which has Jimmy as the lock-screen wallpaper.

She shrugs. "Can't really tell, can you? Unless you're literally wearing their tour merch. The Ark fans could be *anyone*."

"That's true . . ."

A bartender finally notices I'm waiting and I ask him for another J2O. The girl immediately says, "Hey, we're J2O buddies! Don't you drink either?"

"Nah, mate. I'm Muslim. I mean, some Muslims drink, but I don't."

"Oh, cool! I wish I had a mature excuse like that. I just think it tastes like wee."

"Does it actually taste like wee?"

"Well, I haven't ever drunk my own wee, so I can't actually back up that statement."

The bartender brings over my J2O just as the girl says this, causing him to give us a frown. When he leaves, we both snort out a laugh.

"Note to self, don't talk about drinking wee in front of strangers," she says.

"Too late. It's done."

"Man. Great first impression there."

"It's a memorable one, I'll give you that."

She grins at me and asks, "What's your name, then?"

There's a momentary malfunction in my brain where I forget whether I'm supposed to be introducing myself as Fereshteh or Angel. But we're in the Ark fandom right now. The internet in real life. So I go with the latter.

"It's Angel," I say.

"Angel! What a fucking fantastic name," she says. "I'm Bliss."

⇄　◄◄ ⊙ ►►　♥

Bliss is the best person I've met tonight.

It's rare that I meet someone as talkative as I am, but Bliss is most definitely that. Despite having told me she's not really an Ark fan, she's been running around the room with me, speaking to everyone. I introduce her to TJ and Pops and other fans who I know from the internet. I introduce her to Juliet, once I finally find her lurking near the bar, though Juliet doesn't really seem to know what to say to Bliss, who immediately starts talking about Juliet's phone case, which has pressed flowers inside it, declaring that she had no idea flowers didn't just disintegrate within a few weeks of dying, and why were there not just a load of dead flowers lying around in gardens everywhere? Where do the dead flowers go? I just shrug my shoulders exaggeratedly while Juliet widens her eyes at me as if to say, *What the fuck is happening, Angel?*

Bliss doesn't introduce or even point out the friend she came with. I start to wonder whether she made them up.

Eight thirty becomes ten o'clock and I stick with Bliss for the rest of the night. Something about her is different to the other fans. She's loud and chatty, but when we settle in and start discussing complex Ark issues, Bliss hangs back and just listens. Then she whispers a joke in my ear and I feel like I've known her for years.

"I want to work for a charity," says Bliss, leaning so far over the table that her cheek is almost pressed against it. "To save the world."

"What bit of the world, though?"

"Location, you mean?"

"Nah, like, what sort of charity? The world's a bit shit. Can't save all of it at once."

"*Oh.* Greenpeace, I think. I want to help them try to stop climate change before humans destroy the Earth."

"Wow. Will they be able to do that?"

"Probably not. But it's worth a shot." She looks at me. "What do you want to do?"

"Career, you mean?"

"Yeah! Or, like, life, generally."

It takes me a moment to remember what my future plans are. I almost just mention Thursday's Ark concert. My future plans feel very far away right now, like they're not even real. They're just in the inevitable After I Meet The Ark.

There seems to be very little I care about in my life besides The Ark.

"Psychology," I say. "I'm going to uni in October."

"Cool," says Bliss. "I'll save the nature, you save the humans, and hopefully everything will be all right. Psychologist and climate change warrior save the world."

"Damn. I'd watch that Netflix show."

I learn that Bliss is bisexual. She says it with such extreme confidence that I'm suddenly jealous. Lots of people, especially in the Ark fandom, are like that, though. They know exactly who they are. They put it in their blog "about" page, they put it in their Twitter bio. I never know what to put in my Twitter bio, so I usually just put an Ark lyric in there.

I learn that Bliss's surname is Lai. Her dad is Chinese and her mum is white. Her parents tried to raise her Christian, she says, but she just couldn't ever fully believe in God. She asks me a bit about Islam, because, she says, she skipped all her religious education lessons at school. Normally I get a bit annoyed when people treat me like I'm the fountain of all Islamic knowledge—it's not like every single Muslim has the same opinions and beliefs—but I can't seem to bring myself to be annoyed at Bliss about anything.

"It's not really that different from Christianity, is it?" says Bliss, after I've answered her questions. "My boyfriend's best friend is a really committed Christian."

"There's loads of similarities, yeah."

"I really wish I could believe in God and all that stuff."

"Why?"

"Just gives you something to believe in and cling on to, doesn't it? Even when everything else turns to shit."

I nod at her. She's right. "What do you do when everything turns to shit, then?"

"I dunno. Cry?"

"Well, believing in God doesn't stop you crying every now and then."

"It's a bit like all this, isn't it?" she says, gesturing around her. "The fandom stuff. It feels like we're part of a big religion."

I've never really thought of it like that.

I laugh. "Yeah. Man. We'd better go find something to pray to in the hope that Jimmy and Rowan will bless us with another onstage hug."

Bliss laughs at me, and I wonder, for a moment, if she feels sorry for me, for all of us.

"You guys really like the idea of Jimmy and Rowan together, don't you?"

I shrug. "They make me feel like love exists."

That something good exists. That the world shouldn't just disintegrate, right now. That there's something worth me sticking around for.

"Wouldn't you otherwise?"

I try to think of another pair of people who make me believe in love, but nothing comes to mind. I think about my parents snapping at each other.

A school friend who was dumped after she finally had sex with her boyfriend. A couple sitting in silence at a restaurant table.

"Probably not," I say.

⇄ ◄◄ ⊙ ►► ♥

When I next return from the bathroom, Bliss is on the phone, sitting a little away from the crowds of fans. Gone is the bright, confident expression—she looks like she might be arguing with someone, actually.

As I approach, I hear her say, "Well, it's not really any of your business what I do or where I go," and then she lowers her hand for a second so I can see the screen before she hangs up and drops her phone onto the table.

The name on the phone screen was *Rowan*.

Which is kind of ironic.

"Everything okay?" I ask, sitting down next to her. She whips her head up at me, startled, then shoots me a beaming grin as if nothing had happened.

"Yeah, yeah, all's good!" she says. "Just my mum calling. She doesn't like me staying out late."

"Ah," I say, trying to sound convincing, but I think it's highly unlikely her mum's name is Rowan.

"I should go," she says, and pockets her phone. She gives me a big smile. "It was nice to meet you!"

And then she's gone. Before I have the chance to say anything. I feel a bit like I've maybe just met a ghost.

⇄ ◄◄ ⊙ ►► ♥

After a few more chats and another J2O, I decide it's time I reunited with Muliet, but Juliet is nowhere to be found. Mac, on the other hand, is sitting alone in a booth with a pint of beer in front of him, looking slightly like a cheated lover who's come to the pub to drown his sorrows and write some poetry.

"Who was that you were hanging out with, then?" says Mac, after I've sat down opposite him with a fresh glass of J2O. He appears to be on at least his third beer.

He looks a little bit lonely, sitting in a booth by himself, and I kind of feel sorry for him.

"I dunno. Some girl I just met."

"You just met her? Looked like you were BFFs."

I shrugged. "We got along, I guess."

There's an awkward pause.

"Well, I didn't realize you were some sort of fandom celebrity," he says with the fakest smile I've ever seen.

I laugh at him. "That's a massive overstatement."

He raises an eyebrow. "You joking? Literally *everyone* here knows who you are. People keep coming up to you to take selfies."

I shrug. "It's just the internet."

*"Just the internet."* Mac laughs. "Sometimes I think the internet is more real than the real world."

I realize suddenly that Mac is not in a good mood.

What a shame.

"Where's Juliet got to?" I ask. "You not hanging with her?"

The mention of Juliet seems to marginally cheer him up. "Yeah! Yeah, she's just gone to the loo."

"Ah."

There's a pause.

I stare at him across the booth, trying to suss him out.

"I haven't met many people like you who like The Ark," I say, taking a sip of J2O.

He looks back at me. "No?"

"Nah." I narrow my eyes. "How'd you get into them?"

"Oh wow, I don't know. Found them on YouTube?" He taps his near-empty glass with one finger. "Can't remember now."

"I'm surprised," I say. "The Ark don't really seem like your style."

"I like all kinds of music."

"True," I say. "You're not really super involved in the fandom, though, are you?"

"Well . . . no, I guess not. I really like their music, though." He takes a swig of beer and looks away from me.

There's a pause.

"Looking forward to seeing them this week?" I ask.

He nods. It's not nearly as enthusiastic as it should be. "Yeah, definitely."

I put my elbow on the table and lean on one hand. "What songs are you looking forward to?"

He laughs. "What is this, a questionnaire?"

I smile. "Just being friendly, my guy. We haven't talked much today."

"All right. Well, 'Joan of Arc,' obviously. 'Magic 18' and 'A Place Like This' are two of my favorites."

"Hm." "Magic 18" and "A Place Like This" are also two of The Ark's biggest hits. Most people know those songs off the radio. "I'm kind of hoping they play 'The 2nd Person,' you know, off the *Kill It* EP? Or anything from the *Kill It* EP. I know it came out, like, three years ago, but, you know. There's always hope."

Mac stares at me and nods. "Yeah, definitely." He looks dead behind the eyes. He has no idea what the *Kill It* EP is.

And that's the moment that I realize.

That's the moment I realize he doesn't actually like The Ark.

He's been faking it this whole time just to get Juliet to like him.

I smile at him. "You really like Juliet, don't you?"

He sits up in his seat like a zombie rising from the grave. "What?!"

"Dude," I say, then narrow my eyes. "Come on, my man. Come on."

"What?"

"Juliet."

"What?"

"You shouldn't pretend to have interests just to impress a girl. She'll find out the truth eventually. Not worth it."

"*What?*"

"You don't have to lie to me!" I lean forward. "I'm Angel. I'm cool. You can trust me. You don't have to force yourself to like The Ark if you *don't*. I'm not gonna judge you. I'd rather you were just honest with me."

He stares at me for a long moment.

And then he says, "Please don't tell her."

⇄  ◄◄ ⊙ ►►  ♥

By eleven o'clock, everyone apart from me is drunk.

Can't say I didn't expect it. We're a group of young people, aged from fifteen to twenty-nine according to the people I've spoken to tonight, and we're at a pub. Cue drinking.

Time to get out of here.

I escape the group of people I've found myself in with a hearty "Gotta pee, be right back," and start hunting around for Mac and Juliet. They'll probably want to go home by now. Since I forced him to admit he's not an Ark fan, Mac seems to be having the worst time in the world. I keep spotting him in the crowd. He looks grumpy as fuck. And I've barely seen Juliet—just a few quick glints of ginger hair here and there.

I wander around Spoons, pushing through the crowds of what has now become groups of girls and lads getting ready for a night out, or old drunk men drowning their sorrows in beer and football. I circle the whole of the first floor, then have a look upstairs as well, but can't see Mac or Juliet anywhere.

I stand in the entranceway and call Juliet while the Spoons bouncer stares at me like I'm doing something highly suspicious. But Juliet doesn't pick up.

I leave a voicemail.

"Hey, it's Angel. Just wondered where you guys are and whether you wanted to go home yet, or . . . yeah! Call me back pleeeease."

Two minutes later, I don't get a call back, but I do get a message.

**Juliet Schwartz**

Hi sorry!!!! We left a bit early. We felt like checking out a couple of other nearby bars!! Hope that's okay!! You were chatting to some other people so we didn't wanna interrupt!! Nan will let you in if you wanna go back to mine, or you can come join us?

I read the message, and my stomach sort of drops.

They just left without me.

Juliet just left with Mac. Without me.

I mean, okay.

Guess it was sort of my fault. I was talking to other people. Didn't really talk to Juliet at all this evening.

**Angel Rahimi**

Ah, no worries!! I'm not really into the drinking scene so I'll just go back to yours :) Have fun!

I consider turning round and saying goodbye to the people I've met in real life this evening—Pops and TJ and all the others—but . . . no. They're all drunk. And I'm tired. I just want to leave now.

$$\rightleftarrows \ \ \blacktriangleleft\blacktriangleleft \ \textcircled{\scriptsize\blacktriangleright} \ \blacktriangleright\blacktriangleright \ \ \blacktriangledown$$

When I sit down alone on the tube, I reread the message from Juliet. She hasn't seen the message from me at all. I thought she was starting to see through Mac and his lies. I thought she wanted to spend time with me.

Maybe it was my fault. Maybe I shouldn't have talked to Bliss for so long. Maybe I'm just disappointing in real life.

When the tube leaves Leicester Square and my internet connection goes, I put my headphones in and listen to The Ark and try to just stop thinking about everything, anything. I had a good night. I spoke to people. I had a good night. Hard to think that way, maybe, when you're sitting alone on a London tube train at half eleven on a Tuesday. I wonder why I feel sad. All that talk about the future and careers and stuff? Why would that make me sad? I just don't like thinking about it. So what. Who cares. Don't need to think about it. Everyone seems like they have it together except me. Silly. I'm fine. I have it together. I'm going to uni. Just me being negative. Just negative. I can stop. Need to stop listening to a sad song. Change track. This one's better. This one will make me feel better. My boys always make me feel better.

When I see them on Thursday, everything will be better.

I'm brought out of my thoughts by a light tap on my arm.

I glance up, ripping my headphones from my ears. Who the hell is talking to me at half eleven at night on the London Underground?

An old woman is sitting next to me.

"Whatever it is," she says, "it's all God's plan, and He knows what He's doing."

"Sorry," I say, smiling. "Did I look sad?"

"You look like it's the end of the world, my love," she says.

I like to think God does have a plan for everyone. But I also think there's too much shit in the world for all these plans to be perfect ones. Or maybe God doesn't have time to write a plan for everyone. And some of us are just trying our best and getting it a bit wrong.

"Definitely not that serious," I say.

"Serious is relative," she says. "That is for the Lord to decide."

She points upwards, and I sort of follow her hand and look up at the ceiling, but just find myself looking at the faulty, flashing light bar of the tube carriage.

# JIMMY KAGA-RICCI

Our bathroom light won't stop flashing. Could be worse, I guess. I mostly thought we'd get back and find that someone had broken in and stolen everything we own, or there would be a fire and we'd get back and there wouldn't even be an apartment anymore. I was so worried about it that I bought a very expensive and very large theftproof/fireproof safe before we went. As soon as we walk through the door, I run straight towards the safe and open it. Everything's still there, though. My journals, my guitar, my main laptop, my childhood teddy bear, and the knife that Grandad gave me for my sixteenth birthday.

That's what I grab first. The knife.

It's a family heirloom. It was passed down from my great-grandfather to Grandad, and then to me. Grandad didn't *say* it was an heirloom that had been passed down only through the men of the family, but I'm pretty sure that's why he gave it to me. Kind of a sexist concept, but still. It meant a lot.

"To remind you of who you are," he said with a smile, "and where you're from."

It'd be useless as an actual weapon, since it's completely blunt—you can run your finger along the edge and not even get a scratch. But it does make me feel safer when I've got it with me. Like I've got a little piece of home with me wherever I go.

Rowan obviously thinks it's ridiculous and wishes I would just put it in a drawer and never take it anywhere. When I walk out of my bedroom with the knife in my hands, he gives me an eye roll from the hallway.

I search thoroughly round the place to check no one's been in here. We've got this pretty spacious three-story apartment—five bedrooms, three bathrooms, a big open-plan living room/kitchen, a gym room that only Rowan uses, a cinema room that only I use, and an office that no one uses. All high up in London. We bought it as soon as we all turned eighteen. Doesn't look like anyone's been here, though. All my Blu-Rays are still scattered over the cinema room floor. *Whiplash* is open on top of the Blu-Ray player.

How could someone have broken in and taken that photo while we were actually in the flat? *Months ago?* We have an alarm, we have secure windows and doors. Remind me to pay someone to install CCTV as soon as possible.

I try to put it all out of my mind as I have a shower. I wash all the hairspray out of my hair, still there from last night's performance. I wash off all the airplane sweat and the crusty remnants of foundation from my face. I brush my teeth and clean my ears and rub the sleep out of my eyes. I inject my weekly testosterone into my thigh and stick on a Band-Aid that has Dennis the Menace on it—a present from Grandad. I wrap myself in a fluffy towel and sit down on the edge of the bath for a few minutes. The bathroom light keeps going off every few seconds, leaving me in the dark.

⇄ ◄◄ ⊙ ►► ♥

Turns out it's only 6:30 p.m. by the time I'm out of the shower, which I at first think is a good thing—an entire evening to do what I want, aka sleep—but then Lister says, "Guess I'll invite some people round, then."

I've changed into pajamas and am making a cup of tea, Rowan has not moved from the sofa he collapsed onto half an hour ago, and Lister has taken all his clothes off bar his boxers, lain down on the rug, and is eating a packet of Monster Munch.

"Fuck off," I mumble. "You're not inviting people round."

"Bliss is coming round, though."

"That's different. Bliss is Rowan's girlfriend."

"It'll only be a few people."

I bring my cup of tea over to the sofas and sit down. "I thought you wanted to rest?"

Lister rolls over towards me. "This is resting."

"You just wanna get drunk."

Lister blinks. "Well, yeah, pretty much."

Before we got famous, Lister showed little sign of being into the party lifestyle, beyond being mildly disruptive at school. But as soon as we started making money, Lister's love for the finer things reared its head. He started throwing lavish parties. Buying expensive cars and designer clothes. Hooking up with people left, right, and center. And drinking lots and lots of alcohol.

"Just do it by yourself," I say.

"Jimmyyyyyy." Lister starts stroking my leg. "Why are you so grumpy all the time?"

"Can't you throw parties when I'm not here?"

"Why do you hate parties so much?"

Because I am a neurotic, highly anxious, and unsociable boy with very serious trust issues and a low tolerance for personal space invasion. And I have had a really awful day.

"I just do."

"I'll hire security."

"You'd better."

Lister stares at me for a moment, and then turns to Rowan. "Any objections, Rowan?"

"Yes," says Rowan, but doesn't say anything else.

"Right, then. I'm calling everyone."

⇄  ◄◄ ⊙ ►►  ♥

The number of people who know where our apartment is causes me a very large amount of concern daily. We don't get people knocking at our door, thankfully—one of the benefits of living in a posh apartment block with decent security—but most gossip magazines and blogs know. A strong percentage of fans know. And a lot of celebrities know, mainly because of Lister's parties.

Lister Bird knows everyone. Lister knows musicians and singers and rappers and bands. Lister knows producers and models and actors and the aristocracy. Not that he particularly goes seeking it. Everyone just wants to be friends with Lister Bird.

They want to be friends with me too, but it's not like I'm gonna let that happen, am I?

"Everyone," as Lister usually refers to it, turns out to be around fifty people. Our apartment goes from haven to club in approximately two hours. Lister gets the Bluetooth speakers working and puts on a playlist. By 7:30 p.m., Lister is buzzing people in every five minutes, and by 9 p.m., our apartment is unrecognizable. The first time this happened, I had someone fit a lock on my bedroom door the next day.

"You should have told him no," says Rowan. We're sitting on a sofa in the living room again, but there are about thirty other people in here too, drinking and laughing.

"I did," I say.

Rowan sighs, and then looks at me. "We could just go and sit in my room, if you want? Play some *Splatoon*?"

I shake my head. "People will wonder where we are."

"Oh, who cares?"

I wish I didn't care.

"When's Bliss coming?" I ask.

Rowan sinks back into the cushions. "Should be here soon, I think." He pauses. "I told her not to come, what with all these people around. But you know what she's like." He puts on a voice. *"You already invited me round, and if Lister can fucking invite fifty fucking people round your fucking house, I can fucking come round whenever I fucking like!"*

I laugh. "I miss Bliss."

"Me too."

I keep seeing people walk past and sneak a look at us. A lot more than normal.

"I think I might call her, actually," says Rowan. He fishes his phone out of his pocket and stands up. "She said she'd be here half an hour ago."

He walks away from me and starts talking to Bliss, but I can't hear what he's saying. His expression quickly drops and gets annoyed, as it often does when talking to his girlfriend.

⇄ ◄◄ ⊙ ►► ♥

"Fucking *hell*," says Bliss when we let her in at the door. She is wearing an oversized All Time Low T-shirt and ripped black jeans. "Where's Bird? I'm gonna kick his ass."

Rowan met Bliss Lai at a charity event when we were all sixteen. She was a youth volunteer; we were special guests. She had absolutely no idea who we were, and she was, in our opinion, much more entertaining than we were—ushering us round the TV studio like we were misbehaving cattle, playing Rock Paper Scissors with us for the last packet of Wotsits in our dressing room, sneakily dancing behind us while we were on sound check.

Bliss Lai actually deserves to be famous.

But Rowan and Bliss don't want that. And I sort of agree with them. If people knew Rowan had a girlfriend—that would be it. Fandom insanity, media insanity, and Bliss would become internationally famous literally overnight. Thankfully, Bliss doesn't seem to give a shit about fame. One time we snuck her into a TV awards show and she accidentally spoke to David Tennant, without having any idea who he was. David thought she wanted a selfie, when in fact she was just trying to find the nearest toilet.

"Wait, don't tell me," says Bliss, holding up a hand. "He's already throwing up in the bathroom. Or he's already found someone to have sex with."

Rowan sighs. "Hopefully neither of those."

Bliss turns to me and pats me gently on the cheeks. "Jimmy! How are you? I've fucking missed you. Are you eating properly?"

Another thing to add about Bliss: She is the only person who is more heavily parental than Rowan.

"I'm okay, and I . . . eat food sometimes?"

"Well, that'll have to be good enough, I suppose." She claps her hands together. "Now, there'd better be some fucking Capri Suns somewhere around here."

⇄ ◄◄ ⊙ ►► ♥

Rowan, Bliss, and I hang around the kitchen for a bit, staying in a little huddle so that not too many people try to talk to us. People keep coming up to us, though, but no one I know particularly well, only people I've seen from afar at events, maybe been introduced to once, seen pictures of on the internet or on TV or on magazine covers. Rowan introduces Bliss to everyone as a publicity assistant—her usual cover. Everyone always believes it.

Rowan and Bliss were a perfect couple at the beginning. Rowan liked Bliss's total disregard for the power of fame—she didn't see him as any better than her. Bliss liked Rowan's maturity and intelligence—he was like a wise old man trapped in a sixteen-year-old's body. When they were together they both seemed to stop worrying about everything else in their lives— Rowan was no longer an overworked band boy and Bliss was no longer a struggling student. They were just *together*.

Unsurprisingly, that didn't last long. Relationships can only get so far on the infatuation wave.

Nowadays, things are far rockier. I don't know whether it's the pressure of being mostly long distance and rarely seeing each other, or whether they're just bored with each other, but whatever it is, whenever they see each other things usually end in an argument. Which is what's happening right now.

"Why would you be hanging around people like that, though?" Rowan shakes his head. "What if they found out who you were?"

Bliss apparently spent her evening at an Ark fandom event or something, simply because she was *curious*, which is a very Bliss thing to do.

"How would they find out?" Bliss rolls her eyes. "Come on. I'm not stupid. I was just intrigued to see what these people are like. Some of them were actually kind of cool, I met this really cool girl called—"

"They're *fans*. They don't care about you; they don't care about anything except The Ark. Do you know what they'd do to you if they found out who you were?"

"Fucking hell, you make it sound like they're serial killers or something."

"They're not far off."

They continue to argue and I open another beer. I like Bliss, and I love Rowan, but honestly? I wish they would just break up.

⇄ ◄◄ ⊙ ►► ♥

I try to get drunk but obviously don't try hard enough because by 10 p.m. I'm only on my third drink and don't feel anything.

The music's louder than it was earlier and people have started to dance. The floor vibrates; expensive clothing and expensive people flash under the changing colors of our LED lighting, bright white smiles, sparkly drinks. A cloud from the smokers hangs overhead like mist. I go and open a window, stick my head out, forgetting it's raining, and get my shirt wet.

"Hey, Jimmy," says a voice, and I turn round and find myself face-to-face with Magnet, real name Marcus Garnett, who was the most recent winner of *The X Factor* and who hasn't been doing too badly; he's had a couple of charted singles now. Ballads, I think. He sat on our table with us at the BRITs this year.

I hold out a hand. "Oh, hey, Magnet, you all right, mate? How's it going?"

He shakes it and nods. He's got a soft-looking face, a little bit teenager-ish. I think that's why we got along. Everyone else I meet looks and behaves about ten years older than us and it just makes me feel like a baby.

"Yeah, I'm pretty good, thanks, mate, yeah." He grins sheepishly. "Hey, you don't wanna head upstairs, do you? The music in here is bloody loud, innit."

I chuckle. "Yeah, sure. Lister's just slowly making our neighbors hate us."

"This his idea tonight?"

"Ha, yeah, you know what he's like."

Lister's reputation for partying isn't a well-kept secret.

We wander up the stairs, past groups of people chatting and drinking. I spot Rowan and Bliss sitting in a corner, talking and laughing. Rowan looks more relaxed now. Maybe they'll be all right after all. I don't know.

"You just got back from your European tour, right?" asks Magnet. The tenth or eleventh person who's said those near-exact words this evening.

I tell him we have one more tour show to do on Thursday. We stop and stand in the upstairs corridor. The music is quieter up here, but my ears are still buzzing.

"You've had an eventful few days, haven't you?"

A door slams somewhere, making me jump.

"Yeah, I guess . . ."

"It's not true, is it?" asks Magnet, smiling. "You and Rowan."

"What? No . . ." I go to take another swig from my drink, only to find I'm holding an empty glass.

Magnet laughs. "The shit the fans come up with, am I right?"

I almost want to laugh. As if this guy knows anything about having fans like ours.

"Yeah."

The track downstairs changes and everyone screams.

Magnet puts his hand on my arm. "If you need someone to talk to." He smiles, but it looks weird now, not as soft anymore. "You can always call me up, yeah?" He rubs my arm.

"Er . . ." The alcohol all seems to be hitting me at once. "Yeah."

Magnet moves towards me slightly. "You need to have friends in this business, you know?" He moves his hand up to my shoulder. "People you can trust."

"Mm."

"You can trust me, Jimmy."

"Mm."

He puts his hand on my cheek. Why is he doing that?

"You're so hot in real life," he says under his breath, as if he didn't think I'd hear.

I laugh, like he's joking. The buzzing in my ears gets louder.

*"In real life,"* I say.

Then he leans in and presses his lips against mine.

Oh. Okay. Fine. This is fine. Can't say I realized this conversation was going in this direction, but fine. The buzzing is so loud. Don't know what I'm doing. It's not like this is the first time this has happened with some random guy at some random party. I don't know. Don't remember. Don't care. He's got his hands on my face now. I don't really feel anything for this guy. But maybe this is all I'll ever get. Oh well. Who cares.

"Oi, Jimmy."

I stop kissing Magnet, turn round, and see Lister standing at the end of the corridor, leaning against the wall. He shakes his head at me. "Come on."

I pretty much just start walking away from Magnet, without saying bye or anything, but he grabs me by the arm again and says quietly, "Hey, you wanna go somewhere with me?"

I look at him again. "Not really. Sorry."

He pulls a little harder on my arm. "What, are you with Lister, then?"

I frown at him. "No. What the fuck?"

"What's fucking *wrong* with you?" he asks me. Nastily. "Saving yourself for marriage?"

I don't say anything.

"What a joke," he says. "You were throwing yourself at me at the BRITs party."

"Jimmy, come on!" Lister shouts from the other end of the corridor.

I try to focus on the knife inside my jacket. Remind myself who I am. Go home in my mind.

"Am I not good enough for you? You Ark clones think you're the fucking kings of the world, don't you? But the only reason you have so many fans is because they all want you and Rowan to fuck each other."

The swear word makes me wince.

He sneers at me. Where his face had looked soft before, he looks like a monster now. "Sometime soon something's going to knock you down from your pedestal. And then you'll come crawling back to the people who tried to be nice to you."

I shake my head wildly and just walk away from him.

⇄  ◄◄ ⊙ ►►  ♥

When I reach Lister, he gives me a little pat on the back and then shoots a look at Magnet, which is weird. Much more protective than usual.

He pulls me away and down the stairs, one arm round my shoulders.

"Alcohol makes you a slut now?" he asks. I know he's joking, but the word still pisses me off.

"Don't," I say.

"He wasn't even attractive. We've met him, like, once."

I shrug. "Oh well."

Lister stops and looks at me. "Jimmy. Come on, mate. Since when did you have that attitude?"

"I don't know. I don't know."

I realize suddenly that Lister isn't that drunk. If anything, I'm drunker than him, which never happens. Lister is the one who actually likes these parties, likes alcohol and spending money and hooking up with people. But something's different tonight.

I'm too drunk to work out what.

"You're not like that," he continues. "You don't just run around kissing anyone who appears in your immediate vision."

"I didn't initiate it."

"But you went along with it!"

"Yeah, well, maybe I felt like getting off with someone. Why do you care?"

Lister doesn't say anything.

I let out a deep sigh. "I just want to be a normal teenager sometimes," I say.

"But we're not."

I meet his eyes.

"Why are *you* judging *me*?" I ask. "You're the one who does this stuff all the time."

"Oh, do I?" Lister laughs and shakes his head. "You and Rowan . . . God . . . you still think . . ." He trails off, and when we reach the bottom of the stairs, Lister walks away from me.

⇄ ◄◄ ▶ ►► ♥

I don't see Magnet for the rest of the night, and when the alcohol starts to wear off, my anxiety suddenly goes full throttle and I have to go and sit down in a corner and try to do some deep breathing, but it's not really working. Maybe I'm having a heart attack. Wouldn't surprise me. Magnet's not the first guy I've kissed and he's probably not going to be the last either. Drunk Jimmy makes terrible decisions. But I don't care whether anyone knows about me being gay, anyway. What more can people do to me?

Sometimes I wish I was a normal teenager. I could go to a normal party and maybe kiss a boy and work out all that stuff like normal people do.

As soon as I think that, I hate myself for complaining.

I've really got nothing to complain about.

"Do you ever feel trapped?" I ask Rowan.

He frowns. "Trapped how?"

"Like you can't do anything without people watching."

"Why does it matter whether people watch?"

I shrug. "Must be nice to just . . . be a person."

Rowan stares at me. The flashing lights reflect in his glasses. "But we're gods, Jimmy. What's better than that?"

# ANGEL RAHIMI

As soon as I step out of the tube station, my phone informs me I have missed three calls from home.

Since Mum and Dad are normally asleep by this time, I call back immediately. Just in case it's an emergency.

Dad answers. "Fereshteh?"

"Hi, Dad."

"Ah, what a *relief*. We were getting so worried."

"Why? What's up?"

"You didn't call. We thought you were going to call every evening."

Oh.

"Oh," I say.

Dad pauses.

"Everything okay?" I ask.

"Fereshteh," he says, "all of this . . . feels such a shame."

"What? What d'you mean?"

"You worked so hard, my darling. For your exams. We know you struggle with academic study. We know it's not for you. But we wanted to honor this achievement with you."

"It's not important," I say. "The leavers' thing. It's not important."

"Okay, so it isn't important," says Dad. "But we're still saddened that . . . you simply don't seem to care about your achievements or want to celebrate them. You don't value that part of yourself. You just . . . care about this boy band."

"You're blowing this *way* out of proportion!" God. He's actually starting to annoy me now. "Dad, why would I want to celebrate myself when I'm so extremely *average*? You've got Rostam's uni graduation coming up soon— just go enjoy that."

There's a long pause.

Then Dad sighs. "Is this a big, important thing for you, Fereshteh?"

"Well, yeah. I really like this band."

"And what will you feel when you get home? When is the band obsession going to end?"

"Why does it have to end?"

"Because this is your life," he says. "Not the life of a band."

I stop walking, and stand very still in the street. I'm almost at Juliet's nan's house and there isn't a single person in sight. Just the dull yellow light of the streetlamps and the rain pattering against the pavement.

"I just want to go to a concert," I say. "And then I'll feel better."

"Were you not feeling good before, my girl?" he asks.

I don't think I've ever felt anything except The Ark.

# JIMMY KAGA-RICCI

"My Jim-Bob! What are you doing, calling me at this hour? Tell me what's wrong."

It's hard to talk because I'm kind of crying. Didn't mean to. Someone started playing Frank Ocean over the speakers and then I started thinking about Grandad dying (it's going to happen at some point) and then I went to find Rowan but he was standing in his bedroom with Bliss, Rowan with his arm round Bliss, Bliss's head on Rowan's shoulder, both of them staring out of the window at the rain. So I just turned round and started crying because I felt alone. It just happens sometimes.

"Jimmy, Jim, talk to me, son. What's going on?"

"I . . . just wanted to talk to you."

Grandad sighs over the phone. "Oh, Jim-Bob. Come on, lad. What's wrong?"

I sit down on my bed. "I . . . just felt sad."

"Why are you sad, boyo?"

It's hard to say proper words when you're crying. Embarrassing.

"Has something happened?"

I shake my head. "No, nothing's happened."

"Then, what's going on, Jim-Bob?"

"I think I'm lying to everyone . . . and I don't want to lie to anyone anymore."

Grandad sighs again. "Oh, Jimmy. You don't lie to me, do you?"

". . . No."

"Then that's not everyone, is it? What's this about?"

I wipe my eyes. "I don't know who I am. Everything I do feels like a lie. I wake up every day and I have to be *Jimmy Kaga-Ricci*, this famous guy, and I have to smile at the camera and say hi to people but . . . I don't even know who I am underneath that."

Grandad chuckles. "Jimmy . . . you're young. You're only just starting to figure that out, lad."

"I hate myself."

"Why would you do that?"

"Whoever I am . . . it's bad."

"Why would you say that?"

I shake my head. "I don't know. I just am. I'm lying."

"But what are you lying about?"

I reach inside my jacket and take out Grandad's knife. It has my great-grandad's name on it—Angelo Ricci. Holding it makes me feel real. It reminds me that I was born. That my life is something other than this birdcage I'm trapped in. Isn't it?

"Everywhere I go, everything I do . . . I'm lying. I'm pretending. And everyone's watching me . . . waiting for me to get it wrong."

"Jim-Bob . . . that's normal. You put on acts for people. Everyone does that. It's not a bad thing. It's protection, son. You've got to protect what's important to you. Especially when you're someone like you."

"It makes me feel horrible."

"That's the life you've got, my boy."

This makes my eyes water again.

"I don't want it, then."

"Don't say that, Jimmy."

"I don't want it."

"Jimmy. Are you drunk?"

". . . No."

"Now *there's* a real lie, boyo. Is Rowan there?"

"No."

Grandad huffs. "Jimmy . . ."

"I can't do it by myself."

"You're going to have to one day, Jim-Bob. I'm eighty-four years old. We all have to do this by ourselves eventually."

"I can't. When you're gone . . . I don't want to be here anymore."

"You'll be all right," says Grandad. "You'll be all right, Jimmy. Are you listening to me? Jimmy? You'll be all right, son. Come on, don't cry. Shh. I'm still here. Come on, boyo. Shh. Grandad's here. You'll be all right. Everything's going to be all right."

# WEDNESDAY

**"GOD FORGIVE US: WE HAVE BURNED A SAINT."**
**—A SOLDIER AFTER THE EXECUTION OF JOAN OF ARC**

# ANGEL RAHIMI

There's nothing quite like being woken up by a Twitter direct message that reads:

It was you

Despite having not read who it's from, nor having any idea who it's from, the sinister nature of the message makes my heart jump so hard that I'm immediately fully awake, and I jolt upright, in a fashion not dissimilar from yesterday morning's Jowan revelation. I rub my eyes and focus in on my phone and read the name above the message.

**Bliss Lai**

Okay. So. What the fuck?
I read the full message.

**Bliss Lai**
It was you, wasn't it. You told them.

What was me? What have I done?
The bedroom door creaks open, and I whip my head round. Juliet is standing there, dressed and ready for the day.

When I hauled myself out of bed to pray at dawn, Juliet was in bed next to me, asleep. I hadn't heard her come in, but it was a relief to know she didn't sleep in Mac's bed. Still, when I got back into bed afterwards, I couldn't fall asleep for a whole hour.

She looks at me and holds up her phone in front of her so that the screen is shining at me through the dim light.

"Rowan's got a girlfriend," she says.

She sounds like someone's died.

I laugh at her. "Shut up."

"Angel," she says, snapping, like she's angry. Then, remarkably, her eyes tear up, and her lips wobble. "This isn't a joke." She wipes her eye with one hand.

"I don't understand," I say.

I don't want to understand. I don't want any of this to be happening. I want to go back to when everything in my mind was real. When I could read a story and it would be real and real life didn't matter, real life was inferior.

Real life has arrived to punch us all in the face. Maybe I'm at that age now.

"Everything from yesterday . . ." she says. "Jowan. It wasn't true."

Juliet walks over to me and shows me some pictures, and they're all of Rowan Omondi and his girlfriend, Bliss Lai.

# JIMMY KAGA-RICCI

"My girlfriend's being attacked by paps in the fucking street on her way into work and you want me to fucking *calm down*?!" Rowan screams at Lister so loudly that Lister actually recoils. "Fuck off, thinking you can help us, thinking you have any fucking understanding of what it means to care about someone, you fucking sex addict!"

It probably doesn't help that Lister's only wearing his boxers and smells quite badly of weed.

I shoot Lister a look that says *please go away*. He stares at me and then turns and leaves the living room.

I didn't really sleep much last night. I locked the door, I looked under my bed and in my wardrobe and in my en suite, I searched on my chest of drawers and in the corners of the ceiling for hidden cameras. I didn't find anything, but that doesn't mean nothing was there. I lay in bed and tried to rest but I couldn't relax. It never really felt like home here in the first place.

I was woken up this morning by Rowan throwing one of the house phones at a wall, because his and Bliss's relationship is out.

It was Dave, obviously. The evil interviewer. Because we fucked up that interview, he decided to run the story he wanted. And he had *everything*. Photos from various parties they've attended together, photos from private family gatherings, even photos back from the charity thing where they first met.

Bliss Lai is the number one trending topic on UK Twitter.

Okay. What do you do when people are upset? What do people do when I'm upset? I'm usually the one who's upset, so I never normally have to deal with this. I don't think I've ever heard Rowan scream at someone before. He doesn't seem like himself. He hasn't all week, really.

I walk over to him and put my arm round him, but he just shrugs me off and says, "Just fucking leave me alone, Jimmy; there's nothing anyone can do about this."

He slumps down onto a sofa and starts trying to call Bliss again. Okay.

I walk away into the kitchen and start making three cups of tea, despite knowing it's probably only me who's going to drink any. The kitchen clock reads 12:36 p.m. How did this happen in the space between going to sleep and waking up? How did the entire world find this out in the space of a few hours?

I hear a strange whining noise and it takes a few seconds for me to realize that it's Rowan crying quietly into his hands. Sort of makes me want to cry too. Sort of want to hug him, but I don't think he wants that.

"How did that interviewer get all the photos?" I say to no one in particular. Rowan doesn't answer.

We can't trust anyone.

We're being stalked. Watched. Followed to private events, parties, *everywhere*. They're selling photos of us to the press. Sharing them on private gossip blogs and group chats.

Someone got into our house. They've been here. I can *smell them*.

"Jimmy," says a hushed voice—Lister's—making me jump and turn towards him. Thankfully he's put a hoodie on.

"What?"

"Cecily had someone drop this off this morning."

He hands me a wad of paper. The top of the front page reads:

This contract (hereinafter referred to as the "Agreement") executed and effective this _____ day of _____, 20___, by and between

**THE ARK** (hereinafter referred to as the "Artist") and **FORT RECORDS** (hereinafter referred to as the "Company"):

It's our record contract.

"Oh," I say. "Have you read it?"

To my surprise, Lister nods. I don't think he's read a book since GCSE English. "It's a bit confusing to read, but . . . yeah." He makes a face. "It's all just . . . *more*."

I glance back at Rowan, who is still sitting, head in hands, on the sofa.

There's nothing I can really do to help him right now, I guess.

I open the contract and start to read.

Some of it seems normal. Or at least, what I assume to be normal. I never fully read our first and only contract; we were fourteen and a little clueless, and we just had a lawyer and our parents read it (in my case, Grandad).

But a lot of sections catch my eye: sections asking us to do more interviews, go on longer tours, write music faster.

It takes me a full twenty minutes to read it all.

I knew that we'd have to spend more time on the band, on publicity, on music, but this is *extreme*. I knew all of this already, but seeing it here, written in such official, complex, legal language, it's all so much more than I thought it would be. It's all so much more *real*.

I've barely had any time to myself as it is. I barely see Grandad more than once every couple of months.

"What's Cecily doing about this?" I say.

Lister shrugs. "Nothing, as far as I know."

We'll be internationally famous, but what's the point if you have to give up everything else in your life to get there?

"We can just say no," I say, starting to ramble. "We can just have a similar contract to what we have now. This one's been fine."

"And give up breaking America?" asks Lister. "We won't get big in America unless we take on this contract."

"Then we go with a different record company."

"It'll be the same wherever we go, Jimmy. At least people at Fort Records know us and slightly care about us. Everyone else just thinks we're a money machine."

I look at Lister. He's sitting at the breakfast bar, staring blankly at the cup of tea in front of him. I didn't know he'd even been thinking about this stuff. Rowan is quiet now, sitting totally still with his head in his hands.

"It's not fair," I whisper.

What's the point in being in The Ark if we're going to get stalked, harassed, have photographs leaked, privacy stolen, and never, ever be at *peace*?

I've been gripping my cup of tea so tightly, I don't realize how hard I slam the mug down on the counter, sending shards of ceramic flying all over the kitchen. There's a sudden pain in my palm and I turn it towards me to find I've cut my hand open. Blood trails down my wrist and plops onto the floor.

# ANGEL RAHIMI

So, the latest is that I'm struggling to process that the person I met last night was the person who has been in a relationship with Rowan Omondi for at least, if sources are accurate, the past two years.

She spoke to him on the phone right in front of me.

I mean, it's her, all right. It's really bloody her. If the name wasn't enough—what's the bet there's another Bliss Lai in the world—the pictures confirmed it. There she is. Exactly the person I met last night: the pout, the sleek black hair, the soft cheeks and rounded curves. Always pictured with a cheeky smile.

I spoke to her for ages.

And I had absolutely no idea.

Oh, fuck.

I showed her the picture of Jimmy as my lock screen.

I talked to her about Jowan.

She probably thinks I'm absolute fandom trash.

Juliet has left the room, probably to go and mourn on her own for a bit, leaving me to deal with The Message.

I start by having a look at Bliss's profile. Her username is just her name: @blisslai. Her bio reads "I do a lot of stuff and I like a lot of things." Her tweets are a jumbled mix of university complaints, TV show reactions, and articles about social and political justice.

Everything would seem perfectly normal if she didn't have over fifty thousand followers. No doubt she'd only had a few hundred at most yesterday.

I'm half-tempted to leave it for a bit.

No. No.

If I leave it now, I'll leave it forever.

**Bliss Lai @blisslai**

It was you, wasn't it? You told them. You saw Rowan's name on my phone.

**angel @jimmysangels**

i swear to god it wasn't me. i had absolutely no idea who you were. i'm so so sorry this has happened but i swear i did not know that you were rowan's girlfriend.

After a minute or so, the little tick symbol shows up, meaning that she's seen it. She's read it.

She doesn't reply after that. Fuck. What do I do? What do I do? I don't want her to hate me. I don't want her to think I would do this.

**angel @jimmysangels**

i promise this is the truth. if i'd known you were anything to do with the ark I would have been freaking out right in front of you. seriously. i'm just a normal fan, i would never do something as extreme as this.

**Bliss Lai @blisslai**

You underestimate the power of fans hahaha I know how extreme they can be

What am I supposed to say to that?!

**angel @jimmysangels**

i don't know what i can say to make you believe me

**Bliss Lai @blisslai**

Neither do I

What am I supposed to say to *that*?

**Bliss Lai @blisslai**

I don't know what to do

**angel @jimmysangels**

are you okay? are you somewhere safe, at least?

**Bliss Lai @blisslai**

Well not really, I'm at work. There are people with cameras waiting outside.

**angel @jimmysangels**

oh my god

**Bliss Lai @blisslai**

Yeah haha

**angel @jimmysangels**

can you get rowan to help you???

**Bliss Lai @blisslai**

Not really, him coming here would just make things worse. I don't want to go out there alone. they'll surround me.

**angel @jimmysangels**

could someone at work maybe leave with you?

**Bliss Lai @blisslai**

Not really . . . they just want me to make the photographers go away.

Oh God. I'm really about to do this, aren't I?

**angel @jimmysangels**

do you . . . want me to come and find you?

**Bliss Lai @blisslai**

Fuck, would you??

**angel @jimmysangels**

if you needed someone, yeah. i don't have anywhere to be today.

**Bliss Lai @blisslai**

It's just to help me get out of the throng of paparazzi. You're really tall so that should help haha

**angel @jimmysangels**

i will warn you, i am weak. like no muscle. also scared very easily.

**Bliss Lai @blisslai**

Better than nothing though

**angel @jimmysangels**

you say that now!

**Bliss Lai @blisslai**

You're really gonna come here?

**angel @jimmysangels**

you really want me to?

**Bliss Lai @blisslai**

You're not just doing this to try to meet The Ark, right?? Because you won't meet them.

**angel @jimmysangels**

no!!! honestly, i just want to help!

Why do I want to help? Why am I doing this?

**Bliss Lai @blisslai**

Okay that's good because otherwise I might have to live in HMV forever

She works in an HMV? That's not exactly what I expected from someone so confident and ambitious. How old is she anyway? She seemed five years older than me, but if she's Rowan's girlfriend, maybe she's closer to my age.

**angel @jimmysangels**

okay well that sounds traumatic. send me the address and i'll be there as soon as i can!!

She sends me the address. I look up where the nearest tube station is. I get dressed. I go downstairs.

Juliet and Mac are eating breakfast in the kitchen. Juliet looks like she'll never enjoy food again. Mac looks like a guest at an awkward family dinner. Dorothy is standing at the kitchen counter, writing in a notepad.

I make up some excuse about agreeing to meet with a friend in London, but neither Juliet nor Mac seem particularly fazed and they don't ask any questions. I walk out of the house without a second thought. Off to rescue the girlfriend of one of the three boys who have kept me alive for the past five years. You know. Just a casual, normal Wednesday.

# JIMMY KAGA-RICCI

It's not normal for us to get a day off from The Ark. Most days are spent at interviews, meetings, rehearsals, studios, concert venues. And even on the rare day we get to spend sightseeing during our Europe tours—they're not days off. Not really. Not when the fans track you down, somehow, impossibly, to wherever you want to go. Not when someone is asking for a selfie every five minutes, snapping photos, screaming, always screaming.

The fans gave us everything we have. I love them. I love the fans.

I love them, I love them, I love them, I love them.

Days spent at home are our real days off. When did we last have one? Maybe three, four months ago? I Skyped Grandad, called my mum and dad. Rowan Skyped his family, spoke to his sister for hours. Then we ordered pizza and played *Splatoon*. Lister . . . I don't remember what Lister did.

Today isn't anything like that, anyway.

Rowan is inspecting the cut on my palm, checking to see if any shards of ceramic have been embedded into my skin. He holds my hand up to the kitchen light, squinting at it.

"I think there's a bit in there," he says.

My hand stings.

"Oh," I say.

"I think we're gonna have to get it out."

"Oh."

"Do you want to do it or do you want me to do it?"

He looks at me. Right in the eyes.

"Jim?" he says.

"You do it," I say.

"Do we have tweezers?"

Tweezers. I feel a bit ill.

"I think so. In the bathroom."

Rowan puts my hand down on the breakfast bar and walks away towards the bathroom. I just stand there, waiting, my hand open in front of me like it's not really attached to my body, blood still seeping out of the open wound. I look down and realize there's blood splattered all down my pajama shorts and on my legs.

I laugh.

Why've I got blood all over me?

What the fuck.

"Jimmy?"

Rowan's back, holding the tweezers. He picks up my hand and grips my wrist tightly.

"This will hurt," he says.

"Yeah," I say.

Rowan digs the tweezers directly into the wound.

I make a strangled screeching noise in the back of my throat and try to move my hand, but Rowan keeps it still. My eyes start watering again.

"Sorry," Rowan mumbles, poking the tweezers at my palm now.

I'd say it's fine, it's all fine, he shouldn't be sorry about anything, he's the one going through seven tons of shit this week, but all I can manage is a pained laugh.

"Nearly got it," he says, clenching his teeth. Rowan doesn't like blood. When we had to dissect a kidney in a Year 8 biology lesson, he threw up.

"There!" He holds up the tweezers triumphantly. There's a tiny reddish sliver of ceramic in between the pincers. Rowan puts it down on the counter-top. "Now you won't get poisoned."

"Thanks," I say, wiping my eyes with my uninjured hand.

"Wait here, I'll get a bandage."

"I can do that—"

"Not with an injured hand, you can't."

Rowan leaves again.

The blood falls with a soft *plip* onto the table. Almost indiscernible from the rain falling outside.

The fact of the matter is there's no way to fix this. The information is out, the photos, all the evidence of Rowan and Bliss's relationship. There's no way to erase the memory of every single person in the world. I can't go begging to Cecily to fix this one. I can't pay anyone to stop. I can't do anything.

I just have to sit and wallow in it.

The punishment for the truth.

At times like this, when horrible stuff happened, I used to pray, and talk to God, and He'd talk back to me. All that stuff.

These days, though, it's a lot harder to get a response.

"I couldn't find a plaster big enough, but we did have some bandages." Rowan grabs my hand again, pulling it towards him, and pushes up his glasses with his free hand.

"Do you think it needs stitches?" I say.

Rowan starts wrapping it in bandages. "I don't know. Do you want to go to the hospital?"

"No. This is our only day off."

"True."

He rips the bandage and ties it. The blood has already started to seep through the thin white cotton.

"How does that feel?" he asks.

I lie. "Fine."

He chuckles. "Liar."

I look at him. "It hurts."

He looks at me. "Don't smash mugs, you mug."

"I didn't mean to."

"I know."

We both stand there at the breakfast bar. Rowan starts scooping all the shards of ceramic into a pile in the middle of the table. I move my fingers around. It hurts.

It all hurts.

"Are you okay?" Rowan asks me.

"Are you?" I ask.

"No," he says.

"Me neither," I say.

He sits down on a bar stool, spinning gently from side to side.

"I wish we could go outside," he says.

"We can," I say.

"No, we can't."

The pain on his face makes my pain feel worse.

I spot movement in the corner of my eye, and look up, only to see Lister darting away into the corridor. I'd forgotten he was even in the room.

"How did that interviewer get those photos?" Rowan asks, shaking his head. "Who would want to mess with us that much? And *why*?"

"It's got to be a fan," I say.

Rowan nods. "Yeah. One of the extreme ones. They're the sort who'd do something like this. Just stalk and collect pictures and post them just to create drama. First that *Jowan* photo and now *this*. God, I *hate* them."

I gaze at him.

He sighs. "It's fine." He pats me on the arm. "We're in this together, aren't we?"

"Yeah," I say, my voice little more than a whisper.

God.

At least I have him.

He looks at me. "You okay, Jim? You look like something's wrong."

Rowan is the only person in the whole world who knows me. Rowan was with me when we were eleven and desperately strumming at guitars in a tiny school music room. Rowan was with me when I was twelve and crying because people were bullying me, girls were sneering at me, boys were spitting at me, teachers frowning in confusion at their class register when I corrected them with my real name, Jimmy, again, and again and again and again. Rowan was with me when we were thirteen and watching YouTube videos in my bedroom and saying, hey, maybe we should do this, maybe we could do this. Rowan was with me when we were fourteen, fifteen, when paparazzi locked me in my own family's house for two days, and when we were sixteen, seventeen, when I passed out because I hadn't eaten enough after a week of press interviews, when I had a panic attack immediately after our BRITs performance.

But my best Rowan, my favorite Rowan, is the Rowan I knew seven years ago, sitting next to me, plucking at a guitar.

"I miss home," I say.

He looks confused. "We are home."

"No, we're not," I say.

# *ANGEL RAHIMI*

I have been Ready to Die at many points in my life. The day before my A-level chemistry exam, for example. And yesterday morning, probably, upon waking to find all my dreams—all one of them, I guess—had supposedly come true.

And this is another.

Walking down a busy London high street, going to meet Bliss Lai, who is Rowan Omondi's girlfriend.

I mean, logically, this shouldn't be affecting me at all. I met Bliss yesterday. We got along normally. Two very normal people. Just a fangirl and the girlfriend of an internationally famous member of a boy band.

Totally normal.

I check what I'm wearing. I always feel better if I'm wearing something good. Thankfully, I'm wearing some skinny jeans and a baggy shirt over a long-sleeved top. I look cool. Clothes distract people from how uncool you are on the inside.

Google Maps takes me closer and closer to the HMV shop in which Bliss is trapped, but I don't really need to look at it, because there is a group of men huddled outside the building holding various large cameras. They actually seem fairly chilled out at the moment—sitting on benches and bins, leaning against walls, chatting happily to each other.

Waiting. Waiting like a group of balding vultures.

I slip past them and head inside HMV. If it weren't for the group of men, everything would be perfectly normal—there are shoppers wandering around the aisles, shop workers roaming in their HMV T-shirts.

Bliss, however, is nowhere to be seen.

Okay.

Right.

You can do this.

I take out my phone and message her.

**angel @jimmysangels**

i'm here! look for a confused hijabi standing next to the new releases DVD chart

**Bliss Lai @blisslai**

On my way

She replies almost instantaneously. My palms are kind of sweating. Please don't freak out. Please don't freak out. Please, just, please, please be chill. Just for this.

A door in the far corner of the shop opens, and there she is.

Bliss Lai.

This is fine.

She sees me and shoots me a weak smile, winding through the aisles towards me. She looks almost exactly the same as yesterday—the only real difference is the purple HMV shirt she's wearing—but she's lost all the mystique she had last night. She's frowning. She's gripping her bag. She just looks scared.

"Hey," she says once she reaches me.

"Hey," I say, and smile at her. "You okay?"

"I'm shitting myself," she says.

I nod at her. "I mean, fair enough."

She genuinely does look a bit like she's gonna shit herself. She keeps glancing around, checking no one's spotted us yet.

"I haven't even got any fucking makeup on," she whispers.

"Don't worry," I say, but I would be extremely worried if professional photographers were going to run at me with cameras when I had zero eyeliner on. Reassuring her that she looks perfectly fine probably isn't the most helpful thing to say either. "It doesn't matter what you look like."

She laughs. It's more of a panicked cackle. "You're right. I could look like a gecko and they'd still run the same story."

I snort. "A gecko?"

"A small lizard."

"Well, you don't look like a small lizard."

"That's because I'm wearing my human skin right now."

We both laugh.

"What's our plan?" I ask. "Shall we just leg it?"

She takes a deep breath and then nods.

"Have you got any sunglasses?" she asks.

"Oh, yeah!" I give her my aviators. She puts them on. She looks a bit like a baby wearing their parent's sunglasses. "Sorry, they're much too big for your head. I have a massive head."

"The more of my head they conceal, the better."

"Where do you want to go?"

"Tube? Just down the road?"

"Sounds like a plan."

She takes another deep breath. "I'm just gonna run. Can you, like, I don't know . . ."

"I will try to remain in between you and the group of scary men at all times. Most of them are shorter than me. And I'm wearing heavy boots. If they get near us, I'll just kick. Like a giraffe."

She claps her hands together in faux prayer. "You are a saint."

"Don't you mean . . . an *angel*."

We both say "*Aaaaaay*" at the same time, and I think that means we're friends.

We approach the front of the shop. Bliss remains hidden, since she's short enough to hide behind the displays, and the paps don't seem to be paying attention to me or anything else anyway.

Bliss looks me directly in the eye, the corner of her mouth twitching into a nervous smile.

"On the count of three," she says.

I nod. My stomach churns. I can't remember the last time I full-on *sprinted*. Might have been Year 11 PE.

"One," she says.

I bounce up and down on the balls of my feet. Really hope I don't trip over. Could do without that being photographed by professional paparazzi.

"Two."

What are they going to do? Are they actually going to chase after us? Are they going to not notice us at all? How do real-life celebrities deal with this?

*"Three."*

Bliss just legs it. She vanishes from in front of me in a flash of purple. And then I'm running too. Running around the aisle out of the shop and down the road, my boots slapping against the sidewalk, rain stinging against my cheeks, my eyes, praying I put enough pins in my scarf this morning.

They're behind us. I can hear them running. Shouting. Shouting for her. Up ahead, Bliss dares a quick glance back, and there's panic in her eyes, and so I look back too and nearly fall over in the process, because the paps are only a few meters behind me, running with their cameras, trying to take pictures and shout and run all at the same time. I shriek out a laugh and try to run faster but I'm already getting out of breath and I nearly fall over again after narrowly dodging a lamppost.

People on the street are staring at us as we run past. I catch eyes with an older woman who reminds me strongly of my Year 9 maths teacher, and I almost think she's going to shout at us for running, but then she gives me a nod, and after Bliss and I run past, she sticks out her leg, sending at least three of the paps crashing to the ground and bringing the rest of them to a halt behind the pile of men and cameras.

I scream "THANK YOU!" at the woman, wishing I could stop and talk to her properly, but we can't, we keep going, laughing, laughing so hard it hurts, and we run the rest of the way down the street until we're safely inside the tube station, through the ticket barriers, and stopped just before the escalator, panting, my throat feeling like it's on fire.

"I am not . . . fit enough for this," I say.

Bliss is leaning her whole body weight against a wall, chest heaving up and down. "I really hope . . . I don't have to do that every time."

"Did you see that woman who tripped them up?"

"Hell yeah! What a fucking legend!"

We both start to laugh, and then I need to sit down, because my thighs are shaking.

Bliss smooths her hair, tucking it behind her ears and sorting out her parting. She glances down at me, then sits, joining me on the tube-station floor.

I'm busy checking my scarf in my phone's front camera. If I'd known extreme athletics was on today's agenda, I most definitely would have chosen a more practical hijab style this morning.

"You're losing a pin," says Bliss, reaching up and adjusting one of my pins. I can see myself in her sunglasses. "Oh, thanks!"

I put my phone away, and then we sit still for a moment.

"Now what?" says Bliss.

Now what.

"I don't know."

"Me neither."

We sit there.

"Don't you want to go home?" I say.

Bliss rubs her face, wiping away the rain. "My mum said don't come home. They've found out where I live."

"God, already?"

"I fucking hate the internet."

We continue to sit there.

"What about Rowan? Do you want to go and find him, or . . . ?"

Bliss chuckles. "No. He wants me to go to his, but I shouldn't be seen with him. That's exactly what the paparazzi want. And the fans will get angry at me."

"Why would the fans get angry?"

She raises an eyebrow. "Haven't you been on Twitter? Most of the fans *hate* me."

Oh. That makes sense. The fans want Rowan to be with them, or to be with Jimmy. Anyone else must die.

"Can't Rowan help you somehow? Can't you go meet up with him somewhere safe?"

"I don't *know*," she says, then puts her head in her hands. "I don't know what to do."

Without warning, she lets out a heavy groan, punches the floor, then puts her head back in her hands.

It hits me then how serious the situation is for Bliss Lai.

Her life will never be the same ever again.

"Do you . . . do you want to come back to mine for a little bit?" I say.

Bliss's head snaps up to look at me.

"I mean, I'm staying with a friend right now, but I'm sure she won't mind . . . She really likes The Ark as well, but . . . I mean . . . if you don't mind a bit of fangirling every now and then . . . I'm sure she'll understand—"

"Why would you want to help me?!" she says abruptly. She shakes her head and laughs. "Genuinely. Like, you know you're not going to get to meet them, right? You're not gonna get to meet The Ark because of this."

"I'm just a wonderful human being, to be honest," I say, but the sarcasm is too obvious.

"Seriously, though," she says. "Why?"

Why would I want to help her?

Part of me knows it's what God wants. It's the good thing, and the right thing, to help someone in a horrible situation.

But another part of me knows that this is because of The Ark.

Because I fucking live to serve them too.

"I just want to do something good," I say.

"Living up to your name," says Bliss, smiling.

"Not yet," I say. "Hopefully one day."

"I think you're doing well so far."

I want to say that she's the only one who believes that, but I don't, and instead, I take out my phone, find Juliet's number, and call her.

"Hey, Angel, you okay?"

"Juliet," I say, "you might wanna sit down for this, my guy."

# JIMMY KAGA-RICCI

"Hey, Jimmy, you okay?"

Lister is standing in my bedroom doorway. I am lying in bed, trying to watch *Brooklyn Nine-Nine* on my TV, but I can't concentrate on it, and I have no idea what's going on. I just keep laughing at random things Holt says without really understanding the joke.

"Yeah," I say.

Lister frowns. He's still only wearing boxers and a hoodie. He has a cigarette in one hand.

"Don't smoke," I say. "You'll die."

Lister looks at the cigarette, as if unaware that it'd been there.

"Yeah," he says, looking back at me.

He wanders over and falls onto the bed next to me, mousy hair spilling over the pillow. He puts out his cigarette on a coaster on my bedside table.

"What've you been up to?" I ask.

"Not much. Just called my mum and . . . you know . . . sent her some money . . ." His voice trails off.

We lie in silence for a few moments, before he takes my injured hand and lifts it into the air, studying the bandage and the few spots of blood that have seeped through.

"You're an idiot," he says.

"Yeah."

He places my hand gently back on the bed.

We lie there and watch the TV for at least ten minutes before anything more is said. As much as Lister gets on my nerves sometimes, having him here is comforting, in a weird way. It's the same with Rowan. Though Rowan and I have always been closer, the three of us are family. We're the only ones who know what it's like to be in The Ark.

The sound of Rowan playing the piano in the living room drifts through my open bedroom door.

"I can't believe you fancy *Magnet*," says Lister.

I roll my head towards him, immediately annoyed. "I don't."

"Yeah, you do. Or did. Whatever."

I look away.

"He's a pretentious fame whore," Lister continues. "He'll have three singles and then he'll disappear from the Earth. In ten years he'll be working as a real estate agent."

That I can actually agree with.

"It was a mistake," I say. "I thought he was like us."

Lister is silent for a moment.

"No one's like us, Jimmy," he says. "I think we're your only dating options."

"Rowan's straight."

"Oh. Just me, then."

I whack him on the arm and we both laugh.

We return to comfortable silence for a few minutes before I speak again.

"How d'you get away with it?" I ask him.

"With what?"

"Getting with so many people."

He's silent for a moment.

"You don't really know anything about me, do you?" he says.

"What?"

"You think I just fuck everyone, don't you?"

I look at him. His forehead is creased, his eyes unblinking.

"Well, don't you?" I say.

He sighs. Then he chuckles. Then he rolls away and laughs hard.

"No, Jimmy," he says, and then sighs exaggeratedly again, grinning. "No!"

"Well, a lot of people, then."

"No, Jimmy!"

He bops me suddenly on the nose, making me flinch. He's still smiling.

"Why do you all think that?" he asks.

"Well . . ." I begin, but don't really know where to go from there. "I mean—you always disappear at parties and . . . you're always flirting with people."

"But you've never actually seen me having sex with all these people you think that I've had sex with."

I snort. "No, I've never actually seen you having sex with anyone."

Lister smirks up at the ceiling, tucking his hands behind his head. "Shame. It's quite a sight."

"Shut up, you dick."

I don't really know what to say after that, so we just lie there for a bit again. What's Lister trying to say? That he doesn't have sex with quite as many people as we all think he does? So what? That doesn't change anything.

"Five people," he says suddenly.

"What?"

"That's how many people I've had sex with."

"At once?"

"*No!* Jesus fucking Christ." He blinks. "I mean, that sounds highly appealing, but no."

I shove him, nearly making him roll off the bed. He laughs, then readjusts himself, and we fall back into silence again.

Only five people?

I mean, that's higher than average for most nineteen-year-olds. But it's a *lot* less than Rowan and I thought. We thought he was having sex with someone, or several someones, at every party we went to. And we've been to a *lot* of parties.

"I know you all think I'm a druggie bisexual slut," he says. "The classic bisexual stereotype. Just because I like more than one gender, that opens up my dating options, and consequently I sleep with everyone on sight. That's what you think."

"We . . . we don't . . ." But we do. We did. And I can't lie to him about it.

"Well, news flash, not all bisexuals are having sex every five minutes." Lister snorts.

I decide to turn the TV off.

I can't remember the last time Lister and I talked like this. There's always been a sort of barrier between us. Between him and Rowan too. Maybe because he's that little bit older. Or maybe because Rowan and I have been friends for longer, have always been closer.

"And also," he continues, "most of those were a couple of years ago."

"Oh."

"I'm not like that anymore," he says with more seriousness than I'm used to. He stares into my eyes. "I just want you to know. I don't do that sort of thing anymore."

"Really?"

"Yeah."

"Why?"

"*Why?*"

"Yeah."

He suddenly can't meet my eyes. He rolls his head away, back to staring at the ceiling.

"It just got boring," he says, but it sounds like a cover-up for something. I decide not to press him for more.

We don't ever talk about deep stuff, me and Lister Bird.

"So who've you slept with that I know?" I ask, trying to lighten the mood.

Lister's face immediately breaks out into a more familiar boyish grin.

"You wanna know?"

"Hell yeah. Give me the gossip."

"D'you remember the lighting director from our second UK tour?"

"Kevin?"

"Yeah. Him."

"Bloody hell." I strain to remember Kevin's face. He must have been about twenty-five, at least. "Okay."

"I wish I hadn't, actually," he continues. "It wasn't very fun." In a smaller voice he says, "He was the first *guy*, and I think he thought I was more experienced than I was."

"Oh." I think that's what we all thought. I wonder if I should ask him to talk about it more, but he quickly moves on to the next name, which is a member of an extremely famous girl band.

"You're *joking*," I say, moderately scandalized.

"No. We'd been chatting a lot on Twitter before that." Lister chuckles. "She invited me back to her hotel after the BRITs party this year. She's the most recent person I've been with, actually."

I say nothing because I'm still so surprised. I've had a few conversations with that girl before. She's always in the news. Wouldn't have suspected a thing.

I don't even remember Lister disappearing after the BRITs party. Maybe because I was talking to Magnet in a corner.

"It was just a hookup, though," he says, glancing at me, almost *nervous* for some reason. "Didn't mean anything, really."

I roll over so I'm facing him fully now. It's easy to see why so many people want Lister Bird. He's got all the classic features of a male model—the sharp jawline, slanted brows, straight nose, piercing eyes, and he's naturally slim too, without having to exercise like Rowan does. And he's white, so he's got the edge with the racists of the world. He was voted number one in this year's *Glamour*'s 100 Sexiest Men, MTV's 50 Sexiest Men Alive, and various sites' 100 Hottest Men in the World, all of which it was finally acceptable for him to qualify for, since he's over eighteen now. He's commonly cited as a "celebrity crush," even by straight men, and he rejects modeling opportunities weekly.

Everyone wants to have sex with Lister Bird.

"Who was the first one?" I ask.

"First time I had sex?"

"Yeah."

He pauses again, as if debating whether to tell me.

"It was when I was sixteen," he says. "With some woman we met at a recording studio."

"Woman? How old was she?"

Lister laughs.

"She was thirty-two," he says.

My mouth drops open in horror. I sit up, leaning on one elbow. *"Thirty-two?"*

"Yeah, but it's fine. It's not like I didn't want to do it. I mean, I was nervous, but, like, she didn't force me, or—"

"That's not right," I say.

"What?"

"That's too young."

"I knew what I was doing."

"No, you didn't," I snap. "She did. She took advantage of a teenager who didn't know what he was doing and probably thought that he was getting an actual relationship out of it. A few months younger and that would be legally classifiable as *rape*. Imagine if you'd been a sixteen-year-old girl and she'd been a thirty-two-year-old man?"

Lister lies very still as I speak, his face expressionless.

"Are you angry at me?" he says.

"Do you just have sex with people to make them like you?"

"What? No!" He sits up too. "No, and I don't do that anymore anyway—"

"Well, you had sex with that girl at the BRITs this year—"

"*God*, you're just like Rowan," he spits out, then climbs off the bed and away from me. "I didn't think you'd react like this as well."

My stomach drops a little. "You told Rowan?"

He doesn't say anything.

"Why did you tell Rowan and not me?" I ask, just confused now. What's his problem with *me*?

"I didn't want you to know about it," he mumbles. "I didn't want you to judge me. But I guess you did."

"I'm not judging—"

"Neither of you get it. It's different for me." He turns to me with one last pleading look. "You and Rowan have each other, but you have to see that it's different for me. Being Lister Bird."

I just shake my head. "What does that *mean*?"

The final bit of hope in his expression drops, and he walks away from the bed and towards the door.

"Why else would anyone want to be around me?" he says. "I'm Lister Bird. Why else would anyone want to be around me other than to *get with me*?"

# ANGEL RAHIMI

Juliet peers round her front door with a mix of fear and disbelief on her face.

I ended up telling her the truth about the situation over the phone, but she hadn't believed me. She thought I was joking. Even when I told her that it wasn't a joke. Three times.

"You weren't joking," she says, speaking to me but staring at Bliss Lai, who is standing next to me.

"Well, no," I say.

Juliet still looks like an eighteenth-century widow in mourning. She's legitimately wearing black—black jeans, black T-shirt—and her eyes are a bit red. I almost feel bad. Has she been crying about this? I know she loves Rowan, but . . . she didn't think she had a shot with him, did she?

"Hi," says Bliss, cutting through the silence. She puts one hand on her hip and grins sheepishly, as if this whole situation is an administrative error. "So sorry about this."

Juliet takes a long look at Bliss. Then she stands up straight, flicks her hair back, and says, "*Don't* be sorry—none of this is your fault. Whatever dickhead leaked those photos deserves to go to prison."

Bliss relaxes at Juliet's words, and Juliet ushers her inside, taking her bag, asking her if she wants tea, laughing and joking and generally acting like she's known Bliss for years. Bliss follows her, a little confused but visibly relieved, and she shoots a quick grin back at me as she follows Juliet into the house.

I breathe a sigh of relief and wonder why I ever doubted Juliet. I make friends with good people.

⇄ ◄◄ ⊙ ►► ♥

The three of us are standing in the kitchen, chatting casually and getting to know one another, when the door creaks again and Mac peeks his head round the frame.

He's grinning.

"I was feeling lonely in the living room all by myself!" he says. He enters the room and leans jauntily against the kitchen counter.

Bliss gives him a weird look and then looks at me as if to say, *Who is this and why is he here?*

Juliet points at Mac. "Oh, this is Mac, by the way. He's here to see The Ark too."

"Hi!" says Bliss.

"Wow," says Mac, smiling. "So, you're famous now. I'm jealous."

There's a pause, and then Bliss laughs awkwardly.

"Not sure there's much to be jealous of, bud," says Bliss, "unless you wanna date Rowan Omondi."

Mac immediately starts spluttering. "Oh, no, no, erm, no, I'm not—I mean, I like The Ark, but I'm not—It's not—I'm not—"

Bliss raises her eyebrows at him. "Is the word you're looking for 'gay'? It ain't poisonous."

Juliet widens her eyes at Bliss's bluntness.

"Erm, yeah. I'm not," stammers Mac.

"S'fine, man. Chill."

I glance at Juliet, trying to keep the huge grin off my face. She's staring at Bliss, somewhat amazed.

"Erm, *anyway*," says Mac, determined to keep the conversation revolving around him and only him, "so, you must have had a crazy day!"

Bliss chuckles. "Yeah, I guess you could say that."

"Can't Rowan help you?"

Bliss rolls her eyes. "I don't need his help."

Mac chuckles. "Well, I mean, wouldn't it be easier if you just . . . went and hung out at his place or whatever?"

Bliss shrugs. "Not really. Why would that solve anything?"

"I don't know . . . he's rich and powerful, he can do something, can't he?"

"*Rich and powerful.* You make him sound like a dictator."

I can't say I fully understand why Bliss doesn't want to go and see Rowan. Surely if they're in a relationship, he'd be the first person she'd seek help from, not some random Ark fan she met in a Wetherspoons less than twenty-four hours ago.

Finally sensing he's not wanted, Mac says, "Erm, well, I'm gonna nip to the loo while you ladies drink your tea." And he speeds out of the room.

Bliss turns her head slowly towards me and Juliet, her eyes wide and a big smile on her face.

"Okay, not being funny, but why do you have the human embodiment of a mosquito in your house?"

I let out a snort. Even Juliet smiles a little in the corner of her mouth.

"He's not *that* bad . . ." says Juliet, but it's half-hearted.

"Mate," says Bliss. She wanders over to Juliet and pats her on the shoulder. "Please, please God, do not tell me Junior Conservative of the Year is your *boyfriend*?"

"Erm," Juliet says.

"Please no."

"Well, technically no."

"*Technically* no?"

"Erm . . ."

"Oh no. Oh no no no no *no.*" Bliss looks at me and puts her hand on her heart. "Have you been letting this happen?"

Juliet looks up at me, mildly embarrassed.

"Well," I say, "it's not really my place to comment on my friends' romantic interests."

"Excuse me, it's your place as a friend to tell them when they're almost dating a guy who can't even use the word 'gay' without spontaneously combusting."

She's probably right.

I look at Juliet. "Er, yeah. He's a bit of a dick."

Juliet doesn't say anything. She looks *betrayed*.

"Yikes," says Bliss.

"Can we not talk about it?" asks Juliet, turning round and starting to clear up our empty tea mugs.

Bliss raises her eyebrows at me.

When Mac returns I take him out into the corridor and tell him a dramatic story about how Juliet will feel *so much better* after this morning's events if she could *just have a milkshake from Sainsbury's*. I don't even have to finish my sentence before Mac is volunteering to go. I'm not even sure whether he wants to impress Juliet or whether he just wants to get away from Bliss before she says something so blunt that he starts to cry.

Bliss, Juliet, and I sit on the carpet in the living room with an open tub of mini brownies in between us.

Bliss has her fingers clasped together like a village elder and is somehow staring down at the both of us, despite being shorter than me.

"So," I say, "what's it like dating Rowan Omondi?"

"Ugh, let's not talk about *that*," says Bliss.

I shoot a glance at Juliet, but she's zoned out again, like she did earlier.

"Oh," I say, "er . . . sorry?"

"No, no, it's just, I don't know." Bliss rubs her forehead. "I don't know, man. I feel like my life revolves around Rowan. And I don't want it to."

"Oh."

"I guess I can't help it now."

"Can't help what?"

"My life revolving around my *boyfriend*." She says the word "boyfriend" like it's a particularly bad swear word.

"Oh."

Juliet is now eyeing Bliss carefully.

"I had plans," says Bliss. "Plans for my life. And now . . ." She starts to laugh. "What's gonna happen to me now? All I'm ever gonna be known for is being a band boy's girlfriend."

"It'll die down," I say. "Stuff like this is only hot news for, like, a week, isn't it?"

"This is The Ark we're talking about," says Bliss. "Come on. You're in the fandom. You know what it's like."

She's right. This won't die down in a week. The Ark fandom will be talking about it for the next three years, at least. People will track down Bliss's every move. She won't be able to move house, go to university, go on holiday, go *anywhere* without someone spotting it, posting about it, talking about it.

And they'll hate her. The ones who are in love with Rowan, anyway, which is a lot of them. They'll *hate her.*

"Everything will be all right," I lie.

She laughs. "You're sweet."

"Maybe you should talk to him," says Juliet in a small voice.

"And say what?"

"I don't know, tell him how upset you are?" Juliet fiddles with her hair nervously. "Maybe he'll be able to do something."

"I don't *need his help.*"

"But . . . he's your boyfriend. You act like you're not even friends."

Bliss frowns. "It's different. We don't see each other very often because he's always busy."

Juliet looks away with an eyebrow raise. "Okay."

"Look, I know you're just skeptical because you've got a thing for Rowan."

Juliet's head snaps back towards Bliss. "What?"

"Yeah, Angel told me yesterday."

Both of them look at me.

"Oh wow," I say. "You're not about to start arguing about a *boy*, are you? Because then we'd have reached a new level of pathetic in this conversation."

Juliet sighs. "No." She looks back at Bliss. "I'm not, like, in love with Rowan. I mean, he's hot, yeah, but I ship Rowan more with Jimmy than anything else. I think I'm more upset about that." Her voice quiets. "This week has been a roller coaster."

Bliss chuckles. "Oh yeah. I forgot that was a thing." She shakes her head. "He really hates that."

Juliet puts her head on her knees. "I don't want to talk about boys anymore."

Bliss nods. "I don't want to talk about boys ever again."

I look at them both, feeling quite glad that I don't have to deal with this sort of situation in my life.

"They do love each other, though," says Bliss. "Rowan and Jimmy."

My heart does a little leap.

"Not in that way," she continues, "just in a friend way. But . . . I don't think that's any less special."

Oh. I guess I never thought of it like that.

Juliet nods. And then she smiles.

"You seem cool," she says to Bliss.

Bliss grins. "So do you. We should be friends now."

"Yeah. Fuck these boys."

"And not in a sexual way. In a 'throw them in the bin' way."

"Yeah."

Bliss holds up a hand for a high five, and Juliet reciprocates, and they both laugh a little and then look at me.

I think of Jimmy and feel like a traitor, but then I meet Bliss's high five too.

Bliss stays for the whole afternoon. Every time we suggest she might want to call Rowan, or her mum, or a taxi, she says no.

I think she just wants to pretend that nothing is happening.

When it's afternoon prayer time, it finally hits me that she's here, and I helped her, and that has to be a sign.

It has to be fate that we met.

The good news is that Bliss being here takes Juliet's attention away from Mac almost entirely. The three of us bond over watching ridiculous Jowan fan videos on YouTube—extra dramatic ones comprised of sad Hozier tracks and slow-motion glances between the two boys—which Bliss finds even more hilarious than we do. We sit for a while and talk about our lives, Bliss telling Juliet all the things about her that she told me yesterday—her school life and wanting to save nature and her horrible HMV job—and Juliet telling Bliss about her dream of being a theater set designer and all the private-school pranks she's been a part of. Then we all decide to play Cards Against Humanity, which I win spectacularly after I match a card that says *This is the prime of my life. I am young, hot, and full of* ___ with a card that says *Poor life choices*. Juliet doesn't even drink the milkshake Mac went out and got her. It just sits and gets warm on the kitchen counter.

"Oh dear" is Dorothy's reaction when the situation is explained to her.

"Oh dear, indeed," says Bliss. She laughs, but I think she's crying on the inside.

"Well, you're welcome to stay here for as long as you'd like," says Dorothy, linking her fingers together on the kitchen table. She'd been out for most of the afternoon at a "health club." I have absolutely no idea what a health club is, but I hope I can spend my whole retirement at one. "I've rather been enjoying having so much excitement in the house."

Bliss smiles at her. "That's so kind . . . I should probably go home, though. My mum's just texted and she's getting pretty worried. And the paparazzi have mostly gone away for now."

"Well, if you're sure. But the house is open if you need to escape anytime."

"Thank you, I really appreciate that."

It's nearly dinnertime when Bliss gets into a taxi and leaves. Juliet and I wave her off, like we're saying our final farewells to a deployed soldier. The car disappears round the corner, and then it's just Juliet and me, standing out in the rain. Little droplets make a dotted pattern in her shirt.

"You'd think her life would be perfect," says Juliet. "She has *the guy*. You know? The ultimate fantasy dream." She turns to me. "Do you know what I mean?"

She means that Bliss is living the dream of millions of girls around the world. And yet, she still isn't happy.

"I know what you mean," I say.

"I feel like . . . the dream . . . The Ark . . . it's not helping anymore," she says.

I'm so confused by the statement that I don't even ask what she means. She looks at me, and I wonder whether she's waiting for me to say something, or ask something, I don't know. What does she want me to say? What am I not doing right? Why aren't we happy and enjoying ourselves in this week that we've been waiting for since last year?

"God, today has been the worst," she says.

I look at Juliet and almost recoil. She looks *devastated*. I mean, we've all had a bit of a *day*, but I don't think I've ever seen her so miserable.

"Yeah," I say. "This Rowan-Bliss thing just came out of nowhere."

She looks up at me, a sad, almost disappointed expression on her face.

"Yeah," she says. "The Rowan-Bliss thing."

But I just say nothing and she walks inside, leaving me out in the rain.

# JIMMY KAGA-RICCI

I should probably go and apologize to Lister, but I don't know what to say.

I wish it was tomorrow already. I want normality back.

Even if normality is waking up at 5 a.m., sitting in a chair for an hour while someone does your hair and makeup, eight hours of press events and interviews, then an evening of sound checks, rehearsals, and then a concert in front of twenty thousand people.

I'd rather have all of that than this.

A house of silence.

It's 9 p.m. now. As far as I know, Lister and Rowan have been in their rooms for hours, only wandering out when it's unavoidable to go to the bathroom or get some food. I've been dozing on and off since about four o'clock, Netflix still playing episodes of *Brooklyn Nine-Nine* one after another, but I might as well give up trying to sleep, since it doesn't seem like it's going to happen.

I'm starting to remember how claustrophobic it is in here. In this apartment.

Which is awful, really. Ungrateful. Twenty people could easily live here.

I just wish we could go outside.

I roll out of bed and stand up. All the blood rushes to my head and immediately I'm hit with a headache. Great. Just what I need.

Maybe I should go and say sorry to Lister.

No. I didn't do anything wrong. Did I?

Maybe I should go and talk to Rowan.

I don't want to talk to Rowan.

Don't want to think about this mess.

Don't want to think about anything.

I head out of my room and make my way to the kitchen, passing Lister's bedroom on the way, which is closed and silent. The living room is dark, even though the sun hasn't fully set. On the kitchen counter is our new record contract, open from where I'd been reading it earlier. Is that our future? Is that my future? We're supposed to be signing it in *two days*.

Don't want to think about that either.

I fill up a glass of water and drink the whole thing, then fill it up again and walk over to the window. The rain doesn't relax me in the way it normally does. It feels like it's trying to get in. Flood the room.

I look down at the street below. We live in a residential part of London, but there are always people walking around. If I could choose where to live, I'd choose a house in the Lake District. A solitary building without another man-made object within fifty miles.

I want to go outside.

About a year ago, Cecily told us to stop going outside without a bodyguard. Rowan, Lister, and I had tried to go to the cinema. Just us three, after a meeting at Fort Records. We were going to walk there—there was an Odeon just round the corner. But there were so many people wanting to meet us in the street that we didn't even make it there. There were so many people, such a huge crowd, that I'd started to panic, and Rowan had to be very rude and start shoving people out of the way, and someone grabbed Lister to stop him from leaving.

After that, we stopped going outside without a bodyguard.

I open the window and stick my arm out, just to feel the rain for a bit. Cool air rushes inside. I take a deep breath. Hadn't even noticed how stuffy it was in here.

What if I just . . . went outside?

Just for a minute. If I wear a hoodie or a cap or something, I'll probably be fine. Just want to stand out there for a minute. Fresh air.

I grab a hoodie and a cap, just for good measure, and I open the apartment door, walk down the corridor, and get in the lift. My stomach drops as the lift goes down, like it does on roller coasters. It feels freeing.

As soon as the lift door opens, I'm running. Run out of the building, through the door, down the steps, and—there. Fresh air. Light. It's so light. The rain is cool and clean and pure. The rain isn't going to hurt me.

"Mr. Kaga-Ricci!"

The sound of a voice makes my heart hammer in my chest and I spin round—but it's only Ernest, one of our apartment block's doormen. He's hurrying towards me down the steps outside our building as fast as he can, which isn't very fast, because he is eighty-two years old.

"Mr. Kaga-Ricci, should you be outside by yourself?"

I blink very slowly as he approaches. "What?"

Ernest produces an umbrella and holds it above my head.

"You should come back inside, sir, it's pouring. And you shouldn't be outside on your own."

I hate it when Ernest calls us "sir." He's over four times our age. He witnessed the Second World War.

"Are you all right, sir?" He frowns at me. "What's all that blood doing on your shorts?"

I glance down. Oh. Shit. There's still blood all over my shorts.

"I . . . er . . . cut my hand. On a mug." I vaguely wave my bandaged hand.

"Well, you rather look like you've had a bit of a rough and tumble, if you ask me." Ernest chuckles. "Not fighting with your friends, are you?"

"No," I say, which is much easier than attempting to explain the truth.

Ernest sighs heavily. He reminds me so much of Grandad. And a bit of David Attenborough. Both are reasons why I befriended him in the first place.

"What are you doing out here, eh?" he asks.

"I wanted to go for a walk."

"In the pouring rain?"

". . . Yeah."

"I'm not sure that's a good idea without a bodyguard, sir."

". . . I know." I look at him. He's gazing at me sympathetically. I wish I could give him a hug. "Can you come with me?"

Ernest chuckles. "I'm not allowed to leave the building, I'm afraid."

"Oh." I shove my hands into my pockets. "I'll just go on my own, then."

"Sir, I really don't think—"

"I'll just walk around the park. I'll only be ten minutes."

"But if someone recognizes you—"

I've already stepped out from underneath his umbrella and started walking away. "I'll be fine."

I don't care. Ernest's voice fades away into the rain.

I open the gate into the park. It's not really a park, it's just a long strip of grass, trees, and flowers in between the rows of apartment blocks. You're only supposed to enter if you're a local resident, so I should be fine. Plus, it's getting dark now. Not that there's any level of sunset visible through the thick gray rain clouds.

There's no one around.

I sit down on a bench, pull back my hood, and take my cap off. The rain patters against my skin, against my forehead and cheeks and knees. It's therapeutic. I rub my face, washing it with the rain, getting the sleep out of my eyes. I run a hand through my hair, which is soaked and soft. I look at my hands. My body feels like it's mine again.

A squirrel darts through the grass in front of me and clambers up a tree. It climbs all the way up to the top, then disappears. I smile.

Then I see someone approaching.

Fuck. No. What do I do? Run? Should I go? Should I hide? Are they going to recognize me? Probably. I shouldn't really be seen looking like this.

They might guess where I live. Call other people. Everyone will know. Everyone will—

"Have you seen those gloriosa daisies?"

I snap my head up. I must have been panicking for longer than I thought.

But it's just an old woman leaning on a walker. She looks very, very old. Older than Ernest. And Grandad. Her skin looks so worn and wrinkled, her hair wispy and white. She's wearing a big purple raincoat, and her glasses are so thick that her eyes are huge. She's walking about four times more slowly than most people.

She grins crookedly at me. "Aren't they lovely, eh?" She points shakily at a big bunch of yellow flowers growing in one corner of the park. "They'll be bringing butterflies and bees here once this rain clears up."

I don't say anything.

She laughs. She sounds so happy.

"Beautiful," she says. "What a world we live in!"

And then she walks away.

The sky gets darker and darker, and then it's nighttime. I didn't bring my phone, so I have no idea what the time is. Streetlamps shine into the park between gaps in the trees, giving the whole area a dim yellowish glow, the rain blurring everything, lights sparkling off the water, and when I next open my eyes, nothing seems very real anymore, just dark and melting, everything's just melting into yellow slush, and I stand up, my knees aching a little from sitting for so long, and I walk out of the park, mud sticking to the soles of my shoes. It's not cool now, it's cold, and I don't want to be here anymore. I want to be warm and dry and I want nobody to talk to me, ever—

"Oh my *God*, is that—"

Fuck. Don't look. Pretend you didn't hear.

"Jimmy! Jimmy Kaga-Ricci!"

I glance to one side and—there they are. Across the street. The girls. Our girls.

They run up to me. "Jimmy! Oh my God, oh my God." It's hard to register who is talking. There's four of them. Now all talking at once. One of them has started shaking very visibly. Another is just making squealing noises.

"Hi," I say, though it's not much more than a croak.

"I honestly love you so much," says one of them. "You've kept me going, like, throughout all of secondary school."

They don't love me. They don't know me.

"Can I get a selfie?" says another girl.

"Would it . . . ?" I start to ask if it would be okay if we didn't, but she's already turned round and taken a picture of herself next to me on her phone.

"Oh my God, what did you do to your hand?" one asks.

"I broke a mug and cut it by accident," I say.

"Awww," one says.

"Okay, I've got to go now," I say in a tone I hope isn't as rude as it probably is. The panic is rising in my chest, my breath shortening.

"Wait, wait," says a girl. "I just want you to know, like, how much you've changed my life. I really, really love you, and you've helped me through so much personal stuff over the past few years. So, thank you."

I blink at her. I am so tired.

"How can you love me when you don't know me?" I ask.

And suddenly they all stop talking at once.

"We—we do know you," says one, and another says, "We do love you."

"Not real love, though," I say.

"It is real!"

"How can you love someone you've never even met in real life?"

"This is real life," one says.

"I meant before that. All until now. When I was just a photo on the computer."

None of them knows what to say.

"I'm glad I helped you," I say, and then I walk away before they can stop me, before they start grabbing me, before they call their friends and they all get together and mob me, because they "love" me.

"We do know you, Jimmy! And we love you!" they call after me, but even though they meant it in a nice way, it still terrifies me; it terrifies me that they all believe that what they feel for me is *love*. God, what have I done? What have I done to them? By the time I get back to our apartment, sit down on the floor with my back against the front door, I'm actually having a panic attack. I can't breathe, shaking, probably going to die, something's going to kill me, someone's going to kill me, how am I going to save myself? How am I going to save myself? How am I going to save myself?

"Jimmy."

Maybe it would be better if some fan stalker just killed me while I was asleep, made all this stop—

"Jimmy, look at me."

God, please, please help me, please let me be happy—

"You're having a panic attack. Look at me."

Yeah, no shit. I focus. Rowan is sitting in front of me.

"Breathe with me," he says, and then breathes in deeply. "Breathe in—"

I try to take a deep breath in but it just turns into three very quick, shallow breaths, like I'm drowning. I think I'm gonna throw up.

"Breathe out."

Another three quick breaths. I can't do it. Everything is wrong. Bad. Everything is bad.

"Breathe in."

I try again, but it's still too quick, too shaky, too shallow.

"Breathe out."

Rowan repeats it more times than I can count. I don't know how long it's been when I can finally breathe properly again, and Rowan manages to persuade me to stand up and walk over to the sofas. He brings me a towel, because I'm drenched in both rain and sweat, and a glass of water. It splashes around when I hold it. My hands are still shaking.

"We don't live in the real world anymore," I say.

"Do you want to talk about it?" says Rowan.

"No," I say.

But God, I do. I always do.

# THURSDAY

**"I AM NOT AFRAID; I WAS BORN TO DO THIS."**
**—JOAN OF ARC**

# ANGEL RAHIMI

Today I am going to meet The Ark.

I was in my thirteenth year when I first heard an Ark song. I was tucked up in bed one evening near December and I was on another routine spiral through the endless abyss of YouTube. And I found their first YouTube video.

It only had a couple of thousand views back then.

They were all around my age. Thirteen and fourteen. Jimmy's hair was a messy brown mop. Rowan still had dorky rimless glasses. Lister's jeans were always too short.

A musical explosion in a family garage.

They played a cover of Eiffel 65's "Blue." In their own style of course, more rock-ish, but with Jimmy playing all sorts of synth sounds on two different keyboards.

It went viral a few weeks after that.

I like knowing that I've been there since the beginning. I'm part of something. I've been part of this for five years. When I open Twitter and see photos of them performing in Manila, Jakarta, Tokyo, Sydney—I am part of that. I am one of the few that has seen them through this and been there every step of the way.

It doesn't matter that they don't know me.

Being a fan isn't always about the thing you're a fan of. Okay, well, it *sort of* is, but there is much more to it than just going online and screaming that you love something. Being a fan has given me people to talk to about the things that I like for the past five years. Being a fan has made me better friends online than I've ever encountered in real life; it has entered me into a community where people are joined in love and passion and hope and joy and escape. Being a fan has given me a reason to wake up, something always to look forward to, something to dream about while I'm trying to fall asleep.

And people sneer. Sure. I get it. Adults especially. They see all these teenage girls and they think it's because we're stupid. They only see the tiny percentage of fans who take it too far—the stalkers—and they think we're all like that. They think we only love the band because of their looks; they think we only like their music because it's relatable. They think all of us are girls. They think all of us are straight.

They think we're dumb little girls who spend all our time screaming because we want to marry a musician.

They don't understand half of it. Any of it. How could they? Adults don't think teenagers can do anything, anyway.

But despite everything in the world being terrible, we *choose* to stand by The Ark. We choose hope, light, joy, friendship, *faith*, even when our lives aren't perfect, or exciting, or fun, or special, like the boys from The Ark's are. I might be a disappointing student, without many close friends, with a life of mediocrity waiting for me back at home—an average degree from an average university, an average job, and an average life—but I will always have this.

In an otherwise mediocre existence, we choose to feel passion.

# JIMMY KAGA-RICCI

"Lister," says Rowan, sighing heavily as Lister walks out of his bedroom wearing a jumper that appears to be made of plastic. "Not that I'm not passionate about grunge, but you look like a bin bag."

"Looks good, though," I say. "I mean, if anyone could get away with wearing a bin bag, it'd be you."

Rowan shoots me a *don't encourage him* look.

It's 10 a.m. and our apartment has transformed into a clothes shop in the space of half an hour. This is the routine every time we do a show. Tasha and her crew of stylists have clothes delivered from a variety of designers, and then we choose what we want to wear. With some advice from the stylists of course. Right now, me, Rowan, and Tasha are all sitting on the back of the sofa, watching Lister twirl like a kid in a party dress.

Lister puts his hands on his hips and lunges deeply. He's wearing very tight jeans. Rowan puts a hand up to block the view.

"So are we voting yes or no?" Lister asks.

"No," says Rowan.

"Yes," I say, making the "okay" signal with my non-bandaged hand.

"No, sweetie," says Tasha. Her American accent makes her feel almost motherly. "Come on, you look like trash. Where's that bomber jacket I got you? The Vetements one! It's from this year's spring/summer collection!"

Lister sighs. "I just thought it'd make a *change*."

"This is the last tour stop. You can't look like trash on your final show of the tour."

Lister winks at us. "Come on, Tash, I *never* look like trash."

Tasha chucks a shoe at him and he laughs and retreats into his bedroom.

"Jimmy, have you chosen?" asks one of Tasha's team.

I shake my head. I'm terrible at choosing what to wear because there's always too much choice. I love everything. All of it. The ripped jeans and sloganed hoodies and button-ups and military boots and Vans and earrings and soft cotton T-shirts. Sometimes I enjoy choosing what to wear for a show more than the show itself.

"How about this?" Tasha wanders over to one of the clothing racks and withdraws an oversized black hoodie with a black-and-white photo of Jake Gyllenhaal in *Donnie Darko* on it. On one sleeve the word *TRUTH* stands out in white bold lettering, and on the other sleeve the word *LIE*.

"That looks good," I say.

"With some ripped black jeans?"

"Yeah, definitely."

Rowan suddenly appears, wearing only boxers. "Hey, Tash, you got that dress that I wanted to wear?"

"Sure, hun, check the rack near the door. To go with the Metallica jumper, right?"

"Yeah, that's the one. D'you think black leggings or jeans?"

"Leggings, I think."

"Sick."

Lister reappears wearing what can only be described as a cape.

Tasha folds her arms. "Now you *know* I didn't order whatever *that* is."

Lister starts running around the lounge, cape billowing behind him, singing the Batman theme.

Tasha picks up another shoe and hurls it at him, and when she misses does it again. Lister shrieks and dodges, then runs towards us and throws the cape over me, so both of us are concealed under it. I can't stop myself laughing, trapped under the cape, and I catch a glimpse of Lister grinning at me, a soft smile, one that reminds me of years ago, back when this was all new and exciting and fun, back when we really were *children*. Then he yanks the cape and skips away.

"When I dump you all and start my solo career, I'm wearing all the capes I want!" he calls.

"You go ahead," Tasha calls back. "But that isn't tonight, sweetie."

Rowan's bedroom door opens and he emerges wearing his concert outfit, which is a dress with leggings underneath. All in black, obviously. He looks like a saint.

He's also holding a large cake with candles on it and is looking at me.

The lights dim, and everyone suddenly turns to look at me, and then they start singing "Happy Birthday."

To me.

Wait.

What?

What's the date?

They finish singing, by which time Rowan has made it across the room to me. He grins. "You forgot again, didn't you?"

"I never know what the date is . . ." I mumble, feeling very embarrassed from the sudden attention. Lister's grinning at me as well, cape wrapped round him like a scarf, clapping his hands together softly.

"Make a wish, then, Jimjam," says Rowan.

I look at the candles and wish for what I always wish for, which is to be happy. Then I blow them out. Everyone cheers and claps.

"How long we got, Tash?" calls Rowan as he carries the cake over to the breakfast bar.

"About half an hour, hun."

"Sweet."

Music starts playing over the surround sound. Lister fiddles with the volume controls and changes track to one of our old favorite bands, The Killers. We used to sit and listen to them in music practice rooms and in each other's bedrooms. Back in the day.

I can't help but smile.

Lister starts jumping up and down and singing along immediately, cape flapping about behind him. He skips around the room again, trying to persuade various stylists to join in, even trying to get Cecily to join in (which of course she doesn't, because she's too busy tapping away on her phone). Then he comes up to me and takes my hands, pulling me around, galloping across the floor, then pulling me up onto the sofa and bouncing up and down in time to the music like we're on a trampoline. Rowan used to have a trampoline in his back garden. Well, I guess it's probably still there.

"COME ON, RO!" shouts Lister through harsh breaths as we bounce up and down. I start laughing at Rowan's expression—his classic eyebrow raise. Despite this, he runs across the room and leaps up onto the sofa to jump with us, throwing his arms round me. I stagger and nearly fall over, and laugh again.

The music blares all around us and we start screaming along to the chorus. We all still remember the words, despite it being months, maybe years since we've heard this song. I forget our own songs in shorter times than that.

"How does it feel to be *nineteen*?" shouts Rowan over the music.

"That bit closer to death," adds Lister.

I feel happy, maybe. Just for a little bit.

Maybe my wish came true.

# ANGEL RAHIMI

Things felt awkward when Bliss left last night. There was a space between me and Juliet again and not even Mac could make up for it anymore.

Which in some ways is a good thing, but mostly it just meant there were too many awkward silences.

And despite Bliss's warning about Mac, Juliet still left to go to Sainsbury's with him fifteen minutes ago while I was doing my makeup. Without telling me.

I kind of have a little cry about it for five minutes. Just a minor cry. Which is stupid, because all she's done is gone to a supermarket without me. Didn't think I was that clingy.

After that I sit in the kitchen and catch up on some Tumblr discourse from last night.

The theories about Jimmy, Rowan, and Bliss are getting pretty wild. People are coming up with some hilarious explanations for the Jowan photo and the Rowan/Bliss reveal, such as it's a ploy by their management, out to stir up some extra publicity to keep attention on The Ark once their tour ends, or that both reveals were calculated by Jimmy and Rowan themselves, a passionate cry for help, a desperate attempt to out themselves and tell the world about their secret love affair and the burden of Rowan being forced into a fake relationship.

A lot of people agree with me. Rowan and Bliss are in a relationship. And Jowan is just a fantasy.

A lot of people are devastated. Like Juliet was yesterday, I guess. And I thought I would have been too, but while it was a surprise, it didn't destroy me in the way I thought it would when the news eventually came that Jowan, love itself, wasn't real.

Maybe I sort of knew it was a lie all along.

⇄  ◄◄  ⊙  ►►  ♥

"You seem to be in a good mood."

I have a minor heart attack while washing up my cereal bowl, and then turn round.

It's Juliet's nan, wearing a dressing gown and holding a mug. She smiles at me and sits down at the table, taking a sip from the mug.

"I'm in a *very* good mood," I say, which is hilarious, because I was literally crying about ten minutes ago.

"Excited about tonight?"

"*So* excited."

Dorothy sips on her mug again and says, "Do you mind if I ask you something?"

I grab a tea towel and say, "Yeah, sure!"

"Are J and Mac . . . together?"

Oh.

"Erm . . . well . . ." How exactly do I explain this? "They *might* be, but I think . . . because they've only just met each other in real life this week . . . I think it's got a bit . . . er . . . complicated."

"I see . . ." Dorothy nods and looks down. "I see."

There's a pause. What do I say? What should I say?

"She's always talked about this *special friend* that she had on the internet," Dorothy continues. "But . . . I'm not actually sure whether that's *him*, or whether that's *you*." She looks at me and smiles sadly. "I'm just trying to make sense of it all, you know?"

Aren't we all.

"What did she say about them?" I ask.

"Just that she finally had someone she loved talking to." Dorothy shrugs. "J's been through so much, and she doesn't like to talk about her problems. She's always had difficulty making strong friendships. So I was really happy to hear she'd made such a good friend . . . even if it was just online. Online friendships are real too, aren't they?"

*Been through so much?* What does that mean? It feels rude to ask.

"Absolutely!" I say.

"Yes . . ." She shakes her head suddenly. "Anyway, excuse me, prying into my own granddaughter's private life through one of her friends!"

"It's . . . it's fine . . ."

"She's just not the most communicative to me, and I want to be there for her, now more than ever."

"Oh . . ."

*Now more than ever?*

Dorothy sighs. "And of course she had another unpleasant phone call from her parents yesterday morning."

Unpleasant phone call? Yesterday morning? I heard nothing about that.

"I'd better go off and get ready for the day." She stands up and leaves the room.

I'm still standing there with a tea towel in one hand. I know Juliet isn't as chatty as I am, but we *have* talked about serious stuff. What's Dorothy talking about? Juliet would have told me if something serious had happened. We're best friends. Aren't we? Pretty much, anyway.

⇄  ⏪ ⏯ ⏩  ♥

"Hi, Dad," I say, sitting on Juliet's bed with my phone against my ear. I won't be able to call home tonight, as I'll be at the concert, so I'm calling now.

"So, today's the day, hmm?"

"Yeah."

"Are you excited?"

Am I excited? Well, yeah, I guess. But it feels like more than that. I'm excited and scared and hopeful and I think I'm going to cry again at any possible moment, and, God, I think that I might ascend when Jimmy looks me in the eyes.

"Definitely," I tell him.

There's a pause.

"What is it you like about this band?" he asks.

"I like their music," I say.

There's another pause.

I guess the leavers' ceremony is happening right now. My classmates will be lining up in the assembly hall, waiting to shake our head teacher's hand and get a "well done," two words for two years of effort.

"Are you sure?" he asks. "Is it just because they're good-looking?"

"No." I bite my lip. "It's more than that, Baba."

"More?"

"Just . . . more."

"We don't understand, Fereshteh. Help us understand."

"You . . . can't."

They can't understand. Some things are impossible to explain.

# JIMMY KAGA-RICCI

Preshow routine is always the same—arrive, sound check, food, meet-and-greet, break, then the show—but I do usually find a way to worry about it anyway. Today isn't so bad, though, since we've performed at the O2 Arena seven times before, so I know my way around and there really shouldn't be any major surprises in store. Hopefully.

We don't have to wear our nice clothes until the meet-and-greet, so all three of us are back in joggers. In the car on the way there, Lister falls asleep on my shoulder, mousy-brown tufts tickling my neck. I flick him on the forehead when he starts to drool on me.

Sound check passes quickly. Playing our songs when the entire audience is empty is always a laugh, because we're just playing for ourselves, and we can deliberately get stuff wrong and play games like Lister trying to get us out of time and Rowan adding in harmonies where there aren't normally and me changing the lyrics of our most famous songs.

After that we sit and chill in the dressing room for a while with Cecily and the hair and makeup people and some frantic, nervous O2 employees running in and out, asking us if we need anything every two seconds.

It's a stuffy room. Very posh, of course—this is the O2—but it's too hot. I stand up and start walking around, wandering over to the table laden with snacks and drinks, inspecting the artwork on the walls and the potted plants and the giant mirror. One of the walls is adorned with a giant Baroque painting print. Something Christian, definitely. I try to guess which part of the Bible it's depicting, but I guess my Bible knowledge isn't good enough, because I'm not sure, and then I feel really bad.

I go and sit next to Rowan, who is having his hair done by Alex at a dressing table.

Rowan looks downcast. He joined in with our silly riffing during sound check and my mini birthday party earlier, but every time the laughing stops, his expression drops and he looks like he's about to cry.

"You okay?" I ask.

He flinches, not realizing I'd been sitting there. Alex makes an exasperated noise and tells him to sit still.

"Oh," says Rowan, "er, yeah."

"No, you're not."

He sighs and holds up his phone.

"Bliss just won't talk to me," he says, and then looks at me in the mirror. "Why won't she talk to me?"

None of us have seen or heard from Bliss since the morning the news broke. Rowan told us that she refused to come to our apartment, and then she stopped answering his calls.

"I've called her, like, fifty times," says Rowan, chuckling sadly. "I get that she'd be upset, but . . . it's not like this is *my* fault . . . Why doesn't she just want to talk to me about it?" He looks down at his phone again. "Where is she?"

"Maybe she just wants to lie low for a while," I say.

"We're in a *relationship*," says Rowan, and then his voice lowers to a whisper. "What sort of relationship is it if you can't even talk to each other when something bad happens?"

Not a good relationship.

That's what it is.

But I don't want to say that to him.

"After we sign the contract tomorrow . . ." he begins, then stops.

"What?" I say.

He stares blankly at himself in the mirror. "We're gonna have no time at all. I'm gonna have no time to see her ever."

"I mean . . . we'll probably have *some* time . . ."

"If it's even less than we have now, it's basically nothing," he says.

Alex stares firmly at Rowan's hair, but the expression of pity on his face is unmissable.

$$\leftrightarrows \quad \blacktriangleleft\blacktriangleleft \; \textcircled{\scriptsize\triangleright} \; \blacktriangleright\blacktriangleright \quad \blacktriangledown$$

"Where's Lister?" asks Cecily, who is sitting with one leg crossed over the other on a sofa in the middle of the room. "He should be getting his hair done by now."

No one answers her.

"Did he go to the bathroom?" I ask.

No one answers again.

"He's probably there," says Cecily. "Can you go get him, babe?"

"Okay." I open the door and leave the room.

This dressing room is one of many on a long gray corridor. I wander down to the right towards the bathroom and enter. This bathroom is just for us, and, like the dressing room, it's fancy—all shiny marble urinals and ornate mirrors and a figurehead glaring down at us from above the hand dryers.

"Lister, are you in here?"

A loud clunking noise sounds from the stall farthest from the door—a bottle hitting the floor—then a whispered, "*Fuck.*"

Lister.

I walk towards the stall and stand in front of it. What's he doing in there? Why does he have a bottle?

"Are . . . you okay?" I ask. "You've been in here for a while."

"Can't a man poop when he needs to, Jimmy?" Lister laughs but it sounds horribly forced.

"Is that definitely what you're doing?"

He doesn't answer me for a moment.

Then he starts to laugh.

There's another clinking sound. Definitely a bottle.

What is he *doing*?

"Can you open the door?" I ask. Maybe I should go back and get Rowan. Something's not right.

To my surprise, he obligingly slides open the cubicle lock and pulls the door open.

He's sitting on the toilet—lid closed and joggers pulled up, thankfully— with his phone in one hand and a nearly empty bottle of red wine in the other.

"What d'you want, then?" Lister leans forward and narrows his eyes. "I'm in a very important meeting."

I feel suddenly very small. He's been here, in the bathroom, drinking.

"Did . . . did you drink all of that just now?" I ask, pointing at the bottle.

Lister looks at it as if he'd forgotten it was there. "Oh. Yeah. Just a little preshow . . . er . . . just to calm the nerves."

He's drunk. Not obscenely drunk, not dangerously drunk, but drunk enough.

On a show day.

He's not supposed to do this on show days.

"You're not supposed to drink on . . . on show days," I stammer.

Lister snorts. "Come *on*, it's the last show of the tour." He leans his head against the side of the cubicle. "After that, I can drink every day."

"You can't be drunk at the show. At the meet-and-greet. People will notice."

"Naah, I'm *fine*. Look." He stands up so quickly that I take a couple of steps backwards. He flicks his hair back and puts his hands on his hips. "Look. No one will suspect a thing."

To be fair, he's right. He looks perfectly normal, bar maybe a slight haziness of the eyes, the way they're not quite focused, and the way his mouth keeps twitching into a smile.

"Why do you do this?" I ask.

"Do what?"

"Get drunk all the time."

He steps out of the cubicle, pushing me farther backwards. His smile drops.

"What's wrong with that?" he says, his eyes widening and staring off somewhere over my head. "What's wrong with drinking? What's wrong with having parties and having a good time and *enjoying* what we have?!" He laughs. "We're rich and famous, Jimmy. Do you understand how good that feels when you grew up like *me*? *We had nothing.*"

I stay silent.

"No," he says. "You don't. Because you didn't have to worry about money before all this started. I *did*. Me and my mum were *this close* to being on the street. And now you're telling me off for actually *enjoying* having money and being *happy*. You're just getting angry at me."

"I'm not angry—"

"I'm fucking tired of you and Rowan thinking you're so much more *mature* and *sensible* than me. You think you've got it all sorted but you don't! You're just the same as me. You're both just as bad as I am. So, stop fucking acting like you've got the higher ground."

I don't say anything.

He steps forward, edging me back so I'm pressed against the sinks. "Sorry, sorry, I didn't mean to shout at you. I'm just tired." He puts the near-empty bottle down on the sink next to me, and then pats me gently on the cheek. "Hey. Jimmy. Sorry." Then he wraps his arms round my shoulders and hugs me tightly. "Sorry for always being shit."

I still don't say anything. I don't really know what to say. I can't even follow his thought processes.

I pat him gently on the back.

"You're an alcoholic," I tell him, realizing this properly for the first time. I wonder whether anyone's told him that before.

He snorts. "I know, right?" He thinks I'm joking.

He moves back so he can look me in the eyes. He stares at me for a moment.

"Hey . . ." He's blinking slower than normal. He brings up a hand and runs his fingers along the neck of my jumper. "Do you want to . . . ?"

He doesn't finish the question. He just leans in and kisses me.

My stomach lurches. Not because I'm excited, but because I'm *shocked* and I'm getting flashbacks of the last time I did this. Never my idea, is it? I want to, I want to kiss a boy in some dramatic way . . . but I also *don't*, not when it doesn't feel right. It's never the way it should be, the way it looks in the movies. That sort of starlight romance doesn't exist for me.

He doesn't taste good and he pulls me against him by the waist and holds me there and I freeze, both because I don't know what to do and because he's taller and stronger than me, and even though he's gentle, and important to me, I don't . . . I've never thought of him that way . . . have I?

And even though I could kiss him just because he's attractive, even though I could kiss him because I so badly want to feel wanted, wanted in a good way, not how the fans want me, not how everyone else wants me, even though I lean into it for a brief second, suddenly high on the feeling of being with someone who knows me, the *real* me . . .

I don't . . . I just . . .

I can't.

I lean back, pulling away with a startled, "Don't, don't do that."

"Oh . . ." He gazes at me, unmoving. "Oh God, I'm sorry. I'm so sorry."

Then he hugs me. And it feels real. Despite the alcohol.

"I'm so sorry," he says, and he sounds like he's apologizing for humanity itself. "I . . . That's not . . . I didn't want to do it like that."

"Do . . . do what?" My voice is little more than a hoarse whisper.

"Tell you," he says.

My stomach lurches again. This can't be happening now. This is the wrong time. He's never . . . I'd never have guessed—

"You don't have to . . . like me back," he says, and his voice breaks but I can't tell whether he's laughing or trying not to cry. "But please don't hate me."

"I—I don't hate you," I say, because I can't get out what I really want to say, which is that I love him, but not really in *that* way, I mean, not right now at least, and I want to help him, I don't want him to keep drinking all the time, but we're all dealing with shit, and I don't know anything about the world, and I thought the three of us would be friends forever. I can't deal with these unsaid feelings. I don't want to know about them. I don't want to think about them.

Eventually he pulls back and steps away from me, releasing me from where I'm trapped against the sinks. He turns away from me without another word and starts walking towards the door.

"Only one more show! Then we can rest in peace!" He sounds cheerful but I'm still reeling from what just happened and "rest in peace" keeps ringing around my brain, again, and again, and again.

# ANGEL RAHIMI

"I'm gonna die," I say again as we're walking out of the tube station towards the O2 Arena. "I'm gonna die. I'm literally gonna die."

"Wouldn't recommend that," says Juliet, as if she's been on a two-week holiday to Death and gave it two out of five on Tripadvisor.

There are The Ark fans all around us, also walking towards the O2. Though we may be typecast as screaming twelve-year-olds, The Ark fans are in fact a hugely diverse crowd of people. There are tweens wearing Ark T-shirts and face paint and holding big handmade signs saying *I LOVE YOU, LISTER* and *ROWAN, JIMMY, LISTER* in a big heart. There are teens with colored hair, wearing all black, thick biker boots and ripped skinny jeans and denim jackets. There are older teens dressed like they're going out to a club, makeup sharp and edgy, wearing heels and holding sparkly clutches. And there are even adults—younger adults, sure, but adults nonetheless—here because the love for The Ark still burns in their hearts, because they still scream along in the car when The Ark are on the radio, because, like all of us, they don't care what other people think; they're just here to be happy.

That's the common theme, I think. We are all here to be happy.

Well, maybe apart from Juliet.

Juliet has been in a bad mood all day and I don't know why. Why wouldn't she be happy today, *the* day that we've been waiting for?

She's been hanging out with Mac, hasn't she? The love of her damn life?

What exactly is her problem?

The meet-and-greet area is a huge room with a roped queue and a curtained-off area where we get ten seconds to say hi to the boys and take a photo with them.

I am wearing one of my most edgy and best outfits, which includes a button-up baseball shirt with the word *Angels* on it (an incredible find from my aunt and uncle's holiday to Los Angeles last year) over a long-sleeved top. While it's not really making me any less nervous about meeting The Ark, I at least feel like myself, which is the most important thing.

I've also rehearsed (in my mind) exactly what I'm going to say to them.

Jimmy/Lister/Rowan: Hey, how are you?

Angel: I'm great, thanks! I'm so happy to be meeting you guys! I've been listening to your music since I was thirteen.

Hopefully Jimmy: No way, really!

Angel: Yeah, you guys have allowed me to make some amazing friends and you've shaped all my teenage life with your music. I hope you'll continue to make music forever!

Hopefully Jimmy: That's our plan! Thanks so much for coming!

Then I'll ask them for a photo in which Jimmy and Rowan are holding my hands and Lister is doing a peace sign behind my head.

And then I can rest in peace.

The room is already half-full, despite it being over two hours before the meet-and-greet starts at four o'clock. I spot a couple of people I know from

Twitter, and a couple of others who attended Tuesday's meetup, but I'm too fidgety to go and say hi. I just keep babbling to Juliet and Mac, even though Juliet isn't saying much and Mac looks like he'd rather be at the dentist.

Ten minutes into the two hours we have left to wait, Juliet says, "I'm going to the bathroom" and disappears, leaving me and Mac alone.

I'm not going to let anything get me down.

I'm not going to let Mac wind me up.

I'm going to see The Ark.

And then I can die happy.

"How long do we have to wait again?" he asks.

"Two hours," I say.

He makes a face of disgust. "*Two hours? We've got to wait for two hours?*"

I feel my smile twitch.

"Got a problem?" I ask him.

He shrugs and looks away. "No."

"Good."

We stand in silence for a moment.

"She doesn't know yet, then?" I say.

He looks up at me in alarm. "Know what?"

"Know that you hate The Ark."

"I don't *hate* The Ark."

"That you're not a true fan."

He snorts. "*True* fan. You talk about them like they're a religion or something."

"What are you even going to say to them?" I ask. "Hi, I'm Mac, I've never actually listened to your music properly, I'm only here because I lied to get a girl to like me—"

"Just lay off, this isn't any of your business—"

"Juliet is my *best friend*, so, yeah, I think it's my business—"

"Best friend?!" Mac laughs. "*Best friend?* You only met her *this week*."

"We've been talking to each other online for years—"

"So? That doesn't mean *anything* compared to real life."

"How are you any different to me?" I feel myself snapping. I don't want to, but God, I hate this guy. "We're in exactly the same position."

"No," he says. "I wanted to meet Juliet so we could get to know each other better. You wanted to meet her because you have this selfish need to have someone to talk to about the things you care about. Are you even interested in properly being *friends* with her? Talking to her about *anything* apart from a fucking *boy band*?"

He abruptly stops talking and glances behind me, and I turn and see Juliet gloomily making her way back through the room.

I try to think of a clapback, but nothing comes in time.

⇄  ◄◄ ⊙ ►►  ♥

The queue is almost full now—almost everyone has arrived and the excitement is real.

I wish Juliet would wake up and enjoy this with me.

I wish Mac would stop glaring at me behind her back.

There are only ten minutes before The Ark are supposedly going to appear. I can't imagine what it's going to be like, seeing them this close for the first time. I don't know what I'm going to feel.

They will be good feelings. That I know.

I feel like I've come to the end of a pilgrimage.

"What are you gonna say to them?" I ask Juliet. Maybe we just need to talk about it a bit. Get her hyped up. Then she'll be more excited about it.

Juliet blinks slowly. "Oh, er, I don't know. I haven't really thought about it."

Oh.

"Are you gonna get a selfie?" I ask her.

"Yeah, probably."

I bite my lip.

"Aren't you excited?" I ask, and instantly regret it.

She turns to me, eyes wide, almost like she's about to cry.

"I've just . . . There's been . . ." she begins, but then swallows and looks away. "Yeah, yes. Yes, I'm really excited."

Maybe she's just nervous.

⇄  ◄◄ ⊙ ►►  ♥

It is two minutes till four. There are only two minutes to go until we see them for real, in the flesh, living and breathing and three-dimensional.

The boys.

Our boys.

I get chatting to a group of girls, a bit younger than us, in the queue behind us. They're German, and have traveled here from Germany after failing to get tickets to the Germany tour dates. Even I think this is kind of crazy, but I guess some people actually have money to do things like get trains and planes to go to other countries. I only managed to get to London because I saved all my birthday money and Eid money.

"It's nice that you've got a boy with you," says one of them in incredibly perfect English. I'm terrible at languages and immediately feel jealous. "It's a shame that there aren't many fans of The Ark who are boys." She points at Mac, who turns round to look at her.

I glance at Mac. "I know, right!" I pat him on the shoulder. "This is Mac. He's a big fan, all right!"

Mac chuckles nervously. "Yeah!"

I notice Juliet start paying attention to our conversation.

"I wonder why that is," I say. "Why girls like The Ark more than boys."

"I think it's because they're nice," says one of the German girls. We all look at her, and she shrugs. "You know that they're good people, from their YouTube videos and their interviews. They're not like normal musicians. It feels like they're our friends and they understand us and care about us."

The girl's friends all nod and voice their agreement.

"And that's what girls like," says another of the girls. "Boys that are nice and good. Not *attractive*."

They all laugh. Mac forces himself to join in.

"So, Mac," says another girl, "which Ark boy is your favorite?"

"Oh . . . er, well . . ." He pauses and I see the panic flash across his face.

Everyone looks at him.

"Probably . . . Owen?" he says.

There's a long pause.

"Owen," I say, and then laugh. "I sure do love Owen from The Ark."

The German girls laugh and start chatting among themselves again.

"Wait—" says Mac. "Hang on, I meant—"

"We know what you meant," I say to him.

And then I look at Juliet.

If she'd been grumpy before, she's distraught now.

"Owen . . . ?" she says.

"I meant . . ." says Mac, but he can't even remember Rowan's name.

"I know exactly what you meant," says Juliet. She nods and laughs. "I know *exactly* what you meant."

For someone so small, she suddenly looks terrifying.

"You're not really an Ark fan, are you?" she says.

"What? That's—I—"

"You just lied about it to me this whole time because you fancy me, don't you?" she says.

Mac goes a deep red color. "It's not . . . like that . . ."

"What is it like, then?" Juliet grins at him. It's vicious. "Go on."

But he can't think of anything to say.

"Bliss was right," she whispers, almost to herself. "Oh my God."

The silence after that is broken only by screams, and I already know what is happening before I turn to look.

The Ark are here.

# JIMMY KAGA-RICCI

"There's queue ropes, right?" I ask whoever's listening—Rowan, Lister, Cecily, a random O2 employee, our security guard. "There's, like, a fence, or, like, a gate . . ."

We are standing in a corridor outside the meet-and-greet room. There are several security guards and O2 employees around us going through what's about to happen. I'm trying to talk while also doing deep-breathing exercises, which is not working.

Rowan squeezes my shoulder. "Jimmy . . . come on, calm down."

"Do you think they're going to ask us about . . . like . . . the stuff that's happened this week . . . the Jowan photo . . . ?"

"You don't have to answer anything they ask you, Jimmy. You don't have to talk if you don't want to. There are three of us."

"Do you think they're gonna read something into this hoodie?" I hold out the *TRUTH* and *LIE* sleeves of my hoodie. They always overanalyze stuff like that.

Rowan shakes his head. "Come on, it's just a hoodie, for God's sake."

"They'll want me to say *something*. They're gonna want me to say something." I can't control my breathing. Everyone else has started to notice. "About the photo or Rowan or Bliss or—"

"Hey, Jimmy," Lister interrupts, leaning heavily onto my shoulder. He's sparkling; he's a beacon of contemporary beauty. I don't feel like I'm here. "Don't worry. If any of them ask you about the photo, I'll change the topic and start talking about my affair with—"

"Are you drunk?" Rowan hisses at him. The slurring in Lister's voice is unmistakable.

Lister narrows his eyes and frowns.

"Probably," he says.

"What the *fuck*?" Rowan shakes his head.

Rowan pulls me away from the group and puts his hands on my shoulders.

"I know a lot of shit's happened this week," says Rowan in that very parental voice he puts on when I'm freaking out about something unnecessary, "and I know that makes your anxiety worse, but you've got to calm down. Nothing bad has happened to you, Jimjam. Nothing bad is happening to you."

"Everything's bad."

"Nothing bad is going to happen to you."

But it feels like it is.

"*I am not afraid*," says Rowan softly. "Remember?"

"I am not afraid," I whisper, but the second half of that quote, *I was born for this*, swirls around my mind and makes me want to run.

I can hear the rain outside. Wait—no. That's not rain.

That's the fans.

⇄  ◀◀ ⊙ ▶▶   ♥

The screams mean that they are very happy that we are here.

I focus on the air a few meters ahead of me so that the horde of fans goes blurry. We are standing at one end of the room and the fans are gathered in a roped queue that winds all the way around the room. I smile at the blur and salute at them, the things I always do. I faintly register Rowan waving on my left and Lister waving on my right. Lister calls out, asking them how they're doing, but they just scream back at him. Lister says we're looking forward to meeting them and we'll be just behind this curtain and he hopes they've been having a good day so far and he hopes they're looking forward to the concert tonight. And then we are turning away and walking behind the curtain and my smile can drop and once we're totally out of sight Rowan is squeezing my hand but I'm gone, I'm already gone, I'm up above the three of us and gazing down at the three bodies and wondering who on Earth decided that these three pathetically flawed human beings deserved so much worship.

Then the first girl appears from the other side of the curtain and she is so happy. And we are so happy to meet you. Have you had a good day so far? Would you like to take a selfie?

# ANGEL RAHIMI

They are so happy.

They look so much happier than they do in photos.

Jimmy's smile is so wide—a youthful, dreamlike grin—as he gazes over the crowd, almost *surprised* even, surprised and happy that so many people would want to come here to see him. He's wearing a hoodie with *Donnie Darko* on it. God. I love him. I love him.

Rowan's smile is close-lipped but there is light in his eyes and he looks proud, so proud to be here, so proud of all the things that he and his two best friends have achieved throughout their lives together.

Lister is the one doing the talking this time. I'd hoped it'd be Jimmy, but I don't mind really, not when Lister looks like Paradise itself, glowing, warm and alive.

They are so beautiful.

How could three people so beautiful exist in a world like this?

Once I have looked at them all separately, I look at the trio together. There is something inexplicable tying them together. Rowan and Lister stand symmetrically waving, Rowan always on Jimmy's left and Lister always on Jimmy's right. Both that little bit taller than Jimmy, who is the heart and the center of The Ark. Rowan and Lister revolve around him like the three make up a solar system. I feel an inexplicable fear of them separating. Imagining them on their own is impossible.

Then they disappear behind the curtain. And all is right in the world.

# JIMMY KAGA-RICCI

I quickly lose count of how many people we've met and greeted and watched disappear again behind the curtain. We quickly find a routine where the three of us say exactly the same thing each time. The fan walks towards us, Lister says hey, how are you, they reply, Rowan answers them if they say anything that needs a response (for example, if they tell us how much they love us, or how we've changed their life, etc.), and then I say how glad we are that they came to see us. Then Rowan suggests he take the selfie, because he has the longest arms.

And then they're gone.

And everything is fine. Everything is okay.

Rowan was right. Of course. Nothing is going to happen.

Almost everyone wishes me happy birthday. And a lot of the fans ask me what I did to my hand. I tell them I accidentally smashed a mug.

"I heard about that online," says someone, which hits me so off guard that I fail to say anything in response, and Rowan has to quickly interrupt with another "Do you want me to take a selfie? I have the longest arms!"

I have no idea how long we've been going when we're offered a five-minute break. Sometimes we don't take breaks when they offer them, but Rowan takes one look at me and says, "Yeah, just five minutes, if that's all right," and someone gives me a bottle of water, which I drink half of in about ten seconds.

Lister sits down on the floor.

"How you doing?" Rowan murmurs to me.

"Fine," I say.

I want to tell him about Lister and that I'm terrified of the fans and what's the point of being in a band when all it's doing is causing us misery?

"Really?" he says.

"Yeah. It's fine."

He seems to believe me.

# ANGEL RAHIMI

We are three people from the front of the queue and a large group of girls near the back of the line seem to be causing a fair amount of unrest. I keep hearing shouts of "Can you *stop* pushing?" and the space between each person seems to be getting smaller and smaller. We're all fairly packed in now, actually. People are starting to get agitated.

Despite how the media paints us, fandoms are actually very supportive and respectful places. Fans will stick up for each other and look after each other in a way that normal strangers don't. I think it's because despite who we are, where we came from, and whatever we've been through, we all have a very big part of us in common.

Of course there are always a small number of fans who are not good people.

There are always those who lack any empathy whatsoever.

"Why is everyone pushing?" Juliet mumbles. The first thing she's said in about half an hour.

The next person walks towards the curtains. Two more to go.

Mac looks like he wants to die. He hasn't said anything either. I've been distracting myself by talking to the other fans around us, talking to people who actually care about being here.

"I might get out of here," he says suddenly.

Juliet says nothing.

"Someone else deserved your ticket," I tell him.

He looks at me like I'm from another planet.

And then there is a sound.

A loud crack.

And a terrified voice rips through the air.

"What the *fuck*, what the *fuck*—"

And Rowan stumbles out from behind the curtain with blood cascading down one side of his face.

# JIMMY KAGA-RICCI

I am wearing my happy face again and everything is fine and then suddenly it isn't.

A girl walks round the curtain and everything is normal and then it's not.

Instead of smiling and holding out her phone for us to take a photo, she withdraws a brick from her bag.

A brick. Like the ones you'd use to build a garden wall.

Security aren't superhuman. The girl throws the brick at Rowan before they can jump on her and it hits him on the side of the head and he stumbles backwards with a cry of pain, hands flying to his face, and the girl, some random girl we've obviously never seen before, is screaming. The girl is screaming that she hates him, she hates what he did, why did he have to have a girlfriend, why did he have to destroy her life, but security are pinning her to the ground and I'm looking at Rowan again and his face is a mess of blood. He takes his hand away from his face and looks at it. He just stares at the blood—he can't believe this is real. I can't believe this is real. And then he stumbles blindly away, out of the curtained-off area, probably meaning to head towards the door we came in from but instead veering towards the crowd. I haven't moved.

It all happens in under ten seconds.

Rowan. I start walking after him, ignoring Lister's attempt to get me to stop, to stay where they can't see us, but I'm gone, I'm out of the curtain, and I see Rowan, just in time for both of us to be consumed by a plague of bodies, screaming, screaming our names.

# ANGEL RAHIMI

I'm ripped away from Juliet and Mac as the queue ropes are trampled by bodies. Those who want to get to The Ark push forward and those who know we should give them space can't fight back and the crowd of two hundred fans crush themselves into a screeching, swarming mass of bodies. Queue ropes seem to disintegrate. My view of Rowan and the blood dripping cinematically from his eyebrow is torn away as I'm swept across the room by the tide. I drop my meet-and-greet ticket, which I'd wanted them to sign. When I struggle to breathe, too many people crushed against my chest, I start panicking. I stop wanting to be here. I want to get out. Now.

I let the tide of bodies push me towards a wall. I try to spot Juliet—she's small, she could easily be pushed under and get trampled—but I can't see her, there are too many people. I get pushed again. Someone's bag scratches my arm. Someone stands on my foot. The screaming is so loud.

The screaming isn't the same as normal, though.

Screams of fear are very, very different.

I know there are bad people in fandom but I've never actually seen them—the people who stalk them to their hotels, the people who keep trying to track down their address, the people who don't care about the boys' comfort, personal space, happiness. The people without empathy.

Most fans aren't like that. Most fans would take a bullet for The Ark. Most fans would defend them until their last breath, form an army to keep them from harm or discomfort.

But when one person does something like this, it's no wonder everybody hates us.

I'm gradually being pushed farther down the wall, and as soon as I feel a handle sticking into my back, I take my chance and disappear behind the door into what appears to be a disabled bathroom.

I fumble for the light and go and look at myself in the mirror. My scarf has been pulled slightly askew, so I quickly fix it, and wipe up the smudges of eyeliner under my eyes. Aside from that, you'd never have guessed I'd just been caught in a mob.

I sit down on the closed toilet lid and try to calm down.

If I just wait here for a while, the security guards will sort everything out, and then I can leave and go to the concert as planned.

Or maybe it'll be canceled.

If Rowan is injured.

I didn't get to meet The Ark.

I didn't get to tell them anything.

I didn't get to thank them.

All I have is the image of Rowan's bloodstained face.

# JIMMY KAGA-RICCI

They are all around me. They are touching me. Reaching for my arms, my hands, my face. I can't move. I can't breathe. I close my eyes. I put my arms over my face. I don't want to see them.

I am dragged into the flood.

I try to stop listening but I can hear them all. Someone screaming that they touched me, laughing, they got to touch me. Another screaming away from me, telling people to move, give him space, stop pushing. Someone is saying, "Don't worry, Jimmy, we'll help you, we'll get you out." Someone else is saying, "Oh my God, he's so beautiful in real life. Jimmy, we'll help you. Stop pushing. Give him space. He is so beautiful."

I try not to make any sound but I can't breathe and I'm scared. I'm going to die. I get pulled one way by the flow, yanked another by someone's fist on my hoodie. I feel it rip. I can't stop the tears emerging from my eyes, I can't make my heart stop pounding, I can't do anything, I can't do anything—

"ROWAN!"

One single bellowing cry of Rowan's name sounds above everything else, despite the noise. It's so loud, so full of panic and pain and so different to the other shrieks, that I lower my arms from my face and open my eyes to look.

Cecily Wills has risen above the crowd like Poseidon emerging from the ocean.

She must have climbed on someone, or found a chair to stand on or something, because she's at least two meters above the ground. She reaches out with one arm over the crowd, which I then realize is in the direction of Rowan, who has somehow almost made it to the door. Rowan reaches out his hand towards her over the heads of the crowd, his hand and arm smeared with blood, but can't quite reach far enough, and the tableau of them both reaching their arms out towards each other reminds me of that Michelangelo painting, *The Creation of Adam*, where God is reaching out to man.

The bodyguards fight through the crowd, pick him up round the waist, and carry him towards the door.

In the time that this is happening, two girls seem to have been trying to fend off the rest of the crowd from coming near me. They're both a lot smaller than me, and look younger too, and I'm not really hearing anything they're saying anymore, but they keep pushing away the people who are either forced closer to me or are trying to reach me. I've finally hit a wall and I keep my back to it, feeling the cool wallpaper on my fingers, and then start edging along it, not really sure where I'm going, just that I need to get away.

When my hand finds a door handle, I open it and fall back inside without a further thought, slamming the door and locking it, and then I spin round, intending to find a corner to hide in or a sink to crawl under, but instead I am faced with a girl.

# ANGEL RAHIMI

I nearly shit myself when the door bursts open, and then nearly shit myself again when I realize who has entered the bathroom.

I am faced with none other than Jimmy Kaga-Ricci.

Jimmy Kaga-Ricci.

The heart and soul of The Ark, the band that has ruled my life for the past five years.

He is only a couple of meters away from me.

Looking right at me.

This cannot be real.

I must have hit my head.

Or I'm dead.

My head wouldn't make up something like this, would it?

I know I have a lot of daydreams and fantasies, but I would never imagine Jimmy like this. His hoodie has been ripped and there are tears glistening on his cheeks. He's got a bandage wrapped round his hand—did he just do that now, or did he have that when he got here?

He looks scared too. He doesn't look like himself without the airy smile that I always see in the photos and videos. He's frowning, eyes wide and alert, like a frightened rabbit. He doesn't seem to be able to catch his breath—he's breathing abnormally fast—and he's shaking. Visibly.

Of course he looks impossibly beautiful too.

I desperately want to hold him.

But he doesn't know who I am. Of course. He has no idea who I am.

I'm just another featureless face in the sea of people screaming his name.

I take a small step forward and start to say, "Are you okay?" but I only get to "Are you—" before he stumbles back against the wall and stammers, *"D-d-don't come near me."*

# JIMMY KAGA-RICCI

*"Don't come near me,"* I say, unable to stop myself. Fuck. I need to be polite. I try to reach inside myself and pull out the Jimmy who smiles, says hello, how are you, would you like to take a picture, but I can't. He's gone; he's dead now. I can't breathe properly. Please, God, please help me.

What if she hurts me? What if she takes a picture of me? What if she tries to kill me? She doesn't look scary, but they never do—she's tall, though, taller than me, so she could probably kill me with a few punches. She's smiling. *Smiling.* Is it a nervous smile? A sympathetic smile? I'm panicking too hard to tell.

I sink down onto the floor, my legs giving way. She's not moving. She's not coming any closer. Good. Please. I look at the door. It'd be worse out there. I can hear them shouting. *Jimmy's in there. Don't go in there, Jimmy's in there.*

I look back at the girl. She doesn't look scary but I'm scared. God, please, don't let her hurt me.

She suddenly crouches down so that she isn't towering over me. I don't want to look anymore, so I put my hands on my head and hide my face against my knees, curling myself into as small a space as possible. I try to think about Rowan and the way he tells me to breathe when I'm having panic attacks. Breathe in. Breathe out. I can't. It's not the same when he's not here. I can't do it on my own.

Someone will come. Someone will come to help me.

"Jimmy . . . are you okay?" she says. She's got a loud, deep voice. Or maybe my brain is just making things up.

She shuffles a little more towards me. Closing in. I can't breathe. She's going to kill me.

I don't know what to do.

Instinctively my hand goes to the back of my jeans to Grandad's knife and I hold it tight and I say, *"Please don't."*

# ANGEL RAHIMI

*"Please don't,"* he says, holding something out. It takes a few moments for me to realize what it actually is.

It's a knife.

Not a butter knife or even a kitchen knife. It's a knife designed for cutting people. A dagger, to be honest. It's even got an ornate handle.

I stand up faster than I thought I could and stagger backwards so that I'm as far away from Jimmy Kaga-Ricci and his dagger as I can possibly be. As soon as I do this, I realize my mistake. I can't get to the door now. He's right in front of it.

Wait. What? Jimmy Kaga-Ricci isn't going to *stab* me. Is he?

He's Jimmy. He's *sunshine*. He's the dreamlike center of The Ark, a little aloof but always shining, always lovely. He's been through hard times of course, but he's surrounded by the love of his two best friends, and his fans, and he's performing his music, his passion, to the world.

That's Jimmy Kaga-Ricci. Isn't it?

Not this. Whoever this is. Shaking and crying on the floor in front of me, waving a dagger around like he thinks I'm going to attack him or something.

This can't be him. It can't. He can't. This is wrong. This isn't what I know. This is all wrong. I don't understand.

This isn't how we were supposed to meet.

"What are you doing?" I say. God, my voice is shaking. I'm scared. Why am I scared of Jimmy? My Jimmy? I love Jimmy. I've loved Jimmy for years.

His breathing sounds like he's just surfaced from water. The hand holding the dagger is unsteady. He's hidden himself behind his knees.

"Just . . . *stay away*," he croaks at me, his voice scarily quiet.

He's afraid of me.

*Me*. Me. The human embodiment of a caterpillar.

"I could . . . I could leave?" I suggest, pointing vaguely towards the door, but the sudden movement of my arm makes him flinch.

"*No*," he snaps, raising his head. "You're gonna—You'll just bring more of them." His eyes are wide and fearful. The beauty that I'd admired there has gone.

"Well . . . I . . . Can you tell me how to help you?" I ask. Is he having some sort of . . . I don't know . . . episode? Maybe he has a health condition that I don't know about. Asthma? Epilepsy? I don't know enough about either of those things to be able to do anything to help.

"I—" He chokes on his own sobs. His fear is contagious and I'm catching it fast.

I've never seen anyone this terrified.

He lowers the dagger a little. I dare myself to look at it a little closer. It looks like some sort of war antique and the actual blade is worn and . . . blunt? Could this thing even break skin?

"What do you want me to do?" I say, not because I'm scared of him, but because he clearly needs help.

But he doesn't even respond.

# JIMMY KAGA-RICCI

"What do you want me to do?" she asks quietly. God, I'm being weird and scary and I hate myself so, so much.

"S-sorry," I say, holding up my free hand, trying to shield my face. Sorry for being weird and scared and a disappointment of a human being. "I'm not gonna—I won't, I just—" I can't explain what I'm trying to say. That I know I'd never actually stab anyone. I can't.

It just makes me feel like I'm really here. Holding this piece of me in my hand.

"P-please–" I say again, but she doesn't move. Her face moves from fear to confusion, and then to pity.

"What is wrong with you?" she asks.

I need to tell her that I'm just having a panic attack, that this is something that happens, but all I say is "Please help me."

"How can I help you?!" she practically cries out. "Tell me what I need to do!"

The shouting just makes it worse and I can't say anything.

"I don't understand," she says. "God, I don't understand."

I can't let her leave. She'll bring them all here. The fans. I can't let any more of them see me like this.

Breathe in. Breathe out.

# ANGEL RAHIMI

He starts trying to breathe in and out very slowly but can't quite manage it, his breath breaking and stuttering mid-inhale.

Wait. I think I know what this is.

I think he might be having a panic attack.

I've never had a panic attack. I've never seen anyone have a panic attack. I don't even know much about panic attacks other than they are, well, an attack of panic.

He's still holding the dagger but he's dropped his arm down to the ground, as if it's too heavy to hold up. He's not actually going to stab me.

I crouch down near to the floor again.

"My name's Angel Rahimi," I say very slowly, introducing myself as Angel before I realize what I'm doing. Maybe that's who I am now.

He looks at me then, eyes narrow. "What?"

"My name is Angel Rahimi," I say. "I'm a fan of The Ark. I came to your meet-and-greet today. I want to help you."

"Angel?" he says. "Your name is Angel?"

"Well . . ." I begin, but why make this any weirder and more confusing than it already is? "Yeah, yeah, it is."

He doesn't do anything but stare.

"I'm not going to hurt you," I say.

"What?"

"*I'm not going to hurt you.* I'm very harmless. I can't even kill spiders."

More staring.

Then he says, "Okay."

"Are you . . . are you having a panic attack?" I ask. Maybe he's tripping on drugs or something. It's not like I'd know.

He nods very slowly.

"S-sorry . . ." he stammers through short breaths.

What's he apologizing for? The panic attack?

God, I want to hug him. I want to hold him and let him cry gently into my shoulder.

At least we seem to be communicating now.

"Maybe try taking a few deep breaths?" I suggest. I demonstrate by taking a comically deep breath. "Breathe in." I exhale with a loud whoosh. "Breathe out."

To my amazement (as I hadn't expected him to do it), he tries to mirror my breathing, his eyes so round and wide and watery and cutting through the air to look at me. He can't quite manage it, instead taking about three breaths in the same time that I take one. Though I'm still shaking quite a bit, I manage to smile at him and say, "Yeah, that's it! That's it!" Like a parent cheering for their kid on sports day.

While doing this, his hand loosens from the dagger. Once he gets down to two breaths for every one of mine, he manages to say something else.

"Why are you helping me?" He sounds more like himself in this question than he has done throughout this whole terrifying meeting. His voice is so familiar to me. I hear it every day, I think about it all the time, sometimes I *dream* it. Sometimes I dream him, bright and shining, reaching out to me with one hand. Wouldn't surprise me if this was a dream.

"I love you," I tell him.

His expression drops. He looks down at the floor.

"You don't love me. You don't know me," he says. "Do you even know what love is?"

Not the response I expected. Then again, I hadn't intended to tell him "I love you" like I was reciting a romantic confession, or something pathetic like that. Because it's not a romantic confession. It's so much deeper than that.

*Love* sometimes doesn't feel like the right word. The feelings I have for The Ark are what keep me going every day. They get me out of bed, even when everything is shit and I'm feeling worthless. And it always is and I always am. If you think about it, it's really no wonder someone like Jimmy can't understand. When you have a life like that, why would you need to cling on to something like a band? A celebrity? When you have a life where you have everything, where every day brings joy and passion, traveling around the world with your best friends, why would you need to spend your time thinking about anything apart from yourself?

He'll never know what that's like.

Needing, desperately, to think about anything apart from yourself.

"Do *you*?" I ask him.

But he has no time to answer. The door's lock is smashed in, the door swings open, and a huge bodyguard just picks Jimmy off the floor like he's a misbehaving toddler and carries him out of the room. I scramble off the floor and watch him leave, several other bodyguards shoving fans out of the way to get Jimmy across the room.

And then I just start to cry.

# JIMMY KAGA-RICCI

I don't exactly black out, but I just stop registering what's happening around me. It's not really happening to me. It's all just happening to this body that people call Jimmy Kaga-Ricci. The body that people call Jimmy Kaga-Ricci isn't really me, anyway. Never has been. People look at Jimmy and they don't see *me*. They see Jimmy Kaga-Ricci. Smiley, dreamy musician Jimmy Kaga-Ricci. Not the actual Jimmy.

Before I know it, I'm back in our dressing room and everybody is shouting. Cecily is shouting at O2 staff, O2 staff are shouting back, the rest of the tour management team are shouting at our bodyguards, and Rowan is shouting at me, angry, asking me why I disappeared, where did I go, it's dangerous, and Lister is shouting at Rowan, telling him to calm down, stop shouting, it's not Jimmy's fault, he's clearly shaken up, leave him alone.

Leave me alone.

Rowan has gauze on the side of his forehead. You can kind of see the blood starting to seep through, just like the cut on my hand from yesterday.

"Is it okay?" I say, not answering any of his questions. I point at his head.

"Fucking hell, yes, I'm fine, but—" He starts to repeat his questions, but I just walk over to the sofa and sit down next to Lister, who is downing a bottle of water.

He looks at me as I sit next to him.

"You okay?" he asks.

I just laugh at him.

"What happened?" he asks.

"Someone called Angel helped me."

"An angel helped you?" Lister raises his eyebrows. "Wow. Maybe I should become religious after all."

⇄ ◄◄ ⏵ ►► ♥

"We're *doing* the show," says Rowan. Everyone—me and Lister, Cecily and the tour management, the O2 staff and our bodyguards—is silent.

Then Cecily says, "Rowan, babe, I really think you should get to the hospital—"

"It's literally just a cut. It doesn't even hurt anymore."

I can tell he's lying. His voice goes all high-pitched when he's lying.

"It's not safe," says Cecily, sounding desperate. "This is a serious breach of security. Who knows what else they could let through the bag checks!"

This is actually a good point and makes me immediately paranoid.

But it only seems to increase Rowan's rage.

"Look," he says, his eyes wild. "The fans? They have taken *everything* from me. They have taken my privacy. They have taken my girlfriend. They've taken the fucking world from me. Do you understand that? I can't even fucking *go outside* anymore."

Cecily and the tour management just stare at him.

"The last thing I have is this band," Rowan continues. "The music. They're not having that as well."

Cecily lets out a heavy sigh, and then turns to the rest of the crew.

"We're doing the show," she says.

⇄ ◄◄ ⏵ ►► ♥

"Who was this girl who helped you?" asks Lister. We're still sitting on the sofa, though someone is doing Lister's makeup while we're talking.

"Angel," I say.

"Yeah. The *angel*."

"She wasn't a real angel."

"Yeah, okay, I got that."

We both laugh. It feels weird. I must not have laughed for a while.

"She was just some fan who came to the meetup. She just wanted to help me calm down, but I was . . . I was acting weird."

I don't really feel like going into detail. Like how I got Grandad's knife out (which Lister still doesn't know I carry around) and she helped me calm down while I was having a panic attack.

I shouldn't carry the knife around. I should just leave it at home. It's stupid. I'm *stupid*.

Lister frowns. "She didn't just . . . ask for a selfie or whatever?"

"No, she didn't ask for anything. She seemed like she genuinely wanted to help."

"Wow."

"Yeah."

It's rare. The fans always want something from us.

"Lots of them were trying to help, actually," I admit.

"What d'you mean?"

"Like, I mean, there were some who just wanted to touch me, but, like, lots of them were trying to kind of . . . protect me."

Lister snorts. "Protect you? Why?"

"I don't know. But they were trying to push away the people who were trying to get near me. Saying stuff like 'Jimmy, don't worry, we'll help you.'"

"Wow."

"Yeah. Has . . . has anything like that happened to you before?"

"No. They usually just want a selfie and to touch my hand or something."

"Yeah. Same."

We both stay silent for a moment. Rowan is having a heated conversation with Cecily in the corner of the dressing room; they're both making big hand gestures. I'm not sure what they're arguing about.

"I don't think Rowan would believe you if you told him," says Lister.

"I don't think so either," I say.

The makeup person finishes and leaves, and then me and Lister are alone again.

"By the way," Lister begins, but it takes him a moment to say anything else. I turn to him. He looks down, and then up at me. "Sorry about earlier. I . . . don't want you to think . . . erm . . . I expect anything from you . . ."

I'm taken aback. I'd mostly thought that we were both going to pretend that it never happened.

"It's fine."

"No, hang on, just listen," he says, turning his whole body towards me. "I don't want to make our relationship weird."

"It's not weird."

"Jimmy—"

"No one can do anything to surprise me anymore," I say, and start to laugh at him. It's funny because it's true. "No one can do *anything* to surprise me anymore."

He frowns. "What—what d'you mean?"

"I'm not in here anymore," I say, pointing at my chest. "This is all happening to someone else."

"Are you . . . okay?"

I laugh at him again.

Alex is redoing my hair. He's not trying to talk to me, which I appreciate. I'm now wearing a different black hoodie—a plain one, without any pictures or text on it.

I keep thinking about the girl who helped me.

Angel.

Don't remember her last name.

But her name was Angel.

Makes me feel like she *was* some sort of sign from God.

That's silly, though.

I mean, it's too obvious.

Is she going to tell anyone about what happened? Probably, if she's a fan. It's probably going round Twitter already.

Who cares?

What more can they do to me?

At least when this is all over I will be able to buy a house in the Lake District, far away from anybody else, and stay there, and nobody will know where I am, nobody will talk to me, nobody will touch me. I can sit on my doorstep and play the guitar and there will be nothing but the sound of the music and the birds. Maybe I'll meet a farmer my age, or maybe someone working on nature preservation, and he'll have no idea who I am because he doesn't own a television and there's no internet in the forest, and I'll serenade him with some songs I wrote especially for him and then we'll fall in love and live in a tiny stone cottage with the deer and the rabbits and the birds until we're old men.

"You'd better go and get your microphone set up, Jimmy," says Alex. He pats me on the shoulder and gives it a little squeeze. I realize I've just been sitting in the chair for a good few minutes, lost in thought.

I stand up and say, "Yeah."

"You gonna be all right, tonight? You had another panic attack, didn't you?"

"Doesn't matter," I say.

"You've been having a lot of those lately."

"I know."

"What's going on with you boys? You seem a bit"—Alex makes a gesture with his hands—"disjointed."

I just shrug and say, "Yeah."

# ANGEL RAHIMI

The show is still on. Or at least, I assume so. There've been no announce-
ments saying it's canceled. Nothing has been said about the incident at the
meet-and-greet. But everyone knows, of course. It's being passed from fan to
fan and it's trending on Twitter. Photos and videos of the crush are plastered
all over the internet. A photo of Rowan, bloodstained and terrified, is posted
again and again and again. I see someone being carried out of the O2 on a
stretcher. There are whispers of broken ribs. Everyone's saying they saw
Jimmy cry.

But the show is still on.

I feel sick and empty.

I don't feel excited anymore.

I walk around the O2 for several minutes before realizing that I could
just call Juliet. Once I've made it to the arena entrance, I sit down on the
floor and fish my phone out of my pocket, and call her.

She doesn't answer on the first ring, but she does on the second.

"Hello?"

"Hey, it's Angel," I say. "Are you okay? Where are you?"

There's a pause.

"I'm fine. I'm good."

I can hear the murmur of voices. People around her? Or is she talking
to someone?

"Where are you?" I ask again. She must not have heard me.

There's another pause.

"I think I'm gonna go home," she says.

Home? What?

"What?" I say. "Why?"

"I . . . That was all a bit . . . insane . . . I'm just not feeling it. I just want to go home—"

"But it's still on! They haven't canceled it!"

"No, I know, but—"

"Why do you want to go home?"

"I just do."

We both stop talking. She wants to *go home*? And miss The Ark?

We've been waiting for this for a year.

This was the entire point of me coming to stay with her.

"Look, Mac's going too," she says.

"Well, we both know *Mac* doesn't want to see The Ark, don't we?" I snap without thinking. And who cares what he wants? He's the one who lied just to get to meet Juliet in real life. That's not something a friend does. Or a boyfriend. Or whatever their relationship is. I don't give a shit.

"Yeah, I know. I get it. I'm sorry, all right?"

I suddenly feel kind of bad. "Don't be *sorry*—"

"Well, you clearly think this is my fault. You've had a problem with him for the whole week." There's a pause. "And me as well."

"What?"

"From the moment you met me in real life and I didn't live up to your expectations. Well, I'm sorry I don't want to talk about The Ark *all* the time. I'm sorry I actually wanted us to get to know each other as *people*, not just Ark fans."

"I at least thought you'd be excited to see The Ark, but I guess you're *not*."

"There are more important things going on than a *boy band*."

"Like *what*?" I shout, and several people close to me turn round to look.

"Er, I don't know, like friendships and relationships and actually making real human connections?!"

"If you want that so badly, then why don't you just go hook up with Mac, then?" I say, but want to take it back immediately.

She says nothing for a moment.

"Is that what you think I want to do?" she asks.

I splutter as I talk. "I—I don't know! You leave me to go off to other bars with him, spend a whole night with him when we were supposed to be hanging out at the meetup *together*, you invite him in the first place without telling me! *And*—" I feel my eyes welling up. Fuck. I don't want to cry. Not now. Not today. "And he's your special internet friend that you've been talking to your nan about all this time."

*"You were the special internet friend."*

I don't say anything.

"But I could have been anyone because you don't care about my life or anything about me," she continues. "You don't care about anything or anyone apart from The Ark."

I stand up.

"How are you going to go through your life loving nothing as much as you love a boy band?" she says.

And she hangs up.

⇄ ◄◄ ▷ ►► ♥

I lost my meet-and-greet ticket but my concert ticket is thankfully still in my bag. I go inside without stopping at the merch table. Even if I could afford it, I don't think I'd want to get anything. Just not in the mood to queue up and talk to people.

I'm in the standing area, but since I haven't been queuing for eight hours, I'm not very close to the front. I weave through as much as I can (one advantage of being alone). The gaps between bodies get smaller and smaller the closer I get. At the front, despite it being still an hour and a half before the supporting act comes on, younger fans are stumbling from side to side, being moved by the pull and flow of the crowd. I think I should be able to see them okay, which is what matters.

This is the point where I thought I'd be jumping up and down, shaking Juliet by the shoulder, both of us grinning with excitement. But there's no one next to me and I don't feel anything.

My phone is on 12 percent battery, so I shouldn't use it to check Twitter anymore. I don't have a charger with me. I turn my phone off and zip it into my bag.

It's dark in here. There are a few spotlights zooming around, and occasionally they flash over me, but then they're gone, and I'm plunged into darkness again. I try not to look at anyone around me. The last thing I want is anyone talking to me. They're all chatting and laughing. They've been waiting for this day for a long time. Just like I have.

I stand for the next hour and a half until the support act arrives, trying to absorb the excitement of the people around me, but the more I hear it, the faker it sounds.

I try not to think about anything but I end up thinking about everything. Juliet, angry on the phone. I'm going to have to leave tomorrow and go home. Jimmy, broken and crying on the floor, Rowan covered in blood. The fans tearing at them, reaching out for them, rising from the flood.

I'm sure that when The Ark arrive, I'll feel happy.

I know that when The Ark arrive, I will feel happy.

# JIMMY KAGA-RICCI

I'm sure that when we start playing, I'll feel happy. I always do. Even if I'm nervous, no matter what—I always, always enjoy playing our music.

I'm watching the supporting act from backstage. He's a YouTube musician. Trans guy too. My suggestion. I started chatting to him on Twitter a while back after he tweeted me, asking for advice about trans guy voice changes. I get a lot of messages from trans guys about that sort of thing. It's one of the few things I like about being on the internet.

I start checking Twitter while we're waiting and Rowan is going through the set list with Lister for the fourth time. My notifications are spammed with what happened earlier. Most people are telling me they hope I'm okay.

I hate that they all saw me like that.

But it feels freeing too.

I don't want to have to smile all the time.

I wonder whether Angel is going to post about what happened.

"You all set, Jimmy?" asks Cecily, standing near me with her arms folded. She glances pointedly at my phone.

"Yeah," I say, and put my phone in my back pocket.

And that's when I realize.

My knife is not there.

It's gone.

Cecily sees the immediate change on my face. "What? What've you forgotten?"

"N-nothing," I force out.

No.

No.

It must have fallen out in the dressing room.

When I was sitting down, or—

But it didn't, did it?

I never picked it up when I was escorted out of that bathroom.

I need to go and get it.

It'll still be there, right?

I have to go, now.

They can't start without me.

I start running.

There's a moment, and then everyone is shouting after me. Someone starts running too, I don't know who, but I'm already out of the backstage area and down the corridor and past the dressing rooms and at the conference rooms and through the door, thank God it's open, and it's empty, crushed bottles and tickets and a couple of posters littering the floor, and I'm pulling the door to the disabled bathroom open and dropping to the floor, but there's nothing, it's empty, there's nothing there.

It's gone.

"*Jimmy*," Rowan heaves out, coming to a halt in the doorway. "What the *fuck* are you doing? We're on in like thirty seconds!"

I turn to him and say, "It's gone."

"What's gone?" He looks around the bathroom. "Wait, is this . . . is this where you were?"

Don't cry. God, please, don't let me cry. I don't want to cry again.

"It's . . . She must have it," I say. Yes, Angel must have taken it; she was the only one in here. She must have taken it as a memento. The day she met Jimmy Kaga-Ricci and he had a meltdown.

Rowan holds out a hand. "Jimmy, we haven't got time for this."

I take his hand and stand up.

"Sorry," I say.

"What have you lost?" he asks.

Everything, I want to say.

# ANGEL RAHIMI

They rise out of the stage like they're here to guide us into Paradise.

They are immediately everything. The center point of the world. They dispel air and light and the fans flock to it, reaching out, pleading.

The Ark are here.

Jimmy and Rowan jump down from their platform, leaving Lister alone on there, where he clambers onto his drum stool and holds both of his drumsticks in the air, pointing upwards. I look up, but nothing is there. The lights turn bright white, and then orange, illuminating the dry ice and shrouding the trio in a glowing mist. One long, low electronic bass note vibrates around the arena.

Jowan walk up and down the front of the stage. Jimmy skips and smiles, but now that I've seen the other Jimmy, it doesn't seem real anymore. Rowan wanders, nodding, staring down the crowd. He knows they are the kings of the world.

The bass note continues.

Jimmy's black wing feathers are sewn across his hoodie. Rowan's got a small but visible plaster on his forehead, but he still looks exceptional. He's wearing a dress. I love him, I love him. Lister stands on his drum stool, very still, watching, waiting. The light illuminates his hair. A halo.

They climb back up to the top platform where all their instruments are. Lister picks Jimmy up by his thighs, holding him up to the light, and

Jimmy stretches out his wings. Fans around me are crying, screeching, begging.

I'm weighed down by what I know.

How can they just carry on after what happened today?

Which is the real Ark? This one or the one I met in the bathroom?

I want to believe in this one, but I think it might be a lie.

The stage doubles up as an LED screen. An image of Joan of Arc wielding her sword flashes on and off, like a strobe.

"*London*," Lister says then in his low voice, and it echoes around. London screams back at him, but it doesn't have the same magic.

The bass continues and then comes the voice that always begins their show.

*I am not afraid, said Noah*

The flashing lights and spotlights that have been moving around the crowd all stop at once. One of them stops directly on me. I hold my hand up, blocking the light from my eyes.

*I was born for this*

The Ark have taken up their positions by their instruments, staying very still, dreamlike through the orange mist. I strain to see Jimmy's expression, but he's just a winged smudge in the light.

*Born to survive the storm*
*Born to survive the flood*

I get the urge to cry again.

Why do I feel like he's died when he's right there in front of me?

*Believe in me*
*Said Noah to the animals*


Though they're near invisible now, it's impossible to miss Rowan raise a hand and pat Jimmy on the shoulder. Jimmy doesn't move. They love each other. At least that belief of mine is real . . . right? Please, God, please, I want to believe. I want it to be real more than I want to be alive.

Somehow, I expect that most of my beliefs were fantasies.


*And two by two, they ascended*
*Onto the ark*


I turn round and look back at the arena. Phones are dotted lights in the darkness like stars. I can't see any faces.

They start playing the opening bars of "Joan of Arc." I feel nothing. I just turn back and stare up at them, waiting, praying for something good to happen, something good to make me feel okay again, just as it always has until today.

But I don't feel anything.

# JIMMY KAGA-RICCI

I thought something would be different, but the show is normal and I can smile fine and of course, of course, nothing changes. I don't forget any lyrics or chords or anything. Lister doesn't even forget the set-list order. That's just how it is, isn't it? Everything carries on as normal.

I've dropped down to the lowest platform on the stage. The closest I can get to the fans. Smudgy blobs become real faces of real people, some of them smiling, some of them crying, some of them singing along with me. For a second I forget everything again and smile with them.

Then I see her.

A glint of light on a shiny headscarf.

She is not singing. She is not singing or crying or even smiling.

I almost stop singing. Almost.

I could go for it right now. I could jump into the audience and grab her by the arms and beg her to give me my knife back, tell her I'm sorry, I'm sorry she had to see who I really am. I could call out to her right now in front of twenty thousand people.

I watch Angel. She watches me back. I feel suddenly like she understands me more than any person I have ever met.

She knows now. She knows that the smiles, the romance, the sparkly boy-band dream—it's all just fantasy. Fantasy and lies.

But I can't do anything.

A hand on my shoulder steadies me. Rowan, playing his guitar without even having to think about it, has joined me on the lower platform. He widens his eyes at me, barely visible through the light reflected from his glasses, silently asking, *Are you okay?*

I smile at him.

It makes the audience scream.

I open my mouth to start the final chorus.

# FRIDAY

"IT IS TRUE I WISHED TO ESCAPE; AND SO I WISH STILL;
IS NOT THIS LAWFUL FOR ALL PRISONERS?"
—JOAN OF ARC

# ANGEL RAHIMI

I expect Juliet to be there when I wake up, but she isn't. She slept in the other spare room last night. I don't even know whether Mac is here.

Maybe he escaped, back into his other life.

I don't feel bad for him.

I think about Bliss and wonder where she is. Has she escaped to her other life too? Gone back to Rowan? Crossed the dimensional void into celebrity land?

I feel like I've wandered into the void—the empty no-man's-land between the fans and the celebrities—and now I don't know how to get out.

I check my phone. It's nearly half seven in the morning. Missed Fajr prayer and I don't even want to get up so I can pray. That's how I know I'm in a bad mood. I barely remember getting back here after the concert. I left before they came back on for the encore. Didn't want to watch anymore. It was just making me feel numb.

Like I was watching a puppet show where you can clearly see the hands.

I don't know.

I'm just being dramatic probably.

Maybe by tomorrow I'll feel a bit more normal about all this.

Maybe by the end of the week.

⇄ ◄◄ ⊙ ►► ♥

"I'm sensing you're not in such a good mood today, Angel."

Juliet's nan wanders into the kitchen, dressed and ready for the day. How do old people always seem to be on top of things? Always up early, always doing chores and phoning people and generally living productive and positive lives. Maybe it just takes seventy years to get the hang of being alive.

I'm sitting at the table with a cup of tea in front of me, staring blankly at the fridge door. I smile weakly up at her. "Oh, no. Sorry."

Dorothy sits down opposite me. "How was the concert, then? Did you all have a good time?"

I barely know what to say.

I force out a squeaky sort of "Yes" and hope it sounds convincing.

"When I was your age," says Dorothy, "I was big into the Beatles. They were *huge* in the sixties. Girls used to queue up for hours just to meet them, send them love letters in the post, throw their panties at them onstage, screaming like banshees at their concerts. *Beatlemania*, they called it." She rests her arms on the table. "I'll never forget what dear old John Lennon said: *We're more popular than Jesus now.* They attacked him for that, I'll tell you. But he was right. It was a religion."

I listen on in silence.

"It's very easy to see why it happened. These Beatle boys—they were unthreatening. Their music was good and fun, yes, but they looked kind. They were attractive, but not in a scary, very masculine way that many young girls find intimidating. They had floppy hair and skinny frames— you know, that sort of thing. Which is very fashionable now, but wasn't really back then. They gave these girls something very safe to love. Something that would never bite them back. In the sixties, everything would bite you back if you were a girl."

I wonder whether that's why I love The Ark. Because they're safe.

But they're not, are they?

They still managed to bite me back when I got too close.

"It was absolute mayhem and nobody knew what to do about it. Especially the poor Beatles themselves. Did you know they just stopped touring in

1966? They just completely stopped because it was too much. The fame, the press, the girls. It was all too much."

Dorothy sighs.

"But they always blamed the girls. The media, I mean. They said the girls were hysterical because they were failures in other parts of their lives—they were single, childless, jobless. They kept harking on about their screaming. Oh, goodness me, those male media types, they couldn't *stand* all the girls screaming." Dorothy chuckles. "Which is funny, really. They kept trying to put these girls down by saying how pathetic they were, but in reality the girls were more powerful than anybody."

I don't feel powerful. I think I'm the saddest and most pathetic person in the world.

"One of the reasons they stopped touring," Dorothy continues, "is because the girls were screaming so loud that nobody could hear the band playing or singing. The screaming just drowned it out entirely."

"Were you part of Beatlemania?" I ask her.

She chuckles again and looks down at the table.

"Well, that was a long time ago," she says.

# JIMMY KAGA-RICCI

I probably would have been able to sleep for a long time—maybe a full eight hours—if I hadn't had to stay up until 4 a.m. for the post-tour after-party, and then wake up at 8 a.m., because we're doing a chat show recording this morning.

I'm not at our apartment. I'm in a hotel room by myself. Somewhere close by the O2. I lie there for a full minute, staring up at the unfamiliar ceiling, trying to remember what I'd just been having a nightmare about, before recalling that it had been a dream about losing Grandad's knife, and in actual fact that had also happened in real life, and I should probably just go back to sleep and never wake up ever again.

My phone buzzes on the bedside table. A text from Cecily telling me to wake up.

Today we sign our new contract.

I'm glad I'm not in my apartment, anyway. Not safe there. Anyone could come in and take a picture of me.

Here isn't much better, though.

God.

I don't want to do stuff like this anymore.

Please.

I just want to stay in bed.

⇄ ◄◄ ⊙ ►► ♥

We never eat breakfast in hotels. Sometimes someone picks us up some food from somewhere, but we can't eat in public places. Sometimes that means we just don't eat.

By nine o'clock, we're all in the car and on the road towards the TV studio, which isn't technically that far away but driving through London is always a nightmare. Lister has a glass bottle of water in his hand and keeps holding it up to his forehead. Rowan keeps drifting off, his cheek pressed against the window. Outside, it's raining.

Every time I remember about Grandad's knife, I get the strong urge to grab Lister's glass bottle and smash it on the floor. Instead, I opt for digging my fingernails into my palm, which turns out to be a very bad idea when I remember that there's a big cut in the middle of my hand.

Once Lister and Rowan are asleep, I slide up the shutter between our section of the car and the driver's section. I take out my phone and dial Grandad's number.

"Hello?"

"Hi, Grandad, it's Jimmy."

"Jim-Bob! I didn't expect you to call today. How are you doing?"

"We're in the car on the way to a TV thing . . . and then we're signing our new contract."

He chuckles. "Ah yes, the *new contract*. Are you excited?"

I wish I was.

"Yeah," I say.

"Did you have a good birthday yesterday?" asks Grandad. "Did you do anything special? We're going to have to celebrate the next time you come and visit your old grandad, you know!"

"Yeah . . ." Oh yeah. It was my birthday yesterday. "Yeah, they . . . Lister and Rowan got me a cake and . . . everyone sang 'Happy Birthday.'"

When am I going to get to visit Grandad next? Who knows when I'll have my next day off? What if he dies before then? What if I've already seen him for the last time?

"Lovely. I knew I could count on those boys to celebrate with you, even if you're all very busy," says Grandad. "I've got your present all wrapped up on the kitchen table, ready for you to unwrap next time you're down here."

If I wasn't in a car, I would run there right now.

"I can't wait," I whisper.

"Everything else okay, boyo? Not feeling as down as you were on Tuesday?"

"Grandad, I've—"

I start the sentence with the intention of telling him about his knife. But I can't. I can't admit that to him. Admit what a fucking useless, terrible, pathetic excuse for a grandson I am. I lost the one precious thing he gave me, the one thing I was going to keep for my entire life, just as he kept it for all of his. It was special. Important. And now it's gone.

"I'm feeling fine," I say, trying not to let my voice waver. "I've got to go now, though."

"Ah, very busy, I see! Not to worry, lad. Give me a call at the weekend, won't you?"

"I will do. I love you."

"I love you too. Bye, now!"

"Bye."

I hang up and wipe my cheeks on my sleeve.

# ANGEL RAHIMI

I get dressed, pack up my stuff, and leave the house without saying goodbye.

Okay, I leave Dorothy a note saying thank you, but I say nothing to Juliet.

It's not like we live near each other. It's not like she's going to talk to me online ever again. No use sticking around and making things awkward.

I'm not a big fan of facing things like this head-on.

Would much rather just put it out of my mind and think about something else.

Friends come and go. Right? I've been through this already so many times before. Friends are good for a while, but eventually, you have to move on. "Best Friends Forever" is an imaginary concept. No one can be friends forever.

Not with me, anyway.

Doesn't matter.

It's all good.

I've still got The Ark.

When I get home I can watch some of the videos people took at the concert.

Yeah.

Good.

I'm excited.

I'm happy.

I've got something to look forward to.

I put The Ark on once I get on the tube. Jimmy's voice in my ears, singing to me. But the lyrics don't sound like they used to. They sound like a cry for help.

⇄ ◂◂ ⊙ ▸▸ ♥

"Hello?"

"Hey, Dad, it's me."

"Fereshteh! Oh good, I was hoping you'd call this morning. Your mother thought you were going to message us last night and obviously you didn't so she barely slept and woke up *so* grumpy this morning—"

"I'm coming home, Dad."

There's a pause.

"Coming home? Really? I thought you were staying until Sunday!"

"Yeah . . . I'm not now."

"Fereshteh . . . Did something happen, my girl?"

I sigh. "Er . . . yeah, sort of."

"Oh no. What—"

"It's fine, Dad. It's not a big deal. I just want to come home now."

"Of course, of course. I'm working from home today, so I can pick you up from the station anytime."

"I don't know what train I'm getting yet. I'll call you from the station."

"Well, okay, then. Are you sure you don't want to talk about it?"

The way he says it makes me well up a little bit.

"Not right now," I say.

"Did you enjoy the concert at least?"

God, I didn't. I didn't. And it feels like my whole life has gone to waste.

"Yeah," I say.

"Do you . . . ?" He pauses. "Do you want to talk to your mother?"

Mum. Is she still angry? She's going to be smug when she finds out I had a horrible time this week. *I knew it wouldn't end well,* she'll say. *That'll teach you to care so much about a boy band.*

"Does she want to talk to me?" I ask.

Dad sighs. "Of course she does."

"Well, I'll talk to her when I get home, anyway."

Dad sighs again. "Okay."

The train doesn't leave for another half an hour, so I have some time to kill. I buy a cup of tea from Starbucks and sit down on a stool, facing out at the rest of the station. I've still got The Ark playing through my earphones. Their third album, *Joan of Arc.* It's not really my favorite, but maybe I just haven't listened to it enough.

I'm halfway through my cup when I spot someone familiar in the crowd. I squint through the window at the figure. Puffy hair, skinny jeans, button-up shirt. He's walking towards Starbucks when he stops and stares directly at me, eyes widening.

Oh.

It's Mac.

Oh God.

I can't deal with this confrontation right now.

I slip out of Starbucks, pretending I haven't seen him, and start walking in the opposite direction, round past the various station shops and cafés. I sneak a glance back and—oh God, he's seen me. I walk a little faster and slip into a WHSmith, heading towards the back of the shop. I pretend to be perusing the sweets section (which is, at least, very characteristic of me), when I hear:

"Angel!"

I turn. Mac is walking into the shop, waving at me. I wave cautiously back at him and he starts walking towards me, swerving round the shoppers and the aisles.

"Hi," I say.

"Hi," he says. He looks vaguely out of breath, like he's been walking very fast.

There's an awkward silence.

"Why are you here?" I ask.

"Well . . . I thought I'd see if I could catch you before you left, actually," he says.

"Did Juliet send you?"

"No."

Oh. That's weird.

He senses my confusion and smiles sheepishly. "Well, when we woke up and we found out you'd left from your note, Juliet was really upset, so I wanted to—"

"You wanted to come and find me and bring me back in some sort of valiant attempt to get back in Juliet's good books," I say.

He chuckles. "Is it so bad to want to do something good for someone you like?"

I shrug at him.

Juliet was upset? Even after our big argument?

I thought that was it for our friendship.

Fuck. Have I fucked up?

"This is like that movie trope where someone has to run to the airport and stop their romantic interest from leaving," I say.

Mac smirks. "Except you're not my romantic interest."

"Yeah, no shit."

He snorts and looks down. A couple of people push past us.

"Let's . . . let's go find a bench or something," I say.

⇄　◄◄ ⊙ ►►　♥

We leave the shop, walk in silence towards a bunch of nearby seats, and sit down next to each other. I stare up at the departure board, becoming distinctly aware of the crowds of travelers swarming around us, walking from cafés to escalators to platforms. Everything's swirling and moving. Nothing stays still for more than a second.

"Why'd you do it?" I ask him.

"Do what?"

"Lie."

He looks away.

"I wish I hadn't done that," he says.

"Well, you did."

"I know."

"Did you just really fancy her, or . . . ?"

*"Fancy,"* he scoffs. "I'm not twelve."

I raise my eyebrows. "Okay, then."

"Sorry, just hadn't heard anyone use that word since, like, Year Seven."

"Okay. How about *deeply in love*? Is that better?"

He huffs out a laugh. "Are those the only two options? 'Fancy' or 'deeply in love'?"

Oh God, he is really starting to piss me off.

"Why don't you explain your feelings, then?" I say, leaning back into my seat and folding my arms. "Settle in, my guy. Let's make each other really uncomfortable."

He pauses. "Well, okay. So, I like her."

"Now, is that a *like*, or a *like like*?"

"Oh my *God*, you sound like my mum. I had a crush on her, okay?"

"Okay, okay. Just clarifying."

"We were talking on Tumblr messenger quite a lot. And obviously I could see from her Tumblr that she was mainly interested in The Ark. So I just . . . sort of . . . *suggested* that I liked them too, which, you know, wasn't a *full* lie, I liked a couple of their songs I'd heard on the radio! But . . . the lie just, like, went on from there. Got bigger and bigger until I was paying literally a hundred quid to go to their concert and come down to London just so I could see her."

"And how did that work out for you?" I ask.

"Well, I really could have bloody used that hundred quid for something else." He laughs.

Someone who deserved to go to their concert could have got that ticket.

"I think we were getting along really well in real life," he continues, "er . . . until we went out after the meetup on Tuesday."

"Did something happen?"

"No. Nothing specific." He rubs his forehead, then looks at me. "It just became very apparent that she'd rather be hanging out with *you*."

I blink. "D-did it?"

"I mean, firstly, she talks about you literally *all* the time." He folds his arms. "We'd start talking about something, and she'd always find a way to bring you into it. You were like . . . this constant presence in all of our conversations."

I say nothing.

"Secondly," he continues, "she started to sense that I didn't like The Ark as much as she did. And it's not like she wanted to talk about The Ark all the time, like *you*, but when we did talk about them . . . she could tell that I wasn't that interested."

"Good," I say. Good. I'm glad Juliet could tell. She's not stupid.

He looks at me. "Honestly, I thought it was just . . . a band she liked."

Just a band she liked.

Imagine if The Ark was just a band we liked.

"Sometimes you need to lie." He runs a hand through his hair. "Do you ever feel like nobody knows the *real you*?"

When I don't respond, he laughs again and looks away.

"That's what I feel like," he says. "Back at home, in the real world. I . . . I'm not myself. I just say and do things to make people like me. Not even my closest friends know anything important about me." He shakes his head. "And I don't know why I can't just be myself around anyone . . . whoever *that* is."

I stare at him.

"And then I started talking to Juliet online." His eyes glaze over. "And she liked talking to me. She was excited about talking to me. And I could be *myself*. I could talk to her about all sorts of things and we had stuff in *common*. And I just thought . . . if I could just reach out to her and get to know her in the real world . . . maybe I could have someone in my life who knows and likes the *real me*."

He breathes out harshly looks away again.

"But I made a mistake," he says. "I get it. The lie. Just one little lie slipped in, just one thing I had to lie about to get her to really like me. Just like I've always done to everyone I meet. Lie to make people like me. But I get it. You can't make friends or . . . or relationships based on lies. And in the end the whole thing was a lie anyway. Our relationship. The idea that I had in my head. It was all something I'd just . . . fabricated. To make me feel a bit better about myself. So I had something to just . . . believe in."

I open my mouth to say something snarky, but close it again.

"Anyway, it doesn't matter," he says. "I'm not gonna start, like, begging for forgiveness or whatever."

I lean forward and put my head in my hands.

Fuck.

Why is nothing ever simple?

After a few moments, he says, "Er, you okay?"

I sit up again. "I get it."

"What?"

"I get why you lied." I smile weakly. "I do stuff like that too. Back at home, with my school friends. I just say things to be liked and . . . stay silent about stuff I care about. Because I feel like no one cares about the 'real me.' But with Juliet I felt a bit more like myself."

"Oh."

"We're both a bit shit, aren't we?"

Mac chuckles. "Juliet's probably the purest out of all of us, anyway."

"Yeah."

"Well, I came here to tell you to go back to her," he says.

"I can't. I've already fucked up our friendship."

"*No.*" He slaps his hand down loudly on his knee. "No. Juliet needs a friend like you."

"What, one who won't shut up about a boy band?"

"*No*, one she can actually get along with and have fun with." He shakes his head. "Like, considering her home life now, she really, really needs you. Like, now more than ever."

Wait. What's he talking about?

Home life? Now more than ever?

"What?" I ask. "What d'you mean?"

"You know," he says. "Her parents?"

I properly sit up now, a faint throb of panic sitting in my chest. "What are you talking about?"

He frowns. "Are you . . . joking?"

"*No, I'm not fucking joking, Cormac!*" I say, nearly shouting by this point. "Please explain what the absolute fuck you are talking about!"

And then he says something earth-shattering.

"Juliet's parents kicked her out," he says. "She's had a horrible relationship with them for years, but her refusing to do law at uni was, like, the final straw. You know her parents are big-time lawyers, right? And so are her older siblings? So her parents just kicked her out, said she could make her own way. That's why she's living with her nan right now." Mac shakes his head. "It's really fucked her up. You really didn't know about that?"

No.

No, I didn't.

"She's, like, all alone in the world."

I get flashes of conversations. Me complaining about my mum to her on the train. Juliet's expression as I got off the phone with my dad. Her trying to tell me something, again and again and again, but me changing the subject, bringing up The Ark; always, always talking about The Ark instead of anything actually important.

"Why . . . didn't I know that?" I say, my voice hoarse.

"Maybe you never asked," says Mac, but I'm already standing up, yanking my rucksack open and digging around in there, searching for my phone, because I need to call her. I need to call and tell her I'm sorry and we don't have to talk about The Ark anymore, we can talk about this, she can tell me, God, I'm so sorry—

But my hand closes round something else instead.

Jimmy's knife.

# JIMMY KAGA-RICCI

"Can you just step back a little bit for me, Jimmy? That's it. Yep, just back a little bit. There we go. Need to make sure you stay in shot in the aerial camera."

TV studios are always much, much smaller than they look on TV. Much too hot under the lights.

We run through our numbers a couple of times while the sound team adjust microphones and instruments and soundboards and other things I don't know the name of. We're performing "Joan of Arc," obviously, and also a cover of "All the Things She Said" by t.A.T.u., which is one of our favorite songs, but in the first sound check I forget the second-verse lyrics, and in the second sound check I get the "Joan of Arc" chord sequence all muddled up. When we're done, Rowan mouths "You okay?" at me. I never normally get music stuff wrong.

We're not recording until eleven, so there's time for a short break after the sound checks, when we're introduced to the host. When we get to our dressing room, Lister immediately starts rummaging through the drinks they provided, but when he discovers there's no alcohol, he just sits down in a chair and doesn't move.

Rowan and I don't say anything, but from the look on Rowan's face, I think he might know what I know. About Lister probably being an alcoholic.

We'll have to deal with that at some point.

When we have time.

We get called back into the studio half an hour later. Apparently there was some fault with the microphones during the sound check and they need us to do it again.

We play "All the Things She Said" once through, then stand and wait while the sound techs are fiddling about with buttons and wires. I glance to one side at Rowan. He's spaced out, staring into the air. Holding his guitar like a soldier with a gun against his chest.

He looks worse than he has all week.

Sometimes I look at Rowan and can't remember what he used to look like. We were in primary school when we met. We were placed next to each other in class and told to learn five facts about the person sitting next to you. All I remember about Rowan's was that his favorite band was Duran Duran. All he remembers about mine was that I'd never broken a bone.

He had rimless glasses and short tight curls. His jumper was way too big for him. As soon as we both learned that we each wanted to be in a band, we were best friends.

The boy next to me now isn't anything like that boy. Not bright-eyed and excited to tell me about the new guitar he got for his birthday. Not dragging me to the music block to show me he could play the bass line for a Vaccines song. No laughter. No wonder.

We got what we wanted in the end, though. Didn't we?

We wanted to be in a band.

"Where is Bliss?" says Rowan, after several minutes of silence. He knows neither of us know. But he's asking anyway.

Lister starts tapping out a quiet jazz beat on the drums.

"Rowan," he says, which is weird, because he always calls Rowan "Ro." "Do you really want to be with Bliss?"

Rowan snaps his head towards Lister, immediately agitated. "What d'you mean?"

"I mean that you argue. Both of you. All the time."

Rowan freezes. Then he turns away again.

I start pressing the buttons on my Launchpad in time with Lister's beat. It isn't on, so it doesn't make any sound apart from rhythmic clicks.

"I do love her," he says.

"So?" says Lister.

"I just . . . wish there was a way for us to be together like normal people," says Rowan. "Without . . . you know. All this." He gestures around him at the studio. "And the new contract."

"You know we've got a bit of leeway with the new contract; we can negotiate—" Lister begins, but Rowan interrupts him.

"I know, but I *want* the new contract," he says. "It's gonna spread our music worldwide. But Bliss . . . our relationship . . . this is just the price of fame."

Lister chuckles and lowers his head. "So dramatic."

Rowan starts plucking a few notes in time with my button-pressing and Lister's beat.

"One day we'll be able to do what we want," says Rowan.

"When's that?" I ask.

"One day," says Rowan.

Lister starts singing under his breath.

*"And when he gets to heaven,"* he sings—words I don't know, and a tune that goes somehow perfectly with the chords Rowan is making up on the spot—*"to Saint Peter he will tell: One more soldier reporting, sir. I've served my time in hell."*

"Can we have 'Joan of Arc' one more time, then, lads?" shouts someone from the soundboard.

We stop jamming and I turn my Launchpad on.

⇄  ◄◄ ⊙ ►►  ♥

"It's contract-signing time," says Cecily, slamming several copies of the contract down on the table in the middle of our dressing room. "Who needs a pen?"

"Hold on, I thought we were doing this after the recording?" asks Rowan, confused.

"No, babe. Fort Records canceled our meeting later, so they want the contracts posted ASAP. Might as well get it out of the way now."

I pick up a copy of the contract from the table and flick through it. It looks just as garbled and dramatic as it did when I last looked through it. All the less favorable bits keep catching my eye, all the bits about us having to do longer tours and more publicity. It's all just *more*. It's so big that we can't control it any more.

It's like The Ark isn't even ours anymore. It's just a brand. Not real.

I look up and Rowan already has a pen in his hand and is swirling his name along the dotted line of his copy. His face is blank.

"Jimmy?"

I turn and find Cecily holding a biro out to me. I look at the pen.

"You okay, babe?" she asks, looking me directly in the eyes. I can't remember when I last looked her in the eyes. She might be the mum of the band, but sometimes I feel like I barely know her.

"Erm," I say.

The pen. I need to take the pen and sign my name and sign my life away.

"What's wrong?" she asks.

I look back at Rowan. He's chucked the contract away, leaned back in his chair, and closed his eyes.

"Erm . . ."

Lister is flicking through his copy, frowning and shaking his head, tapping his pen against his forehead.

More. It's all more. So big I can't hold on to it anymore. So big that it's not ours anymore. And what will we get in place of that? Lies. More lies. More fake smiles and forced interviews and fans who will lap up the lies and take photos of us and stalk us and hate us—

"I need to go to the bathroom," I say.

Cecily withdraws the pen. She suddenly looks concerned. It's an expression I don't recall seeing on her before. "Okay. Don't be long."

⇄  ◄◄ ⊙ ►►  ♥

I splash some cold water onto my face before realizing that I've already had my makeup done. Whoops.

I think I'm losing it.

Going off the wall.

Is this why celebrities eventually get addicted to drugs? Because it all gets a bit too much?

Sometimes I think about taking drugs. Sometimes I think it might help.

When I see Lister smoke and drink, I know it's bad, but I understand why he does it. It's so he doesn't have to think.

I hate thinking.

The bathroom door swings open and Lister enters the room. He does a little double take at seeing me standing there with a wet face, but then smiles and says, "We seem to keep meeting in bathrooms, don't we?"

I chuckle. "We do."

"I'm not here to assault you this time."

"You didn't *assault* me. You just misjudged. You stopped when I said no."

"Well, I didn't exactly ask for permission, did I?"

He laughs sadly. Has he been genuinely upset about what happened yesterday? I've barely thought about it at all.

He walks over to a urinal, unzips his jeans, and starts peeing.

"I'm surprised you're not angry at me about that," he says, mid-pee.

"I'm not angry," I say. "I know it was a mistake."

He pauses. "Mm."

He zips up his jeans and then goes to wash his hands. He glances at me. He's all dressed up and made up for the recording—his hair's been straightened and hairsprayed, he's wearing an expensive denim jacket, and if you look closely, you can see the face powder on his skin. But I know him too well. He's tired. There are shadows under his eyes, still visible through the makeup. His eyes are a bit bloodshot too.

He turns the tap off and looks at me.

"What's wrong?" he asks. He knows.

"The contract," I say. "It's . . . I don't like it."

He nods. "Yeah. It's got some dodgy bits."

"Do we . . . ?" I dare myself to ask. "Do we really have to . . . go ahead with it?"

Lister raises his eyebrows. "Er . . . I guess I never thought about that."

"Never mind," I say, turning round to walk towards the door. "Doesn't matter."

"No, hang on." He grabs my arm, pulling me back. "Are you okay? I mean . . ." He shakes his head a little. "You seem . . . kind of . . ." He makes a weird gesture above his head. "Out of it."

"I'm fine," I say immediately.

"Are you . . . still thinking about that Jowan photo?"

"It's fine."

"Okay, well . . . what are you doing in here?"

"In . . . the bathroom?"

"Yeah."

"I was just . . . peeing."

He nods and steps back a little. "Sorry. I'm just . . . being weird."

Then he chucks a crumpled paper towel at me. I dodge it, laughing.

"You've got a wet face," he says. He walks up to me and starts dabbing my face with another paper towel. "You haven't been crying, have you?"

"I just . . . I just splashed some cold water on my face."

"Why?"

"Because . . . I was . . . I don't know." I start laughing. "I don't know."

He finishes drying my face, throws the paper towel into the bin, and then before I know what's happening, he wraps me into a warm hug. He squeezes his arms round my shoulders and brushes his temple against my head.

"You know I love you, right?" he says, his voice sounding different, low, right next to my ear. "I know you and Rowan have always been a team, but . . . I love you too . . . okay?"

"O-okay—"

"Please don't hate me."

I run my hands over his back. "Why would I hate—"

But he steps away before I finish my question. He's smiling. I can't read it. I can't read him at all.

He might be a mess, but he is good. How can someone as good as Lister like someone as terrible as me?

"What are we talking about?" he says, and laughs, and then moves to perch on the edge of the sink. What *are* we talking about? Is he drunk again? There wasn't any alcohol in the dressing room, though.

I lean against the wall next to the dryer. There's a big window opposite us, wedged open a little bit. It's raining again, but it's sunny too. There might be a rainbow out there, but the window is frosted, so we can't see the sky.

"Do you ever imagine what would happen if we just . . . ran away?" asks Lister suddenly. I glance at him. He's looking at the window too.

"What d'you mean by *ran away*?" I ask.

Lister points at the window. "I mean, if we just climbed out of that window right now and left. Got in a taxi, went to the train station, and disappeared."

Everyone would freak the fuck out. They'd probably get the police looking for us. And people would find us anyway. People on the street, cashiers, taxi drivers, train guards. Everyone knows who we are.

Celebrities can't disappear.

"I think about it all the time," I say.

God, I want to try it.

"Do you?"

"Yeah."

God, I just want to go.

"I should try it," I say, intending to say "one day" as well, but I don't get that far.

Lister laughs. He thinks I'm joking. "I think Cecily would hunt you down and kill you."

"Do you think this window opens far enough?" I walk over to the window. It's got two frames, one on top of the other, so I undo the latches at the top, and sure enough, the whole bottom half of the window slides upwards. The rain starts to fall into the room, pattering on the tiled floor.

Lister is silent. I glance back at him.

"Well . . . that's definitely big enough," he says cautiously.

I could go and see Grandad. We could celebrate my birthday and he could make me hot chocolate and we could play Scrabble.

"I might just go," I say.

Lister laughs again but it's shorter, smaller. "Don't joke."

I stick my head out of the window. We're on the ground floor. Outside is a sidewalk, then a big car park with only a few cars dotted here and there. I can't see any people.

"Jimmy . . ."

I pull myself back inside.

Lister has moved forward from the sink. He looks worried. "You've . . . you're all wet again now!"

"It's fine," I say.

And then I stick one leg out of the window and step down on the other side. I duck my body under the window frame and move myself outside into the rain. Then I lift my other leg and bring it outside too.

And then all of me is outside.

Lister walks right up to the window.

He's grinning but he's scared. I know him. I can tell.

"Jimmy, don't—Tash won't like you getting that hoodie wet . . ."

I step backwards, away from him, away from the window.

"I think I'm gonna go," I say.

His grin drops. "Jimmy . . . are you joking?"

I step back a little more, dropping down from the sidewalk. My heart is beating so fast. It feels so fucking good.

"No," I say.

Lister grabs the window frame and sticks his head outside. "Jimmy, *don't*! I was only joking about running away! I'm serious! This isn't funny anymore—"

I could go and find Angel. I could go and get Grandad's knife back.

"What about the contract?! And the recording?!" Lister calls. He has to shout for me to hear him now. "We need to go back!"

I turn round and look at the near-empty car park. It's silent apart from the pattering of the rain.

"Where are you going?!" he shouts at me.

Oh God, I could go anywhere.

# *ANGEL RAHIMI*

Here's a weird thing I think about in situations like this:

What Would Jimmy Do?

Obviously I pray and stuff, like, to actual God, but often I find thinking about Jimmy is a bit more useful, because I can visualize his personality and imagine how exactly he might deal with this precise situation. Asking for help from Allah is all very well and usually does make me feel better, but it doesn't usually help me make any immediate decisions.

What would Jimmy do in this situation?

Would he go back and apologize to Juliet and be there for a friend who is clearly going through a rough time?

Or would he focus on the task at hand—returning Jimmy's knife?

Except . . . the Jimmy in my head isn't Jimmy, is it?

I don't know what Jimmy would do at all because I don't know anything about him.

God.

This isn't helping, is it?

I keep thinking that maybe I imagined what happened yesterday.

Wouldn't surprise me.

Maybe I've lost my mind a bit.

Maybe the monotony of my life has been getting to me.

"So . . . are you coming back?" Mac asks after I've been sitting there for a few minutes, going over both the options.

Juliet or Jimmy.

My best friend or The Ark.

"I . . . don't know," I say, my voice hoarse. I don't know. I don't know what to do.

Mac sighs. He takes this as a no.

"I'll leave you to decide, then," he says. "I'm going back to Juliet."

And he gets up and leaves.

⇄  ◄◄ ⦿ ►►  ♥

As soon as he's gone, I shine my phone flashlight into my rucksack so I can take another proper look at Jimmy's knife.

I mean, it's a good thing I took it. It would have got lost forever if I'd just left it. Someone would have found it and thrown it away, or sold it, or whatever. And it looks precious. It looks important to him. It's got "Angelo L. Ricci" engraved on the side.

Angelo. Sounds almost like Angel. Kind of funny, isn't it?

It must have belonged to his grandad or great-grandad or something. His Italian side is on his mum's side, so it can't have been his father's. It looks older than that, anyway. It looks pretty antique.

I wonder how much it's worth. Probably a lot, if it's old.

I need to give it back to him. I'll message him. I'll tell him I have it.

I glance up at the departures board. I've got twelve minutes until my train home leaves.

Juliet or Jimmy?

It's an obvious choice, right?

I need to talk to Juliet.

Jimmy will have to wait. I can message him on Twitter later. He'll probably never see it anyway.

Juliet is the priority today.

I need to talk to her.

I need to repair the mess I've made.

I stand up, swinging my rucksack onto my back and taking my suitcase in one hand. I turn to start walking away to the door.

That's when my phone buzzes in my pocket.

I fish it out and look at the Twitter direct message on the screen.

**Jimmy Kaga-Ricci @jimmykagaricci**

want my knife back. where can you meet me?

# JIMMY KAGA-RICCI

**Jimmy Kaga-Ricci @jimmykagaricci**

want my knife back. where can you meet me?

Wasn't hard to find Angel on Twitter.

I typed *The Ark Angel* into the Twitter search bar, and then scrolled through the results until I found her—various tweets about coming to the concert, and a selfie of her and a few other girls at a pub tweeted a couple days ago. She's got a photo of me as her own display picture. Why do they do that? Why don't they use their own face as their display picture?

Even her Twitter handle is "jimmysangels." That doesn't make any sense.

I send the message with shaking fingers.

I don't even have the energy to feel embarrassed. I mean, I should be. Messaging a fan and asking for my knife back. What's happening to me?

God, I could do anything right now.

I've walked all the way across the car park and am now walking down the sidewalk next to a road. Up ahead are various hotels, mostly for the people who come to the studio to work, and a big restaurant area. And there, just outside a Nando's, is a taxi bay. With several taxis waiting inside.

Oh my God, I'm doing this.

My phone starts ringing. Rowan.

I click the reject button.

I start running towards the taxi bay. There are only a few people walking around. They won't notice me. It's fine.

I pull my hood up and over my forehead.

I'm going.

Oh God.

I'm running and grinning too. Is this happiness?

$$\rightleftarrows \quad \blacktriangleleft\blacktriangleleft \enspace \circledR \enspace \blacktriangleright\blacktriangleright \quad \heartsuit$$

"Where to, lad?" asks the taxi driver as I open the door and sit inside. He's an older man, graying and large, with a thick northern accent.

"Er . . ."

Fuck. Which bit of London would Angel live in? Does she even live in London? I check my phone again. She hasn't messaged me back yet.

"Just . . . just to King's Cross." That's safe. There'll be more taxis there.

The man doesn't reply, so I look up, wondering if he hasn't heard me. He's looking at me curiously in the rearview mirror, squinting.

"You're from that boy band, aren't you?" he says. "The one that got famous on the internet."

"Er . . . yes."

"Haven't you got your own taxi to take you places?"

"Er . . . not right now, no."

The man looks at me for one more second. For a moment, I feel a sudden fear. He's big. I'm small. He's a gruff, northern, older white man, and I'm a posh, transgender, mixed-race boy wearing very tight skinny jeans. But then he just shrugs and says, "Well, all right. You seemed nice enough when you did that *X Factor* performance last year. You've got a nice voice, I'll tell you that. Well, better than the nob-heads they put on that show."

". . . Thanks."

He pulls the taxi out of the bay.

"You know, my wife is a big fan of *The X Factor*, but I reckon if Simon

Cowell and his crew want to find the real talent, the internet's the place to go, ain't it? That's where the younger generation are, ain't it?"

The taxi driver continues talking, without leaving room for me to reply. I glance down and look at my phone. The missed call count is up to fourteen. And Rowan's started texting me. Can't bear to read them.

Instead, I check my Twitter DMs. And there she is.

Angel Rahimi.

**angel @jimmysangels**

I have it!! Can you get to st. pancras?

Btw I only took it because I thought someone would steal it if I left it

It looks really precious

Anyway yes I'm at st. pancras!! Will happily return it to you if you can get here! Or I can come to you!

Whatever you want!!!

# ANGEL RAHIMI

**angel @jimmysangels**
Whatever you want!!!

I'm dying. Dead. Deceased. Rest in peace, Angel.

Jimmy messaged me. Which means he must have remembered my name and literally *searched* for me on Twitter. Thought about me, decided to message me, typed out my name, and clicked on my profile.

I mean, the circumstances are understandable.

And I know that the boy I've been fangirling about for the past five years isn't exactly the real Jimmy Kaga-Ricci.

But, still.

I'm grinning uncontrollably.

And it won't take long, will it? I just give him the knife, say goodbye, and then I can go back to Juliet, sort everything out, and make things right again.

I don't have to choose between them. I can have both.

⇄  ◀◀ ⏵ ▶▶  ♥

I head into the nearby Starbucks and buy another cup of tea. I almost get a cake as well but decide that I don't want to accidentally have cake in my teeth when Jimmy shows up.

God, I'm not even wearing good clothes today. I'm wearing travel clothes. Just a pair of slim joggers and an oversized hoodie.

Shit.

Okay. Calm down. It doesn't matter what I wear. Jimmy probably won't care. He just wants his knife back.

I sit down at a table and open my rucksack again, looking at the knife inside. I've wrapped the blade in one of my jumpers. It's an antique and I don't want to scratch or break it. Don't want to do anything that might make Jimmy upset.

I take a sip of the tea and check my phone again. There's a little tick underneath it—he's read the message.

I know I shouldn't feel happy, but I do. Despite the fact that he clearly isn't the Jimmy persona that I've loved for years and years and years. Despite everything, I feel so, so happy.

Which is kind of sad, really.

**Jimmy Kaga-Ricci @jimmykagaricci**
Okay will be there in about 30 mins

# JIMMY KAGA-RICCI

**Jimmy Kaga-Ricci @jimmykagaricci**

Okay will be there in about 30 mins

**angel @jimmysangels**

Okay!!! I'll wait inside Starbucks!! Just message me when/where you want to meet!!!

Angel is very enthusiastic about this, for some reason. I thought she'd be annoyed at having to go out of her way to give me back the knife.

I didn't think she'd still be a fan of me after seeing me have a meltdown yesterday.

They don't like seeing you sad.

By the time we're nearing St. Pancras, Gary, the taxi driver, has just about told me his entire life story. It was pretty interesting to listen to, actually. Growing up in the outskirts of Durham, the story of his first wife and how she cheated on him with the man who came to fix the boiler, and how his twin daughters are both studying astrophysics and are definitely going to get to space someday. Sometimes I forget that there are people who have good, pure, normal lives that don't involve rather complex lying every single day.

There are a lot of people walking around in London. I duck down a little bit when we start getting into the pedestrian areas and pull my hoodie farther over my face. It'd only take one person to glance into the taxi and spot me and tweet my location and that'd be it.

If I could have any superpower, it'd be invisibility.

"Are you sure you want to stop here, lad?" Gary asks. "It's a bit busy, ain't it? Won't someone recognize you?"

He's right. I'm not disguised at all. In fact, I look completely like myself, since I'm all made up for the recording—skinny jeans, hair done, under-eye shadows concealed, wearing a signature hoodie.

But I'm going.

I'm going to get my knife back.

"I'll be fine," I say.

**Jimmy Kaga-Ricci @jimmykagaricci**

Arrived. Coming to find you

**angel @jimmysangels**

Okay!! I'm in starbucks!! Or I can meet you somewhere else??

⇄　◀◀ ⊙ ▶▶　♥

"D'you want me to wait for you, lad?" Gary asks.

"No . . . no, I think I should be fine from here," I say. I can just get another taxi when I've got the knife. Don't really want Gary asking any questions, to be honest.

I pay Gary what I owe him and then get out of the car.

Just before I shut the door, he says, "Whatever's troubling you, it'll go away."

I look back at him and say, "What?"

He taps his fingers on the steering wheel. "I know it can't be easy being someone like you. D'you have friends around you? People to support you?"

I mumble something about being fine and close the door. Enough of that.

⇄　◀◀ ⊙ ▶▶　♥

I start by just walking, my hood pulled as far as it'll go over my forehead and my phone clutched in one fist. But it doesn't work.

There are people everywhere. Walking to and from the station, getting in and out of cars and taxis, crossing the road, standing around.

A swarm.

Can't remember the last time I've been around this many normal people at once.

I get a few glances at first. A couple of people catching my eye and *realizing*. Once I've walked ten meters or so, someone behind me murmurs, "Doesn't he look like Jimmy Kaga-Ricci?" Once I'm nearly at the station steps, someone in front of me points and says, "Oh my God, that's Jimmy from The Ark!"

I try not to look and I walk faster.

I'm inside the station.

Someone behind me pulls on my arm, forcing me to a halt. I turn, even though I know I shouldn't, and it's a girl asking for a selfie.

"I can't, sorry," I say, and pull my arm away, only to be faced by *five* other girls, holding their phones. Someone is videoing. They're asking for selfies. They're talking to me. I need to get out.

Another group appear—boys and girls. A woman and her daughter. A group of men in their twenties.

I start just posing for selfies. Like it's a fucking reflex.

I can't just leave. I can't just say no.

They start cramming closer to me. Someone reaches out and brushes their hand down my arm. I feel myself flinch and I hope it doesn't show.

I'm shaking too.

I'm starting to panic.

Deep breaths.

Don't let it show.

Don't let it start.

"Can I have a selfie, Jimmy?"

"Your music got me through the whole of school."

"What are you doing here?"

"I really love you."

# ANGEL RAHIMI

I look up from the very intense game of *Rolling Sky* on my phone to discover that there is a huge swarm of people converged in the middle of St. Pancras.

It can only be Jimmy.

Didn't he bring a bodyguard with him? What was he *thinking* coming here by himself? He's probably one of the most famous people in the entire country, for God's sake.

What do I do?

Should I try to help?

Should I find a station guard? Security?

Yes. Yes, they'll be able to help.

I grab my bags and rush out of Starbucks, looking around wildly. Passengers, but no security guards. No policemen either. Oh, fuck. Do I have time to walk around and find one?

I look over at the group of people again. It's *huge* now. It's a human tornado and he's at the center. I can't see Jimmy at all, so I don't know for *sure* whether he's in there, but a couple of twelve-year-olds walk out of the group staring at their phones and screaming, so I'd say it was a pretty good guess.

I take a deep breath and pull my hood up firmly over my head.

And then I walk straight into the human tornado.

I get cries of annoyance and rude comments as I barge past people, but my height and my boniness do have their advantages. My elbows are probably my greatest weapon. I accidentally gave my brother a black eye with my elbow when I was eight.

It takes a solid minute, and I do end up on the floor at one point, but I'm eventually propelled into the center of the group, where Jimmy is facing away from me, taking a selfie with someone. I tap him politely on the shoulder and say, "Er, Jimmy?"

He turns round. The panic on his face is unmistakable, though he seems to be doing slightly better at containing it than in the bathroom yesterday. His eyes are wide and he's biting down hard on the insides of his cheeks.

Is he even going to recognize me?

"Angel," he says.

I guess he is.

And then he says, "Help me."

Help him.

I put my arm round his shoulders and shout, "OKAY, JIMMY HAS TO GO AND CATCH A TRAIN NOW!" I start pulling him out of the crowd, but people are following, snapping photos in his face, shouting at me and him. Someone shouts, "Who the fuck are *you*?" and I say, "I'm . . . his *bodyguard*," which is probably the most unbelievable statement anyone has ever made, since I have the body shape of a twig and look three years younger than I actually am. Probably should have gone with "manager," but too late now.

As we're forcing our way out of the crowd, Jimmy clutches on to my hoodie with one hand, like a scared toddler. Is this weird? Probably. I love him more than my own fucking life.

And then we're free.

And that's twice this week that I've saved people from being harassed because they're famous.

What even is my life?

# JIMMY KAGA-RICCI

She appears in the crowd like I've conjured her out of the air.

Angel Rahimi.

She's kind of lanky, with a thin, bony face. A small tuft of black hair shows just beneath her headscarf.

I'm too busy trying to remember how to breathe to pay attention to what she's doing, but suddenly we're out and walking fast through the station. She's got one arm round my shoulders but it doesn't feel constricting. Instead, it feels oddly *comforting*. Like she's my mum or older sister.

"Just . . . we'll just keep going until we get somewhere quieter," she says, but I don't think she has any more idea where we're going than I do. People keep staring, and a couple of people snap photos. Can't stop them. Can't do anything.

She walks us all the way through the station until she ducks left into a shop and pulls me right to the back of the room.

"I think we've lost them," she says, glancing behind her. Then she laughs. "Wow. I've always wanted to say that." She puts on an American accent. *"I think we've lost 'em."*

Why am I holding on to her hoodie? I quickly drop my hand.

"Thanks," I say, but it comes out all croaky and weird.

"Are you okay?" she asks. There's genuine concern in her eyes. "That was pretty intense."

"I'm fine," I say, but I'm not fine, not really. My heart is still racing and my hands are sweaty and shaky. Typical. Why am I like this? "Are . . . you okay?"

"Dude, I'm *fine.*" She shakes her head in amazement. She's bouncing up and down on the balls of her feet. "That was ridiculous, though. Why didn't you bring a bodyguard with you?"

"I . . ."

What the fuck have I done?

The contract. The recording. Rowan. Lister. I just up and *left.*

Angel holds up both of her hands. "Don't worry, sorry, you don't have to explain any of it. Like, I'm one to talk, aren't I? I'm the most ridiculous person alive."

She doesn't give me time to say anything in response. She swings her bag off her shoulders and opens it up, then withdraws a jumper.

It's in there. Oh, thank God. She's got it. She wasn't lying.

It's not lost.

"Probably best not to . . . get it out in the middle of a train station," she says, grinning, and then laughs at herself. "That sounded like a euphemism." She holds out the jumper. "Just . . . just keep the jumper. It's old. I don't need it."

I cautiously take the jumper from her. I can feel the knife inside it. I can feel the exact shape of the handle.

Thank God.

"Okay . . . I'll . . . I'll leave you alone now," she says, still smiling. She steps back slightly and slings her rucksack back on. "It was . . ." She takes a deep breath. "I know this was probably very awkward for you but . . . I'm really happy that I got to meet you and talk to you."

The sincerity in her voice is different to how the normal fans sound. It's different from the screeching way they say our names, from the forced extremeness that they think that we changed their lives.

"I'm really glad I got to help you," she says. "After all you've done to help me."

"I . . . haven't done anything," I mutter.

"You have," she says, smiling. "I promise you have."

And then she nods and turns away.

And I find myself grabbing her hoodie sleeve again.

"Wait," I say.

She turns back, confused. "Y-yes?"

"Can you just . . . stay with me for a bit?"

"Yes . . . yeah, sure . . ." She stays very still. I drop my hand from her arm.

"I . . . don't want to be on my own," I say.

"That's okay," she says. "I hate being on my own too."

We stand there for a moment.

"Are you sure you're okay?" she asks.

I hug the jumper against my chest.

"Not really," I say.

"Could you . . . could you call someone?"

"No," I say.

"What do you want to do?"

What do I want to do?

And then it hits me.

Grandad.

"I want to go home," I say.

"Home?"

"I want to go home."

"Like . . . like your apartment?"

"No," I say. "*Home*. My actual home. Where I grew up."

"*Oh*," she says, surprised. But then she's nodding like it's the best thing I've ever said. "Yes. Yeah. Of course. You should do that."

"Will you come with me?"

I ask the question before I've thought about it properly.

It just comes out, like a reflex.

I want Angel to come with me. I don't know why, but I do. Is it because I know I won't be able to get out of here alone? Maybe. Is it because I just feel drawn to her? I don't know. I don't know why I feel anything anymore. Maybe it's just because she's the only fan in the world who knows who I really am.

I don't want to just say goodbye and never see her again.

"Of course," says Angel, her eyes wide and unblinking, as if she wouldn't mind if I wanted to go to Australia. To Pluto. To Heaven itself. "Wherever."

"You're not busy?"

"*Busy*," she scoffs, as if the notion is ridiculous. Then her expression turns serious again. "Does . . . does anyone know where you are?"

"You mean apart from the hundred people who just mobbed me?" I laugh bitterly.

"I mean . . . like Rowan and Lister. Or your manager?"

"No. No, they don't know."

I don't want to think about them right now. I don't want to think about any of that.

"Can we go?" I ask.

She straightens out her hoodie and nods.

"Yeah. Let's go."

# ANGEL RAHIMI

Somehow I have ended up on a train to Kent with my son, Jimmy Kaga-Ricci.

I jokingly refer to him as my "son" online all the time, but the more time I spend with him, the more I'm starting to feel like his actual parent. My sunglasses are massive on his head when I suggest he uses them as a disguise. I have to buy our train tickets for us using his card because he's too nervous to talk to anyone.

Also, he seems to be going through some sort of emotional breakdown.

I mean, I think I might be as well.

I only remember once we've been on the train for ten minutes that I should probably text Dad and tell him I'm not coming home after all.

Is everything okay? he texts back.

I send him a thumbs-up emoji.

⇄  ◄◄ ⊙ ►►  ♥

Jimmy doesn't talk much. Hardly at all, in fact. The soft, smiley persona from all the videos and photos I've seen appears to be imaginary.

But, despite everything, he's still Jimmy Kaga-Ricci.

Before we leave, he says, "You don't have to come with me."

But I'd go anywhere with him, wouldn't I?

I love him. I don't know how else to describe the feeling I have for Jimmy

Kaga-Ricci. It's not a crush. Not infatuation. I mean love in the "I will think about you every day for my whole life" sense. Love, like the desperate ache to hold on to something useless, even though you know that if you threw it away, nothing would change.

How did that happen to me?

# JIMMY KAGA-RICCI

"Man, how far out is this house?" asks Angel as we're sitting in another taxi, driving through Kent. We've long since left Rochester station, and we've been driving for at least half an hour. Grandad lives in the countryside.

She's peering out of the window, though we can barely see anything through the rain.

"It's far," I say.

Angel shoots me a look. "How *mysterious*."

"I'm not gonna give you the address. Sorry. It's not safe."

"Ha, d'you wanna blindfold me as well? Like they do in the movies? Okay, yeah, that would make this way creepier than it already is."

I don't reply.

"You kids picked the wrong day to come down the moors," says the taxi driver, an older woman with a different but as strong an accent as Gary. "They say flooding's on its way."

I say nothing again, so Angel, who seems to be literally incapable of putting up with a conversation pause, says, "No way, is the rain that bad?"

She's got this fake voice. It's easy to tell the difference between the things she really means and the things she's just saying to be polite, or to make people like her, or to carry on a conversation.

They talk about the weather for a bit and I zone out. My phone has run out of battery.

"Where d'you want dropping off, kids?" asks the taxi driver when we enter the village. It's pretty small, bordered by thick woodland and rolling fields, and the houses are all custom-built, each one markedly different from its neighbors. Grandad's house is on the other side of the village, about a ten-minute walk. My house, I mean.

Angel looks at me, waiting for me to respond, since she has no idea where we're actually going.

"Just here is fine," I say. Don't want the driver knowing exactly where my house is. Just in case.

I pay her and we get out of the car. Angel seems almost cheerful. I think it might be an act.

I think everything she does might be an act, really.

It's not dark yet, but the sky is so gray that the streetlamps have come on. The sidewalk and the road are dotted with puddles, and after a couple of minutes we're completely soaked. Neither of us has an umbrella, or even a coat. My jeans are freezing and sticking to my skin. Angel keeps tentatively adjusting her hijab. I offer to carry one of her bags for her, but she flat-out refuses to let me.

She talks the entire while we're walking.

Most of the time she doesn't seem to require a response. She talks about so many things and so quickly too, jumping from family holidays to school trips to old friends to internet videos without any pause. Is it a sort of nervous tic? Is she just attention-seeking? I don't think I've met anyone who talks so much.

It's vaguely comforting, I guess. I'd rather this than silence and my thoughts.

"So your family lives here, right?" she asks, after she's flown through twenty different topics.

"Just my grandad," I mumble.

"Where do the rest of your family live?" she asks.

I pause, but then say, "Not near here."

She realizes she's touched on something she shouldn't, so there's a rare pause while she tries to come up with a different topic. It's kind of funny, really. She seems to be terrified of angering me.

"My family live in a big town, so seeing this sort of place is so nice—"

"My grandma's dead," I say.

She stops talking.

"My mum and dad have always worked. They're divorced and they've both got big business careers that take them all over the world, which is why I've lived with my grandparents since I was little. But because of that I've never been close to them. They don't really care about me that much, so I don't speak to them very often."

She doesn't talk. Our shoes splash against the road.

"My older sister goes to university in America. We don't really talk. She doesn't like people knowing that we're related."

"I didn't know you had a sister," says Angel.

"No," I say.

We walk past the village's only bus stop—the one I used to wait at every morning before school. Feels like an alternate reality.

"So you only have your grandad, really?" she asks.

"Yeah," I say.

That silences her for a full minute.

⇄ ◄◄ ⊙ ►► ♥

"I'd . . . just like to take a detour, if that's okay," I say as we pass the village pub and turn a corner.

"You're not going to murder me, are you?" she asks.

I look at her. She laughs, but also sort of looks like she's genuinely asking.

"No?" I say.

"Okay," she says, and laughs again.

"Why did you come with me if you think I'm going to murder you?" I ask.

"I don't *actually* think that," she scoffs.

I look at her. She glances at me, and laughs when she sees my expression.

"I don't know. I mean, I don't think getting murdered would be that bad if you were the one killing me." She seems to realize how weird the statement is just after it leaves her mouth. "Er, I mean . . . I . . ."

"Are you all like this?"

"Who? And like what?"

"Fans. Are you all, like . . . Would you just do whatever I said?"

She thinks about it.

"No, I don't think everyone would," she says, and leaves it at that. "Where did you want to detour to?"

"Oh . . . I just wanted to go to the church." I point up ahead at a church partially hidden behind some willow trees. It's a tiny tenth-century crumbling building, but it's pretty much the only church I have left.

Angel seems to only just notice that it's there. "Ah, yeah, sure. Cool."

"I won't be long. You don't have to come in if you don't want to."

"Nah, I'll come in. No one will mind, will they?"

"No."

"Cool. I've never been inside a church."

"Not even in school?"

"Nah, my schools weren't that religious."

"Do you go to . . . like . . . a mosque?"

She chuckles, making me realize what a dumb question that was. "Yeah, I go to a mosque sometimes."

"Well, I've never been inside a mosque."

"They're pretty nice. Would recommend."

"Do you get to go very often?"

She stares at the road. "No, not very often. Only on special occasions, really. Do you get to go to church a lot?"

"No."

"Ah."

We fall into silence again, and she doesn't try to fill it this time. We just walk and listen to the rain.

⇄ ◄◄ ⊙ ►► ♥

The church is just as I remember it. A huge wooden door opens into a cold stone building with wooden rafters and a single stained-glass window at the far end. If the schedule is the same as it was when I was little, there's a service at 7 p.m., but that isn't for another couple of hours, so it's completely empty right now.

"They don't keep this place locked?" Angel asks.

"We don't exactly have a crime problem around here."

"Hm." She loiters behind me, looking around. "Interesting."

I watch her eyes move from the faded cushions stuffed behind the pews to the plaque of vicars dating back to the fourteenth century and the small statue of Jesus on the crucifix behind the altar.

"It's not really as grand as I expected," she says, eyebrows raised. "No offense."

"Catholic churches are more decorated than this. This is a Church of England church."

"Ah." She wanders past me, then turns and sits down on a pew, swiveling so she's facing the front of the church. "This is nice. Bit creepy. But nice."

"Creepy?"

"Well, it's a good murder location."

I huff out a laugh and sit down in the pew opposite her. "I'm not gonna murder you."

"Exactly what a murderer would say."

We catch eyes across the aisle and both laugh at the same time. The sound echoes around the empty church.

"I used to come here with my grandad a lot. Like, before all the band stuff happened."

Angel crosses her legs. "Yeah?"

"Yeah. Everything sort of feels okay for a bit while I'm here. Like, I can just stop thinking about it all for a while. Nothing else really matters."

Angel nods and looks away. "I know what you mean."

She doesn't say anything else, so I say, "D'you mind if I just . . . go and sit at the front for a bit?"

"No, of course, go for it."

I go to the front of the pews and sit, and for the first time in weeks, months, I don't know how long, reach out to God. He's waiting. He always is. No matter how long I go, no matter how shit it all gets, at least I have one or two things waiting for me. God doesn't care whether I have one pound or one hundred million. God doesn't care if I make a mistake, if I fuck up again and again and again. God asks me, "How are you?" and I just start crying. I try to be quiet but I can hear my sniffs echoing from the stone walls. God says, "Say something," and I tell Him that I don't know what to say, and He says, "Anything you've got." But I just cry some more. God tells me, "Everything that happens is making you stronger," and I want to believe Him but I can't. "I love you anyway," He tells me. At least someone does.

⇄ ◀◀ ▶ ▶▶ ♥

We exit the church and start trudging through the wet grass of the graveyard. I decide to stop and visit my grandma's grave. The gravestone still looks relatively new compared to the huge old stones around it, despite it being over five years old now. Grandma didn't see any of this band shit happen to me. For some reason, that makes me glad.

Across the churchyard and fields beyond, the sun is finally setting, though it's almost impossible to tell through the rain.

"Whoa, some of these are from the seventeenth century!" says Angel. She's walking around, reading all the gravestones, lighting them up with her phone flashlight. "This is amazing. You can't even read some of the inscriptions."

I look down at Grandma's grave. There are some flowers laid there, a little disheveled from the rain, no doubt put there by Grandad. Wish I had some flowers to add. All I have on me is a dead phone, my debit card, and a knife.

*Here lies*
*Joan Valerie Ricci*
*a treasured wife, mother, and grandmother*
*1938–2012*
*I sought the Lord, and He heard me, and delivered me from all my fears.*

"What do you think about when you pray?" I ask Angel.

She wanders over and looks down at Grandma's grave. She realizes suddenly what she's looking at and stops moving.

"Lots of things," she says, still looking at the grave. "Or sometimes nothing. It's more about feeling than thinking. For me, anyway."

I guess I'd say the same. But I don't say anything.

"Joan," she says suddenly. She points at Grandma's grave. "Your grandma's name was Joan?"

I nod. "Yeah."

"Did you write 'Joan of Arc' about her?"

I nod again. "Yeah."

"Everyone thinks it's a shippy song about you and Rowan."

I laugh. I want to cry. "Yeah."

# ANGEL RAHIMI

I'm teetering on the edge of sobbing but of course I don't. I keep smiling at him and trying to keep things light. I think I want to sob just because I'm overwhelmed. Or maybe seeing Jimmy at his worst is making me think about my own life too much.

Gross. Don't wanna think about *that*.

I'm starting to get kind of hungry, so when we arrive at Jimmy's grandad's house—an adorable brick bungalow with a huge front garden—I'm praying that Jimmy's grandad is the sort of old person who will not let a young person out of their sight until they're well fed.

Jimmy knocks on the door so loudly that I'm almost scared he's going to smash the glass.

"He's a little bit deaf," he says in explanation, "and he always has the radio on."

The door opens to reveal a very tall and thin elderly man. He reminds me immediately of some sort of headmaster character from an old film or an aging university academic—he's wearing quite a formal shirt and some trousers, what remains of his hair is slicked back, and his glasses are thick and rounded.

He looks at Jimmy, not even seeming to notice me, and his face lights up in the most incredible, unexpected smile I have ever seen.

"Jim-Bob!" he cries, and immediately pulls Jimmy into a warm hug. "Oh, Jim-Bob, I didn't expect to see you this evening!"

"My—my phone ran out of battery," Jimmy mumbles into his grandad's shoulder.

"That's okay, that's all right. You can come and see me anytime. You don't have to call beforehand."

Jimmy pulls back, though his grandad keeps his hands on his shoulders. "So . . . I brought my . . . my friend Angel with me."

*My friend Angel.* My heart pretty much skips a beat.

Jimmy gestures towards me, and I experience a brief panic in which I'm not sure whether I should offer to shake his grandad's hand or not. Thankfully, he doesn't offer, but he does smile kindly at me.

"A friend! Well, Jimmy hasn't brought a friend over since he was fourteen years old."

I imagine Jimmy, a normal fourteen-year-old, bringing a friend over after school to play video games. Seems like an alternate dimension.

"Hi, yes, I'm Angel Rahimi," I say. Why did I feel the need to add the surname? "Er, sorry there wasn't any warning . . . erm . . ." I shoot a look at Jimmy. What exactly am I supposed to be saying? Even I don't really know why I'm here.

"It's really no trouble at all. I really do enjoy having visitors, especially friends of my grandson. I'm Piero Ricci." He steps back and opens the door wide. "Look at you both, you're soaked! Let's get you inside and get some toast on the grill."

⇄ ◄◄ ⊙ ►► ♥

Piero has given me some of his dead wife's clothes to change into while my own clothes are drying on a radiator. Everything in my bags is completely soaked through.

"I only kept the really special outfits," he says with a wink, and holds up a dotty button-up shirt. "She used to love this. Said she felt like the night sky. She'd have had a big old strop to see this go to the charity shop."

He then gives me some gray trousers. Joan must have been about five foot three, because they only reach halfway down my calves. I pull my socks up extra high to try to make up for it.

I leave the bedroom to rejoin Jimmy and Piero in the kitchen, but halt just outside the door as I hear them talking.

"Found it in a charity shop," says Piero, and there's the noise of a page turning and a finger tapping on the paper. "Look, this is a good one."

"Yeah, I like how they all really capture the person's expression," says Jimmy, more animated than I've heard him in the entire time that I've known him in real life.

"I've been saving it for your birthday. I think you'll find it really interesting."

"Yeah, thank you!"

I enter the room, immediately spotting the art book by some unknown artist on the table between them. Jimmy shuts it, like it's so precious that I'm not allowed to read it, and looks up at me.

"You certainly are a tall one, aren't you?" remarks Piero, chuckling at the length of my trousers. "You'll have to mind your head on the bedroom doors."

I'm also now using one of Joan Valerie Ricci's flowery scarves as a hijab. I actually think it's a pretty good look. Nice one, Joan.

Jimmy's wearing clothes that seem to fit him, so they must be his. But they look like they've come straight from five years ago—the loose beige chinos, a similarly loose polo shirt. For someone who is internationally considered a fashion icon, appearing in fashion and gossip magazines and blogs pretty much every day, it's almost unnerving to see him dressed like a fourteen-year-old trying to be cool.

"What d'you fancy, my love?" asks Piero, heaving himself up from the kitchen table. It seems to take him a great deal of effort. "We've got eggs? Baked beans? Toast? Hot drinks?"

I sit down at the table opposite Jimmy. "Oh wow, all of that sounds amazing—"

"I can do that, Grandad," says Jimmy, immediately standing up from the table, which is so endearing I feel like someone has used a staple gun directly onto my heart.

"Oh no, you sit down, boyo. I'm not letting you in charge of food." Piero flips the kettle on and starts rummaging in a cupboard. "Look at you. You're wasting away."

Jimmy sits resignedly back down. "I am eating," he grumbles.

"Not enough, lad. Growing boys need to eat a lot. I'm going to have to have a word with Rowan, the next time I see him. Make sure he's keeping an eye on you."

I'm halfway through my meal when the question I've been fearing is finally asked.

"So how do you know my Jimmy, then, Angel?" asks Piero, warming his hands on his mug of tea.

I share a look with Jimmy. He just shrugs at me and continues nibbling a dry slice of toast, signaling me to make up something. Thankfully, this is one of my greatest skills.

"Well, I was just a normal fan of The Ark . . . but Jimmy and I happened to meet and strike up a conversation at . . . at a . . . after one of their concerts. And we got along fairly well, so . . . we stayed in contact and . . . now we're friends."

It's weak, but it's actually not too far from the truth.

"I see," says Piero. "That's nice. Jimmy doesn't really get the chance to make many new friends, these days."

The statement strikes me as odd. Surely Jimmy must have a *ton* of famous, rich, successful friends.

"And why did you decide to come and visit your old grandad, eh, Jim-Bob?" asks Piero, clapping Jimmy on the shoulder as he shuffles past to open a cupboard.

Jimmy has been sitting silently all the while Piero has been speaking to us.

Jimmy opens his mouth to say something, but then shuts it again.

And then he just starts crying.

It takes a moment for Piero to notice, as he's busy stirring the teas. Then he turns, with a questioning "Hm?" and his eyes widen. "Oh . . . Jimmy, come on now," he says gently. He walks back to the kitchen table and sits down next to him. Jimmy puts his face in his hands. Piero wraps his arm round Jimmy's shoulders. "Come on, lad, you're all right. It's all right now."

He starts offering comforting words, nothing of any real substance. I don't really know what to do, so some time in the midst of this, I slip out of the room and go and sit in the living room. Doesn't feel right for me to be in there, and seeing Jimmy cry makes me more uncomfortable than I could ever have anticipated. I've read about him crying in fanfiction hundreds of times. But real life is different. Crying has no romance or drama in real life. It's just sad.

A radio is on in the living room. Other things in the room: several potted plants and cacti, a large TV, an iPad, a reading lamp, heaped bookshelves, a grandfather clock, and photographs of family members all over the walls. I approach and have a look. Jimmy is there again and again and again. Sitting in a woman's lap as a baby. Running around in a garden as a toddler, long brown hair flowing behind him, holding a daisy in one hand. A primary school photo in a bright red jumper. A twelve-year-old Jimmy with spiky hair and black cargo trousers, singing and playing guitar in a pub. There's even a photo of two adults who I can only assume are Jimmy's parents—a short, serious-looking South Asian man in a business suit and a tall, thin-faced woman with scraped-back hair. Jimmy doesn't resemble either of them very much.

In one frame, there's The Ark's *GQ* magazine cover from last year—"THE REINVENTED BOY BAND"—Jimmy in the center in sharp focus. In another, there's what looks like a poem written in primary school, and it catches my eye, because the title is "The Angel." I start reading it.

*When all was bad in Jimmy Land*
*He wished for someone to rescue him*
*To make him part of a famous band*
*And fight off things dark and grim*

"Jimmy's gone off to bed now."

Piero's voice makes me jump and spin round.

He chuckles. "Oh, sorry, my love, did I make you jump?"

"It's fine," I say, smiling. "I was just snooping around."

"Looking at all our memories?"

"Yeah."

"Wrote that gem when he was about seven, I think." Piero sits down heavily into an armchair and pushes his glasses up his nose. "Always had a knack for words."

I sit down on a sofa. "Is he . . . okay?"

Piero barks out a laugh. "Well. No. No, he's not."

There's a pause. What should I say? It's clear that Jimmy's having some sort of emotional breakdown.

"He's had a very severe anxiety disorder for several years," says Piero with a heavy sigh. "Panic attacks. A lot of paranoia. Started fairly soon after his grandma died, then got worse as all this band malarkey got more intense. Used to see a lot of that when I was a boy. My father had it after the war."

I guess I knew that he'd got some sort of mental illness after I saw the panic attack. Piero makes it sound way more serious than I'd been thinking, though.

"Runs in the family, I think," Piero continues. "My daughter has it mildly. It killed my father in the end, though. He didn't tell anyone. Refused to talk about it. Never cried. When he popped off, they said it was natural causes, but it was too early for that, in my opinion. I could see it. It was the anxiety. After leaving his home country as a boy . . . after that bloody war . . . it was too much. He found being alive excruciatingly painful." Piero nods towards a sepia photograph of a man in a suit. "Angelo Ricci, his name was. Almost like your name, eh?" He chuckles.

"Yeah," I say.

"So it's a good thing to see the boy crying," says Piero, almost cheerfully. "Jimmy thinks about everything. Overthinks, really. He's got a very strong imagination. He'll imagine things that aren't ever going to happen and convince himself that they will. It hasn't been this bad for quite some time." He looks at me. "But at least he lets it out. It's ten times worse if you just keep it inside."

It sounds kind of like he's telling me something, but he continues talking before I can think about it too hard.

"Do you know whether there might have been anything to set it off?"

Of course. The Jowan rumors, the Rowan and Bliss fiasco, the mob at the meet-and-greet, his meltdown in the bathroom.

"The Ark are going through a bit of a crazy time in the news," I say, not too sure how much I'm allowed to reveal to Piero.

Piero nods. "I see."

There's another pause. Piero stares blankly into the fireplace before suddenly saying, "And why are you really here, my love?"

"What—what d'you mean?"

He chuckles. "Any fool can see you and Jimmy aren't friends."

I swallow a nervous laugh. "Oh, er . . . well . . ." I look away. Shit. What do I say? The truth is too weird. Maybe Jimmy wouldn't want him to know the truth about the knife.

"I don't know why I'm here," I say. "Nobody knows I'm here."

"Oh really?" Piero crosses his legs. "Just felt like it, did you?"

"Yeah." My voice lowers. "I just . . . wanted to help. Help Jimmy, I mean. He needed help and . . . well . . . I love him, so . . ."

"You love Jimmy?" He raises his eyebrows.

"Not like . . . not like I'm *in love* with him. I just . . . he's just . . ." I can't explain it.

"I thought you weren't his friend?"

"I'm not. I'm just . . . I'm just a fan."

"Ah." Piero nods. "And you wanted to help Jimmy."

"He needed help and . . . I was the only one who could help."

"How gallant."

"Maybe that wasn't the right thing to do," I whisper.

Piero shrugs. "I don't think there was a right or wrong there. There rarely is, in my opinion." He leans forward suddenly, linking his fingers together over his knees. "You know what I think, my love?"

"What?"

"I think that Jimmy needs to solve his own problems. And I think you need to solve yours."

He doesn't say this in a mean way, like he wants me to leave or anything. He says it in this gentle tone, like he feels *sorry* for me.

"I know a fair bit about the fans of Jimmy's band," says Piero. "I may be eighty-four, but I keep myself informed about what goes on in this world."

He pauses.

"And the saddest thing about you fans," he says, "is that you don't care about yourselves."

I stare at him.

"You would give your lives for these boys. You cling to them like you're reaching out to a god. They practically keep you alive. But beneath that, and if you took all that away, you fundamentally do not value yourself." He sighs. "All your love is given away. You leave nothing for yourself."

"I—I don't think we're all like that," I stammer.

"But I think you are," says Piero, looking directly at me.

"You . . . you don't really know me."

"I know that you came to a tiny Kentish village, from London, with a boy you barely know in real life, without telling your friends or family, just because he seemed a bit unsettled."

I feel a pang of sudden dislike for Piero Ricci.

"I know he asked you for help," says Piero, "but the trouble is, while asking for help is always good, it's impossible to keep relying on others to solve your problems for you. There comes a point where you have to help yourself. *Believe* in yourself."

"Are you talking about Jimmy or are you talking about me?" I say.

He smiles and says, "You tell me."

# JIMMY KAGA-RICCI

Grandad was kind of right. I don't *think* I've been under-eating, but my old clothes fit me again, despite me thinking I'd grown and broadened out. How am I just as thin and small as I was at fourteen? It's not like I've been starving myself. Have I?

My bedroom feels smaller. It does every single time I come back here, like it's gradually shrinking and one day it'll crush me completely. I've barely changed it since I stopped living here. There are band posters on the walls. Stickers all over the wardrobe. Stuffed toys on the bed. An old guitar in the corner of the room. The bedsheets are black and white stripes. I add the art book Grandad gave me to the bookcase, then change my mind and put it on my bedside table instead.

I strip out of my clothes, making sure to take my knife out of my jeans pocket. I feel its weight in my hands. Strange how comforted I feel just holding it. Strange how I feel so much for one simple object. Even if I threw it away, nothing would change.

I put it on my bedside table too and then get into bed in just my boxers. I'm still kind of damp, and my hair is still wet, but the duvet is thick and warm and snuggly. Feel like I'm sinking and I could keep on sinking until I disappear into the bed and emerge into another universe.

I've done something stupid, coming here. Just to have a little cry on my grandad's shoulder. My own little pity party.

I've done something even more stupid, asking some fangirl to come with me, just because people on trains scare me and I thought she was a nice person.

But there is one thing I am sure of. One thing I know is the right decision now. Not stupid. Not sad. Not pitiful.

I'm freeing myself.

I'm leaving The Ark.

# SATURDAY

"HOLD THE CRUCIFIX UP BEFORE MY EYES
SO I MAY SEE IT UNTIL I DIE."
—JOAN OF ARC

# ANGEL RAHIMI

Everything is chaos from the moment I wake up on an air bed in Piero Ricci's study, surrounded by piles of art books, being stared down by a large painting of Jesus.

I don't even have to go on Twitter to hear the news. I get a little notification from the BBC News app, which I rarely use. The title is:

**_The Ark frontman Jimmy Kaga-Ricci goes missing during chat show recording_**

Bit dramatic. But kind of realistic.

I guess no one knows where he is.

It also appears that I have gone missing too, judging by the number of missed calls, texts, and Facebook messages I have from Juliet.

**Juliet Schwartz**

Angel are you okay?? Fair enough you wanted to go home but are you safe?? Did you get home okay? I'm really worried I haven't seen you tweeting or on Tumblr or anything. did you get home okay? Please just message me or call me back. You've just disappeared and I'm really worried.

There's also a text from Dad.

**Dad**

Heard on the radio that one of your band boys has gone missing? Sounds serious. Hope you're okay. Text me soon. xxx

Thank God he doesn't know where I am. I text him back. Don't worry, I'm fine. Probably just a media overreaction.

There are more texts and messages, but they all sort of say the same thing, until I get to one of the last ones from Juliet.

**Juliet Schwartz**

ANGEL. I just saw a photo of Jimmy on a train and . . . YOU'RE THERE? You're with him??? It's a blurry photo but it's definitely you, I recognize your hoodie . . . What the FUCK . . . please tell me what the fuck is happening. The internet says he's gone to Kent so I assume you're there too?! Why??? What the fuck Angel?? What the fuck are you doing??

I quickly go through all the photos taken of Jimmy on the run; there are only a few that I'm in. And they're blurry. You can clearly tell we're together, but I'm not identifiable. That's good.

God, it's not easy to hide when you're an internationally famous celebrity, is it?

I feel a pang of guilt. Juliet was worried about me. Of course she was. She's my friend. Shit, I should have gone back to her.

I send her a half-hearted message back, not really knowing what else to say.

**Angel Rahimi**

Hi I'm safe everything is fine

Jimmy is still in bed and I am drinking a cup of tea in the kitchen when there are several very loud bangs on the front door of the bungalow.

Piero, who is already up and dressed, sighs and lifts himself up from the table.

"That'll be the boys," he says, and the way he says "the boys" reminds me of the way the fans always call them "our boys." The Boys. Our Boys.

Then it sinks in properly.

Rowan Omondi and Lister Bird are here.

I hear Piero open the door and he starts to say "Hello," but somebody starts speaking over him immediately.

"All right, where the fuck is he? I'm going to fucking kill him. Is he okay? Did he make it here okay?"

The voice changes from stern to deeply concerned so quickly that it's difficult to identify who exactly is talking, but when the figure storms through the hallway and past the kitchen door, I realize that, of course, it's Rowan.

He steps backwards and peers in at me through the door, frowning.

"I've got a fucking bone to pick with you in a minute," he says, pointing directly at me, and then continues walking.

It's absolutely fascinating. I've never seen Rowan *angry* before.

Lister Bird slopes after him, looking freezing and soaked in just a plain white T-shirt and joggers. He shoots me a guilty look as he walks past the doorway, but doesn't say anything.

This really is not exactly how I wanted to meet The Ark—makeup-less, wearing an old lady's clothes, them probably thinking I'm a kidnapper of some sort—but you take what you can get.

# JIMMY KAGA-RICCI

My entire body jumps as I wake up and realize that I am being violently shaken from side to side. I unglue my eyelids and try to focus, a strangled *"Wh-what"* leaving my lips, and realize that the person shaking me is none other than Rowan Omondi.

"You *fucking dickhead*," he shouts too loud. Oh God, what have I done? "You absolute *fucking dickhead*, I can't *fucking believe* you did this to us. *Why* didn't you reply to my *fucking* messages? I can't believe we had to fucking *drive* all the way to fucking *Kent* just to come and get you. Why don't you ever fucking *tell me anything—*"

Lister is standing next to him. He pats Rowan gently on the back. "Okay, Ro, you can stop shaking him like a bloody snow globe now."

Rowan opens his mouth to continue shouting, but then closes it again, and he stops shaking me. Then he sits down on the bed next to me and pulls me up and into a hug.

"Jesus fucking Christ, I thought you'd been kidnapped. Thank God I still remember your fucking home phone number. God, look at you, sleeping in this tiny bed with a *knife* on your bedside table. Like, you could hurt yourself. *God.*"

He moves back from me, keeping his hands on my shoulders. He looks me up and down. I can see myself, blinking and disoriented, reflected in his glasses.

"Are you all right? Did anything happen? Is there something you're not telling me?"

I clear my throat, feeling still half asleep and confused. "Er . . . those are three different questions."

He shakes his head. "Why did you come here, Jimmy?"

Why?

"I don't want to be in The Ark anymore," I say, my voice barely more than a whisper.

Rowan and Lister stare down at me.

"All right," says Rowan, "where's that girl? She's got some explaining to do."

He leaves the room but Lister stays. He rummages in my wardrobe, and chucks a T-shirt at me. I stay very still, not quite able to process what I'm supposed to be doing.

"You're not naked under there, are you?" he says, raising an eyebrow and leaning against the wardrobe.

"What's the time?"

"It's nearly one in the afternoon."

Nearly *one*. I think I was sixteen the last time I slept in until one.

I put the T-shirt on and get out of bed.

"Maybe some trousers too?"

"Oh." I grab my old chinos off the floor and put them on. Lister waits and watches me passively.

"Sorry to make you come here," I say.

"Yeah," he says.

I look up at him. He looks cold and unlike himself. No smile.

"I really am sorry," I say. Well, it's more of a hoarse, sleepy whisper. "I really . . . hate myself. I wish I—"

Lister looks me in the eyes, suddenly fearful.

"Don't say what I think you're going to say," he says.

"Sorry," I say, but he's already worked out what I was going to say. I wish I wasn't alive.

"Like, who the fuck even *are* you? No fucking offense, but who the fuck *are* you?" Rowan is gesturing at Angel aggressively with one hand. They're standing on opposite sides of the table. Angel looks like she's not sure whether she's starstruck or about to cry.

"Can we please tone down the language, Rowan?" Grandad mutters from one corner of the kitchen.

"Yeah, sorry, but *this girl*"—he points at her like she's one of the kitchen chairs—"she's been creeping around The Ark *all week*. She literally spent a whole night at that fandom meetup with Bliss on Tuesday."

I wonder if I'm still dreaming. Bliss? How would Angel know Bliss?

I look at Angel. She is staring, wide-eyed, at Rowan, frozen.

Rowan nods at her. "Yep. I know *all* about that. You think my girlfriend wouldn't have told me that? She's my *girlfriend*. She told me all about you. Your name's *Angel*, isn't it?"

Lister snaps his head round to face Rowan. "Wait—*Angel*?" He looks at me. "Is this Angel? Angel from the bathroom?"

Rowan nods. "Yeah."

Everyone looks at Angel.

She forces a short laugh. "'Angel from the bathroom . . .' Jenny from the Block's slightly more awkward younger sister?"

No one laughs with her.

"And then," Rowan continues, "Jimmy disappears and I see pictures of Angel and Jimmy on the internet and then Bliss messages me out of nowhere, like, *Rowan, I know this girl*—which, by the way, is the first I've heard from Bliss since Tuesday night—and then next thing I know Jimmy's going off with her on the train to *Kent*? Like, I think I deserve an explanation, all right?" He looks around the room, waiting for someone to nod and agree with him. No one does anything.

"It was my decision—" I start to say, but he interrupts me.

"You don't know what you're fucking *doing* half the time, Jimmy. I bet if she hadn't encouraged you, you would have been totally fine. You do realize we had to cancel the whole chat show thing, don't you? And the fucking *contract*. Cecily is freaking *out*." He holds his phone up to me. "She's texting me, like, demanding that I bring you back—"

"Angel didn't do anything; it was my decision to come here and it's my decision to leave The Ark—"

"No, you can't make decisions like that by yourself—"

"You want to leave The Ark?" Angel whispers faintly in the background, but none of us respond to her.

I feel myself starting to shout at Rowan. "Stop treating me like I'm younger and dumber than you!"

Rowan falters, his eyebrows furrowed. "I'm not! It's just . . . you're more fragile than . . . than . . ."

"What? Than you and Lister?"

Rowan steps towards where I'm standing in the doorframe. "Well, yeah, basically!"

"I'm not fragile! Why do you always treat me like a baby?!"

"Because you're the one who does shit like this! Who just up and leaves us right before we're recording for fucking prime-time television!"

Grandad steps forward a little. "*All right, enough.* Arguing like this isn't going to solve anything."

I glance at Angel. She's not crying, thankfully. I thought she might cry. I mean, I would cry if my idol started shouting at me.

"Okay, well, fair enough if you need a break," says Rowan. "Fair enough if you want to see your grandad. Could have chosen a better time, but fair enough." He turns on the spot and points once again at Angel. "But I don't want this *fangirl* anywhere near us. I don't know what the fuck you want, but you're creeping me the *fuck* out, and this is entirely your fault."

Angel opens her mouth and stammers, "I—I can leave . . . It's fine—"

But at the same time, I say, "She doesn't need to leave; she's not what you think. I wanted to come here and she helped me—"

"They're all the *same*, Jimmy," Rowan spits, rolling his eyes. "The fans all just want to take pictures of us, fuck us, or watch us fuck each other. That's all they want."

"Right, I'm not having any more of this," Grandad barks, and grips Rowan firmly on the shoulder. "You go into the living room. Angel can stay in here. I don't want to hear any raised voices or any swearing. We're going to have an adult conversation about what Jimmy wants and what is the best course of action. All right?"

Everyone is silent.

Then Rowan mutters, "All right." He slinks out of the kitchen, giving me a stern look as he walks past me.

"All right, Jimmy?"

I look at Grandad. He reminds me of when he used to tell me off for coming home late after school due to band practice.

"All right," I say.

Lister's tapping his hand rapidly against the side of his leg. He catches my eye, and then turns and follows Rowan and Grandad into the living room.

I look at Angel.

"Sorry," I say to her, hoping that sums it up.

She huffs out a small laugh and then sits down in a chair.

"Not your fault," she says, and it sounds like she's blaming herself.

# ANGEL RAHIMI

So. Rowan hates his own fans. Genuinely did not see that one coming.

It's definitely my fault that all of this is happening. I should have said no when Jimmy asked me to come with him. Then maybe he wouldn't have gone, he wouldn't be trying to leave The Ark, and Rowan and Jimmy wouldn't be literally destroying their relationship in front of my eyes.

Rowan shouting at me wasn't too bad. But watching Rowan and Jimmy argue was like watching the world tear itself into two. What can I do? God. I can't do anything. What if they stop speaking because of me? What if they fall out of love because of me? What if they hate each other because of me?

Oh God.

What have I done?

Everything is my fault.

Why am I here?

What is my life?

I stand up from the kitchen table, shoving the chair back. Everyone else is in the living room. No one sees me run to the study, shove all my not-quite-dry clothes into my suitcase, and put a jumper on. No one sees me hoist my rucksack onto my back and pull my suitcase down the hallway. No one sees me open the door and walk right out without saying a thing.

It is still raining. So heavily now that you can't actually see very far ahead. It feels like a nightmare.

Maybe this is all a nightmare. Or is it a dream? I can't tell the difference anymore.

I pull my suitcase down Piero Ricci's driveway and onto the empty road. It lands with a splash that completely soaks my socks, and when I look down I realize that the road is pretty much one giant puddle. Maybe the taxi driver was right about the flooding. Across the road are a few more cottages, but beyond that are just blurry fields. The world seems deserted, dissolving in the rain.

I stop walking.

What am I doing?

Where am I going?

Who am I without The Ark?

I fish my phone out of my pocket and call home. Someone picks up after two rings.

"Hello?"

I wipe rain out of my eyes. It's Mum.

Didn't realize how much I missed her voice.

"Hi, Mum, it's me."

Is she still angry? Is she going to shout at me? I thought Dad would pick up the phone.

"Fereshteh." She waits for me to speak, but I don't. "Your dad said you aren't coming home until tomorrow after all."

My knees feel weak suddenly, like I really need to sit down.

"I don't know what I'm doing, Mum," I say.

"Fereshteh, what is it? Tell me. Tell your maman. I'm here, my girl. I'm here."

"Are you still angry with me?"

"I was never angry, my darling. Only scared."

"Why . . . were you scared?"

There's a pause.

"Because I felt that I suddenly didn't know you," she says. Her voice is so quiet, or maybe the line is dodgy due to the rain. "Hearing you so angry, so determined to see this band . . . and not caring about your own achievements. I wondered whether you were growing up to be a girl who valued nothing about herself. Only a boy band."

I realize then that I'm crying.

I'm just standing in the rain, sobbing.

"I met The Ark," I say to her, choking on my own breath.

"The band? Your band?"

"Y-yeah . . ."

"Was it . . . not good?"

The whoosh of the rain makes it hard to hear her.

"It wasn't . . . wh-what I expected . . . I thought . . . it would make me happy to see them and meet them . . . but I just realized . . . that . . . there's nothing happy or good in the world . . . nothing that is truly good or truly happy . . ."

I can't speak anymore after that because I'm just sobbing. I'm not even making any sense. I crouch down on the sidewalk.

"I—I can't—I don't know wh-who I am without them." My free hand curls into a fist and I bring it up to my face. I want to punch myself. "My whole life is . . . is The Ark . . . b-but . . . I can't believe in it anymore . . . and now I have n-nothing good in the world . . ."

"My girl . . ." Mum whispers, and God I wish she were here, I wish she could hold me, cuddle me like she used to do when I tripped over as a toddler and scraped my knee.

"Do you think it's stupid?" I say, my voice hoarse. "Do you think I'm a stupid teenage girl?"

She does. She must do.

"No, Fereshteh," says Mum. "No. I think you are the girl with the deepest heart."

I put my hand over my eyes.

"I don't have anything left to believe in," I say.

"Allah is with you," she says, "and I am with you."

And I want to explain that while both of those are true, or at least I hope they are, it's not the same, and they can't fill the hole that The Ark has left endless and vacant.

"And you have yourself," she says. "Fereshteh. My—"

The call suddenly ends. I whip my phone from my ear and look at the screen, only to find that the signal bars have gone.

⇄ ◀◀ ⏵ ▶▶ ♥

"Hey, Angel."

A voice makes me look up from the ground.

Meters away from me is none other than Bliss Lai. She's wearing the same jeans as she was in on Wednesday, her sleek hair kept mostly dry by a huge umbrella.

"Having a meltdown in the rain?" she says, and grins at me. "How very relatable."

"How . . . why . . . what . . ."

"I know," she says. "I have that effect on people."

She sits down on the sidewalk next to me, holding the umbrella over both of our heads.

"So what's up with *you*?" she asks.

"Having a crisis," I say.

"Same," she says.

"Where've you been?"

"At home. Hadn't been outside since Wednesday. The paparazzi have been loitering around my house."

"Why are you here?"

"Thought it was time to come out of hiding," she says. "And sort out the mess that is my fucking life. Rowan messaged me saying you'd all be here." She chuckles. "Not that I replied to his message."

"Oh."

"And why are you here? Bit random. You're not stalking Jimmy, are you? Because that would be weird and I thought you were cool."

I open my mouth to try to explain, but close it again. Impossible. I just shake my head at her.

"Cool," says Bliss, and we sit there, under the umbrella, while I get out the rest of my tears.

# JIMMY KAGA-RICCI

Grandad puts a property show on the TV as if watching a middle-aged man talk about house prices is going to calm anyone down. None of us are calm at all. Lister is pacing around the room, staring hard at the floor. Rowan has seated himself firmly in an armchair and has folded his arms. I sit down on the sofa and start fiddling with my collar.

How am I going to explain anything I'm thinking?

"Now," says Grandad, "I'm going to go and make everyone a cup of tea. And you're not allowed to start talking about anything that has happened until I get back. All right? I think the three of you just need a few minutes to sit and *think*."

Rowan starts to protest but Grandad leaves before he can say a full sentence, so he just slumps back into the chair and taps his foot.

I can see the questions burning in his eyes. Why did you do this? Why do you want to leave The Ark? Do you hate me and Lister? How could you do this to us? What's wrong with you? Don't you enjoy the fame and money? Can't you just put up with it for a bit longer?

They're all questions I've already asked myself.

"Can you *please* stop *pacing*," snaps Rowan in Lister's direction after a couple of minutes.

Lister doesn't even argue. He just stops and stands very still.

Then he says, "D'you remember Jimmy's fourteenth birthday party?"

Both Rowan and I turn to look at him.

Lister nods, looking up at the ceiling. "It was just us three that year in here. Joan baked us that huge cake and we all had those little bottles of blue WKD, which Joan thought was just some kind of fruit squash. Not that we got drunk. We all pretended we were drunk but we really weren't."

Neither Rowan nor I speak.

"And then," Lister continues, "we'd been planning to watch the *Lord of the Rings* films back-to-back, but instead we spent four hours in the garage coming up with our own electro version of 'Happy Birthday.' And Joan and Piero came and watched and clapped." He grins suddenly, manically. "Oh, man. Jimmy, does Piero still have the old drum kit in the garage?"

He doesn't wait for an answer from me, he just walks straight out the door and into the kitchen, calling for Grandad. "Hey, Piero, d'you still have my old drum kit, by any chance?"

Rowan leaps up, following him, spluttering some sort of protest.

I get up and follow them too, to find Grandad standing in the kitchen, perplexed, holding a tea bag in one hand.

"Oh yes," he says, "well, I didn't really know what else to do with it, so it's still there."

"*Sick.*" Lister practically bounces down the hallway and swings the door to the garage open, Rowan and me following in silence now, baffled. Lister turns to look at us and gestures towards the garage. "Come on, lads. Band reunion tour starts here at Tiny Miscellaneous Village in the north Kent marshes."

Rowan sighs, but the agitation in his voice has dissipated. "Lister . . . what the fuck are you doing?"

Lister doesn't answer, so we follow him into the garage. He turns the light on and there it is, our original band setup, the place we used to write music, rehearse, and record all our first YouTube videos. A rusty old drum kit stands at the back, the stool ripped and faded. Two painfully plastic keyboards are propped up to one side, and there's even our old spare acoustic guitar, complete with My Chemical Romance stickers and an engraving (by Lister) of a hand sticking its middle finger up.

Lister immediately skips over to the drum kit and sits down, rummaging around his feet until he finds the drumsticks. He taps on the drums tentatively, and I feel like I've gone back in time. I remember the sound. I'm fourteen again.

"Come on!" he says to the two of us. "Let's jam."

Rowan looks down at the old guitar. Compared to the top-of-the-range bass guitars he usually plays now, this thing looks like it was found in an alleyway. Nevertheless, he picks it up and sits down on a chair, strumming at it. We all wince upon hearing how out of tune it is, and without saying anything, Rowan starts tuning it, humming the correct notes to himself until the strings match him.

"Jim," says Lister, looking at me now. He points at the two keyboards. "Plug those in!"

I hesitate for a moment, but then I wander over to the two keyboards. They're each on their own stand, but one is slightly higher than the other. What I used to do was set each of them to play different sounds, then I'd play both of them during our songs. It created quite a cool effect, and I didn't know anything about Launchpads or MIDI controllers or sequencers or any software stuff, really. That came later.

I plug the keyboards in and switch them on. I'm surprised they even still work, being out here in the garage for over five years.

Lister starts playing a simple beat, nodding his head in time. I quickly realize he's playing the version of "Happy Birthday" we came up with all those years ago. Rowan raises his eyebrows but quickly catches on and starts playing the chords. They don't sound quite as cool on an acoustic rather than an electric, but still, it's not too bad.

I turn to the keys. I pick my two old favorite sounds, "Soft Electric Guitar" and "Bass Synth." The notes come to me seemingly out of nowhere. I hadn't even realized I'd stored this silly song we made up in my brain.

*"It's Jimmy's birthday,"* I sing before I realize what I'm doing. I shoot my head up, embarrassed.

Lister is grinning widely. Rowan still has his eyebrows raised, but he's smiling at me in the corner of his mouth, strumming away the chord sequence.

"Erm," I say. "Am I going to have to sing 'Happy Birthday' to myself?"

"No, you are fucking *not*, Jimmy Kaga-Ricci," says Lister, and turns his drumbeat into a run, and with a shout of "FIVE, SIX, SEVEN, EIGHT," we explode into music. We all start singing at once, remembering the stupid variation of "Happy Birthday" we came up with.

*It's Jimmy's birthday*
*The birthday man*
*It's fourteen years*
*Since his life began*

And soon I'm pretty sure Lister is just making up a load of little drum runs in the middle, things he hadn't been able to do before, and then he's pointing at Rowan and Rowan's making up a guitar solo on the spot, it sounding weird and out of place but somehow so *good* on the acoustic guitar, and then Lister is pointing at me with one drumstick and I'm just playing the keys, and Lister is shouting at the top of his lungs,

*Happy birthday, Jim*
*Happy birthday, my guy*
*Love from Lister and Ro*
*Your best pals till we die*

And we all laugh at what a terrible rhythm the lyrics are and I forget everything that's been happening and we just play together, like kids, in a garage, at a birthday party.

⇄  ◂◂ ⊙ ▸▸  ♥

When we step out of the garage, God knows how long later, Grandad is sitting in the lounge, sipping a cup of tea.

Opposite him on the sofa is Angel. She is, for some reason, soaking wet, and has a towel wrapped round her.

And next to Angel is Bliss Lai.

# ANGEL RAHIMI

Rowan's expression drops from a warm smile to shock as he enters the room and sees Bliss.

"What are you doing here?" he says, almost choking on his words. "I mean, what—Why—"

"You told me you were here," says Bliss, shrugging. "So I thought I'd join the party. You might wanna tell Cecily to notify the press that Jimmy's safe, by the way. They all seem to think he's having a catastrophic breakdown."

There's a horrible silence.

"Why haven't you been—" Rowan stops mid-sentence, swallowing.

Piero sighs. "Okay. Kids, why don't we give Rowan and Bliss a bit of space for a few minutes, eh?"

Lister races out of the room before Piero finishes speaking. Jimmy shuffles nervously from foot to foot, before Rowan gives him a nod, and then he leaves. I glance at Bliss. The friendly, jokey smile I came to know earlier this week is completely absent. Instead, she looks like she's just rolled up to a funeral.

I stand up and leave the room too.

⇄  ◄◄ ⊙ ►►  ♥

Everyone apart from Jimmy has gone into the kitchen. He's just leaning there against the hallway wall, empty-eyed and alone. He glances up at me when I appear.

"Hey," he says.

"Hey," I say.

"Have you been crying?" he asks.

"Who hasn't?" I say.

"Fair."

"Mm."

I lean against the wall opposite him.

"You know, you can go home anytime," he says, trying to smile at me. "I'm not . . . I mean . . . I don't want you to feel like you have to stay for me."

He's right. I should go soon.

"Yeah," I say. "I'll go soon."

"Why are you here?" Rowan's voice. We can hear them clearly through the thin walls of the cottage and the open door.

"We needed to talk, didn't we?" says Bliss. She sounds resigned.

"But why now? Why avoid me all week and then turn up now?"

"I needed some time to think."

"Well, thanks for leaving me to deal with it by myself," Rowan snaps.

"I was dealing with it by myself as well."

"You didn't have to. We could have dealt with it together."

"No, we couldn't," says Bliss. There's a pause. "No, we couldn't. We can't do anything good together anymore, Rowan."

I watch Jimmy's expression. At Bliss's words, Jimmy's eyes widen, and he starts pulling on his collar.

"You're right," says Rowan after a moment. "Ha. You're actually right. We just snap at each other all the time."

There's a longer pause this time.

"You know I love you," says Bliss. "I care about you a lot."

"Yeah," says Rowan.

"But it's not . . . a romantic sort of feeling anymore."

"Oh."

"And . . . I think . . . you being in The Ark . . . the fame and the fans and the paparazzi . . . it's not the life I want."

"Yeah."

"That's all I wanted to say."

There's a sniffing sound. Someone's crying. I can't tell who.

"You were the only person apart from Jimmy and Lister who saw me as normal," says Rowan. Oh. It's him. "I want to make it work."

"You know that's not a good foundation for a relationship. And you know we can't."

"Yeah. Yeah, I know." Rowan sniffs again. "Sorry. Sorry for everything."

"There's nothing to be sorry about," says Bliss. "I had a fucking blast, mate."

"Yeah?"

"Yeah. Got to hang around with you and your crazy life for all this time, didn't I? But I can't do this forever. I want to be more than this. I am more than this."

"You are. You always were."

Little more is said. After a few moments, Jimmy nods to himself and wanders into the kitchen, leaving me alone in the corridor.

I am about to join him when my phone suddenly rings. I scramble to pick it up, not bothering to look at who's calling. It must be Mum.

"Hello?"

"Angel? It's Juliet. I'm at Rochester station."

# JIMMY KAGA-RICCI

"What . . . why are you here?" says Angel from the corridor, which strikes me as odd, because who would she be asking that to?

I head back out to see what she's doing, only to find her on the phone, with a look of mild fear on her face. A parent, maybe? Surely her parents must be wondering where she is by now.

There's a long pause while the person on the other end speaks.

"I'm fine, I'm—I'm still with Jimmy," Angel stammers.

There's another long pause.

"No . . . no, I don't think that's a good idea . . . there are lots of people here already, everything's a bit . . . everything's a bit messy . . ."

A short pause. Angel grimaces.

"No, don't do that," she says.

Who the hell is she talking to? It doesn't sound like she's talking to an adult.

"No, wait, hang on, I—" Angel swallows. "Fine. Fine. I'll ask the address. I'll message it to you."

The person she's talking to appears to hang up very quickly, because Angel listens for a moment, then removes the phone from her ear and looks at it in confusion.

"Who was that?" I ask out of sheer curiosity.

"Er . . . that was my friend Juliet," says Angel. There's a pause before she elaborates. "I was staying with her in London when . . . when I came to meet you. She's come to Rochester to find me." Angel looks up at me. "Would it be all right if she came here?"

*Juliet.* I don't know anything about Juliet. Never even heard of her. Is she a fan of The Ark? If I gave her our address, would she spread it around? Why does she want to come here anyway? Does she just want to meet us? Take pictures?

"If not," continues Angel nervously, "I . . . I'd better go and meet her at the station. She's already there. In Rochester."

I don't want Angel to leave. Not while things are like this. She's literally the only one who understands my side of the argument.

"I swear to you she—she'd never share the address. She won't be weird. She just wants to see me. She doesn't even know Rowan and Lister are here."

The weird thing is, I actually trust Angel.

I trust everything she says.

"Okay," I say, and then tell her the address.

# ANGEL RAHIMI

It's nearing two o'clock by the time Juliet gets here. I wouldn't have let her come, but she threatened to call the police and accuse Jimmy of kidnapping me. Not sure how that would have stood up in a court of law, but she sounded serious so I gave her the address.

I open the door to her, having been watching and waiting out of the living-room window. She puts up her umbrella as she steps out of the taxi, though she already looks relatively disheveled—her hair is damp, and she's just wearing a hoodie and jeans.

If she'd come here for Jimmy, she would have dressed up more. Wouldn't she? I don't know.

Do I even know Juliet that well?

"Hi," I say.

"Hi," she says, approaching the door, and there's a slightly awkward moment where I wonder whether we're going to hug, but she doesn't offer, and neither do I, so I just step back and let her go inside. She shakes her umbrella before shutting the door behind her. "You're safe, then?"

"Yep, I'm still alive. Not been murdered." I laugh, trying to keep things light. She smiles at me, but doesn't laugh.

Piero appears out of the kitchen, where he's assigned himself tea duty. I informed him that my friend was coming just after I asked Jimmy for the address. Piero didn't seem to mind at all. In fact, he seemed glad of the extra company.

"You must be Juliet!" he says. "I'm Piero Ricci. Jimmy's grandad. Cup of tea, my love?"

"Yes, please," says Juliet. She's very good at remaining composed, but I can see the slight awe in her eyes.

Piero disappears again, and then Jimmy comes out of the living room. He looks ten times more nervous than Juliet.

"Hi, you must be Juliet?" he says, the same words as his grandad but a completely different tone.

"Yes, hi," she says in the most composed, eloquent, adult tone I've ever heard out of the mouth of someone my age. "Thanks so much for letting me come here to make sure Angel's okay."

Jimmy seems just as surprised as I am by Juliet's complete and total composure. "No problem."

"And . . . I hope you're feeling okay?" she says, asking it as a question.

"Thank you," he says, not really answering. He nods, and then after a pause, he disappears back into the lounge.

Juliet stays very still for a moment, one hand still gripped firmly on to her umbrella.

Then she says, "He's just a normal guy, isn't he?"

Bliss then appears out of the kitchen. She's tied her long hair up into a messy bun and I think she might be wearing one of Piero's cardigans.

Juliet does a comical double take. "Y-you're here too?"

Bliss grins widely. "Why, yes, hello, I am here, and I've just split up with my boyfriend. I'm single and ready to mingle."

Rowan shouts "Too soon!" from the kitchen.

I guess they must be all right after all.

⇄ ◀◀ ⊙ ▶▶ ♥

The three of us—me, Juliet, and Bliss—decide we want to get out of the house for a bit. When Rowan and Lister make an appearance before we go, Juliet greets them like she's making a connection at a business event. They react similarly to Jimmy. I guess when you have girls screaming at you every single day, meeting someone able to behave normally and politely must come as a surprise.

We decide to walk down to the pub at the end of the road to talk. I was starting to feel like I should at least give Jimmy and the boys some space, even if he didn't want me to leave for good.

On the walk down, we don't say anything, even though we're all sharing Juliet's umbrella. We crowd in a row of three on the sidewalk, avoiding the stream that's running down the middle of the road.

The pub is a quaint, cottage-like building with very few people inside, and it feels dim and empty. We order soft drinks from the bartender—a glass of milk for Bliss, a lemonade for Juliet, and a J2O for me—and then go and sit in a corner booth. The rain outside drowns out the voices of anyone else in the building. Juliet keeps tucking and untucking her hair from behind her ear.

There's a lot we need to talk about.

Juliet's voice from Thursday night still rings in my ears.

*How are you going to go through your life loving nothing as much as you love a boy band?*

She was right about that, of course.

I don't love anything as much as I love them. Even myself.

And I guess Juliet doesn't feel the same. I guess she always had larger things going on in her life. Maybe The Ark was an escape for her, like it was for me. But maybe, ultimately, she's strong enough not to make them her everything.

"Well then," says Bliss. "Man. Yikes. Jeepers. Am I right?"

This does actually make me snort out a laugh. Even Juliet smiles.

"What's been going on with you two?" asks Bliss. She points between us. "I'm sensing some tension."

When neither of us answers, she points at Juliet. "Posh girl. Did you dump the fuckboy?"

Juliet chuckles. "Erm, yes." She glances at me. "He went home pretty soon after he got back from the station. We might still talk, but . . . nothing more than that, I don't think."

"Good, good. Excellent." Bliss points at me. "Cool girl. How did you meet Jimmy?"

It's a long story but Juliet doesn't know it either, so I tell it to both of them. The mob at the meetup, being trapped with Jimmy in the bathroom, looking after his knife for him, giving it back to him at St. Pancras, and him begging me to help him get home.

It feels like it all happened to somebody else. Not boring old me.

"Bloody *hell*," says Bliss when I've finished. Juliet sits silently, a little open-mouthed. "I'm gonna need another glass of milk."

She gets up and wanders over to the bar, leaving Juliet and me alone.

"How can any reasonable person just drink milk on its *own*?" I ask, horrified.

"God, I *know*, right?" says Juliet. "It's practically masochistic."

We both laugh, and then fall into silence for a moment before we both try to speak at the same time.

"I—" I say.

"We—" she says.

"No, you first," I say.

"No, no, you go," she says.

I sigh. "I'm . . . sorry. For being a dick all week. You wanted to hang out with me and get to know me but . . . all I cared about was The Ark." I pause. "And . . . Mac told me what's been happening with your parents. That they kicked you out."

Her eyes widen. "He told you about that?"

"I'm so, *so* sorry for not . . . I don't know. For not noticing, or giving you the chance to talk to me about it. I just wouldn't shut up about The Ark all week and . . . going on about my parents being shitty when yours are like actual pure evil . . ." I shake my head and look down. The weight of all the awful things I've done is crashing over me again. "I've been the absolute worst friend."

Juliet bites her lip. "Well . . . I'm sorry for inviting Mac in the first place. This was supposed to be our week, but I was excited about maybe having a boyfriend, and I just . . . I prioritized him over you."

Wait, she's sorry? But this was my fault, wasn't it?

"You're my special internet friend, Angel," she says, smiling weakly. "You know more about me than anyone. I feel like I can at least . . . at least *try* to be myself around you. Even if I can't do it that well at first. And I always enjoy talking to you. And you actually listen to the things I say." It all comes out in a rush of compliments that I'm not ready for. I nearly choke on the ice in my drink. "And I really wanted to tell you about the stuff with my parents, but . . . there just never seemed to be a good moment. And you did just wanna talk about The Ark all the time, which is fine, because, like, I was excited too, but I also . . . I don't know. It's harder to tell people stuff like that in real life."

I stare at her.

"You're my special internet friend too," I say.

She laughs, patting her hair down embarrassedly. "Good!"

"And you can tell me about serious stuff like that. I promise. You can just tell me to shut up about The Ark anytime. I won't be offended."

We both laugh, before falling back into silence again. Juliet starts playing with her straw.

"Meeting The Ark has changed me," I say.

She looks up and frowns. "What d'you mean?"

"They . . ." How can I explain. How do I explain to anyone, ever. "They were my sole purpose for being alive. They felt like the reason I was *born* was to . . . love them." I shake my head. "But I can't properly love something I don't know. And I don't know them. I don't know them at all."

Juliet rests her chin on one hand.

"I've been feeling that too," she says. "I mean, not in the same way, I guess. I've been feeling it for a while."

"Really?"

"Yeah. Sometimes whole days go by where I don't check @ArkUpdates. Sometimes I resent them for making me care so much." She shrugs. "Sometimes I just get this *craving* . . . to break away and have my own life and care about other stuff more. That's why I got so attached to the idea of a relationship with Mac, actually." She sighs. "We talk about other stuff. I felt a bit more like I was my own person for once. I ended up not liking him *that* much, to be honest, but when I talked to him and hung out with him, I felt good because I didn't need to think about The Ark to . . . to cope with other stuff."

I nod. "Yeah," I say. "I get that."

She smiles. "We should just care about ourselves more."

I smile too. "That's a deal, my guy."

Bliss returns with another full glass of milk and says, "I'm shitting you not, the bartender full-on cackled at me when I ordered this." And the three of us laugh. And I imagine this must be what it's like to have real friends.

# JIMMY KAGA-RICCI

It's mid-afternoon by the time Rowan declares that he wants to sit down and talk to me and Lister about the band again. Bliss, Angel, and her friend Juliet (who, by the way, seems refreshingly calm) have returned from their trip to the pub, where they were gone for over an hour. Grandad's listening to an audiobook in the kitchen while doing something on his laptop.

The three of us go to my bedroom. We're too old and too sad to be in here. Feels like we're doing our past selves wrong—the three kids who used to jam on secondhand instruments in here, scribbling down lyrics into the back of school exercise books.

Lister and I sit on my bed, Rowan sits on my desk chair.

He takes a deep breath and asks, "Why do you want to leave The Ark?"

All my thoughts come out, tangled up with each other, not making any sense. "It's all a big lie. It's all fake; the magic of fame isn't real anymore. I don't enjoy anything. I feel like I'm lying every single day. I can't even do things I want. I don't feel safe in my own apartment and I can't leave it either. I've been feeling this for so long, but after that Jowan photo this week, I've just . . . I'm just . . . I'm going insane." My voice gradually gets louder as I speak. "I'm just . . . I'm just going insane."

Lister has found alcohol, by the way. He has a large glass of wine in one hand.

Rowan stares at me. "Right."

We all sit in silence for a minute. Lister puts down his wineglass, picks up my old guitar, and starts plucking at it.

"You can see it's not the same as it used to be . . . right?" I ask desperately. Echoes of our past selves are dancing around us. Lister jumping on my bed, banging drumsticks on my wall. Rowan grumbling when he can't get a microphone to plug into my computer. "You can feel it's . . . it's not the same?"

"Why should things stay the same?" Rowan asks.

"Well . . . maybe they shouldn't, but they're getting worse. The contract, the fans, the rumors . . . it's all getting *worse*."

"What, getting more rich and famous? Millions more people loving our music? That's worse?"

"Is that what you want?" I ask. "Wealth and fame?"

"*No*, I just . . ." Rowan shakes his head. "I just can't understand what's bothering you."

"It bothers me that I can't go for a walk when I want to," I say. "That I can't go and see my grandad when I want to."

Rowan watches me.

"It bothers me that I don't enjoy being in a band anymore," I say.

Lister glances up at this, stopping strumming on the guitar.

"Okay. Okay. I get it." Rowan sighs. He rubs his forehead with one hand. "Look . . . Jimmy, I'm not trying to tell you that any of that is fair. But . . . it's just the deal we've been dealt. It's what we have to put up with in return for being, let's face it, some of the most privileged people on the planet. I know you want everything to be perfect, but nothing is ever going to be perfect. You've just got to put up with the bad things and wait a bit longer until our waiting pays off. In a year's time we'll be famous in America and you'll look back and wonder what the fuck you were ever worried about!"

"And what if I keep waiting and it never gets better?" I ask.

"It *will*."

"No, you don't fucking *know* that, Rowan." I raise my voice. "I'm not going to just sit and wait for things to change anymore. I'm changing things. I'm doing what *I* want for once."

"And you don't give a shit about what *we* want? You don't give a shit about all the stuff we've done together the past six years?" Rowan splutters. "We just played music together and had fun for the first time in months. Maybe years. Don't you care about us anymore?"

"Obviously I do, but it's not good anymore." Why doesn't he understand? Why am I the only one who feels like this? "I can't keep lying every single day. Turning up to events, smiling and waving and pretending to be happy. I can't keep living like this."

"You sound like a baby," Rowan says.

"And *you're* still being a condescending *twat*—"

"Can you both fucking *stop*?" snaps Lister. "Jesus, I haven't ever heard you argue this much in my entire life."

Rowan and I fall into silence.

"This isn't getting us anywhere," says Lister.

"Well, what do you want us to *do*, then, Lister?" says Rowan, rolling his eyes.

Lister takes a large gulp of wine.

"Maybe we should go," he says, looking at me.

"What, me and you?" says Rowan, looking at Lister.

"Yeah," he says. "I don't think Jimmy wants us to be here anymore."

He stands up from the bed and walks out of the room.

Rowan watches him go, and then takes one last look at me, before standing up and following him.

And as bad as it sounds, I feel relieved.

# ANGEL RAHIMI

While I'm glad I got a lot off my chest to Juliet, she's still very annoyed that I don't want to leave and go home with her.

"We shouldn't be here," she says, while we're sitting in the kitchen listening to Rowan and Jimmy shout at each other. "It feels wrong."

I know what she means. It feels like two planets are about to collide.

I find Jimmy in the lounge by himself. He glances up at me as I come in and sit down next to him. His eyes are a bit red.

"Hey," I say.

"Hey," he says.

I feel like we can communicate without talking.

"You still want to leave The Ark?" I ask him.

"Yeah. Erm, yeah. I think so."

I nod and look down. "Okay."

This is it, then.

This is the end.

I have helped to end the only thing I ever cared about.

"Why do you like The Ark?" he asks, looking up at me. His eyes are so big and brown. I know them so well, I know every part of him, the way his hair gets fluffed up at the side, the soft line of his jaw, the slight hunch of his shoulders. And yet, I don't really know anything.

"You are . . . the damn light of my life," I tell him. "When everything is bad, when I wake up and want to go back to sleep and never wake up, you're there for me."

"I'm not," he whispers.

"You *are*." I swallow nervously. "If you want it to end . . . I understand." I pat my chest. "But . . . I guess . . . you're ending a part of me too."

"Part of you?"

"Without you . . . without The Ark . . . all I have is my dull life. You're one of the few things I had in my life that was good and *true*. You're part of my truth."

He blinks. "You're part of mine too."

"Am I?"

"Yeah."

He looks up. I follow his gaze and find him staring at the wall of photographs, his childhood and his parents and his whole life.

"Does this place still feel like home?" I ask him.

He nods. "Yeah."

"You must miss it a lot. And your grandad."

He nods again. "Yeah." He looks at me. "My grandad gave me the knife for my sixteenth birthday. I know it's stupid to carry it around, but it reminds me so much of home."

He reaches into his back pocket, only to make a vaguely panicked face and withdraw his hand, empty.

"Must still be in my jeans from yesterday," he mumbles.

No wonder he wanted it back so desperately.

"Is it an antique?" I ask.

"Yeah, it was my great-grandad's."

There's a silence, and then he stands up abruptly from the sofa, his hand clenching and unclenching by his side.

"I'm just . . . gonna go get it," he says.

I watch him exit the room. I glance back at the photographs on the wall, then get up to have a look, peering at the sepia photographs to find one labeled "Angelo Ricci." I finally lay eyes on a man with high cheekbones, dark doe eyes, and a lost expression.

He looks just like Jimmy.

⇄　◄◄ ⊙ ►►　♥

The sound of Jimmy's voice draws me out of the room. I wander into the hallway, only for Jimmy to storm past me, followed by Piero, shaking his head.

"I don't understand," says Jimmy. "You must have taken it out of my jeans pocket and put it somewhere." He halts by a radiator in the middle of the hallway, where the jeans he wore yesterday are drying. He pats them down, but his knife clearly isn't there.

Piero chuckles. "I haven't seen it, lad! I know I'm old but my memory isn't failing me that badly quite yet."

"Well, that's the last place I had it. In my jeans. Which I took off last night and you put on the radiator this morning."

"Could you have dropped it outside somewhere?"

"*No*, I had it last night! In my room! And it's not there either!"

Rowan steps into the hallway. He's got a coat on, phone in one hand, and looks like he's just about to leave.

"What's going on?" he asks.

Jimmy stuffs his jeans back onto the radiator. "It's gone."

"What's gone?"

Jimmy doesn't answer. He just walks back down the hallway and disappears into his bedroom.

Juliet and Bliss appear behind Rowan, looking confused.

Piero sighs. "He's lost his knife."

Bliss's eyes widen. "*Knife?* Wait, that family heirloom thing? Shit. Rowan told me about that. What does he want it for?"

"It's important to him," I pipe up, and everyone looks at me. Rowan frowns at me, apparently still very annoyed that I'm here.

"Well," says Rowan, "me and Lister are leaving now." He peers down the hallway towards the bathroom and shouts, *"Allister! We're going now!"*

Wait . . . they're going?

They're leaving Jimmy behind?

Lister fails to materialize, but Jimmy appears again out of his bedroom, looking markedly more ruffled than when he went in.

"It's not there," he says. His fists are curled tight and his eyes are moving frantically around the hallway, searching the dark corners and nooks.

"It'll turn up," says Rowan.

Jimmy stops suddenly, and looks at him.

"You took it," Jimmy says.

"What?"

"Didn't you?" Jimmy steps closer to him. "You took my knife."

# JIMMY KAGA-RICCI

Rowan has taken my knife. It's gone from my bedside table. He must have seen it in my bedroom when he came to wake me up, or maybe later when we were talking in here, and decided that it'd be best if he took it away for good.

He overreacted. Typical Rowan. He turned up to the house thinking I'd had a massive breakdown and was now a danger to myself, and the first thing he saw when he stormed into my room this morning was the knife on my bedside table. So he took it.

That has to be it. That *has* to be it.

"Are you having a fucking joke?" Rowan shakes his head. "What are you talking about?"

"My knife has gone. You're the only one who would take it."

"Why would I take it?" Rowan says. "I don't even want to touch that thing." He looks around. "Come on. Why would I take it?"

Why is he *lying*?

"Piero!" Rowan gestures at Grandad, who is leaning against the hallway wall, arms folded. "You must have taken it off him, yeah?"

Grandad shakes his head, baffled. "No, no. It's not mine to take."

Rowan drops his hand.

"Jimmy, you can *search me*; I swear I don't have it—"

"Just *give it back!*" I shout.

"I *don't have it!* I bet you fifty thousand pounds *she* has it." He points aggressively at Angel, who is also in the hallway, and then at her friend Juliet. "Or her fan friend."

Angel lets out a hysterical laugh, which probably doesn't help their cause.

Rowan starts laughing too and walks towards the front door. "Look, I'm leaving—"

"*No.*" I grab his arm, pulling him back from the door. "Don't fucking do this to me. Just give it back."

He yanks his arm back. "Do what? What could I possibly do to you that's worse than what you're doing to me?"

"Boys, come on," Grandad barks. He looks at Rowan. "Come on, Rowan, just give him the knife back."

"I *don't have it!*"

To my side, Angel's friend Juliet murmurs, "Angel . . . do you have it?"

"*What?*" Angel practically shrieks. "I'd never *steal* something of Jimmy's, oh my God!"

Angel wouldn't have it. She's the only one who's been helping me. If she'd wanted to take it, she wouldn't have given it back to me yesterday.

"But . . . you've . . . I mean, you've been acting kind of weird, generally . . ." Juliet doesn't say any more. Angel blinks several times, and then just turns round and goes back into the kitchen.

"You can't leave," I say to Rowan.

Rowan sighs. "I bet you just fucking lost it or something."

"Why don't you just *admit* that you have it?"

"Come on, Rowan," says Bliss, giving Rowan a pointed look. "Just give it back to him."

"I literally *don't have it!*"

"*Right.*" Grandad pulls Rowan by the shoulder and shoves him into the lounge, then grabs me and pushes me into the kitchen. "No one's going anywhere until this is resolved. Anyone can come forward and give me the bloody thing anytime. No questions asked." He lets out a harsh breath. "It was my father's and I don't want anyone to take it either."

I sit down heavily into a kitchen chair. Angel is already there at the table, and she looks up at me.

*You don't have it, do you?* I ask her with my eyes.

She shakes her head at me.

⇄ ◄◄ ⊙ ►► ♥

I decide to get some air. The house has been getting really hot and stuffy with so many people inside and waves of panic were starting to flow over me. I step out into the back garden and trudge through the wet grass, breathing in the fresh air. The rain hasn't stopped all day. I wonder whether the river has burst its banks.

My clothes are getting gradually wetter and wetter, my T-shirt changing from light gray to dark.

Are we all going to be trapped here forever, kept still by indecision?

No one doing exactly what they want?

Wouldn't be much different to being back in the band, would it.

As I wander down the garden, a figure appears from behind a bush. I have to squint through the rain to identify them—it's Lister, a lit cigarette in his mouth, sitting down on a bench that looks out over the woodland and countryside.

"Hey," I say, and he flinches at the sound of my voice, then laughs when he sees me.

"Didn't hear you coming," he says, and takes a drag from his cigarette.

"You shouldn't smoke," I say. "You'll die."

"We're all dying."

"How pretentious."

"I don't want to grow old, anyway." Lister takes another drag. "Seems boring. I've lived enough, thanks. I want my rest."

His voice is slurring slightly. He has an empty glass in one hand.

"Calm down," I say. "You're only nineteen. Not dead yet."

"Nineteen years *too old*."

I laugh at him but can't help hearing the slight sincerity in his voice.

"What's going on?" asks Lister. "What's going to happen?"

I can't answer him. And then he presses his cigarette out on the bench, puts it into his glass, and turns to me. For a moment I think he might want to kiss me again, but instead he just presses his head into the crook of my neck, nestling his cheek on my shoulder, and wraps his arms round my shoulders. He smells vaguely smoky, and a little of alcohol, but he feels so warm.

"I want to change too," he says. A raindrop falls from his hair and lands on my leg. "When I come back in my next life, I'm going to be a normal person, with a normal job. Nobody will know who I am."

Is that a good alternative? I don't know.

"Jimmy . . ." he says, "I'm sorry . . ."

I rub his arm. "What are you sorry for?"

"I . . ." He hides his eyes. "I took the photo."

"What photo?"

"The Jowan photo. From Tuesday."

My stomach drops. It takes a moment for it to sink in.

Lister's voice gets wobbly. "I . . . I genuinely didn't think it was me, but . . . then I found it in my phone . . . and I remembered . . ."

I can't even speak.

He sits up. "Look, Jimmy, I . . . it was months ago. The . . . the Jowan shipping thing, the fans, it was really getting to me." His eyes fill with tears. "The fact that they all wanted you and Rowan to . . . to be in *love* or whatever. It messed me up. It made me feel like I'd never have a chance with you because the fans would be so . . . so *angry* . . ."

"A chance . . . with me?" I repeat back to him.

He continues on like I've said nothing. "I'd liked you for *years* but the fans don't give a shit; they can't see *anything*—they just keep going on about *Jowan*. And then, that night, after one of our house parties, I saw you two lying there in bed looking like . . . I dunno . . . a . . . a married couple or something . . ." A tear rolls down his face. Or maybe it's just the rain. In the quietest voice he says, "I'd never felt so fucking miserable and alone."

I sit still, saying nothing.

He laughs, throwing his arms up into the air. "So I did what I always do! Turned it into a joke. I got drunk and took a photo and texted a couple of friends like 'LOL! Look at this! Don't Jimmy and Ro look like an eighty-year-old couple!!' And obviously one of those idiots leaked it eventually. But it's all my fault, Jimmy." He turns to me. "I'm so sorry. God, I'm so sorry."

This isn't his fault. This is my fault.

This is my fault for being so blind.

"Jimmy," he says, "please don't hate me."

"I don't hate you," I say. "I hate myself." The truth of it overwhelms me suddenly, and I scrunch my hands into fists and cover my eyes. "I hate myself so much. God. I don't deserve to be alive."

Lister's eyes widen.

"I need to be alone," I say. I stand up and start walking back to the house. Lister calls after me, but I don't want to listen to him, to any of this, anymore.

# ANGEL RAHIMI

By early evening, the shouting has started again. Juliet has given up on her attempts to get me to go back with her, but similarly refuses to leave me alone with The Ark, so is sitting in the kitchen with Piero listening to the radio.

Bliss has set up camp at the kitchen table with a book she plucked from Piero's study. She called for a taxi a few hours ago, only to be informed that the sole road leading into the village has been shut due to flooding and won't be reopened for a few hours.

Which means she's stuck here, we all are, until further notice.

I'm sitting alone in the study now, curled up on my air bed. I keep looking at my phone, as if expecting someone to message me, but no one does. I'm thankful Mum and Dad still don't know I'm here. They'd be out of their minds with worry.

No one's found Jimmy's knife yet.

Piero comes into the room a little while later and asks if I want a cup of tea. I say I do, and stand up and leave the room with him.

"You haven't seen Lister, have you?" he asks as we walk through the house.

"No?"

"Hmm." He doesn't say any more.

Jimmy and Rowan are still shouting at each other in the living room.

"Boys, you could get some sleep, you know," says Piero gently.

"I won't be able to sleep when I know someone could stab me at *literally any moment*," says Rowan, glaring pointedly at me as I walk past the living-room doorway.

"All right," Piero says. "Let me know if you need any more tea."

⇄  ⏪ ⏵ ⏩  ♥

"Where's Lister?" a voice mumbles. I open my eyes. It's Jimmy. I've been dozing on the kitchen table, my head in my arms. The radio is still on, crackly voices whispering in the background.

"Haven't seen him," says Bliss, who is already halfway through the book she selected, *Tess of the d'Urbervilles*.

Me and Juliet shake our heads.

"He's not in the house," says Jimmy, scratching the side of his neck. He looks like he needs to sleep for four years.

"Did he go out for a smoke?" asks Bliss.

"I'll go and look."

Piero gets up and rummages in a drawer. "Take a torch, lad. The sun'll be setting soon."

"I'll come with you," says Bliss, standing up.

"Me too," I say.

"Me too, then," says Juliet.

Piero sighs. "All right, nobody panic. Just be careful. There's a lot of flooding just outside the village."

As we leave the room, Rowan emerges from the lounge. He looks exhausted.

"Where are you going now?" he asks, his voice a little hoarse.

"Lister's not in the house," says Jimmy.

We walk all the way round the back garden, and then all the way through the front garden. Rowan jogs up and down the street, even checking the pub, but it has closed early due to the weather.

Lister has disappeared.

We reconvene back inside the house, everyone cramming themselves into the hallway. Jimmy calls Lister's phone, but we hear it ringing from the living room.

Jimmy crouches down, puts both hands on the sides of his head, and starts muttering, "He's gone. He's gone."

"I'm sure he just went for a walk to clear his head," says Bliss, but there's no confidence in her voice at all. "You know what he's like. He's reckless. He does what he wants."

"But he's not *stupid*," snaps Rowan.

Bliss holds up both hands. "All right. Just trying to stay calm and not descend into hysteria. Jimmy." She nudges Jimmy with her foot. "Jimmy. Stand up, mate."

"He can't have gone far, can he?" asks Juliet. "How long's he been gone?"

No one's sure. No one saw him leave. It's nearly eight o'clock now.

"I saw him two hours ago, but that's it," murmurs Jimmy.

"I'm sure he's just gone out somewhere to smoke in peace," says Bliss, still determined to keep everyone hopeful, but everyone's already thinking the worst. It's obvious by the looks on their faces.

⇄  ◄◄ ⊙ ►►  ♥

"Yes, I'd like to report someone missing," says Piero. He's on the phone to the police, all of us seated round the kitchen table. "A young man. Nineteen years old. About five foot eleven, white skin, light brown hair, slim build." He looks at us. "What was he wearing?"

"White T-shirt, gray joggers," Jimmy supplies immediately.

"White T-shirt, gray joggers," says Piero.

There's a pause.

"His name's Allister Bird. Goes by the name 'Lister.'"

There's another pause.

"Yes, I know he's famous. He's a local lad. I'm a friend of the family and he was with me this evening."

Will the police even believe Piero?

"Been missing about two hours."

There's a much longer pause. Piero's face drops.

"This is serious," he says. "There's flooding in our area, and we're really concerned, and—"

We're all holding our breath.

"I see," says Piero. "Well, thank you for your time."

He hangs up, and we all realize simultaneously what has happened.

Two hours isn't long enough to report a missing person. Not *nearly* long enough.

Jimmy makes a low groaning noise and puts his head in his hands again. Bliss makes a loud tutting sound.

"We'll go and look for him, then," says the last person I would expect to make such a statement—Juliet. She links her hands over one knee and flicks her hair back. "It's getting dark, but we've all got lights on our phones. It won't be that hard."

Rowan stares at her.

"I'm still not totally sure who you are," he says, "but you're right."

"I'm *Juliet*," says Juliet in a very irritated tone, which actually makes me smile. I thought she'd be a mess around Rowan. Instead, she's looking at him like he's an annoying little brother.

"Right, then." Bliss claps her hands together. "We're going." She looks at me and Jimmy. "Angel and Jimmy? You in?"

We both stand up and say "Obviously" at almost exactly the same time.

# JIMMY KAGA-RICCI

It's my fault that Lister is gone. He's been hinting at not being okay again and again and again. And I didn't notice, even after he tried to explain about the photo. Was I even listening properly?

I'm always so consumed by myself. Why don't I notice anything that's happening to anyone else?

Grandad's the only one staying home. The five of us set out—them with their phone flashlights, me with an actual flashlight because my phone is out of battery—into the garden. Grandad lent Rowan his only pair of wellies, since they wouldn't fit anyone else. The rest of us are in trainers and plimsolls, which get covered in mud in under five minutes.

The sun is beginning to set now, though it's barely noticeable. The clouds are just turning a slightly darker shade of gray.

"Where would he have gone?" asks Juliet. "How do we know where to look?"

"There are some muddy footprints here!" calls Bliss from the end of the garden. We go and join her, and sure enough there are footprints in the wet earth. "I guess he went in there?"

She points towards the woodland path. We used to walk Rowan's old dog there sometimes, or play manhunt, or make secret bases.

There's water running down the path in some places. Tiny streams. What happened to the summer?

*"LISTER!"* Rowan has the loudest voice and is doing most of the shouting. We've been walking for nearly fifteen minutes now, farther and farther into the woodland.

The three of us even camped out here once. I remember my way around, but everything looks warped and wrong in the rain and the darkening sky. Grandad's house has long disappeared out of view.

*"LISTER."* Rowan comes to a halt and turns to us. His skin, soaked from the rain, shimmers under the dimming light. "I . . . I really don't think it's safe to go any farther. We're getting so close to the river."

What? We're not just going to *give up*. Anything could have happened to him.

But Bliss nods in agreement. "Yeah . . ." She shines her flashlight farther down the path. "Look, the path down there has flooded completely."

The light reflects off a rush of water.

To my surprise, it's Angel who speaks next. "We—we can't just *leave* him out here."

"To be fair," says Juliet, who is shivering quite violently, "we don't know for sure that he's out here."

"But what if he *is* . . . ?"

Rowan stays very still, staring at the ground.

Then he turns round and bellows Lister's name so loudly that the rest of us all flinch and Juliet puts her hands over her ears.

"This fucking rain," Bliss mutters.

"How about we split up?" I suggest. We need to keep looking. Anything to keep us looking. I'm nearly crying again. This is entirely my fault. We need to find him. We're going to find him.

"No, that won't do any good," says Rowan. "We're better together."

It's true. We are.

Bliss lets out a heavy sigh. "Fine. Let's just keep walking for now."

And so we do.

⇄  ◄◄ ⊙ ►►  ♥

Rowan and I end up at the back of the group, side by side.

"Why?" he murmurs. "Where did he go?"

I glance at him, and I can't tell whether he's crying or whether there's just a raindrop falling down his cheek.

"I can't deal with you both leaving me," he says.

Am I really going to leave him?

I don't know.

I don't know anymore.

# ANGEL RAHIMI

I don't know how long we've been walking when we finally come to a stop. We stopped shouting a while back. The light is quickly fading, and we all have our flashlights on now. The path ends, opening out into a seemingly interminable wheat field. Lister could have gone in any direction from here.

"So now what?" asks Jimmy.

No one speaks for a moment.

"Maybe we should go back now," murmurs Rowan.

Jimmy immediately protests. "No, no. We can't." And he's right. We can't go back. We can't just leave Lister out here.

Bliss and Juliet don't say anything.

"You can go back," says Jimmy. "If you want. But I'm not."

"Where else are you going to look?" asks Rowan. "He could be literally anywhere out there!"

"We should just keep going," I say.

Everyone looks at me. Jimmy's eyes light up.

"Yeah," he says, nodding at me. "Yeah. If we spread out across the field, he might—"

"It's not *safe*," says Rowan.

"Yeah, well, Lister isn't *safe*," Jimmy shouts. "And it's my fault! So I'm not going back until I find him."

"I'm staying too," I say. Jimmy glances at me again.

"Well, we can't just leave you here!" says Rowan, looking at us both.

"Choose, then," says Jimmy. "Stay or go."

We're all interrupted by a lightning flash, and then there's a low rumble of thunder. The rain seems to start falling harder.

"Hey, everyone," calls a voice. We all turn and spot Juliet crouched down by some bushes at the edge of the pathway. She stands back up and holds out an object. "Isn't this what Lister was drinking earlier?"

We approach her. It's a large, empty bottle of red wine. Jimmy takes it from her and looks at it, then looks into the bushes. They've been trampled on and pushed aside, creating a murky tunnel.

"Yeah," he says, his voice a croaky whisper.

He drops the bottle and runs straight into the woods.

Everyone cries out, telling him to come back, but I don't hesitate. I start running right after him.

# JIMMY KAGA-RICCI

Even without the flashlight, I can see the exact path he's taken. Flattened grass and still-visible footprints in the mud. I call after him. He's going to be dead, right? Something's happened. I push through branches and thorns, feel them scratching at my skin, I don't care, I don't care anymore. What have I done?

There's someone behind me. Is it Rowan? I turn and—No. It's Angel. She cares. Why is she doing this?

Why is she here with me?

Why did this happen?

"We'll find him," she says to me as we run, and it's like a real-life angel has promised, a real-life angel knows exactly what is going to happen for the rest of time.

We burst out of the brambles and Angel grabs the back of my shirt just before I topple down a slope—we've reached the river, though it's shallow here, only a few centimeters deep, more of a creek than a river. The bank is both high and steep, and the mud is smeared like somebody has slid down it, and so we look over the edge, both of us, and there at the bottom, lying in the shallows of the water and covered in mud, is Lister Bird, with my knife embedded in the left side of his stomach.

# *ANGEL RAHIMI*

Jimmy freezes, unable to do anything but stare down at Lister and the knife. I stop thinking entirely. I step down, digging my shoes carefully into the mud before transferring my weight so that I don't slip, and start climbing slowly down the bank.

He must have slipped and fallen. Probably drunk. Did he fall onto the knife? Was he holding it when he fell?

The closer I get, the more I can analyze the situation. His head isn't in the water, thank God, but his eyes are closed. Once I get even closer, almost at the edge of the creek, I can see his chest moving up and down. Faintly, but definitely moving.

Thank God, thank God, thank God.

"He's—he's alive," I call back to Jimmy. I shoot a quick look behind me. Jimmy's already climbing down after me—a lot slower than me, but he's on his way.

I turn back to Lister and look down at his body. The knife is definitely inside him. Oh God. Oh shit. Are there any important organs there? It's kind of in his side. Is that where the kidneys are? Intestines? Oh God, I got a D in biology GCSE.

I shine my phone flashlight on him. It isn't just mud all over him. It's blood too.

"No no no no no." Jimmy's voice breaks through my frantic thoughts as he scrambles to reach Lister. "Why—why did he have the knife?"

"Doesn't matter."

I start patting Lister's face. Need to keep him awake, right? I don't know. I'm running through all the thriller films I've seen in my head.

Lister stirs and his eyes flutter open. There's a small moment where he might just be waking up from an afternoon nap, but then it hits him all at once. He makes a horrible screaming noise in the back of his throat and tears start rolling out of his eyes.

"It's okay, we're here," I say, but he's started shaking violently, and nothing is okay at all.

"H-hurts . . ." His voice is so small it's almost inaudible over the rushing water.

Jimmy crawls to the other side of Lister so he's sitting in the creek. He starts stroking Lister's hair, saying, "It's okay, you're gonna be okay," but his voice is shaking and he doesn't sound sure at all.

I shine my flashlight over the rest of his body. His leg seems to be twisted at a strange angle. It makes my stomach lurch just looking at it. How long has he been lying here?

"I think he's broken his leg as well," I say, but this just seems to panic Lister more.

"Do we take the knife out?" says Jimmy, looking at me wildly.

"Won't that just make him bleed more?"

"I don't know?! It can't be good that it's in there! He's shaking; it's cutting him!"

He's right. Now that Lister's awake, every time he moves, the knife is digging into him a little harder.

There's no time for us to argue.

"We can't take the knife out," I say. "He might bleed to death. Just keep him calm so he doesn't move too much."

Jimmy takes Lister's face in both his hands and turns it slightly so that Lister is looking at him.

"P-please, p-please," Lister stammers, his voice little more than a whisper. His whole body is trembling from the cold, and I realize suddenly that it's because he's partially submerged in the icy water of the creek.

"You're gonna be okay," says Jimmy, lowering his face towards Lister. Lister's eyes are wide now, wild, trying with all their might to focus on Jimmy. "Just keep looking at me."

Jimmy flashes his eyes at me.

"We—we need to get an ambulance," I say. I frantically wipe the rain off my phone with one hand and dial 999, but I can't get a signal. I try again, and again, but my hands are shaking, and it won't work. It's not working, and I don't know what to do.

Lister starts crying. It's nothing like I ever imagined. It's scrunched up and painful and makes me angry.

"S-sorry," he croaks, rolling his head so that he's resting on Jimmy's legs. "I'm sorry . . . an accident . . ."

"I know, I know. It's okay." Jimmy keeps on stroking Lister's hair.

Lister's breathing gets a little calmer, and I realize he's passing out again. Jimmy slaps his face quite hard, and Lister's eyes spring open again. "Stay awake, Lister, please stay awake."

The sound of shoes pounding against mud interrupts him. I turn round and look up, only to see Rowan, Bliss, and Juliet, staring down at the scene from the top of the bank.

"Someone call 999!" I shriek up at them, and Bliss whips out her phone without another word.

"I j-just . . . wanted t-to help . . ." Lister mumbles, his eyes starting to shut again. He's losing too much blood. "You said . . . y-you hated y-yourself . . . Didn't want you to . . . d-do anything . . . b-bad . . ." His voice dies away into nothing.

"I can't get any signal!" Bliss screams. Juliet gets her phone out too. Rowan skids down the riverbank and joins us at the bottom.

"Why did he take the knife?" Rowan breathes.

Jimmy shakes his head. "I don't know."

"Ambulance!" Juliet yells into her phone. She must have gotten a signal. Thank God.

Rowan pushes me aside as he crawls towards Lister's face. "Come on, Allister, stay awake." He shakes him a little by the shoulder, but stops as soon as Lister lets out a high-pitched whimper. "We need to get him out of the water!"

"We can't," Jimmy snaps. "We can't move him when he's losing this much blood!"

"M-my friend, he's fallen down a slope. He's broken his leg and he's . . . he's been impaled by . . . by something," Juliet stammers into her phone. The word "impaled" makes me want to throw up.

"Where are we?!" Juliet shouts. Rowan shouts back the name of the area.

I stand up and step back. I'm just in the way, really. The rain is already cleaning the blood and mud from my hands.

"They're sending an air ambulance!" Juliet shouts down at us.

Jimmy kneels in the water and lies down next to Lister, sliding his arm underneath Lister's head. "There's an ambulance coming. You're gonna be fine. You're gonna be okay."

I step back farther again and tread into the creek. It's only just deep enough to reach my ankles. I kneel down and put my shaking hands in there, watching as the blood rushes away into the cold water.

# JIMMY KAGA-RICCI

Lister's skin is ice cold by the time the ambulance arrives, and even though
he's breathing, we can't get him to wake up. Everything after that happens
in a blur. When we hear the air ambulance flying above us, Juliet and Bliss
wave their phone flashlights towards it, hoping that they'll notice where we
are. What feels like hours later, though is only really a few minutes, two paramedics are strapping Lister to a board and heaving him up the riverbank.

We run with the paramedics out of the woodland to where the helicopter
has landed in the field. We're not allowed to go on the helicopter with him,
and next thing I know Rowan's holding me back, pulling me down into the
wheat, while they take Lister away. No, I need to be with him, I need to be
there in case, just in case he . . .

For a while, all I can do is sit there. And cry.

And pray.

# SUNDAY

**"BUT TO SACRIFICE WHAT YOU ARE AND TO LIVE WITHOUT BELIEF; THAT IS A FATE MORE TERRIBLE THAN DYING."**
**—JOAN OF ARC**

# ANGEL RAHIMI

"Here, I bought you a Sprite and a packet of Haribo," I say, holding the two items out to Juliet as I wander back from the nearby shop. We're back at Rochester train station, though I barely recognize it at all.

Juliet accepts the items with a surprised laugh. She tucks her hair behind her ear and smiles at me. "How did you know I like Haribo?"

"You definitely mentioned it like ten thousand times in our Facebook convos."

"Oh God, do I actually talk about Haribo that much?"

"Yeah, yeah, you do. I mean, maybe Haribo is your special internet friend."

"Wow. Too soon."

Our train won't be here for another twenty minutes, so we wander through and sit down in the waiting area. We sit in comfortable silence, Juliet munching on her Haribo and me taking sips from the milkshake I bought for myself, watching the people go by. I could definitely get into people watching. Wondering where that guy is going. What's that woman worried about? What's that person's greatest fear? What's their greatest desire?

I don't know. Everything seems a bit more interesting to me now than it used to.

"Did you get me anything?" asks a voice, and I turn to my other side and smile at Bliss Lai.

"Hell yeah, I did," I say, and pull a milkshake out of my bag. "Here you go, milk girl."

"Okay, 'milk girl,' not the best nickname. But *excellent choice*." She unscrews it and takes a sip.

"How's our boy?" asks Juliet, mid-chew.

I check my phone.

"No new messages," I say.

We all stay silent for a moment. I take a deep breath and lean back in my chair.

⇄ ◄◄ ⊙ ►► ♥

Last night, Jimmy and Rowan left for the hospital in a taxi as soon as the road out of the village was reopened. Both of them were eerily silent. Jimmy wasn't crying anymore. We barely said goodbye even. Jimmy just looked at me as he reached the doorway, and then turned to go, and it struck me that I would probably never see him again.

Apart from in photos. And videos. And on the internet.

Rowan kept Bliss updated with texts. None of us—me, Juliet, Bliss, and Piero—could sleep. Piero sat at the kitchen table with the radio on. Bliss and Juliet sat together by the window. I escaped into the study to pray. Pleading to God to let him be okay.

We heard at 11 p.m. that they'd reached the hospital safely, and at 11:30 p.m. that Lister was already in surgery.

Then we heard nothing for over four hours.

And then, at 4 a.m., we had a call from a shaky, small voice. Jimmy.

Lister was going to be okay.

He's gone in for more surgery this morning, on his leg this time, but he's no longer on the verge of death. Jimmy and Rowan are still there, and somehow the fact that Lister is in hospital has made headline news, though no one seems to know exactly what happened.

No one in the world except us.

"Doesn't it all feel like a dream?" I say.

"Yeah," says Juliet. "Or really bad fanfiction."

We all laugh.

"No one would have written Lister like that," I say.

"Or Jimmy."

"Or Rowan, to be honest."

"Real life is weird," Juliet says.

"Yeah."

We sit in silence for a little longer, drinking and eating and watching the world.

What are we going to do now?

What's life going to be like now?

"So, you dumped Rowan?" says Juliet. I realize that Juliet hasn't talked to Bliss about that yet.

Bliss shrugs. "Yeah. We weren't good together. We'll still be friends, but . . ." She pauses. "Actually, I think we'll be a *lot* better as just friends."

"You think you'll still talk to him, then?" I ask.

Bliss frowns. "Why wouldn't I?"

She has a point.

"Oh, hey, Angel, I got something for you too," says Juliet. She yanks her bag onto her knees and unzips it, rummages with one hand, and pulls out a folded-up piece of lined paper. I frown and open it up.

It's a poem entitled "The Angel," written in childish handwriting.

By Jimmy.

"Piero gave it to us, actually," says Juliet. "I think . . . I think he knew we'd probably never see Jimmy again, and . . . he wanted us to have something as a keepsake."

I can't find any words.

I didn't read the second verse of the poem before, so I read the full eight lines from start to finish.

> *When all was bad in Jimmy Land*
> *He wished for someone to rescue him*
> *To make him part of a famous band*
> *And fight off things dark and grim*
>
> *The Angel came down and said, "Now, now,*
> *I can't do everything for you, can I?"*
> *Jimmy jumped up and said, "Then show me how!"*
> *But the Angel flew off with a "Bye, bye!"*

Juliet and Bliss peer over my shoulder.

"I'm glad Rowan is in charge of lyrics," Juliet says. "No offense, but these are some dodgy rhythms."

"This is a sassy angel," Bliss says, nodding her head. "Absolutely savage. She's like, see you later, bud. I got my own shit to do."

"Kind of motivational in its own special way," I say.

"True," says Bliss.

I fold up the poem and put it in my bag.

At least I'll always have that.

"Guys," I say.

They both look at me.

"My real name's not Angel. It's Fereshteh."

Neither of them say anything for a moment.

Then Bliss says, "Well, fuck me."

"My real name's not Juliet," says Juliet, and this makes me actually gasp out loud.

Bliss puts her hand over her mouth. *"Fuck me."*

"It's Judith," says Juliet, wrinkling her nose. "And I really, really hate it."

I'm too shocked to say anything.

Bliss looks from me to Juliet and then says, "Well, sorry to disappoint, but my name is actually Bliss and not, like, Veronica or something."

And then the three of us just start laughing. Really hard.

⇄  ◄◄ ⊙ ►►  ♥

"I'm coming home, Dad!"

"For real this time?"

"Yep." I nod against my phone. "For real."

"What've you been up to? You know I'm going to make you tell me *everything* when you get home. I need it for my novel."

"Dad . . . I think you're supposed to make stuff up for novels. Not just use my life for inspiration."

He laughs. It sounds warm.

"You sure you're okay, Fereshteh?" he says. "Mum said you were very upset yesterday. Was this about your band boy going missing? I heard on the radio that they found him!"

"Yeah. No. I mean . . ." I sigh. "Some stuff has happened. But . . . I'm going to be okay. And me and Mum, we . . . I think everything's going to be okay now."

Dad pauses. I can imagine him nodding and smiling.

"Okay," he says.

"Hey, Dad?"

"Yes?"

"This is random, but . . . how do you think people become band managers?"

"I'm a literature teacher, darling. I can answer questions about *The Great Gatsby* or Persian love poetry, but not about the business of music, I'm afraid."

"Don't worry." I smile. "I'll google it when I get home. Would you still love me if I was a band manager?"

"I'd still love you if you were a deep-sea submarine pilot and decided to live in the depths of the ocean for the rest of your days!"

"Now *there's* your next book idea, Dad!"

We both laugh, and God, I can't wait to get home.

"What about Mum?" I ask.

"Now, she wouldn't be quite so happy about it," he says. "But we've got plenty of time to deal with that."

"Yeah," I say. "We do."

⇄ ◄◄ ⊙ ►► ♥

When I sit back down with the girls, Juliet crosses her legs and says, "I think everything that happened was supposed to happen."

"Like, fate?" I say.

"Maybe. The real world, am I right?"

"Yeah, man."

It carries on. The world, I mean. And we sit and we watch. And I know that I did something. Took a risk. Lived a real life.

Me. Angel Rahimi.

Maybe tomorrow I'll do something else. Maybe tomorrow I'll wake up and think about me and what I want. Maybe tomorrow I'll believe in something other than boys on a screen.

"They were just so *normal*," says Juliet. "The illusion's been shattered."

"I know, right."

"Everyone's normal, really, aren't they?" Bliss says. "I mean, everyone's normal, everyone's weird, everyone's just trying to deal with their own life and keep calm and carry on. And hold on to something that'll keep them going."

"Yeah," I say.

"That's why people get into fandom and bands and stuff. They just want to hold on to something that makes them feel good. Even if it's all a big lie."

"I think that's what I did, anyway," I say.

"Seems a bit more sensible than carrying a knife around," says Juliet.

We all smile.

"There are other good things, though," I say, looking at Juliet.

She looks at me. "Yeah, there are."

"Shall we start over?" I say.

Juliet shrugs. "No. This has been an important part of our friendship development."

"It has, hasn't it?"

My phone buzzes. I look at the screen.

"Hey, it's Jimmy," I say, and open the message.

**Jimmy Kaga-Ricci @jimmykagaricci**

Lister awake after leg surgery, he's feeling a lot better

Thank you for everything

Then he sends me a picture of the three of them. Lister is in a hospital bed, his leg elevated and enclosed in the biggest cast I have ever seen, with an IV drip in his arm. Rowan is on one side, making the "okay" sign with one hand, and Jimmy is on the other, making a peace sign.

Juliet laughs. "They look adorable."

"Shall we send a photo back?"

"Why not!"

I open up my phone camera and take a selfie of us. I do Jimmy's peace sign, Juliet does Rowan's okay sign. Bliss smiles wide. I send it to them.

**angel@jimmysangels**

Tell him to get well soon!!

Thank you for everything too x

# JIMMY KAGA-RICCI

**angel@jimmysangels**

Tell him to get well soon!!

Thank you for everything too x

I smile and look at the photo again. They look vaguely happy. Angel's still wearing Grandma's floral scarf. Juliet's resting her head on Angel's shoulder. Bliss looks happier than I've seen her in a long time.

The heart-rate monitor—or whatever the hell it is—beeps rhythmically, just to assure everyone in the room that Lister is still alive. Not that we really need to hear that when Lister is, in fact, sitting up and furiously making his way through a family-sized packet of Doritos.

Rowan wrinkles his nose from where he's sitting on the windowsill. "You're literally covering yourself in Dorito dust."

"Let me have this, Ro Ro. I got accidentally stabbed."

"Is that going to be your excuse for everything from now on?"

". . . Probably." Lister shovels more Doritos into his mouth. "Need to live my life to the fullest. Never know which day might be your last. Et cetera."

"And that involves . . . Doritos."

Lister waves the bag at Rowan. "If I had my way, everything in my life would involve Doritos."

The taxi ride here was probably the worst half an hour of my life. For most of it, I convinced myself that Lister was already dead. Only when we got to the hospital and we heard he was in surgery did I allow myself to hope.

When the paparazzi and the fans started appearing, we were allowed to hide in a staff room. Unsurprising that someone saw us and leaked our location.

Once Lister was out, alive, drugged up and unconscious, we were all moved to a private hospital room for a few hours. Then he went back into theater for surgery on his leg, leaving us alone again, and the whole time he was in there, I felt like I couldn't breathe.

When he got back and woke up a few hours later, I went ahead and had a bit of a cry and apologized a billion times. Lister tried to make me stop, but I definitely haven't apologized enough. In fact, Lister is pretending that he feels completely fine, but every time he moves too fast, I can see his eyes twitch as he suppresses a wince.

And I still hate myself.

Just FYI.

Still think I'm the worst.

But, you know.

That's not uncommon.

I stand from my chair and go and join Rowan at the window. We're facing the courtyard. Rowan seems to be watching a couple of kids playing hopscotch.

We haven't talked about anything yet, but I can feel it about to happen.

"What are we gonna do about him?" Rowan murmurs to me, nodding his head slightly at Lister and his cloud of Dorito dust.

It takes a moment for me to understand Rowan's meaning.

"Oh," I say. "The alcohol."

"Yeah."

"Well, I have a lot of good therapy connections."

Rowan chuckles. "That's good. I think we all need therapy, to be honest."

"Yeah."

"You can still leave, if you want to. I don't want you to be unhappy."

"I don't want to leave."

He looks up at me, shocked. "What?"

"Well, I *do*, sort of," I say.

"Stop contradicting yourself," he says, and then laughs. "Make some sense, damn it!"

"The three of us . . . we were born to be together," I say. "And I can't leave that. I don't want to leave that."

"*Born to be.*" Rowan echoes my words. "Fate, or something?"

"Yeah."

"I'll put it in a song."

"You should. This would all make a pretty good song, actually."

Rowan smiles. "It actually would, wouldn't it?"

"Being in The Ark is really . . . horrible sometimes."

"You said it."

"But leaving that . . . leaving you two . . . would be terrible." I look at Rowan. "You two are the most important thing to me."

"Speak up," Lister calls from the bed. "I'm missing your emotional speech. I think I should be involved, since I'm the stab-ee."

Rowan groans. "Please stop calling yourself the *stab-ee*."

"I won't and I'm not going to for the foreseeable future."

I smile at Lister. "I was just saying that I love you both."

Lister rolls his head onto one side. "Aw! What the fuck! You nearly let me miss that? A rare display of positive Jimmy emotion?"

"And I'm not leaving the band."

"You're not?"

"No."

Lister's smile drops, and he looks at me sincerely.

"You know we're going to change things, though, right?" he says.

"What d'you mean?"

"No more of this . . . being pressured to do things. Being manipulated

346

and forced to act in a certain way. We need to stand up for what we want. What we all want. The new contract can literally go and fuck itself."

"Yeah," murmurs Rowan, looking at me.

"Like . . ." Lister continues, "like that girl Angel. She knew what she wanted. What she believed in. What she loved. And she . . . she just *did it*." Lister shakes his head. "I've never met anyone like that."

Rowan looks back out of the window. "She definitely wasn't what I thought she was."

"She wasn't a maniacal fan, you mean?"

"She was a maniacal fan, but I don't think the maniacal fans are what I thought they were. Well, not all of them, anyway."

"They're just a bit normal, really," I say.

"Or we're all weird."

"You can say that again."

Lister bellows, "WE'RE ALL WEIRD!" so loud that I flinch and Lister actually winces in pain once he's finished. "Okay, that hurt."

"Get some rest, oh my God," says Rowan.

"Rest is so boring," says Lister.

After another ten minutes, he falls asleep again. Rowan and I stay seated on the windowsill, watching the slow rise and fall of his chest, listening to the steady beeps of his heart.

"I think he's got a crush on you," says Rowan.

I look at him in alarm. "What?! How did you—How did you know about that?"

Rowan shrugs. "Just an observation." Then he raises his eyebrows at my flustered expression. "Why, has something happened?"

"Erm . . ." I try, and fail, to stop myself going red. "Erm. We can talk about that later."

Rowan laughs. His laugh always makes him look younger, reminds me of his younger self. "Changes are coming."

I shake my head. "Changes? What changes?"

*"Changes."*

"That sounds very, very ominous."

Rowan lifts his arm and wraps it round my shoulders. "It's good, Jimjam. We're doing good."

We sit quietly until we start to hear screaming and cheering coming from outside the window. Confused, we both turn to look again, and there, in the center, are a small gaggle of girls, waving and screeching as we look down again. I faintly hear one of them shout, "GET WELL SOON, LISTER!" and another of them is just standing and watching, smiling so wide.

I glance at Rowan. He's smiling. He raises a hand and waves at the girls.

"It's a funny old world," he says.

I look at the girls and start waving too. Sending love through the turn of a hand.

# GHOSTED

## A short story by Alice Oseman

A note from Alice:

*Jimmy is one of the two narrators of* I Was Born for This, *and in his part of the story, we learn a lot about his relationships with his two bandmates: Rowan, the boy he's known since primary school, and Lister, the boy he doesn't understand as well as he should. Jimmy has a different kind of relationship with each of them, but I've always wondered what Rowan and Lister's relationship is like when Jimmy isn't around. So let me take you back to the moment where Jimmy climbs out a window and Rowan and Lister are left stranded without him for the first time . . .*

## LISTER

I think I've been cursed by the god of bathrooms.

First, I drunk-kiss my best friend, only to be rightfully rejected, destroying my chance of confessing my feelings in a sensible way at a sensible time. Now I'm watching as he walks into a car park, his body shrinking smaller and smaller, vanishing into the void.

I'm struck with a fear I haven't felt since I was a kid. Like I'm lost in a supermarket, or I'm in the school library and someone turns all the lights off. The car park is so big and empty, and Jimmy is so small, and fuck knows where he's going. Fuck knows where we are, even. I never know where we are. I just get in the car when Cecily tells me to.

Who puts windows this big in bathrooms anyway? Seems like a pretty obvious privacy issue.

"Jimmy," I call out one final time, but there's no way he can hear me. He's too far away.

I've got two choices.

My heart tells me to go after him. But my head tells me to get Rowan. And if there's anything I've realized in the past few days, it's that listening to my heart only results in disaster and disappointment.

So I turn from the window and run.

## ROWAN

The fact that Bliss isn't replying to my texts should worry me. In any good, healthy relationship, one person straight-up blanking the other would be a red flag. I'm not the sort of person who expects an immediate text back, but when it's been over twenty-four hours, I can safely assume that something is wrong.

Yesterday, I was panicking. I called her way too many times. I left a few voicemails I'm already regretting.

But I don't feel much of anything right now.

Some guy is doing my makeup, brushing concealer over my eye bags and acne scars. I keep checking my phone, even though I don't expect to see anything on there.

I understand that being revealed as my girlfriend is Bliss's nightmare scenario. She told me so.

*I never want to be famous.*

She told me that on our first date. It wasn't much of a date—just video games and making out in her bedroom. We'd been joking about which celebrity couples we could compare ourselves too. I said Blake Lively and Ryan Reynolds. She said Shrek and Fiona, and then told me she never wanted to be famous.

I went ahead with the relationship anyway, truly believing that we'd be able to date forever without anybody finding out.

So ultimately this is all my fault.

"Your head," says the makeup guy, looking at the cut on my hairline. He shakes his head. "I saw on Twitter. These fans . . . People can be fucking crazy."

"Yeah," I say. There's a lot I want to say about the brick incident, but I shouldn't confide to random makeup artists. I should save it for when I get a therapist. "You can put makeup on it; it doesn't hurt that much."

I can see Cecily in the mirror. For once, she isn't hunched over her phone—she's just sitting there, her eyes fixed on the pile of contracts on the coffee table.

Before I have time to wonder what she's thinking, the dressing room door bursts open, and Lister tumbles inside, out of breath.

"Jimmy," he heaves out, and I feel a stab of panic in my chest. "He's gone."

⇄ ◄◄ ⊙ ►► ♥

By the time we get outside, it's too late. Jimmy has vanished from the car park—a giant liminal space that looks like something out of one of my sister's horror video games.

I take out my phone and call him immediately. I call him four times, then five, but each one gets sent to voicemail. I leave him several angry voicemails, then a couple of gentle ones, and then one where I'm borderline screaming.

"How could he do this to us?" I say to Lister when we're back in the dressing room, sitting next to each other on a low sofa. I don't expect him to know the answer, but he puts a hand on my arm and squeezes. For a second, I feel comforted by his presence. It hits me suddenly how rare that is—for me to be comforted by Allister Bird.

Cecily re-enters the room.

"I've spoken to the producers. We can cancel, or you two can perform alone."

"We should cancel," I say.

"Yeah," Lister agrees. "Like, who gives a shit about this? Jimmy's—like, shouldn't we be looking for him?"

I nod. "Like calling the police or something?"

"Yeah." Lister's hand is still on my arm.

"We're not calling the police," Cecily says. Then she adds, "Yet."

"So what *are* we going to do?" I ask.

She sighs. "Honestly? I think you two should perform without him. Otherwise we ruin this whole thing. We can just say Jimmy's unwell."

Lister and I stay silent.

Cecily holds up her hands. "That's just my advice. It's your decision. But this is a huge deal, guys. This show is seen by millions of people. And you don't know what I had to do to get you on it."

"Oh, don't try to fucking guilt-trip us into this," I snap at her before I can stop myself.

She looks at me, eyes widening in surprise. We usually just do what she says without question. That's the way it's always been.

"Well," Lister tells her, "I'm not doing it." He stands up, pulls off the Gucci jumper he'd been given to wear, and drops it on the floor.

"Babe," Cecily says, an almost pleading tone in her voice.

"We can't leave Jimmy out." Lister stands shirtless in the middle of the room and spins around on the spot. "Where did they put my hoodie?"

"What do you want to do, then?" Cecily asks. "Drive around looking for him? He probably just got in a taxi and went back to your apartment."

"Let's go there, then," Lister says. "I bet he was just upset about missing Bake Off this week. Can someone give me my hoodie, please?" One of the stylist assistants is rummaging through the clothing racks with a panicked expression on her face.

Cecily takes a deep breath in through her nose, and out through her mouth.

Then she taps on her phone, holds it to her ear, and says, "Get the car."

## LISTER

When we get to our apartment and discover Jimmy isn't there, Cecily realizes that it's time to freak out. She delivers a five-minute rant about how Jimmy has royally fucked up this entire day, especially the contract signing, how the wrath of the record company is going to rain down on her shoulders, and how much she's going to tell Jimmy off when he gets back.

I know she's worried about him on a personal level too. She's known us since we were fourteen—three excitable kids making their first EP. She's not quite like a mum, but something close, I guess.

She's never been good at showing that, though. She just makes a lot of phone calls.

"I have to go save your bloody career. Don't go anywhere," she says through gritted teeth before leaving our apartment. Leaving me and Rowan alone.

Rowan sits on a kitchen bar stool, swiveling gently. I slump onto the sofa. The designer clock on the kitchen wall tells us it's almost six in the evening.

We catch eyes.

"Piero?" asks Rowan.

I nod.

"Shall I . . . ?"

I nod again.

Rowan picks up his phone.

⇄ ◄◄ ⊙ ►► ♥

Piero doesn't answer. So as not to worry him too much, Rowan leaves him a voicemail in which he says, "Hi, Piero, it's Rowan. Could you give me a call back on this number when you get this message? Thanks. Bye." It almost makes me laugh how polite and casual Rowan manages to sound, despite the fact that our best friend is missing.

While he's doing this, I've lain down onto the sofa and I'm thinking about what alcohol I should drink. I'm feeling like it's the time for some vodka shots. But a cold beer would hit really nice right now. Or my classic: a bottle of red wine. I'll probably get around to all of them. But what first? Maybe the vodka.

I know something's been up with Jimmy this week. I only wonder how much of it is my fault.

Getting pissed off with him while we were watching *Brooklyn Nine-Nine*, however justified that had been, probably hadn't helped his mental state. And then the kiss . . .

I shake my head, trying to remove the memory. That's going to be one of those days that I'll be thinking about for years. Decades, possibly. Embarrassing and devastating. Truly one of my lowest moments, and I've had a *lot* of low moments.

Definitely time for vodka shots.

We have a metal bar cart in our living room for our alcohol. A lot of the bottles are gifts, and a lot of them are stupidly expensive when Tesco's own brand vodka would get the job done most of the time. I select the first vodka I see, grab a shot glass, and do two in quick succession. It burns. In a good way.

"Do you think maybe we should . . . ?" Rowan begins but doesn't finish.

I'm sitting on the floor next to the bar cart. "What?"

"I don't know. Go look for him?"

It's only then that I start thinking the worst. What if he's been kidnapped? Or murdered?

"How?" I say, genuinely asking.

"Don't you have a car?"

"Yes," I say, thinking about my Lamborghini. Sometimes I like to take a walk down to the car park and just sit in it, play some music, and drink. It's blue and looks exactly like a picture I found on Instagram when I was twelve, printed out, and stuck on my bedroom wall. "But I can't drive."

Rowan stares at me. "I thought you had lessons."

"I only had three lessons." And then I got bored, or tired, or busy, or all three. Even if I did learn to drive, where would I drive to?

"How did I not know this?"

I shrug at him. "I think this was around the time you and Bliss had just started dating."

His expression goes cold. Whoops. Maybe too soon to be mentioning Bliss.

Rowan stands up from the stool and crosses the room, phone clutched tightly in one hand. "I'm going to shower."

As soon as he's gone, I do one more shot, and then select a bottle of wine from the cart. Fuck this day.


## ROWAN

I keep my phone balanced on the edge of the sink while I'm in the shower, volume turned up to maximum, never letting my eyes leave the screen just in case Piero calls me back.

Or Bliss, I guess. A call from Bliss would be great right now.

I try not to think anything while I shower, or while I'm doing my skin care, or while I'm putting some fresh clothes on. I try to focus on each small task—spreading moisturizer over my forehead, putting a leg into my joggers, squeezing my hair with a towel—to avoid thinking anything at all about Jimmy or Bliss or the fact that we just ghosted a major TV show, which might require more damage control than even Cecily can spin.

But as soon as I step out into the hallway again, it all comes flooding back, and I kind of want to get out of the building and run down the street, run all the way around the city until I eventually run into Jimmy, and everything will be okay again.

Why would he do this to us?

To me?

He'll be okay. He's probably safe. He's probably making his way to his grandad's right now.

But what if he's not?

And why did he want to leave in the first place?

⇄  ◄◄ ⊙ ►►  ♥

Lister is back on the living room sofa, a half empty bottle of wine on the coffee table in front of him. He's put the PlayStation on but he's just staring at the home screen, taking a sip of wine straight from the bottle every few seconds.

"What are you doing?" I ask.

He turns to me. "Uh . . . was thinking about playing *Bloodborne*."

It's absurd, obviously, to be thinking about playing video games when our best friend is missing. But knowing there's little else we can do except wait for Piero to call, or Jimmy to call, or Cecily to come up with a plan, maybe it's what we need right now.

Distraction.

"Can we take turns?" I ask.

Lister shrugs. "Yeah, sure."

I slump next to him on the sofa. He's still wearing his hoodie and joggers, the concealer on his face has gone cakey, and I can tell he's just had a cigarette. I hate the fact that Lister smokes, and objectively the smell is horrible, but, at this exact moment, there's something almost *comforting* about it. It's a Lister smell.

I could just go and sit in my room, but the apartment feels ghostly without Jimmy. Weirdly—and this rarely happens—I want to hang out with Lister.

"If we die, we have to pass over the controller," he says.

"Well, you'll be passing it over a lot, then."

"Is that a comment on my video game skills?"

"Obviously, yes."

"I'm great at this game."

"We'll see about that."

I take one last look at my phone screen. No missed calls. No notifications whatsoever. I put it down on the table on front of us, then pick up the controller in its place.

## LISTER

Rowan and I are into video games. It's one of the few interests we share that Jimmy does not. Jimmy's the binding glue of our trio—always the person in the center, the person both Rowan and I feel closest to. But when it comes to video games, Jimmy has nothing to contribute except occasionally wanting to play Beer-io Kart, a *Mario Kart* drinking game I invented.

It's not like I don't love Rowan or think he doesn't love me. But Rowan and Jimmy were friends first. And I have less in common with Rowan than I do with Jimmy. It's natural that we're not as close.

If we weren't in a famous band together, I'm not sure whether we'd still be friends now.

We play *Bloodborne* for two hours, mindlessly slashing at monsters and having minor debates about which weapons to upgrade. Rowan looks at his phone every couple of minutes, but there are no calls and no messages.

If I wasn't tipsy, I'd probably be just as worried as he is. But the alcohol has numbed my thoughts. All I can focus on is pressing the right buttons at the right time to kill the monsters.

"You're annoyingly good at this game," Rowan says, eventually.

"Hand-eye coordination, Ro Ro. Something you do not possess."

"You do know I can play eight instruments, right?"

"But not the drums, huh."

Rowan folds his arms. "You will never let me live that down."

"Nope. It's like the one thing I can do better than you."

There's a pause.

"What's your favorite video game?" I ask.

He looks at me. "What are you doing?"

"What?"

"You sound like you're interviewing me for a teen magazine."

I roll my eyes. "It was just a question."

"I get that you're a chatty drunk but can we just play the game, please?"

"Sorry, I forgot you hate talking to me."

Rowan frowns. "I don't *hate talking to you*."

I snort. "But you think I'm an idiot who has nothing intelligent to say."

"I don't think that."

"Yeah, you do. You'd much rather I was the one who was missing right now."

Rowan doesn't respond. We both know I'm right.

"My favorite game is *Undertale*," he finally answers.

"We could play that, if you want," I suggest.

"I think I'm done with video games for today," he says, and gets up from the sofa. "And I'd want you to be sober while playing *Undertale*. So you get the full emotional impact of the story."

"Well, you'll be waiting a long time, then," I joke, but he doesn't laugh.

"I wish you wouldn't—" he begins but is cut off when his phone buzzes.

Rowan snatches it from the table, eyes wild.

"It's Cecily," he says, and then he shows me the text.

You guys should probably check Twitter.

## ROWAN

The photo that most people on Twitter are sharing is what I like to call a "creep shot"—a photo of one of us that's been taken without our knowledge. There've been a lot of those, of course. There's the legendary set of photos of Lister eating McDonald's fries on the tube with a weary look on his face, way back when we were less famous. Those photos often get used as memes.

But this is worse. It's not a meme. You can see the panic on Jimmy's face, and he's surrounded by people. Many of them have their phones out.

There's another photo people are sharing too—a photo of Jimmy with a girl on a train. They're leaning together a little, mid-conversation, so it's not like she's just a random girl. Jimmy *knows* her. He's on a train *with* her.

"That's a Southeastern Railway train," says Lister instantly. "You can tell by the seat patterns."

"So he's gone to Kent, then?"

"Yeah. He's probably going home."

Home. Not this apartment—his real home, his childhood home. His grandad's house.

"Who's that, though?" asks Lister, pointing at the girl.

"No fucking idea," I say.

"She doesn't look like a kidnapper." He squints at the screen. "And Jimmy doesn't look like he's being kidnapped."

"I'm pretty sure he's not being kidnapped."

"He could be. You never know. We should be considering all possible scenarios."

I pull the phone away and begin to dial Piero's number. "Allister, this isn't a true crime podcast."

He doesn't answer me. He just rolls off the sofa and starts crawling his way to the bar cart.

Piero picks up on the third ring.

"Hello?"

"Hi, Piero, it's Rowan."

"Ah." The sound of his voice sends me right back to the weekends spent at his house when we were thirteen, playing covers in his garage, Joan making us cheese on toast, watching YouTubers when we got tired.

"Is he there?"

"Yes, he is."

"Did you not get my message?"

"You left a—?" There's a pause. "Ah. Sorry, lad, I must have missed it."

I resist the urge to sigh in annoyance.

"Is he okay?" I ask.

"He's . . ." Piero lets out a breath. "He's in a bit of a state. He's okay, he'll be okay, but he needs some rest."

"Right. Well, we're going to come and get him."

He doesn't speak for a moment.

"I think you should wait until the morning, lad."

I frown. "Why?"

"He needs a night off."

"A night off from . . . what? His entire life?"

Piero chuckles. "Yes."

"We're actually in a bit of a situation right now," I say, keeping my voice as calm and polite as possible. "We're signing a new contract and we've had to cancel a chat show appearance and—"

"I know," he interrupts. "I know all that. But he needs *a night off*. He needs a good night's sleep in his own bed in his own home."

"You know, technically, this is his own home. Here in London."

Piero laughs. "Ah yes. Of course." He's laughing at me, and I realize then that there's no way I'm going to win this argument.

"We'll come in the morning," I say.

"That's a good lad."

After I hang up, I grab the bottle of wine Lister's just opened and take a big swig. It's disgusting. I've never liked red wine.

"I'm going to bed," I say.

Lister blinks up at me from the carpet. "That was good news. He hasn't been kidnapped. He just needed a nap."

"Can you not make a joke about this situation for like one fucking minute, Allister?"

Lister snorts. "Fine, have a strop. I'm sure that'll help things."

"Why are you always like this? You just don't give a shit about literally anything, do you?"

He just starts laughing. It makes me want to shout at him.

"Do you care?" I ask. "Do you care that Jimmy left and we have no fucking idea why?"

Lister gazes at me, his cheek squashed into his hand, and says, "I don't need to answer that."

"Fine."

I turn away. I don't want to argue, not really, but Lister is so *annoying*. Is it too much to ask that someone else takes situations like this seriously?

But he's always been like this. Even when Jimmy's in the middle of a panic attack, Lister always finds some way to make a joke about it. Why do I always have to be the serious one? The worrier? Why can't someone else do the worrying sometimes?

I wish I could be the one who just got drunk and played video games.

"We'll leave by nine tomorrow morning," I say. "Don't sleep in."

Lister gives me a formal salute, a smirk on his face. I leave the room before I'm tempted to shout at him.

## LISTER

Getting into an argument with Rowan isn't a particularly unusual occurrence. Sometimes it's fun, even. Pissing him off just enough to get him to banter with me, or get into a mild wrestling match, or play dodgeball with me on the tour bus using a Gucci slipper as the ball.

I'm sensing, though, that tonight may not have been the best time to try to initiate an argument.

It's how we communicate a lot of the time. Most of the time, even. Snappy quips, or Rowan whining at me, or me bothering him. We save the deep chats for Jimmy. Jimmy doesn't open up very often, but you know Jimmy will listen if you have something serious to say. If I tried to talk to Rowan about serious stuff, he'd probably just roll his eyes or laugh at me.

I head to my own bedroom, bringing the bottle of wine with me. I know I shouldn't be drinking. I usually know I shouldn't be drinking, but, like, who cares? We all have vices. This is mine.

And I love drinking in my bedroom. Just feeling hazy and having no thoughts and finally falling asleep. I deserve it, don't I? After working all day every day?

And it stops me thinking about Jimmy.

I'd do anything to stop thinking about Jimmy.

Being in love with your bandmate fucking sucks.

I collapse onto my bed. I love my bed. It's huge and squishy and the polar opposite of the lumpy single I grew up with. This whole bedroom is something out of twelve-year-old Lister's wildest fantasies—it's spacious and modern, with one floor-to-ceiling window, dark walls, LED lights behind the headboard, and a fifty-inch TV.

I wish Jimmy was here. In my room. In my bed.

No.

Stop it.

I fall asleep for an hour and wake up with a nasty taste in my mouth, so I head out for a glass of water. On my way to the kitchen, I pass Rowan's bedroom. He's shut the door. I can hear the faint whisper of the TV. He's probably asleep already.

My stomach gurgles, and I realize I haven't even had dinner.

And that's what gives me the idea.

⇄ ◄◄ ⊙ ►► ❤

Forty minutes later, I knock lightly on Rowan's door, two large pizza boxes in my arms.

There's a small pause, and then, "Yeah?"

I open the door.

Rowan's room is always tidy. He puts away his clothes at the end of the day and makes his bed in the mornings. But it's not sparse or boring—he decorated as soon as we moved in. A textured wool rug, silk curtains, giant floor lamp, and, in the center, a four-poster bed, all clean lines and dark wood. Rowan loves to criticize me about buying unnecessary things, but all I need to do is remind him of the velvet chaise longue in his bedroom that I'm pretty sure nobody has ever sat on.

The room looks like an expensive hotel suite. It screams Rowan.

"Hey," I say.

He's on his bed, buried under several blankets. The TV on the opposite wall is playing *Notting Hill*.

"Hey," he says.

"I got you pizza. Hawaiian with pepperoni."

He blinks at me. "You remembered my weird order?"

"It's so weird, how could I forget?"

This earns a snort from Rowan. He sits up from the blankets but doesn't say anything more.

"Can I . . . ?" I shuffle on my feet. "Can we eat it in here?"

Rowan frowns. "In my room?"

"Yeah." I shrug. "It's, like, weird in this place. Without Jimmy. It feels . . ."

"Haunted?" Rowan suggests.

We look at each other.

And then Rowan shuffles to one side of his bed, making room for me.

## ROWAN

Lister devours his entire pizza—barbecue meat feast—in five minutes. I've always been deeply annoyed by what a high metabolism he has. I work out three times a week with a personal trainer just to stay toned, but Lister manages to maintain his lean muscle and lightly outlined abs despite all the beer, spirits, cigarettes, and takeaway food he consumes. Genes are deeply, outrageously unfair.

But it's not him I should be mad at. It's the system of celebrity that pressures us into feeling like we need to be muscular and have low body fat.

"Hugh Grant is *so* fucking sexy in this film," Lister says as he's finishing off the last slice. "Like oh my fucking God. The hair."

I'm on my third slice. "What is it with you and nineties romance movie stars? I swear you said the exact same thing about Leonardo DiCaprio in *Titanic*."

"And Alicia Silverstone in *Clueless*." Lister sighs.

I nod. "That one I can agree with."

"People were just more attractive then."

I nod again. "They feel more real. Like . . . famous actors all have the same face nowadays."

"I was reading this thing online—"

"You were reading?" I ask, eyebrow raised.

Lister narrows his eyes at me. "Wow, hilarious. Anyway, I was reading this post about how people are less attracted to, like, 'perfection' nowadays because we see it everywhere. Like on social media and in movies and stuff. People are genuinely more attracted to people who have 'imperfections.'"

"Ah, well." I pat him on the leg. "That's it for you, then. The reign of Allister Bird as World's Sexiest Man is officially over."

"Thank God." He chucks the empty pizza box onto the floor. I mentally add cleaning that up to my before-bed to-do list.

"Do you genuinely hate it?" I ask. "Being considered attractive?"

"It's not *that*." He steals several of my blankets and piles them over his body. "It's just that people sexualize me all the time. And whenever I talk to anyone, I'm just wondering whether they're thinking about having sex with me."

"I assure you not everyone thinks about sex all the time."

"Are you implying that I think about sex all the time? Very biphobic of you, Ro Ro."

"That's not what I meant, and you know it. And *I'm* talking to you and I'm not thinking about having sex with you."

He turns slowly to look at me. Then he waggles an eyebrow. "You sure?"

I swiftly shove him off the bed and onto the floor.

Once he's crawled back into his blanket cave, we watch the movie in silence for a few minutes. To be honest, Lister being considered super attractive by most of the world is not something that weighs heavily on my mind. He has the face of a model, sure, but me and Jimmy are very aware that Lister is seen as the "hot'" one largely because he's white.

I'm sure being seen as a sex object is quite irritating, but we all have shit to deal with in this game.

"Just for the record," he says suddenly, "I *am* worried about Jimmy."

It comes out of nowhere and is possibly the last thing I would have expected Lister to say in that moment.

"Okay," I tell him. "Good. You should be."

"I'm just saying. Like, you think I don't care, but I do."

"Well, you're not very good at showing that you care when you're doing shots and cracking jokes."

"Well, maybe I show my feelings in a different way than you."

I wouldn't call getting drunk a form of showing feelings, but whatever. Lister has alcohol issues. Probably ones that we should probably deal with soon before he ends up in a hospital. But I'm not gonna try to confront him about that right now.

"Honest question," continues Lister, rolling over so his whole body is facing mine. "Do you think you are less fucked up than me?"

"Yes," I say unflinchingly. "Look at my bedroom—I hang up all my clothes. I shower every day."

"But you freak out at literally any minor inconvenience, you're obsessively controlling about every single detail of your life, and you're like . . . I mean, you hate our fans."

"Okay, that's an exaggeration." I take a bite of pizza. "I don't hate the fans. They just display some questionable behavior sometimes." I swallow. "And d'you know what? I have to be the one in control; otherwise we'd all collapse from stress. You go off partying and Jimmy has panic attacks like every week, so *I'm* the one who has to stay on top of everything, who has to always know what we're doing and when, and then make sure you two are okay so we can all do our fucking jobs."

"But don't you see how that's, like, still very fucked-up behavior, Rowan?"

He calls me Rowan. Full first name. It sounds weird in his voice.

"Not really," I say.

He sighs. Then he steals a slice of my pizza. "Fine, then."

And we don't talk again for the rest of the movie.

## LISTER

Ruined it with my big mouth, as usual. I really thought me and Rowan were having an actual *bonding moment*. A moment of progression in our friendship. But I said the wrong thing and fucked it. Classic.

I'm right, though.

And it's scary that he thinks he's completely fine. That this level of stress is normal. That he's a functioning, well-adjusted human who is able to cope with being one of the most famous musicians in the world with absolutely no help or support whatsoever.

At least I'm aware that I'm unhinged.

We watch the rest of *Notting Hill* in silence. When it's finished, Rowan takes our empty pizza boxes out to the kitchen, and I wonder whether I should leave and go back to my own bedroom. He probably wouldn't be surprised if I did.

But the thought of sleeping alone in my room when Jimmy isn't here feels strange. Spooky.

Rowan returns with two glass bottles of Diet Coke, the caps already opened.

"Diet?" I ask as he hands me one. I always go for regular Coke.

"Take it or leave it," says Rowan, getting back into bed. He steals back one of the blankets I've been hogging, and then, wordlessly, puts *Clueless* on.

I think briefly about going to get a beer but choose not to. I don't want to spoil this.

"So," says Rowan. "Jimmy. Theories."

Oh. Shit.

"Uh . . ." I take a swig of Coke. "Maybe he was just missing his grandad."

"He's always missing his grandad."

"More than usual?"

"I just feel like something's been *off* with him this week." Rowan props himself upright with several pillows. "Like his anxiety's been really bad lately, and I just feel like he's . . . I dunno, not telling us something. He's been so emotionally *distant* from everything. And this week has been hell—like that shitty interviewer and that photo getting leaked. All the stuff that went down yesterday must have been the final straw."

My stomach lurches, momentarily thinking Rowan must know about the kiss. But of course he's referring to the rest of it. The carnage at the O2.

"Yeah, it's all been a bit much," I say.

"Has he said anything to you? Like, at all?" Rowan looks me in the eyes.

"No," I say quickly. "I mean, not really."

"What d'you mean, not really?"

I should shut this down now. I shouldn't tell Rowan about the kiss. He'll go haywire. He'll hate me.

"Like . . . technically no," I say.

"Allister," he says.

The thing about alcohol is that even when you're trying really hard to lie, sometimes the truth just slips out. And despite my giant pizza, I'm still kind of tipsy, and although my brain is screaming at me to shut up, my heart just wants to be honest. God damn heart.

"Something happened," I say.

There's a silence.

"What do you mean, *something happened*?"

"I mean something *happened*."

"Allister." Rowan pauses the movie. "What happened?"

"Me and Jimmy . . . we . . . I kissed him."

The silence that follows is horrible. I regret it instantly.

He says nothing. He doesn't move. He just stares at me.

"It was a disaster," I continue. "It was yesterday and I was *so* drunk, and he was probably having an anxiety moment, and we were talking and something in my brain was like *wow, he sure is giving off kissing signals right now*, and I decided to just go for it, and he pushed me off him and was like *er, no*, and, like, now it's fucking awkward."

"You kissed him," Rowan says. "So he decided to climb out of a window and run away."

"I mean, yeah, in summary."

"I assume I don't need to explain all the reasons why you kissing Jimmy is an absolutely batshit idea."

"Uh, no, you do not."

"Christ." Rowan sits back. "Well, there we are, then. It's finally come to this."

"What d'you mean, *finally*?"

"Allister, your crush on Jimmy is the most painfully obvious, embarrassing, and distressing thing I have ever had the misfortune to witness. And I have had to witness it for several years."

I sit up, feeling my cheeks go hot. *"Several years?"*

"Are you joking?" Rowan laughs. "I remember when we were sixteen and you got all moody because that guy was flirting with Jimmy at the British Teen Music Awards after party."

*"Moody?"*

"They were dancing and you were just sitting in your chair, glaring at them!" Rowan is full-on cackling now. "Like you had a storm cloud over your head!"

"Stop laughing."

"And when we were seventeen and Jimmy did that *Vogue Italia* shoot and you kept the magazine in your bunk on the tour bus!"

"I did not do that."

Rowan wipes a tear from his eye. "Oh my God. So funny."

He's properly pissing me off now.

"So it's my fault that Jimmy's gone and fucked up this whole week," I snap at him. "Great. Sorry."

Rowan stops laughing. "I mean . . . okay, yeah, maybe it was a contributor, but a lot of shit has gone down this week."

I sip my Coke. "I guess."

That actually does make me feel a little better about it. Yeah, what I did was awful. But there were other factors at play.

"You're surprisingly self-deprecating," says Rowan suddenly. "For someone who usually seems like he doesn't give a shit about anything."

". . . Okay." I don't know what else to say to that.

"Do you actually think you could make it work with Jimmy?"

I turn to Rowan. He's being serious. Like, that's an actually serious question.

It's a question I've asked myself every day for years. A question I've answered in daydreams, in nightmares, in conversations with myself in the shower. A question I still don't know the answer to, and maybe never will. A question that doesn't need an answer, now that I know for sure that Jimmy doesn't like me back.

"How would you feel about that?" I ask. "Your two best friends and band-mates *dating*."

Rowan pauses. "I'd have mixed feelings."

I don't inquire further.


## ROWAN

It takes a moment for me to realize, but when I do, it hits me like a truck: Lister actually opened up to me about something.

I feel bad for laughing.

Because as genuinely funny—and moderately worrying—as Lister's crush has been for the past couple of years, it's something that's been stress-ing him out a *lot*. And who has he had to talk to about it?

Am I the first person he's talked to about it?

Probably.

That's kind of sad.

And it makes me want to talk about Bliss.

"I don't know if me and Bliss are gonna . . ." I pause. Are gonna what? Make it? Survive this? Ever see each other again?

"Still heard nothing from her?" Lister asks quietly.

I glance at my phone. "Nope."

"That's kind of a dick move on her part."

"Yup."

"Do you want to stay with her?"

"Like, in my heart, I do. I love her. I love being with her. She's one of the few people in my life I feel genuinely close to, who I feel like I can just be myself around and talk to about anything." I glance at Lister, and he's looking at me intently, a serious expression on his face. It's a little unnerving. I hardly ever see him looking serious. "But . . . the circumstances of our relationship are so challenging. We live in very, very different worlds, and our lives are on very different trajectories. And sometimes I think relationships just can't survive that."

Lister snuggles his face into one of my pillows. "That's sad."

"Yeah."

"You should talk to her before deciding anything, though."

"I mean, yeah, I will. When she can be bothered to text me back."

Lister sighs and rolls onto his back. "We're both stuck in limbo."

I laugh. "A limbo where all relationships are doomed."

"Pretty much."

"At least we have each other."

"True."

We turn to look at each other in unison.

"Fuck them all," says Lister. "We'll start our own band."

"Oh yeah?" I grin. "What's it gonna be called?"

"The Lim-bros."

"And we'll write songs about how love is doomed and everything's shit."

"Exactly." Lister holds his hand out for a handshake, and I take it. "It's a deal."

And then we're both laughing. Laughing at how sad and shit this day has been, and how ridiculous the idea of me and Lister forming a band is, and how tired and stressed we are, and how it took all this for me and Lister to just have an honest conversation about our feelings.

We watch the movie for another twenty minutes before either of us speaks again.

"Like . . . I just want you to know that you can talk to me," says Lister. "About whatever you want. Serious shit. You know. I get that I joke about stuff but I'm down for a deep chat. Anytime. Especially when drunk."

"Wow," I say.

"I mean it."

"I know." I pat his arm.

"You're one of my best friends. And I know we're not as close as we are with Jimmy for, like, all kinds of reasons. But I love you."

I look at him. "Lister. I know."

There's a pause.

"You did not just fucking Han Solo me," scoffs Lister.

"What?"

"'I love you.' 'I know.' Like, that just stabbed me in the heart."

"Allister."

"I can't believe you've done this to me in my brokenhearted drunken state. I'm devastated right now."

"*Allister.* Shut the fuck up."

We're both laughing. And then we shut the fuck up.

As we continue watching *Clueless*, I'm reminded of a memory of us at age thirteen. Our first sleepover at my house, the three of us crowded in my bedroom. Jimmy got to sleep in my bed because he got the best score on *Guitar Hero* that day, so me and Lister ended up on a mattress on the floor next to him. Jimmy fell asleep almost immediately, a feat that would become less and less common as we all got older, but Lister and I couldn't sleep because we were too busy watching funny YouTube videos on my phone, muffling laughs into our hands, trying not to wake anyone up.

I turn the lights down as the movie gets close to the end, and I don't know when I fall asleep, but the last thing I remember hearing is Lister mumbling from beneath the blankets. "Alicia Silverstone, man . . . Like, *fuck*."

"Yeah," I mumble back.

## LISTER

I'm awoken by Rowan spraying me with his rose-scented face mist.

"It's eight forty-five," he snaps. "We leave at nine."

"We wha?"

"We're going to get Jimmy. Remember?"

"Jimmy."

Rowan rolls his eyes, and then yanks me out of his bed by the arm.

"Ow! Ro Ro, I'm delicate in the mornings!"

"Shut up and put some fresh clothes on."

By ten past nine, I'm ready to go. No idea what'll await us when we get to Kent.

"Everything's going to be fine," says Rowan, more to himself than to me. He's tying and re-tying his shoelace tighter than necessary.

When he stands up, I do something weird.

I reach out to Rowan and give him a quick, tight hug.

"Oh," he says.

"Everything's going to be fine," I repeat back to him.

And then I step back, feeling pretty pleased with myself.

For a moment, Rowan looks like he's about to make a snarky comment. But then he just nods and says, "Yeah. Let's go get Jimmy."

# ACKNOWLEDGMENTS

*I Was Born for This* was terrifying to write and came at me in a whirlwind. And yet, here we are, with a story I'm so proud of, characters I deeply love, and a book to share with you all.

I wouldn't be anywhere without my champion agent, Claire Wilson, who has supported me for all these years. My first and biggest thanks is to her.

A huge thanks to my editor, David Levithan, and the whole team at Scholastic US who have shown so much love and care for my books. I am so grateful to be working with such a passionate team and so happy that books from my backlist are getting a chance at new life in the US. I was also very excited to have once again been asked to design the cover illustration for Scholastic's edition. Designing my own book covers has been a lifelong dream and I had such fun with it!

In the UK, I was lucky enough to work with Sarah Hughes on this book— an incredible editor who understood exactly what I was trying to achieve and had *so* many amazing editorial suggestions. And a heartfelt thanks to Ryan Hammond for the gorgeous UK cover.

I'm not very good at making friends and I sometimes feel alone in the writer world, but thankfully in 2013 Lauren James messaged me on Tumblr. Nowadays she's not only one of my closest friends but also my first port of call for all my creative projects. Thank you for being there. Can't wait for us to tell more stories and frantically message each other about them.

Huge thanks as always to my family, for nodding politely at my strange ideas, and my friends, even the ones who haven't read my books.

Thanks to Mehak Choudhary and Ahlaam Moledina, who gave me invaluable guidance in writing Angel's religion and culture, and thanks to Vee S, who beta-read this book and gave me such thoughtful and intelligent advice in writing Jimmy's experience as a transgender young man.

A very grateful thanks to those who shared with me their experiences of being transgender:

Max, Kai Smith, Alexander Yeager, Isaac Freeman, Kan, Ezra Rae, Alex, Ell Eggar, Amanda, Ardell A., Alice Pow, Klaus Evans, Al Vukušić, Reeden Ashworth, Eleanor Horgan, Ari Lunceford-Guerra, Blu W, Phobos, Noah, Charli F, Eli, Noodler, Robin, David K, Arthur Blum, Fitz, K. Funderburg, Felix, Alexander, Alec R, Vivian Hansen, Cedric Reeve, Kit Stookey, Jaxon Stark, Phoebe, Ollie, Marianne Orr, Bryn Kleinheksel, Anna, and Jace C.

And to those who shared their experiences of being Muslim:

Sarah K, Aisha Tommy, Amena, Inas K, Mariam Aref, Sara Almansba, Yasmina Berraoui, Shatha Abutaha, Usma Qadri, and Hizatul Akmah.

Your wisdom and insight has taught me so much and brought Jimmy and Angel to life.

I want to thank my readers. A little cheesy, I know, but the truth is I'm still able to sit here and write my books because of you. In particular, thank you so, so dearly to all the people who post about my books and characters on the internet. Your support has kept me afloat through all my existential crises.

And finally, thank you to the fans. All fans. Fans of bands and musicians and Youtubers and actors. Fans of books and video games and films and comics. Thanks for being you. You have so much love and passion inside of you. The deepest hearts.

# *ABOUT THE AUTHOR*

Alice Oseman was born in 1994 in Kent, England, and is a full-time writer and illustrator. She is the creator of the popular Heartstopper series, now a live-action TV show streaming on Netflix. Alice is also the author of four YA novels: *Solitaire, Radio Silence, I Was Born for This*, and *Loveless*. Visit her online at aliceoseman.com.